Jo Watson is an award-winning writer whose romantic comedies were originally published on Wattpad. Her first novel *Burning Moon* won a 2014 Watty Award for being one of the site's most downloaded titles and has now had over 7 million reads. Jo is an Adidas addict and a Depeche Mode devotee. She lives in South Africa with her family.

Follow her on Twitter @JoWatsonWrites and find her on Facebook at www.facebook.com/jowatsonwrites.

Praise for Jo Watson's hilarious romantic comedies:

'Witty, enjoyable and unique' *Harlequin Junkie*

'Found myself frequently laughing out loud and grinning like a fool!' *BFF Book Blog*

'Heart-warming, funny, sweet, romantic and just leaves you feeling good inside' *Bridger Bitches Book Blog*

'Full of pure-joy romance, laugh-out-loud moments and tear-jerkers' *Romantic Times*

By Jo Watson

Destination Love Series
Burning Moon
Almost A Bride
Finding You
After The Rain
The Great Ex-Scape

Standalone
Love To Hate You

The Great Ex-Scape

Jo Watson

HEADLINE
ETERNAL

First published in Great Britain in 2018
by HEADLINE ETERNAL
An imprint of HEADLINE PUBLISHING GROUP

1

Cataloguing in Publication Data is available from the British Library

ISBN 978 1 4722 5776 5

Typeset in 11.55/16.25 pt Granjon LT Std by Jouve (UK), Milton Keynes

Printed and bound in Great Britain by CPI Group (UK) Ltd, Croydon, CR0 4YY

HEADLINE PUBLISHING GROUP
An Hachette UK Company
Carmelite House
50 Victoria Embankment
London EC4Y 0DZ

www.headlineeternal.com
www.headline.co.uk
www.hachette.co.uk

To GP, JJP, WP and DM! (Hopefully, you know who you are!)

The Great Ex-Scape

CHAPTER ONE

Crappiest, crap day of my entire effing life!

I'd been perching on the closed toilet seat for so long that parts of my body had gone dead. It had started in my feet, worked its way up into my ankles and was slowly numbing my calves. Maybe if I stayed here for long enough, everything would go numb? (Wishful thinking.)

My new—and ludicrously overpriced—pink cardigan was officially ruined from the mixture of mascara-stained tears and snot bubbles I'd been pouring into it for the last hour. But it was all I could use to stifle the undignified sounds of my uncontrollable sobs. This was a public restroom, after all!

I had a headache from hell; possibly from tear-induced dehydration, possibly from the half-empty bottle of wine I'd been sipping on for the last hour. But I knew I had to leave at some point. I couldn't hide in a toilet cubicle forever, as much as I wanted to. People would start to wonder where I was. *He* would start to wonder.

This had been one of those monumentally bad ideas from the start. *No*, what was I saying? This wasn't just a "bad idea," this was the worst idea ever conceived of. On a scale of one to "worst idea ever," this would be right up there with DIY open heart surgery (something I was seriously considering, since the pain of it breaking was almost too much to bear).

Going to my best friend's engagement party.

Sounds perfectly benign.

Making a speech at my best friend's engagement party.

Totally normal.

Toasting my best friend and his beautiful new fiancée.

Absolutely acceptable.

That is until you replace the words "best friend" with "the man I've been hopelessly, devotedly and excruciatingly in love with for the past three years."

I glanced at my watch; ten minutes before I needed to make the speech. Ten minutes until I was due to take up position in front of friends and families and deliver the old "thrilled and couldn't be happier for them" platitudes.

I gulped down another more-than-mouthful of anesthetizing wine as my phone beeped. I rolled my eyes when I saw whose name was lighting up the screen. It was my friend Lilly. She'd been on my case for the last week, insisting that this was my last chance to tell him how I felt, even if he didn't feel the same way. I needed to get it off my chest, she said. It would be cathartic, she said. I would finally get closure, she said. I wished to God she would shut the hell up. But then she'd said that other thing too, the one that kept that ember of hope burning: *What if he does feel the same way too?*

But I'd been here so many times before too. Hopes up, only for them to later be dashed, and downright shattered in the flaming pits of friend-zoned hell. I glanced at my phone again; another one of those dreaded phrases was splashed across it.

You have to tell him how you feel before it's too late. What if you're meant to be together and he just doesn't know it yet?

Meant to be? Yeah, that's what I'd thought too. All that hanging out together. Pizza and beer evenings. Staying up all night chatting on the phone. We'd even gone to a friend's wedding together, for heaven's sake. Surely that was date-y? My friends had all agreed . . . it *was* date-y!

I'd certainly interpreted those as very clear signs. We were meant to be together! It was only a matter of time before he confessed his true feelings to me. But as time passed . . . and passed . . . and passed, nothing happened. And then *she* came along. And everything changed.

I needed to snap out of this. I needed to get a grip. I needed to go outside and pretend that everything was totally fine. *More than fine.* I needed to pretend that I couldn't be more thrilled for my BFF. I'd written a speech drenched in a smorgasbord of hideous, romantic clichés that I'd plucked directly from the internet. As it turns out, cheesy one-liners are just a Google search away. But now, I wasn't sure how I was going to manage to say them out loud.

Why had I agreed to this in the first place? But this was only the appetizer; the real main course was yet to come . . .

And let me tell you, it is a turducken of tragedy. One horrific idea rolled into another equally dreadful one and then stuffed into the mother of shitty ideas. Grilled, basted, tenderized and deboned!

Agreeing to help him pick out his wedding suit.

Agreeing to emcee his wedding.

Agreeing to help him choose his romantic honeymoon destination—where they'd have lots of romantic honeymoon sex.

Clearly, I was a sadomasochist hell-bent on torturing myself. But I had to do this. I had no other option.

So I stood up . . .

Pins and needles in feet. Kneecaps crunching. Dead legs. Stomach lurching. General revolting creeping feeling.

I took my first step, but as I did . . . *Whoosh!* It hit me all at once. The alcohol raced through my body, spiking the blood in my veins and making me buzz. I took another step and the buzz gave way to a much more unpleasant feeling.

Suddenly, I felt woozy. *Very woozy.* And this wasn't the kind of establishment for wooziness. The engagement party was being held at *her* parents' restaurant on their award-winning wine farm in the beautiful Cape Wine lands; no expenses spared. Very fancy. It was the kind of super-upper-crusty party that people with surnames beginning with *Vander* and ending in *Child* went to. Many of the guests had been flown up from Jo'burg to be here, including me.

I stared at myself in the bathroom mirror, holding onto the sink for added support. I looked hideous. *What was my mother's favorite saying again?* "I look like the wreck of the *Hesperus*." I'd never known what a Hesperus was, but for some reason, the word seemed to describe perfectly how I looked and felt right now.

"Hesss Perrr Russs." I hissed it out loudly as I leaned towards the mirror and then almost laugh-cried out loud.

I splashed some water on my face to counteract the wooze—it worked a little—and then I grabbed some paper towels and attempted to wipe my tears away. I blew my nose quickly when I realized it was making a disgusting *"squeeeeeee, squeeeeeee, squeeeeeee"* sound on every out breath.

I reapplied my foundation, popped on a bit of mascara and smooshed on some lip-plumping lip-gloss. I'd bought the lip-gloss for *him*. I'd stupidly thought that if my lips were more Jolie, and less me, that he might take notice. I'd been wrong. And now I was 250 rand poorer.

The lobby outside was abuzz with a crowd of overdressed people. *She* and her crowd were of the super-skinny, pearl-wearing, overdressed ilk. Which meant that I always felt somewhat inferior in their presence, and a great deal larger than I knew I really was. *She* and *her* crowd were the kind of people that gave normal women body dysmorphia and made us all feel like large, beached marine animals.

At least eighty people were bustling about in the massive lobby, excessive for an engagement party, if you ask me.

I smiled at everyone as I walked past, trying to do my best impersonation of a happy, non-tipsy person. Soon we were all ushered into the restaurant and instructed to take our seats. I was sitting across from my so-called BFF, Matt. He smiled at me and I melted into my chair. I always melted when he smiled. I always got butterflies when he called and I got downright dizzy when we spent time together. I glanced to his left, and there *she* was . . .

Samantha. Doctor Samantha, I might add. Pediatric oncologist Samantha, to be specific! She saved sick children's lives for a living, for heaven's bloody sake! How the hell could a mere mortal such as myself compete with that?

Samantha caught me looking at her and I quickly shot her a smiley thumbs-up. I've always wondered if she knows how I *really* feel about him. Aren't women supposed to have a sixth sense about these kinds of things? Unless she did have her suspicions but felt *that* unthreatened by me. I wasn't sure which was worse, and I suddenly imagined her and Matt's late-night conversations about me . . .

"You know she's in love with you, right?" she says, lying in bed, silk sheets tussled, body glistening with beads of sweat from post-coital workout.

"I know," he says, equally sweaty and naked from mind-blowing sexcapades. "Don't worry, though," he turns and kisses her softly, "she's no competition for you."

"I know, baby. I know," she says, and I want to imaginary-punch her.

I tried to shake the image from my head and looked down at the handwritten speech in my hands. But my fingers were shaking uncontrollably and the wooziness was hitting me in steady waves that seemed to be building in momentum.

A large pair of invisible hands suddenly reached out and wrapped themselves around my throat. Squeezing. Throttling. I swallowed, but it got stuck. The tightening feeling was growing by the second as Samantha's father was nearing the end of his speech.

"And now we'll hear from Matt's best friend, Val," he said.

I froze. A deathly pause followed as people turned and looked for me.

"Val!" He said it a bit louder this time. "Val?"

What the hell was I going to do?

Three Years Ago

14 Feb.
Dear Diary,

Something amazing just happened. Genuinely amazing. No, it was not the insights I gained while writing my latest article about why "Dairy is the New Gluten." It was the amazing thing that happened in the lift, precisely 7 minutes ago. As you can see, I'm writing this soon afterwards, while the amazing thing is still fresh in my mind, because I don't want to forget any of it.

I'd just come back from my "romantic" Valentine's date with Stormy-Rain, in which she'd spoken all evening about how Valentine's Day was yet another example of the evil consumerist-capitalist agenda. (I still have no idea what she means, and the irony is that she actually does have a boyfriend!) Needless to say, I wasn't exactly in the most "hearts and chocolates" kind of mood when I got home at precisely 2:30 a.m. . . . that is, until I got into the lift and saw him!

Gorgeous. Pitch-black hair. Maldivian-blue eyes that make you want to peel your clothes off and go swimming in, naked. Dark, sexy stubble dotted across seriously sculptured jaw— not in a Ridge Forrester way, though. Tall, broad shoulders, seriously sexy ass and smelling like heaven. In a word, H. O. T.

So, naturally, I tried to exude that cool nonchalance that is always preferable in these kinds of situations. I made momentary eye contact, gave wildly noncommittal nod of acknowledgment, placed hand on hip, and looked in opposite direction.

And, it worked! Because HE started a conversation with ME. I reiterate, this is important, he opened his mouth first . . .

He asked, "Are you coming back from a Valentine's date?"

I replied, "No." (Still exuding cool, aloof nonchalance, although terribly uncool inside.)

And then he said, and I quote, "I find that hard to believe. Someone that looks like you, dateless on Valentine's Day?" And then he locked eyes with me and smiled.

Bam! I melted. Swooned. Felt explosions around us and butterflies inside. Mainly because he was just soooo good-looking. If he'd had a big, shiny bald patch and those gross white sticky patches in the corners of his mouth . . . it would have just been creepy!

For the purpose of this entry, it's probably also worth noting that by this stage, 2:30 a.m., I was pretty well lubricated. I had hit the cocktails, hard. I could tell he was tipsy too—he had that slightly dreamy, dopey look of someone who was buzzing.

And then, fueled with uncharacteristic courage, mainly due to vodka, I asked, in my most flirty voice, "And you? Where's your Valentine's date?"

He replied, "I don't have one."

He took a step forward. Another step. Another. Until he was right next to me. And that's when the truly amazing thing happened.

We looked at each other and then I swear I heard him say—with his mind—that he wanted to kiss me. So, I said it back, using the powers of telepathy that I didn't even know I had. "Kiss me! Kiss me! Kiss me!"

And he did. It was hungry and desperate and loud and

messy and full of arms and legs and backs being flung against walls. A m a z i n g. Best kiss of my entire life. Sparks, fireworks, lightning bolts and atomic fucking bombs went off. And then the lift doors opened and it stopped.

I thought that was going to be the end of it. I thought this was going to become like those crazy movie moments where you land up kissing a stranger under some equally strange circumstances and then part ways—but it wasn't.

He asked, "Do you live here?"

I replied that I did, "number seventeen" (just so he knew exactly where).

And then, lo and behold (I'm taking this as a sign, btw), he said, apartment 18—he'd just moved in! He walked me to the door and then kissed me again. Soft, slow, sexy and delicious. Then he stopped, ran his thumb over my lips and said, "Good night, neighbor. See you soon." I repeat, "See you soon."

Now, do you see why I needed to write this down immediately! Hottest guy I've ever seen before kissed me passionately in lift (and at door) and it was electric. Earth moved. Mountains shook. Skies opened to choirs of little white-haired angels. I can still taste him. My lips are tingling, and I want more. Perhaps I'll stage a walk-past by his apartment tomorrow . . .

More tomorrow . . .

CHAPTER TWO

All the guests were staring at me, but I was frozen.

Matt gestured at me and gave an encouraging little nod. Samantha's father cleared his throat loudly. A general murmur spread through the room.

I can do this. I can fucking do this!

"Maybe she's got a bit of stage fright. Let's give her a round of applause," Samantha's dad called out.

The room erupted into enthusiastic applause. It only made the whole thing worse.

I got up slowly and made my way to the raised platform where a mic was pinned to my dress. I took my place behind the podium and put the paper down on it, smoothing it with my sweaty palms. Hundreds of expectant eyes stared at me. I could feel them boring holes into my face, even though I hadn't dared to look up yet. If I just stuck to my pre-planned speech, it would be fine . . .

"Hi, everyone. For those who don't know me, I'm Val." At that, a few claps and whistles filled the room.

"Well, what can I say about Matt and Sam really?" I continued. "They're perfect for each other." I forced a massive smile before launching into the next part. "In fact, I've known how perfect these two were from the moment I met Sam and saw how happy she made Matt and how very, very, *very* in love he was with her . . ."

I could feel the thoughts in my brain distancing themselves from me. They floated further and further from my grasp and disappeared into the woozy, mucky sludge that had filled my cranium. Suddenly, everything was very jumbled.

"They are just *sooooooooo* in love. Like, a lot . . . I mean, you should see them sometimes, it's like 'Hey, guys, get a room.'" I heard a strange chuckle escape my mouth. A few other people chuckled, but most looked downright shocked.

Things went pretty pear-shaped after that. Why do they say pear-shaped, btw? A pear has such a lovely shape. So smooth and curvy. And nothing about this was even vaguely smooth, or curvy.

"Sometimes, they just hang onto each other so much, that I want to just pry them apart with my little claws . . . hahahah!" I laughed maniacally. A tiny moment of sanity prevailed, and I realized what I'd just said. I took a deep breath—*Get it together, Val*—and exhaled . . .

"Sqeeeeeeeeeeeeeeeee." The nasal squeak reverberated around the whole room and people recoiled.

"Sorry, sorry! My nose, it's um . . . never mind. What I meant to say is that they are very in love . . . Wait, I've already said that . . . sorry, hang on. What I'm trying to say is . . . is . . . uuuhhhh . . ."

Shit. Shit. Shit.

I looked down at the paper. The letters I'd written were

swimming on the page. The words were blurring, and a feeling
was rising. I looked up from the paper and into Samantha's angry
face. She had her arm draped around a very concerned-looking
Matt. I didn't blame him. I was concerned.

My eyes swept the crowd. A few people were snickering. Some
were whispering to each other and that feeling inside me was
growing steadily. Getting bigger, and bigger, and . . . suddenly,
the feeling was too damn big to be contained anymore. It felt like
a massive balloon was being inflated inside me and at any moment
it was just going to burst uncontrollabl—

"*SORRY!*" I shouted. "Sorry! I can't do this. I'm so sorry, I
just . . . I can't . . . I can't."

I launched myself off the platform. My feet hit the wooden
floor with a surprisingly loud thud. And then I ran from the
room as fast as my jelly legs would carry me. I wanted to be
cocooned in my safe little cubicle again, but a bloody butler holding the biggest silver platter I'd ever seen before was blocking my
path to the restroom. I turned around and ran back up the passage, ducked into one of the many lounges and slammed the door
behind me.

What the hell had I just done?

I needed to lean against something quickly before I collapsed.
My whole body was shaking. Dizzy. Nauseous. Hot. Cold.
Sweaty. Woozy and then—

"Val. Are you okay?" It was Matt! "What's wrong? You don't
look well." I tried to look away but he reached out and took my
face between his hands, tilting it up for him to see.

And that was the moment!

That was it. It was all just too much. Too much to keep bottled up inside for a second longer. I'd been locking it away, trapping it and squashing it down for so many years. And now, it was on the verge of escaping and there was nothing in the world that could stop it.

"NO! No, I am NOT okay . . . okay?" I burst into loud sobs.

"For God's sake, tell me what's wrong. You're worrying me." Matt looked genuinely concerned. Friend concerned. My heart snapped and then so did I.

"Don't you see?" I wailed through loud and very messy sobs. "Have you still not got it, Matt?" My sobs grew louder still.

"See what? Got what?" He seemed genuinely confused. *Was he really that blind?*

Have you ever watched a TV program where they show a time-lapse video of a plant bursting out of a tiny seed? It grows bigger, and bigger, until you wonder how the hell something so big could have come out of something so small. It seems to defy all the laws of nature. That's what it was like when I finally opened my mouth. The words and feelings that had been locked away for so long were enormous and endless. They burst into the space between us and filled the entire room.

"I'M IN LOVE WITH YOU! OKAY? IN LOVE WITH YOU. I've been in love with you from the second I saw you, and you kissed me and I haven't stopped loving you every second of every day since then. And now you're getting married to Samantha who is perfect and beautiful and I hate her for it! I hate her because you love her and not me. And we're so perfect for each other. We spend all our free time together, but you still don't see it. Why can't you love me? Love me—"

I stopped when I heard it. It sounded like my voice was echoing through the rooms. Bouncing back and forth. Clearly, I was hearing things. I let out a loud, frustrated wail and it came straight back to me.

"What the . . . ?" I looked up to see where the sound was coming from. Something was very, very wrong here.

"Hello?" I asked tentatively, and my voice answered right back with the same *Hello*.

I opened the door and stepped out into the passage again, trying to ascertain where the hell the sound was coming from.

"Ssshhhhh," I whispered and heard it immediately. It was as if the voice of God was repeating every single word that I was saying . . .

Holy crap!

In one earth-shattering moment, I realized what was going on. I looked down at my dress, and there it was . . . *the mic*. Still pinned to me.

My breath started coming out in short, sharp, ragged spurts, and I followed the sound of it up the passage and into a room.

The room.

Everyone swung around and glared at me in absolute horror. Their faces were smeared with shock and utter disbelief. I felt the hot flames start at my feet, sweeping up my legs, my torso and finally my face. Suddenly, I was as sober as hell. I tried to open my mouth to speak, "I . . . I . . . I . . . Squeeeeeeeeeeeeeeeeeeee."

16 Feb.
Dear Diary,

I'm confused. And mildly alarmed. I staged several walk-bys past apartment 18 in the last two days, but no sign of him. Am starting to wonder if he's one of these moochers that doesn't have a job? Like from the Dr. Phil show, "My 35-year-old moocher son is living on my couch and now he's also hearing voices" kind of thing.

I drew the line at knocking on the door, didn't want him to think I was crazy . . . says the girl who staged multiple walk-bys. *I can't help it, though. Have not been able to stop thinking about that kiss. Something happened during it. I can't quite explain it. But I've never felt anything like it before, and I'm desperate to see him again.*

Anyhoo . . . I need to finish an article about the A-Spot. Yes, that is an actual thing. And did you know, only 11% of all woman have found it? (I'm in that 11%, btw.) Got to run, need to help the other 89% navigate their way in the new sexual, alphabet soup.

More later . . .

CHAPTER THREE

~

$\mathcal{M}$y foot hit the perfectly manicured lawn, and my heel immediately dug into the fresh, wet soil. I felt my body falling forward and there was nothing I could do to stop myself from falling on my . . .

Face. Dammit!

The feeling of cold soil smearing across the side of my cheek was actually a welcome relief to the feeling of nauseating embarrassment that had been surging through me in waves since I'd run from the room. Run away from all of those eyes. Judging eyes, appalled eyes and, worst of all, amused ones. The shock and horror I could (almost) handle—I could certainly understand it—however, it was the amused looks that made me feel the worst.

But clearly, my speedy getaway wasn't exactly going as planned. I crawled onto my hands and knees, trying to pull my shoe free, but it was in too deep. I slipped my foot out of the shoe and took my other one off too, cursing the fact that I'd departed from my usual flats in the first place. I stood up and looked back at the building to make sure that no one had witnessed my fall, only, they had. My stomach plummeted when I saw some familiar eyes staring at me from behind the glass.

I turned as quickly as possible and continued my now shoeless escape. I ran across the lawn to where my rental car was parked.

I needed to get out of there.

I found my tiny red Kia sandwiched between a huge, shiny Lexus with a number plate that read "DIVORCED" and a Porsche 911 with a number plate that read "THE BOSS." Had I been myself, I would have rolled my eyes and made a note to write an article about what personalized number plates *really* said about you. But I wasn't myself. My little Kia and I needed out of there . . . and if I were to choose a license plate right now, it would have to have been FML.

I put my shoes on the bonnet of the car and frantically dug through my handbag for the set of unfamiliar car keys, but couldn't find them.

Shit! Please, please, *please* don't let me have left them back inside. I begged and pleaded with whatever benevolent force was out there—*someone, anyone*—although I seriously doubted benevolent forces were listening to me tonight. *Oh no!* 'Twas the night of dark, malevolent forces. 'Twas the night that hell cracked open the Earth and sucked me into its fiery, flaming pits. 'Twas messed up AF!

Without thinking it through, I tipped the contents of my handbag onto the bonnet of the car, and as predicted—had I been in the right state of mind for such logical deductions—everything, including my shoes, slid languidly down the curved bonnet and bounced to the floor below like dropped marbles.

"Fuck it!" I cursed again and dropped to my hands and knees, trying to reclaim the contents of my bag. But the stuff had spread so far and wide that it would have taken me ages to get it all. So I prioritized; wallet, make-up bag, tampons and shoes . . . *Wait*, where the hell was my other shoe?

I scanned the floor. Good news, I could now see the car keys. Bad news, I had to flatten myself like a pancake and slither under the car to retrieve them, scraping my body on the rough gravel as I went. I looked around one last time for my other shoe, but when I realized that it was truly nowhere to be seen, I climbed into the car as fast as I could and turned the engine on. I would love to say that the beast roared to life with a sense of urgency, but it didn't. It kind of flickered on like a little one-watt light bulb.

I tossed my shoe over my shoulder and heard it thud against the backseat, and that's when I felt the first punch in my stomach and tightening in my throat. *No!* I willed it away as hard as I could and started reversing, but as soon as I did . . .

"*Shit!*"

DIVORCED had parked so close to me that I was barely able to inch my way back. I ground the car into first, I hadn't driven a manual in years. I swung the steering wheel as hard and far as I could—no power steering either—and started inching forward.

"Double shit!"

THE BOSS was also too close. I stared back at the restaurant. I had three options: One, go back inside and find out whose cars these were and ask them to move, *not* going to happen; two, I could abandon the car here, catch an Uber and come back for it in the morning; or three, I could somehow yoga-move my way out of this.

And so I did. I began the tiring near-ten-point turn that I was forced to make in order to extricate myself from the clutches of these cars. I was finally almost out, and maybe it was because I was so desperate to go and so excited that I almost was free, that I collided with it.

The sound of my little car scraping against DIVORCED's rear bumper was ear-splitting and made my teeth tingle, as if I'd just bitten into an unripe banana.

"No! NO! No!" I looked around to see if anyone had seen me—they had!

I begun swinging the steering wheel again as DIVORCED came running out of the restaurant and started darting across the lawn. Shit, she was fast! Being DIVORCED clearly gave her lots of time for things like CrossFit. I saw another figure emerge from the restaurant and start running—it was Matt! I had to get out of here. Suddenly, a third figure emerged, I surmised it was THE BOSS, since I'd just hit his car too. They all dashed towards me and were nearly upon me when I finally managed to maneuver myself free. I pressed my foot down on the pedal so hard that the wheels spun and gravel flicked, and then I flew out of the parking space.

I raced away as fast as the pathetic one-liter engine could take me. Down the long gravel driveway and back onto the main road. There was a loud buzzing sound in my ears, a terrible metallic taste in my mouth, my fingers were tingling and my mind and heart were racing. Not only had I embarrassed myself in front of what felt like the entire world, but now I had also just committed a hit and run. *I was a criminal!*

That feeling struck again. The punch in my stomach and tightening in my throat.

I swung my steering wheel again, veering off the road. I slammed on the brakes, put on the hazard lights and burst into tears.

20 Feb.
Dear Diary,

So, as it turns out, the A-Spot is much easier to find than my neighbor and I'm seriously starting to consider the fact that I may have hallucinated the entire thing. My friends all seem skeptical too and are suggesting some kind of vodka-induced hallucination. This, of course, raises serious questions about my general mental wellbeing as a whole—or my previously held beliefs in my ability to hold my drink. I'm leaning more towards the fact that it DID actually happen, just because I have no history of hallucinations and I'm half-Russian; my grandmother gave me vodka shots to cure a cold once.

Anyway, A-Spot article is really "revolutionary" says new editor. A real "eye-opener, or leg-opener" if you will. New Woman online magazine has just employed a new editor named Davida, pronounced Dah Vee Daaaarrrrr (roll the R). She seems nice, but you know what it's like, these types can turn so quickly—like milk left on the counter overnight.

She wants another article from me asap, still trying to decide what it should be:

1. *How To Get Abs In Ten Days. (Not likely, but readers like abs, especially at the beginning of the year when we're still all encased in that layer of Christmas blubber.)*

2. *Ten Things Men Wish Their Women Knew About Going Down On Them. (Have no idea what those are*

yet, make note to research. But suspect one is, "don't use teeth.")

3. Ten Ways To Tell He Likes You. *(Why do these things always come in tens, let's try sevens next time. Quicker. Less thinking.)*

More later . . .

20 Feb. (later that day)

As it turns out I am not mad and hallucinating and I can hold my drink. Matt (that's his name btw) is very real. In fact, Matt has been away on business this entire time. Because Matt is an actual adult with a real job—unlike myself. Matt, as it turns out, is a Quantitative Analyst. Of course I have no idea what that means, but nodded my head and made a note to Google it later.

(Googled: A quantitative analyst is a person who specializes in the application of mathematical and statistical methods—such as numerical or quantitative techniques—to financial and risk management problems.)

Okay. Now I really don't know what it means. But Matt is also rather confusing. Very.

He claims to only vaguely remember meeting me in the lift and no mention of the kiss. At all. He's not even acting awkwardly around me. I'm not sure if I should be offended. No. Of course, I'm offended that he doesn't remember that kiss. But things are still looking promising, because he did invite me to his house-warming party. Mind you, there's still a possibility that Matt might turn out to be very boring. Very, quantitative-number-crunching boring. He could also be a total asshole. Men that look like he does often are. I've always noted that the hotter the man, the less developed his personality can be.

Anyhoo . . . I've decided to do the article on Ten Ways To Tell If He Likes You *since it will be very beneficial to know these things moving forward. So far this is the list:*

1. He initiates conversation.

2. He listens and remembers what you say.

3. He leans forward when you talk.

4. He makes direct eye contact and smiles.

5. He compliments your appearance.

6. He teases you playfully. (This one reminds me of school days, when a boy would throw a ball at your head or snap your bra strap to convey his feelings. Maybe men really don't change that much.)

I shall look out for these signs at the house-warming. More soon . . .

CHAPTER FOUR

Here's the big, fat universal truth about unrequited love . . .
It hurts. Period.

It holds you in its fiendish grip and it squeezes the life out of you. It makes you feel physically ill and turns you into someone with a single-minded obsession that rages inside your head day and night. *Make him love me. Make him see me, make him love me* . . . It's exhausting and draining and constantly chaotic. And, eventually, it becomes completely all-consuming. It becomes the thing that defines you. Loving *him*, and not being loved back, becomes everything.

Profound, hey? Great insight, don't ya think? I know, because I wrote an article about it once. As a freelance writer for various women's magazines I write all kinds of articles about these very things:

How To Tell If A Man Just Isn't That Into You.

How To Get Out Of The Friend Zone.

And of course . . .

How To Get Over Unrequited Love.

But you think I would take my own advice. What's that saying about the shoemaker's children having the worst shoes? Well, I was like that. Except now I only had one shoe. Not that any of the articles I write have any real basis in scientific fact or proven theory, though. The most research I do is typing something into the Google bar.

I was still sitting in my car on the side of the road. I was squeezing the steering wheel so hard that my fingers were about to fall off. I clenched my jaw; it felt like I might crack a tooth. I closed my eyes tightly and tried to will away the avalanche of tears that had been streaming down my face for the last five minutes. I was like the little Dutch boy with his finger in the dike, desperately trying to hold it all back. But I was failing, and now, it was just spewing forth with the pent-up vengeance that was three, long, painful years in the making.

Because Matt was it.

If I couldn't have him, then there was no one else for me. Of course my friends were all very fond of pointing out how utterly irrational that thought was. But it was what I'd thought every single day, at least ten times a day, for the last three years. I'd thought it so damn much that now I genuinely believed it. If not Matt, then who?

I glanced in my rear-view mirror, there were hardly any cars on the road at this time and no sign of THE BOSS, DIVORCED or Matt. I pulled back onto the road and started driving in the direction of my hotel. Matt and most of the engagement party were staying there and the prospect of bumping into them was more than a little horrifying. So as soon as I reached the hotel, I ran to my room and threw myself in.

But once inside, I wasn't sure what to do with myself. I was experiencing a kind of prickly anxiety that was making me want to pace the room and scratch my arms. And so I did. I walked and scratched the psychosomatic itch that was emanating from the inside, that no amount of scratching could fix.

This was *not* how I'd seen this situation playing out. And, believe me, I'd seen it play out many times before. There had been many nights when I'd lain in bed playing the scenario out over and over in my head. Firstly, in my scenario there had been no audience. And secondly, Matt was meant to look at me adoringly, love emanating from his eyes, open his mouth and . . .

"*Oh my God! Yes. Yes. I love you too, Val. I've always loved you. I've loved you since that day we kissed in the lift* (in my version he remembers the kiss). *I love you! I choose you!*"

Or some such variation of the above. Anything other than what he'd said tonight.

"I'm so sorry, Val, I had no idea. I've never thought about you like that. You're my best friend. You're family."

A stab of pain, mixed with embarrassment, kicked me in the gut again. Although, I'm not sure you can even call this embarrassment. This feeling transcended any normal understanding of embarrassment. This was nothing like the feeling I'd gotten when I'd had my legs up in stirrups at the gynaes, and a strange man had walked in thinking his wife was in that room. Or the feeling I'd gotten when my nephew had found the vibrator in my drawer, turned it on and run around the house with it thinking it was a toy while my parents were visiting.

No, this was nothing like that. This was something else entirely.

25 Feb.

Dear Diary,

He is not an asshole. He is not boring. He is, in fact, one of the funniest, coolest, nicest guys I've ever met. Just come back from Matt's house-warming party. It was very interesting. Matt's friends were all very "finance-y." They all thought it was fascinating that I was a freelance features writer. They asked so many questions, as if I was some kind of exotic species that they had only just discovered living under a mossy fern in the Amazon.

But I did get to spend a lot of time with Matt. And I don't think I'm imagining it, but we really bonded. We have the same sense of humor, the same dislike of French foods: frogs' legs, foie gras, escargots. We both like beer, pizza with pineapple on and watching rugby (maybe me for different reasons to him, though. Truthfully, I only became a fan of the sport after seeing those calendar pictures of the rugby players wearing nothing but strategically positioned balls).

I also watched out for all the signs tonight too, and this is what I think:

1. *He initiates conversation—Check! As soon as I walked in the door.*

2. *He listens and remembers what you say—Yes! At the beginning of the night I told him how I liked my martini, and at the end of the night, he still remembered.*

3. *He leans forward when you talk—Yes. But to be fair, the music was loud. So not 100% sure about this one.*

4. *He makes direct eye contact and smiles—Yes.*

5. *He compliments your appearance—Not sure. He complimented my fitbit—said he liked the color of it and asked if it was any good.*

On a bad note, he still hasn't said a thing about the kiss and I am starting to genuinely believe that he doesn't remember it. More later . . .

CHAPTER FIVE

The knock on the hotel room door happened at precisely 3:33 a.m. I know this, because I was still awake, staring at the clock, willing morning to come so I could get the hell out of there.

"Val, I know you're in there. We need to talk." It was Matt.

Maybe if I ignored him he'd go away?

"Val, pleeeease," he implored me in that oh-so-familiar tone. The tone that was so bloody hard to resist. Like when he'd asked if I minded throwing his laundry in with mine and doing it for him because he was so busy at work. Or when he'd asked if he could borrow my car, because his was in for a service, and I'd said yes and cancelled a coffee with my friends.

But not this time. "No," I finally managed feebly, sounding unsure of myself. Which I was. "NO!" I said it again, a little louder and firmer this time, but still not quite convincingly.

"Please," he whined into the door, and I couldn't help it, but I moved closer. I waddled all the way up to the door—it was hard to bend my bloody, scraped knees—and rested my head against it. I could see the shadows of his feet under the door and I could hear his breathing. He was so close . . . yet he was so, *so* very far away.

"I can hear you," he whispered against the door in that other familiar tone. It was that playful voice, with the lilting quality to it that always made it sound a little flirty. This was the tone that had perpetually fueled my hopes these three years, like petrol to a fire. It was the tone that had me riding a relentless emotional rollercoaster that I was now so dizzy and exhausted from.

"I can't," I whispered back. I heard him sigh. Something about his sigh pissed me off. Why would *he* be sighing? Shouldn't all the sighing and huffing and puffing be reserved for me?

"I need to talk to you," he continued. And because, clearly, I wasn't quite through embarrassing myself for one evening, I opened my mouth.

"Need? Ha! Well, I've needed a lot of things too and I haven't gotten any of them. Now have I? We all need things, Matt. Everyone fucking needs things, don't they?" As soon as I'd finished the sentence, I regretted saying it. There was no need to add any more drama to this already overly-dramatic situation.

Another sigh from him. "I'm sorry. I don't know what to say to you. I don't know how to make this better."

"You can't make it better." My voice quivered and tears began to sting my eyes. "Where's Sam?" I suddenly asked.

He paused for the longest time before speaking. "I waited until she was asleep."

God, he sounded guilty as hell. Like the husband who comes home late after work because he's been in an "emergency meeting" (Miss Scarlet, in the boardroom with a whip).

"Aaah . . . I see." The guilt in his voice made me feel cheap and dirty. Like I was his slutty Miss Scarlet on the side. This wasn't the first time I'd felt this way either. There'd been many a night when Sam had been working late and we'd hung out together and phrases like *"please don't tell her we went out, she thinks I'm at home working"* were thrown around.

"Please leave," I said. There was a long pause and I waited with anticipation for his answer. Truthfully, there was still this part of me that was hoping he might barge through the door at any moment, take me in his arms and tell me what a mistake he'd made with Sam. We'd fall into each other's arms and kiss and then make love all night long.

God, I hated that part of myself and I wondered if it was possible to kill it off somehow?

"I understand if you don't want to talk to me, but at least open the door so I can give you your shoe. You left it on the driveway."

Shit! And under normal circumstance I might have just told him to keep it, but the things had cost a bloody fortune. "Leave it outside," I said.

"Okay," he replied feebly.

I pressed my ear to the door, waiting for the sounds of his footsteps, and when I was confident that he was no longer there, I opened the door and looked down. My one fancy shoe was on the floor and the irony of this moment did not escape me.

This was my Cinderella slipper, delivered by Prince Charming himself. Only, this prince wasn't mine. His heart belonged to someone else. The problem was that he was in possession of my heart, and I had no idea how to go about getting it back.

4 March
Dear Diary,

Matt has asked me around to his place today to watch the rugby and drink beer! And it's just going to be the two of us. We've seen each other almost every day this week, either in the lift, walking past each other in the corridor, or having a conversation in the parking lot. I think he likes me, I mean, why else would he be inviting me to his place tonight? Alone. I have to get ready.

More laters . . .

4 March (later)
Dear Diary,

Okay, quick update, nothing happened. But he did hug me goodbye and I'm sure the hug lingered for a few seconds longer than it should have. Maybe my friends are right, maybe he's just shy around me because he does remember the kiss but doesn't know how to broach the subject?

More laters (hopefully!)

CHAPTER SIX

I arrived at the airport at 6 a.m., four hours before my actual flight. Matt and Sam and the rest of the engagement party were also booked on that flight and I was hoping to avoid them all by getting onto an earlier one. Because I hadn't slept a wink that night, I felt almost drunk on the exhaustion.

The rental car inspection had not gone well. The angry-looking man with the clipboard and clicky-pen had been very displeased when he'd seen the state of the car. I was made to fill out a hundred forms and in my haste and strange, tired state, I didn't read any of them. For all I knew I could have signed my soul away or joined a pyramid scheme and my box of miracle slimming tablets was already en route to my house. But I didn't care. I had much bigger things to worry about today than the silly bumper that had fallen off and was now in the trunk. Yellowstone could have erupted today, I could have learned that ground baby panda bear paws were being used in the manufacture of my favorite face cream, or that the Amazon had been completely flattened for a Trump theme park—and probably still wouldn't have cared.

When I finally got inside the airport I discovered that the earlier flight was fully booked. But I was put on standby, just in case a seat became free. If I couldn't get on that flight, I would need to find a safe place to hide, and then book myself onto a later flight—thus avoiding the engagement party. So I found myself a chair in the far corner of the airport. But I couldn't get comfortable. And it wasn't because the seats were hard and cold and my knees were stinging. I could feel that overwhelming monster of an emotion building. I dug in my handbag, pulled out a piece of gum and shoved it in my mouth; it was all I could do to stop myself from screaming. And that's when I saw it. I reached in and pulled it out. My diary. It flopped open on a page. I swallowed hard. This was where it had all began . . .

20 June
Dear Diary,

I'm in love. I'm totally in love with Matt. I have no idea how this happened so quickly. We've been spending almost every day together, either my house or his. And when we're not spending time together, we're messaging each other constantly. He messages me something boring that happened in his office like, "Board meeting with entire finance department" and I message him back with how I might turn that into an article, like "Seven ways to have an orgy on a boardroom table without being caught by your boss." Okay, it sounds so lame when I write it like that, but it's not. It's so much fun. And it happens all the time.

We already have an inside joke! This has to be a sign that it's more than "just friends." Surely? Friends don't spend all day together and then constantly message each other when they're apart. Well, friends of the opposite sex anyway. I just wish I knew how he felt. I've been dropping hints like crazy and steering the conversations in directions that are conducive to "relationship talk." And I'm not ashamed to admit that I've also steered them to a rather sexy, flirty place once or twice, but I'm not sure he's getting it!

More later . . .

CHAPTER SEVEN

～

$\mathcal{M}$y bum had just started going numb from sitting on the hard metal airport chair when I saw someone familiar in the distance. I recognized the walk immediately. Matt has this cool kind of swagger that makes you think of sexy, lasso-wielding cowboys. Panic seized me and, without thinking, I dove straight onto the floor.

"EX-ca-uuuse me!" the woman sitting next to me said. I glanced up and saw she was looking down at me in horror, as if I'd just committed some monumental crime against humanity. As if I was personally responsible for global warming, world poverty and antibiotic-resistant superbugs.

"What?" I looked up at her.

"Do. You. Mind?" Her eyes flicked from my face, to my hand, and then back again. I followed them.

"Oh. Sorry, I didn't see it . . ." I mumbled, removing my hand from off her shopping bag.

She reached down and picked the bag up angrily. "Oh, now

look!" she moaned, pulling something out of the bag. "I bought this chocolate for my grandson and you've gone and crushed it."

"Hardly," I said looking at the perfect slab.

"Here." She pointed to the corner of it, where a tiny piece of foil wrapping had been ever-so-slightly disturbed.

"Oh, please. I didn't do that."

"Young lady," she said, her voice slightly louder than I would have liked, and I looked up quickly to see where Matt was. He was still walking in my direction and, *oh-no*, Doctor Samantha had just joined him. *What the hell were they doing here so early?* Perhaps they'd also had the same thought; try and get on an earlier flight to avoid me?

"You have destroyed my grandson's chocolate." Her voice got even louder and the man sitting across from us glanced in our direction.

"I'm sorry. Here." I pulled out my wallet and handed her a fifty-rand note. "Get him another one."

"It was the last one," she said, but snatched the money anyway.

"Well, I'm sure there're many other chocolates out there." I didn't bother concealing the sarcasm in my voice.

The old woman sat up straight. "Are you sassing me?" Vocal volume really growing now!

"Shhhhh," I hissed at her, putting my finger over my lips in a desperate attempt to silence her.

"Don't you dare shush me. And what on earth are you doing on the floor anyway?" Too loud! Way too loud. People were starting to turn and stare.

I looked up again. Matt and Sam were getting closer, and I started panicking. I needed to get out of there, unseen. So I shot up, grabbed my bag and started power-marching away as fast as I could, hoping that I wouldn't be seen. Only I was.

"Val?" It was Matt.

Shit! My power-march turned into a jog which soon turned into a run as I scuttled across the airport.

"Val. Wait!" he called. And then I heard another voice.

"Matt, what the hell are you doing?" Sam said. "Come back here. Immediately!" She sounded furious. I didn't blame her.

"Val. Stop!" Matt called out again. But I didn't. How the hell was I ever going to look at him again when just the sound of his voice made me so embarrassed and panicky that I wanted to puke? I picked up pace and took a sharp left, and to my absolute joy, found this section of the airport jam-packed with hundreds of jostling bodies.

International departures. I pushed my way straight into the dense crowd and started weaving through them, going deeper and deeper into the sea of noisy, moving bodies.

When I was satisfied that I was right in the belly of the beast and that there was no way I could be seen, I took refuge behind a large group of Chinese tourists and let out a long, loud sigh of relief.

Behind me stood a very large man with a sunburnt wife the color of a lobster. I could tell immediately that they were foreigners who'd come here on safari. She was kitted out head-to-toe in those trinkets you buy from game reserve shops, including two huge elephant head earrings. I was so intrigued by the way they swung so violently every time she moved her head, that when I suddenly found myself at the counter I was shocked.

"Huh?" I looked at the woman behind the counter who was now talking to me. "I didn't get that?" I said.

"Ticket, please," she replied.

"Ti . . . Oh. No. I don't have one," I said, ducking down a little now that my Chinese protectors were gone.

"Ticket, please," she repeated. Very slowly this time.

"I'm not really catching a flight," I whispered to her. Her face crunched up, and she looked at me as if I were speaking in ancient tongues.

"I know this is a little odd, but please can I just stand here while you help other people? I'm trying to hide from someone." I rolled my eyes and tried to give her a knowing sisterly look. "You know. Men," I tutted. But my attempts at sisterly bonding were not working on this puckered-lipped waif. She glared at me.

"No, this would not be all right," she spat. Her pitch-black hair was scraped back into a perfect ballerina bun. It was so tight that it looked like it was pulling her eyes and forehead back, DIY Botox. Her lips were stained a deep mauve color—very on fleek— and her eyelashes were as long as a cow's.

"Ticket, please!" She sounded like a stuck record now. I bit my lip and shook my head, refusing to move.

"Hey, lady!" the American with the lobster wife shouted out. His deep voice was so loud and booming, that once again a few people turned.

"Miss, I must insist that if you do not have a ticket, you must leave the line immediately." The woman spoke again, her mauve lips enunciating the words.

"Yeah!" The American agreed, and suddenly two other people joined in and the general volume of the conversation increased several more decibels. I looked around nervously and then, much to my horror, I saw Matt again. I turned my back on him and lowered my head to the counter.

"Well?" the woman at the counter asked.

"I . . . I . . ." Terror washed over me in violent waves that made me start sweating.

"Oh, for God's sake, you're holding up the whole queue," someone else from the crowd shouted.

"I'm going to miss my flight if this carries on," another person chipped in.

"Yeah!" the American seconded. "And then I'll have to sue you and the airline."

"Ticket!" the woman behind the counter pressed.

I looked around, everyone was staring at me and then, out of the corner of my eye, I saw Matt's head turn. *Shit!* Our eyes locked for a second and then he started moving towards me. I turned quickly.

"Ticket, I want one. NOW!" I yelled in her face.

"Which flight?" she asked.

"I don't care," I hissed at the woman. "Just get me on the next flight to, to . . ."

"Val!" Matt was shouting now. I vaguely heard the woman behind the desk mutter something about some island somewhere. I didn't care.

"Yes! That one. That flight! Hurry, hurry, hurry."

I turned and watched in jaw-dropping horror as Matt started getting closer and closer, pushing his way through the thick crowd.

"Move it, move it, move it!" I tapped my hand on the counter as the woman typed.

"That will be—"

"I don't care," I cut her off, thrusting my credit card and passport at her. Who the hell cared what it cost? I needed to get out of there.

"Luggage to check in?"

"No. Carry-on."

"Okay, then enjoy your—"

"VAL!" he screamed. I grabbed the ticket from the woman's hands and ran through the international security gates as fast as I bloody could, not stopping to look behind me.

20 Aug.

Dear Diary,

I know it's been a while. But I've been so busy and this Matt thing is all I can think about. It's driving me fucking crazy. It's like I have a song stuck on repeat in my head. And I don't know how many hints I'm meant to drop either? There is only so much laughing and leaning and staring and touching a girl can do before she comes across as a total creep. The only thing I haven't tried yet is taking actual clothing off and cartwheeling in front of him with my lady parts in the air!

I'm starting to wonder if he's even picking up on my signals. My friends think he is and is deliberately shying away from them, because he knows how intense our connection is and that scares him.

But I've watched the movie He's Just Not That Into You. *Isn't that just a thing that friends are meant to say to each other? So as not to hurt your feelings? Although, I do take some comfort from the fact that Ginnifer Goodwin's character got together with that love-cynical bartender guy. But, on the other hand, Jennifer Connelly's character did end up alone. (But that was because Bradley Cooper had an affair with Scarlett Johannsson, I mean . . . who wouldn't? Look at her! I digress!)*

At least this has all given me an idea for work. Have been doing research for a new article "Real friends tell you the ugly truth, not the pretty little lies"—it's about the lies we tell our friends, but shouldn't.

1. *She tells you that your new haircut is cute, "you can totally pull off the pixie cut," even when it makes you look like a boy*

2. *When she changes her profile pic to one that she thinks makes her look sexy, but it's just a little too slutty and try-hard.*

3. *You tell her you totally like her new boyfriend because you don't want to hurt her feelings, but clearly the guy is a loser and totally beneath her.*

Need to run and think of four more lies we tell our friends. Have managed to get lists of seven past editors at the moment. YAY! Anyhoooo . . .

More later . . .

P.S. I AM SO IN LOVE WITH MATT

P.P.S. I HAVE NEVER EVER FELT THIS WAY ABOUT ANYONE BEFORE

CHAPTER EIGHT

I had no intention of boarding any flight bound for any island today. All I intended to do was sit at the bar and wait until I was sure Matt and Sam and whoever else was at the airport were gone. Then I would leave and catch a flight back to Johannesburg.

Yes, yes . . . I knew how cowardly, not to mention expensive, this little mad escapade had just made me look. Running away from the problem, quite literally. But I was running away for a good reason: self-preservation!

I once watched a YouTube video of a snake that pretended to die dramatically by thrashing and twisting around like that girl from *The Exorcist.* I was seriously considering this as my next option if running away didn't work. If I walked out of here and Matt and Sam were still there, I may be faced with no other option but to fake my own dramatic death right there and then on the airport floor.

I felt as if I was in some kind of a strange, surreal daze. Like a big heavy blanket of fog had descended on me. My phone beeped for what felt like the hundredth time, and I looked down at it. My friends had clearly learned of my crashing and burning and were all very concerned.

Annie: You okay? I just heard what happened!

Boy, did bad news spread fast. I turned my phone off and slipped it back into my bag.

"Hey. Hi!" I raised my hand in the air and waved at the barman. My arm felt unusually heavy and somewhat hard to lift. "Another vodka, lime and soda. Please," I said when he turned.

I looked up at the TV behind the bar. A familiar program was playing and I found that somewhat comforting. It was season 3 of the UK's *Big Band Battle*, in which wannabe rock-star hopefuls competed to win a recording contract. The band that was currently playing was called Six Feet Over It.

The lead singer was totally over the top. He was trying very hard to be sexy. He gripped the mic in the way he might grip the naked flesh of a woman, running his hand up and down the mic stand suggestively as he thrust his pelvis and sang passionately.

Their music was definitely of the cheesy, eighties power-ballad ilk, but it wasn't entirely offensive. It was the kind of music that you would probably find yourself singing along to at a wedding, if you'd had a glass of champagne, or seven. The song reached its dramatic crescendo whereby the lead singer threw himself onto the stage floor. He grabbed his chest as if he was having a heart attack and then raised his head, looked directly into the camera and grimaced as if he was having a painful bowel movement. I rolled my eyes. That was taking it a tad too far, methinks.

I downed my new drink when it arrived and realized it was probably a good idea to leave it there. I stood up, slapped some money down on the counter and decided to move on to a duty-free shop. I took a few steps, then, suddenly, I heard my name.

"Valeria Ivanov." It was a woman's voice and there was something warm and comforting about her tone. It was almost motherly.

"Valeria Ivanov." The voice spoke again and I felt compelled to find out where it was coming from.

I walked slowly through the mad rush of people in the airport.

"Valeria Ivanov." The voice called again. "This is the last boarding call for Valeria Ivanov. Please proceed to gate twelve for immediate boarding."

I looked to my left, and there it was. As if this was some kind of sign. As if it had been put there purposefully, just for me. *Gate 12.* A shiny, golden beacon calling my name—literally. I stared at the gate for a while. The pretty-looking woman standing there lowered her mouth to the microphone.

"This is the last boarding call for Valeria Ivanov. Flight F765, departing from gate twelve." The woman gazed around with a concerned look in her eye, and for some reason I felt bad for her and touched by her concern. Then she turned to the man next to her and spoke.

"She's not coming." And with those words, something inside me flicked on. Something inside me screamed to life and I suddenly found myself shouting.

"WAIT!" Everyone around me stopped walking and looked. "Wait for me. I'm coming!" I shouted again. I hobbled towards the gate on still unbendable knees.

"Valeria Ivanov?" the woman asked.

"Yes," I replied passing over my ticket and passport.

She smiled at me. "I'm so glad. We were starting to think you weren't going to make it."

"I'm here," I said, "and I'm going to make it!" I said that line with a kind of poignant reverence. Yes, I was going to make it. *Wasn't I?*

She tore my ticket in half and handed me the smallest piece. I gripped it in my hands and followed her down the carpeted corridor and straight up to the open door of the plane. The air hostess at the gate smiled at me.

"Welcome aboard," she said. And for some reason I wanted to cry at the kindness in her voice. I had to fight the urge not to hug her. I walked down the aisle to what looked like the only empty seat on the plane.

I slipped my small bag into the overhead storage compartment and sat down, buckling myself in. I did a double take when I saw who was sitting next to me; the Americans from the queue. The man shot me a curious eye.

"So, you're coming then?" he asked sarcastically.

"I am." I smiled back at him. "But to where?" I asked.

"Huh?" He looked at me oddly and then glanced at his wife.

"Where are we going, exactly?"

His eyes flashed with surprise. "Réunion," he said slowly.

"Re-who-where?" I asked. I'd never heard of the place in my entire life!

The plane started moving and then it suddenly dawned on me. *What the fuck was I doing?* I'd just boarded an international flight by "accident" and I had no idea where the hell I was going.

15 Sept.
Dear Diary,

Yes! I know. It's been a while. But I've been away, burning in the fiery pits of friend-zoned hell.

Half of my friends think that maybe I need to accept the fact that I could be in the friend zone, and the other half still think that it can't possibly be platonic. Platonic friends don't spend so much time together. They think that maybe he knows how serious a relationship this would be if we got together, and maybe he's just not ready for it? (That's the current working theory from Lilly and Annie anyway.) Jane and Stormy are leaning more towards the whole, "he's not into you" thing.

I don't know what to think anymore. I went to see a psychologist, not because I'm depressed or anything like that, but because I felt like I needed an outside opinion. But apparently psychologists don't like to ever give opinions on things. I thought it was their job to give opinions and help you figure out what the right thing to do was. But NO! She kept saying, "What do I feel should happen?" "What do I think he feels?" "What do I think it means?" "What do I think that will mean for me?"

HELLO . . . If I knew the answers to any of those questions, I would not have come to you.

Anyway . . . Whatever . . . More later . . .

CHAPTER NINE

⚓

*R*éunion Island; a French island in the Indian Ocean. It's known for its volcanic, rain-forested interior, high mountain ranges, coral reefs and tropical beaches.

Well, according to the in-flight magazine I'd browsed during the flying anyway. The flight had been short, only a few hours, I hadn't expected that. Since I'd never heard of this strange place, I was sure it was going to be somewhere far away, like in the Bermuda Triangle. Instead, having it right off the South African coast made the fact that I didn't know it a little embarrassing.

The flight had given me a chance to talk to my new American friends though. Pam and Bob, who hailed from Texas and had come on an African safari to celebrate their thirtieth wedding anniversary. I'd told them my entire story and they'd weighed in, and both agreed. Matt definitely had feelings for me, because there was no such thing as a truly platonic friendship, they said. I felt somewhat better when I finally disembarked. That is, until I realized I had no idea what the hell I was meant to do next.

I stood in the airport looking around. I couldn't quite believe I was here. The people rushing past me all looked like they were in high holiday spirits. I stood there considering my options, before deciding that the best thing to do would be to book a flight straight back to South Africa.

"What do you mean there're only two flights a week and the next one is full?" I asked the woman behind the counter.

She looked at me and repeated the same thing, a little slower this time. "There are only two flights a week between Réunion and South Africa, today's one back is full and the next one is in three days' time."

"Three days?" I couldn't quite believe it. This threw a spanner in my works. I couldn't stay in the airport for three days, could I? At that, Pam and Bob walked past me.

"Goodbye," I called after them. "Where are you staying, by the way?"

"Saint-Gilles," Pam called out as she walked. "It's meant to be beautiful."

"Thanks." I waved at them and then pulled my phone out. I went straight to a last-minute booking website and typed in the location and my desired dates. Suddenly, my screen was full of tropical beaches, bright green palm trees, cocktails with long, twirly straws and carnival-colored fruits. A small smile tugged at the corners of my mouth. Sudden images of me on the beach with my face buried in a colorful drink raced through my mind and made me feel very, *very* happy.

I flicked through the pictures and finally found what I was looking for; white beaches, crystal waters, lush green lawns, a colonial-looking hotel and the kind of breakfast buffet you could

spend an entire day hanging out with. I pressed a few more buttons and just like that, I was booked in. Maybe three days of sea,
sand and fresh air was exactly what I needed to forget this entire
disastrous mess. I'd had to dip into my emergency savings fund,
but hey, if this wasn't an emergency then what was?

2 Nov.
Dear Diary,

A spark of hope.

*It's not all doom and gloom, Matt has invited me to his
parents 50th wedding anniversary party. I know I am not
reading too much into this when I say it feels date-y. All my
friends agree too—even Jane and Stormy have come off the
fence on this one. Even they concur that an invite like this
implies more than friendship.*

*The best part, it's an away party. We'll be taking a drive
down to the Midlands, staying there for two nights and returning on Monday morning. The Midlands are misty and romantic.
And it's cold. Which means raging log fires and gluhwein and
the need to get under fluffy, warm duvets—hopefully together.
So much to do before going.*

To Do List

1. *Get Brazilian. (Remember to put fear of God into
   waxologist after last disaster when hot wax landed in a
   place that nothing should ever go near and the only way
   to get rid of it was to rip . . . just because the Kardashians
   wax down there, doesn't mean you want to.)*

2. *Eyebrow shaping.*

3. *Buy condoms—because you are going to use them! (WHOO-HOO! Fist pump. Be positive. Don't let the fact you haven't had sex in over a year bring your confidence down. It's like riding a bicycle. It's like riding a bicycle. It's like riding a bicycle—repeat mantra throughout day.)*

4. *Get new lingerie—not too slutty, but not too Virgin Mary. Maybe pink. Red is too much. Red might say this is premeditated and that you have been anticipating this. White is perhaps too little. (Maybe it would be cheaper to throw the reds into my washing machine with my whites and see what happens.)*

This is it. I know it. It has to be! If I am here tomorrow this time and I have not told Matt how I feel, then I fear it will be too late.

More cuming soon . . . (terrible pun intended!)

9 Nov.
Dear Diary,

I've waited an entire week to write this because I didn't know how to face you with the news.

Matt and I did not while we were away at the anniversary party. In fact, I hardly saw him for those two days as he buzzed around with all his other friends and family.

I'm wondering if I can return the sexy undies I bought? I really splashed out this time, more so than usual. I probably can't, since I did try them on once and ripped the label off. So I guess they will just go into my underwear drawer with all the others I've bought for Matt. The drawer is overflowing and I don't know what to do with them. I have watched Orange is the New Black *and saw that storyline where the prisoners started selling their worn panties to weird panty sniffers on the internet, that might be a real option for me at some stage . . .*

I'm deflecting with humor here. But honestly, there is nothing humorous about any of this.

More later, but probably not . . .

CHAPTER TEN

~

$\mathcal{I}$t was dusk when my taxi pulled up to the hotel. The drive had been spectacular. On my right, the road wound its way along the idyllic, sparkling coastline, and to my left, huge mountains reached up to the sky. When I finally got to the hotel, I couldn't help the small gasp that escaped my lips. It was gorgeous. It looked like one of those massive plantation houses in Louisiana, hopefully without the creepy horror movie feel. It was set back on rolling emerald green lawns with the tallest palm trees I'd ever seen. I climbed out of the car and was hit by the warm sea breeze. A subtle scent hung in the air too—what was it? Magnolia?

The inside of the hotel was just as spectacular as the outside. It was all so reminiscent of those bygone colonial days. Drinking gin and tonics in white cotton dresses while lounging on the patio and watching the cricket. I felt as if I was being transported back in time.

It was exactly 7 p.m. when I checked in and finally got to my room. The room didn't disappoint either. It was huge and luxurious and had one of those enormous beds that you could get lost in. The bath was a round tub that was more reminiscent of a plunge pool than an actual bath. I suddenly wished more than anything that Matt would magically appear in the bath, and when I realized he wouldn't, I headed straight for the very well-stocked minibar.

No, it wasn't for the alcohol this time. It was the large bag of M&Ms that were calling my name. The giant Twix bars, *extra-long, buy two get one free*, were singing to me right now. Indeed, it was a massive bag of crisps that implored me to eat it.

But the food did little to comfort me, in fact, all it did was remind me of Matt. Our evenings spent on the couch together eating junk food and drinking beer until our pants were so tight and we had to open our top buttons. It reminded me of all those times that I'd sat there loving him so hard, and not having him love me back.

In fact, most things reminded me of Matt. We'd spent so much time together over the last three years that he'd become an integral part of my life. Like a thread permanently woven into a tapestry, and I wasn't sure there was any way of getting him out of it without the whole picture falling apart.

My mind whirled in circles and I went to my bag and pulled out my diary again. I hadn't written in it for a while, but I read it often. I'd spent many a night flipping through it, analyzing the trajectory of our relationship and trying to figure out where it had gone wrong. I kept trying to identify that one moment that should have told me, beyond a reasonable doubt, that he was just *not* into me. I'd thought I'd found it the other day. I opened it and read.

3 Dec.
Dear Diary,

Worst thing ever happened. I am so far in the friend zone that there is no returning from it. While watching a movie together today, Matt farted next to me.

　　Farted.

　　That's all . . .

But each time I thought I had proof, I found something else that contradicted it. I turned the page and continued to read:

20 Dec.
Dear Diary,

Friends offered new take on farting incident: "Maybe he is just so comfortable around you that he can do that? Maybe it really means that he likes you THAT much. That he knows you will accept every part of him."

　　Interesting theory. I did some research on it too, and as it turns out I found a piece called, "He doesn't love you unless he farts around you." Article seemed to confirm friend's suggestions. Maybe farting is not all that bad. Maybe I am not as deep in the friend zone as I thought.

　　More later . . .

Dear Diary (Later)

　　No! I am so deep in the friend zone. So, so deep. Knee-deep? Waist-deep? No, I'm drowning in it. So today I did it, I had to. During one of our regular SMS marathons, I said, "I love you." And his response? Can you guess? "Luv ya too, dude."

Dude!

That should be considered one of the filthy four-letter words. In fact, I'm not sure I've ever read a word that has hurt me so deeply. My friends are starting to change their tune again. I wish they weren't as confused as I was. Now they also suspect he's not into me.

But how can Matt not be my soulmate? We spend so much time together, we have fun together, we are comfortable around each other, we share everything with each other . . . how can this not be a clear sign for soulmate-ness?

Maybe I mustn't give up? Shit! I don't know. I don't know what to do. I'm back in that loop. The song is playing over and over in my head again.

More later . . .

Just reading it was making me exhausted and giving me a headache. I tossed the diary onto the bed and tried to figure out what the hell I was meant to do next. I opened the doors at the other end of my room and walked out onto the patio. The warm sea breeze hit me in the face and it was amazing.

The swimming pool was directly in front of me, its surface rippling in the breeze and glistening in the moonlight. And on the other side of the pool, behind a huge row of softly swaying palm trees, I could see the beach and tranquil sea. I sat there looking out over these various sights, hoping that they might imbue me with some kind of Dalai Lama-like inner peace, but they didn't. Each time the sea water rippled and the breeze blew through the palm trees, I felt like I was going to jump out of my skin. The more I stood still, the more my mind buzzed and hummed, and the more my entire body screamed at me to run. So I kicked off my shoes and stepped onto the soft grass.

I wandered aimlessly across the lawn; past the other rooms, past another small swimming pool, one abandoned slip-slop. I didn't know where I was going. I just knew that I needed to walk in an attempt to escape my thoughts, even though I could feel they were right behind me, following me, nipping at my ankles like an angry dog.

How the hell had I become that girl? The "perfect" Hollywood rom-com-trope girl. The best friend who's been secretly pining for the man who's about to walk down the aisle and marry some-one else. There's a big difference between me and those movies, though. Those movies usually have a happy ending. The hero always lands up dumping the bride at the altar and then running off to pursue the best friend, realizing that he's been in love with her this entire time. But in my case that was never going to hap-pen, and I needed to somehow deal with it. The million-dollar question was how, though?

I heard a rustle in the plants behind me and jumped as some-thing moved in the undergrowth. I turned just in time to see the big, prehistoric head emerge from the bushes. It was a massive tortoise. I got down on my haunches, despite very sore knees, and watched as the huge creature appeared. It looked at me slowly at first, and then stretched its neck out and brought its head all the way up to mine, as if it were trying to communicate with me.

"Hey, big guy," I said to this bizarre-looking creature. There was something strangely wise about it, as if it had seen and done it all and knew everything. *Maybe it did?*

"So what do you think?" I asked him. He didn't move and his stretched neck seemed frozen and then he locked eyes with me.

"Well?" I asked again. "Got any words of wisdom for me? Do you think I'll ever get over Matt?"

And then slowly, and unexpectedly, he opened his beaky mouth and . . .

"Oh my God!" I jumped in fright, fell backwards and then scrambled away as quickly as I could from the eardrum-shattering noise that had just come blaring out of his mouth. It was a strange and terrifying cross between a groan and a roar—*I didn't even know tortoises made noises!* It was disturbing. And then the noise changed. It was different this time, it was almost . . . Wait, *was he laughing at me?* It certainly sounded like it. I glared back at him and I could see it. See it in his inky-black evil eyes. He was judging me!

"You tortoise bastard!" I hissed at him. He looked at me with a serious death stare. I was just about to reprimand him more when I heard another bizarre and frightening sound. *Oh my God, was someone getting murdered?*

CHAPTER ELEVEN

⌒

*T*he light from the full moon was illuminating everything, so it wasn't long before I saw what was making the awful noise. There, on another patio, someone was sitting with their back to me. The sounds the person was making were straight out of a torture scene in a slasher horror movie. I imagined that the person was busy having their toenails pulled out one by one, or their eyeballs injected with acid. I wasn't sure what the hell I was going to see when they turned around. I was terrified. I walked all the way up to the patio and stood there quietly. And then, the person stirred. They began to turn as if they were suddenly aware of my presence . . .

"Oh my God!" I jumped in fright as the person finally faced me.

"What the . . . ?" I was met with the most bizarre sight. It was a man, that much I was sure of. But his face was covered in a thick black mask that he was busy trying to peel off, very unsuccessfully, judging from the cries of agony.

I stood there in silence for a moment, unsure of what I was

really seeing and how I was meant to respond to it. And then, the black mask started moving and words came out.

"It was a sample from a magazine," the man said, it sounded more like a desperate plea for help than an actual statement. "I put it on my face, and now I can't get it off." There was an edge of panic to his voice.

"A magazine?" It took me a few seconds to register what he was saying, and when I did . . . "What?" I almost shouted at him. I was downright shocked. Floored, to say the bloody least. "You should never, *ever, ever* use those free sample things. Everyone knows that."

"They do?" he asked, sounding even more panicked. "Why?"

I shook my head and took a step closer. "Well, they are officially the cheapest things you can find which means that the ingredients they're made from are probably toxic enough to be used in an A-bomb and you can bet that none of them have been approved by the FDA, or any other regulatory board for that matter." I finished my little rant and looked at him. I'd written an article on the strange world of beauty products once and discovered some horrific things. Nightingale droppings and snail secretions were considered legitimate ingredients in beauty products.

"Really?" The man looked at me in horror—well, I thought that was what it was, all I could really see were his eyes. I tried to extrapolate all the relevant information from his body language, since his face was entirely unreadable. His shoulders suddenly slumped and I felt very sorry for him. He'd gotten himself into a rather large spot of black, gooey bother.

"Let me see the sample packet," I said, taking a step towards him. He picked the sachet off the table and passed it to me. I held it in my hands and looked at it, my suspicions confirmed. I shook my head and read out loud.

"*Petrifying peel of mask of blacky charcoals. For glow of youth and freshness in face.*" I paused for added effect. "You're lucky if this was even made on this planet, let alone China."

He shook his head. "Crap. Now what?"

I sighed. "Let me help you," I said, walking all the way up to him to get a better look. On closer inspection, it looked as though the black mask had actually fused with his skin. "You do know that this is an actual thing, right?" I asked, taking my nail and trying to peel back a tiny section of the mask.

"What is?"

"It's become an internet meme, people trying to peel off charcoal masks and screaming in pain while doing it. Much like you're doing now."

"Oh?" His eyes widened.

I nodded. "They're all over YouTube, no one in their right mind would put one of these things on after seeing those."

"And how did they all get them off?" he asked.

I moved away and looked the man in his eye. God, he had amazing steely-gray-colored eyes under all that black crap. "They pulled," I said. "And it hurt."

He nodded and then sat back down in his chair and looked like he was bracing himself. "Do it. Please. It already hurts, my face feels so tight I can barely open my mouth."

"You sure?" I asked, sitting next to him.

"No, I'm not sure. But it has to come off."

I nodded and went back to work, trying to pull enough off to grab between my fingers. It was difficult, but I finally managed to get enough to work with.

"Okay. Here goes." I pulled and heard a ripping sound, like I was pulling the top layer of his skin off. He grabbed the sides of his chair and winced in pain. I could see he was trying to be brave. I pulled again, and this time, the wince became a loud yelp.

"You're kidding!" he said, pushing my hands away.

"I'm sorry." I felt terrible.

"Just do it. Quickly. Please. I have deep regret over this," he said frantically, even though his mouth could barely move due to the tightening of the mask that looked more like a medieval torture device than an actual beauty product. Beauty was meant to be pain, but surely not this much? And all of a sudden, this whole thing seemed very funny to me.

I smiled. I was trying not to, but there was something amusing about this clearly *very* ill-informed man's pain. I wondered if this was what people at the engagement party had thought of me as I stood up there crashing and burning for all to see and hear. Suddenly, my feelings turned again and I felt less amused and more desperate to help this poor soul, unlike how no one had helped me.

"Okay. Can I go for it then?" I asked, gripping some more between my fingers.

He nodded and braced himself again.

I pulled and his entire body shot up out the chair. "Ow!" He almost screamed that part and I didn't blame him. I looked down at my hand and was holding a large piece of what looked like black plastic.

"This stuff is not normal." I shook my head, placing it down on the table. "It can't be good for you."

"Clearly," he said, rubbing the side of his face, trying to ease what I can only imagine was serious pain.

I patted the chair for him to sit back down. "Almost done," I said, although I'd only managed to pull the bottom half off.

"Are you sure you can't wash it off?" He sounded desperate.

I shook my head. "No. Afraid not."

"Okay." He took a sip of the drink he had on the table and then looked at me. "Want one?" he asked.

"No, thanks. Think I should be sober for this."

"Good point." He put his head back and closed his eyes. "Do it all at once. And don't stop until it's all off."

"Okay," I said, and then was almost about to pull when he shot up again.

"I'm Alex, by the way." He extended a hand for me to shake. I took it and smiled at him. This was up there with the top five strangest meetings of my life. Right up there with the time I bumped into my high school principal coming out of an adult shop with a brown paper bag.

"Val, nice to meet you . . . I guess." I shook his hand and he settled back into his chair.

"Okay, Val. Go for it."

And so I did. I pulled. I could tell it was absolutely excruciating. His face crinkled and contorted as the stuff peeled off like a second skin. I could almost feel his pain as his body tensed and shuddered with every pull.

"Nearly there," I said to him as I passed the eyes and was about to hit the forehead.

"Hurry!" I could tell he was holding his breath.

"Breathe," I said.

"I can't."

"If you don't it's more painful," I offered, thinking of what you see in all those TV shows where women give birth and are told to breathe through the contractions.

"Just hurry," he whimpered, still holding his breath.

"Breathe!" I urged, as I was sure he was about to pass out.

"This is not a Lamaze class." He finally took a breath. "Just, please. Get. This. Thing. Off."

"Okay!" I yanked hard and it finally all came off.

"Oh my God!" The relief in his voice was as palpable as mine was. He jumped out of the chair and put his hands on his face, as if he was making sure it was still there and working.

"That was terrible! That was . . . it was . . . wow!" He had a cute British accent; it was the first time I'd really noticed it. He pulled his hands away from his face and then . . . I tried very hard *not* to stare.

From a face totally obscured in black goo, he revealed something entirely different. Something that made me stop and stare . . .

Have you ever looked at someone, and for some strange, inexplicable reason, felt completely at ease with them immediately? As if they give off some kind of reassuring energy that makes you want to sit down, hold hands, be friends with them and tell them all your deepest darkest secrets?

Well, he had that quality to him. But that wasn't all—when one looked at him for a little longer, this friendly, reassuring face gave way to something else entirely. He was good-looking. But not in any obvious way. His looks seemed to defy any kind of category I'd ever seen before. This intrigued me.

His eyes were bright, warm and friendly—despite their cool, gray color. Eyes you could trust, that shone with depth and intelligence but seemed to also have an edge to them, a smoldering kind of edge. The watery gray was framed with black lashes that almost made him look like he was wearing eyeliner, but not in a gothy way, as if he was about to break out with a poem about his inner angst. And when he smiled, I was even more taken aback. It was a gentle, kind smile that created this boyishly sexy dimple on his left cheek. His hair was a salt and pepper color, more salt than pepper actually. Not a look I'd ever found myself drawn to, but on him, there was something distinguished about it. The hair didn't make him look old though, in fact, his face was clean-shaven and youthful-looking; this combination seemed impossible somehow, and yet, here it was. Standing right in front of me.

I was surprised that I was even noticing his looks in such minute detail, since I hadn't done that in a while. But there was something about this man that was hard not to notice.

"Thank you!" He finally let his face go and took a step closer to me.

"I'm glad I was walking past," I said, pulling my eyes away from him.

"Me too," he said. "I was busy contemplating whether or not I needed to call 999."

"Just don't use samples from magazines again." I wagged a finger at him.

"Trust me. I won't. Thanks again! I owe you one. Please shout if you have an emergency."

I chuckled. "I will." I started walking away but bent my knee a little too vigorously and winced.

"What's wrong?" he called after me.

I turned. "I scraped my knees." I shrugged my shoulders as if it was no big deal. I didn't want to explain how I'd gotten them like this. In fact, I'd rather this stranger thought I'd gotten them from carpet burn than the alternative. I turned once more and continued to walk away again.

"Hey, are you staying here?" he called after me.

"Yup!" I shouted over my shoulder.

"Maybe we'll see each other around then?"

"Uh . . . sure. Maybe," I said dismissively as I continued to walk away. I wasn't trying to be rude, but I didn't really feel like making friends while I was here.

1 Jan. 2018
Dear Diary,

It's a new year. And I am making new resolutions.

1. *Lose weight—at least seven pounds which I am sorry to say have all decided to hang out on my hips. Where is the equal distribution, people?*

2. *Get out of active wear—I have no excuse to wear it other than laziness. I am not a mom of three and I do not go to the gym. (Maybe I should. Go to gym, not become a mom.)*

3. *Drink less this year—goes with number 1. Suspect the extra pounds are all the beer and pizza evenings with Matt—which brings me to 4 through to 10.*

4. *Stop spending so much time with Matt! Get a tinder profile and start dating other people. But not if they are gross and creepy—you are not that desperate. Yet.*

5. *Get a hobby so you are not always with him. Matt is not a legitimate hobby.*

6. *Get over Matt!*

7. *Get over Matt.*

8. *Fucking get over him! Okay!*

9. *Just do it. Get over him.*

10. *Matt! Get over him. ASAP! Must. NOW.*

CHAPTER TWELVE

⌐⌐

I woke in the morning feeling physically exhausted, emotionally bruised and battered, not to mention feeling a sense of *dreget* that was so great, I wasn't sure how I was going to get out of bed today. Dreget was a word I'd come up with many years ago. It's the all-consuming combination of regret and dread. Usually in that order. I first discovered this horrific emotion back in my first year of university in my English lit class.

We had this guest lecturer, a semi-famous poet. Of course, in my seriously naïve nineteen-year-old brain, I had thought him to be the most brilliant, enigmatic man I'd ever met. And when he'd started reading his poems out loud in that angsty, emotional way, his long hair falling into his face, his hand clutching his heart, I'd almost flown off the chair and into his lap. And later that night, after several glasses of red wine (I didn't drink the stuff, but I was just trying to impress him by how sophisticated I was), I did land up on his lap. But halfway through the sex, he'd started doing some kind of weird tantric breathing and humming and whispering lines of poetry in my ear and saying things like, "open your Yoni and your soul for me." I'd lain on my back looking up at the ceiling with dregret. Regret for where I was, followed by the dread of what was about to come—*I hoped it would be him, and I hoped it was going to be soon!* (Yoni, I later learned, is the tantric word for vagina—let that sink in, that someone would actually say that to you in bed.)

But my dregret this morning was even greater than that. I felt almost crippled by it. I wished so badly that I could go back in time and stop myself from making such a public fool of myself. I was never going to live that incident down, and I was sure it would become my story. I would forever be "that girl who publicly confessed her love to her best friend at his engagement party." I dreaded what people thought of me, *what Matt thought of me.*

I rolled over slowly and pulled my phone off the bedside table. It was time to check in with my friends—no doubt they were worried—so I left a message, requesting an urgent Skype conference. We did this fairly often. We'd become rather good at these, with Annie in LA, Jane in Greece and the rest of us in South Africa. The only person who was unable to figure the whole thing out was Stormy, whose suspicion and disdain of technology were infamous. Messages immediately started flying back and forth between us all and a time was arranged for the call in six hours. *What the hell was I going to do until then?*

I put on the fluffy hotel gown, walked onto the patio and looked out. I wondered how much dregret Alex the facemask man had this morning. God, I hoped I didn't see him today, I didn't have the energy for any kind of a conversation. I barely had the energy to breathe right now.

But from here, the sea did look rather inviting. I didn't have a bathing suit though. Perhaps the thing to do today would be to track one down and then lie by the beach inhaling cocktails until the dregret was washed away? And maybe I could wash Matt away too? *I had to.* I took in a deep breath, my lungs hurt, *or was it my heart?* I pulled my phone out and Googled the nearest store. It was fairly close so I decided to head out on foot.

* * *

The small shopping section in the village of Saint-Gilles was truly unique. I couldn't compare it to anything I'd ever seen. The buildings were colorful and bright, almost luminous; oranges, yellows, pinks and greens splashed across everything in sight. The place looked like a Pantone paint strip or a drag queen's make-up palette. And everything here was so French. I had no idea how French it all was until now. I was standing on a *rue* opposite a *plage* and was suddenly very thankful for those mandatory two years of French I'd done at school, even though I'd absolutely hated them.

And there were certainly enough shops to choose from. I slipped into the nearest one and found what I was looking for. Rows and rows of bathing suits and bikinis. The very helpful woman let me try half the shop on before I decided on a super-cute yellow bikini. It looked so tropical and so appropriate for the beach—plus it was on sale. I grabbed a few summer dresses, the cheapest I could find, and headed back feeling somewhat determined. *Yes*, I was going to go to the beach, drink cocktails, lie in the sun and let its warm rays melt away Matt, and all the dregret, embarrassment and self-loathing that I was currently feeling. *I could do this!*

I arrived back at the hotel with a semi-limp. My knees were feeling very tight now that the big, ugly scabs had formed and I wished I'd taken a taxi instead. But I was still feeling determined to sea, sun and sand my emotions away. I walked across the lawn towards my room and that's when I saw him. *Again.*

He had his back to me and the last thing I wanted was for him to turn around and see me. So I continued my walk carefully and slowly, hoping to escape his prying eye. But no, as if he could sense me, as if he knew I was there and could smell my fear, he turned and looked straight at me. My blood ran cold under the intensity of his gaze.

"You," I said, wagging a finger at him. "You were wrong. Look." I pulled the bikini out of the bag and waved it in front of his face mockingly. He looked at me with what was clearly disdain.

"I'm going to put this on now, and head to the beach and I'll be over Matt in no time. Ha!" I scoffed at the creature. But he looked unconvinced. So I continued. "I will. Trust me. I am getting over him this time, once and for all." But the more I said it, the less I believed it. He tilted his head and glared at me with a condescending eye.

"Mommy, look, that lady is talking to a tortoise." I looked up and saw a little girl point at me. Her mother stood behind her and looked down at me with a strange look. She put her hands on her daughter's shoulders and pulled her away.

"Come, dear, let's leave the lady," she said, rushing away from me as if she was concerned.

I straightened. *God, was I going mad?*

Suddenly I didn't much feel like lying on a beach anymore, so I walked back to my room and crawled into bed.

Two Years Ago

14 Feb.

OMG OMG! Matt just messaged me and said he wants to tell me something really, really, really important. (He used three reallys in the message which has immediately started making me think certain thoughts!) Am trying not to freak out inside and let my mind run away from me—it is exactly one year since meeting him, after all. But my imagination has run. Am imagining confessions of love, falling into each other's arms, kissing and sex. (NB—get wax before important announcement and put on sexy lingerie.)

14 Feb. (later that day)
Dear Diary,

Sam.
    Short for Samantha.
    That's her name.
    Yes, that is the name of the girl Matt just introduced to me ... as his girlfriend. His girlfriend! That was the really, really, really important thing he wanted to tell me.
    Apparently, he's been on a dating app this entire time, since he's known me, and they have been messaging each other for months. This means 2 things.

1. *My so-called best friend lied to me about a girl he was into—why?*

2. *If he's been on this app since we met, he never, ever had any romantic inclinations and intentions for me. Ever.*

They even confessed love to each other before meeting. She lives in Cape Town so they hadn't met until she flew out for their romantic Valentine's first date. (I wonder if there was sex? What am I saying . . . OF COURSE THERE WAS SEX!)

I feel like such an idiot. I feel so embarrassed. Like a total loser. Might as well go online and order myself one of those male sex dolls that is also AI so it's programmed to be like a real boyfriend too. (*NB—possible article idea there.)

Fuck! FUCK! I can't write about this anymore. It's too damn painful. I had to sit across the dinner table from her tonight and smile and try NOT to show that inside my heart was breaking. There was this painful tightening in my chest. This thick feeling in the back of my throat that made it hard to swallow. I felt nauseous and all I wanted to do was run to the bathroom and throw up. But I couldn't.

I can't. I don't know. Maybe more later. But I'm not sure . . .

SAM!!!! (multiple exclamation marks for added fucking emphasis.)

CHAPTER THIRTEEN

It was Skype time. Their faces all popped onto the screen, and our reactions were all the same.

"Good God, Stormy! What the hell have you done to your hair?" Jane asked.

"I'm going blind," Annie said, covering her eyes playfully.

"It's green," she said proudly, fluffing her long hair between her fingers. As if we couldn't see that. As if that incandescent, lime glow emanating from the small block on the screen wasn't a dead giveaway already.

"Um . . . we can see that!" Jane said sarcastically. "But why? That's the question."

"I'm just really into green these days," she said. "It's a very soothing color, you know."

I wasn't going to point it out to her, but that color was anything but soothing.

"But enough of my hair, back to Val," Stormy said.

"Yes, but we need to hurry. I have to yank out a tooth in ten minutes," Jane said.

"Gee, such a delicate dentist you are," Annie quipped.

"I'm going to do it under anesthetic, you know. I'm not that bad, guys! But Val!" She snapped her fingers at us all now. "What the hell happened? I saw the video."

"What video?" I asked.

There was a collective silence on the call. "What video, guys?" I repeated.

"Your speech at the engagement party," Jane said.

"Oh, God, no!" I hung my head.

"Did you really think something like that could happen and no one would film it?" Jane said so matter-of-factly.

My heart started pounding. Of course someone had filmed it. I might have done the same had I been on the receiving end. "What part did they film, exactly?"

Everyone looked at me blankly, as if they didn't want to answer.

"Oh. I see. The whole thing. The whole, 'I'm in love with you' thing. From start to finish." My mouth suddenly felt very dry.

"Don't worry. It will blow over soon enough," Lilly said, speaking from experience after a very questionable photo of her went viral and generated thousands of memes around the world.

"The tweets don't even have that many likes," Annie added. My stomach tightened.

"What tweets?" I asked. "I thought you said someone filmed it."

"Um . . ." Annie hesitated, "Byron kind of live-tweeted it too."

"He what!" I half shouted. Byron moved on the periphery of our friendship circle like an asteroid in the outer asteroid belt.

"Don't go read them though," Lilly urged, "it will make it all worse."

"I'm not sure I could feel any worse if I tried," I muttered.

"So how the hell did you land up on an island? What's it called, anyway?" Annie asked.

"Réunion." I picked a brochure up from the bed and waved it all at them. "It was an accident. Well, I was trying to hide from Matt at the airport and next thing I knew, I was on a plane."

Lilly burst out laughing. "That's a new one. Even for us."

"Nothing happens by accident," Stormy piped up. "You are exactly where you're meant to be, right now, in the multiverse." She nodded her head and her green hair bobbed about.

I nodded back in agreement; it wasn't worth asking about the multiverse part. I could see everyone else was thinking the same thing.

"So what are you going to do?" Annie asked.

I shrugged. "I don't know. Hide here for a few days. Then fly back home, sell my house so I never have to see him again. Change name and identity, go into the witness protection program and move to a small town in an alligator-infested swamp somewhere."

"Dramatic," Lilly said.

"Hey, well wasn't it you who told me to tell him how I felt?" I asked pointedly.

"Look," Lilly said, "you had to tell him how you felt. You had to finally get an answer, good or bad. It's a pity it happened so publicly. But now that you have the answer, you can work with it."

I nodded. "I wish I didn't have the answer. What did he say, he's never thought about me like that, he sees me as family . . ."

"Ouch," Jane said.

"I think it's good you finally know," Stormy jumped in. "You can't spend another three years hoping for something that will never come. You've wasted enough time on him already."

"I say enjoy yourself," Annie said. "Lie on the beach. Drink cocktails. Take some time for yourself. You deserve it."

"And knowing our history, you'll probably meet the man of your dreams," Lilly added.

I laughed. "Not likely."

"There are other birds in the bush," Stormy said.

"Fish in the sea," Jane corrected.

"What do fish have to do with it?" Stormy asked, looking genuinely confused.

"Never mind," Jane said. "I have to go. But, Val, have some fun, seriously. Take a few days off and try and relax."

Annie, Lilly and Stormy nodded together.

"Okay. I'll try," I said. Truthfully, I needed rest. These last three years had been so emotionally draining and chaotic that I actually felt totally depleted.

"Matt is not it," Lilly added. "And if he doesn't love you he's an idiot." All my friends agreed loudly with this statement. And I wished more than anything that I agreed too.

"Bye, guys." I waved at them all and closed my laptop. And then, because I couldn't help it, I went to Byron's Twitter account and tortured myself some more.

> *@Byron: OMG. Overheard girl confessing love to her best friend . . . at his engagement party! His fiancée can hear it too #awkward*

@Byron: Suddenly worried for his fiancée that he might say he loves her back. Fiancée looking a little worried too. Everyone is holding their breath #waitingwithanticipation

@Byron: BAM! Crash and burn. He doesn't love her back! #extraawkward

@Byron: OMG. She's just realized that everyone can hear her. And when I say everyone, I mean all 80 people at the engagement party #fiancéelookspissed

@Byron: #crashandburn The look on her face is everything. Damn, feel so bad for her right now.

I tried to bite back the tears, but couldn't. I needed to get out of here, I'd been cramped in this room all day and earlier I'd seen a really nice-looking bar on the beach. I could do with a drink. Or ten! Fucking hell, I needed the whole damn bottle at this stage.

15 Feb.
Dear Diary,

Sam. Sam. Sam.

It's been 24 hours since learning about her. And my brain is still not processing the information. Nothing makes sense anymore. 1+1 is not 2. 2+2 is not 4. Matt+Sam is NOT how this was meant to play out.

Honestly, heartbroken doesn't really even describe what I'm feeling right now.

More . . . later . . . shit! I don't know.

P.S. Pitched new article about growing trend for woman to order male sex dolls with robotic penises. Their skin feels soft, they kiss, they cuddle you after sex and you can choose the shape, length and size of penis, as well as customize their looks. Might be a real option for me moving forward! Imagine . . . I get a Matt doll and hide it in the broom cupboard and bring it out at night. OH GOD! I'm losing my mind.

CHAPTER FOURTEEN

⌒

𝒯he bar was on the beach, and the sand was still warm when I took my shoes off and walked towards it. It had that typical dried palm tree roof that made you think of *Pirates of the Caribbean*, rum and Johnny Depp—not necessarily in that order. A few people were sitting around, mostly couples looking romantic, as if they were on their honeymoons. I hated them. But then I saw him . . . not the tortoise this time. *The other him.*

Facemask man, Alex. He was sitting alone at the far end of the bar and was wearing the most bizarre ensemble I'd ever seen. I scrunched up my face involuntarily at the sight of it, it was *that* downright hideous.

But it wasn't so much *what* he was wearing, but more *why the hell?* The outfit seemed so incongruent with the man I'd met the night before. Not that I knew him, but if you'd asked me to guess what kind of clothes he'd wear, this would not be them.

He was wearing a black leather jacket, the kind that had revolting silver studs on the collar, and were those . . . ? *Yes*, black leather tassels hanging from his big, puffy shoulders. His jacket was open, revealing a tight black and purple T-shirt. The T-shirt had a skull on it set against a background of orange flames. He turned his head slightly and something glinted by his hair and, *oh no*, if I thought it couldn't have gotten any worse, there it was, a gold stud earring in his left ear. I almost threw up in my mouth.

And then it got even more bizarre, because around his wrist he was wearing a timeless, elegant-looking Rolex watch. It was the kind of watch that sophisticated gentlemen wore. The top half of him looked like it was trying to go to a Kiss rock concert, circa bloody 1980—except for the watch. I dreaded to see what the bottom half looked like but luckily for me it was tucked behind a big wooden bar. My vote was either crotch-squeezing black leather pants, or ripped stone-washed denims.

I couldn't quite figure this whole thing out; was he trying to invent some kind of a new look? Was this outfit meant to be some kind of a statement, an ironic one hopefully, or did he just simply have the worst clothing taste in the world? Well, he did put a facemask on that he found in a magazine . . .

His hands started moving and I looked down at the bar, and that's when I realized what he was doing. It just took this whole thing from bizarre to science fiction. He was flipping through a pile of what looked like women's magazines while drinking a bright pink drink through a twirly yellow straw. *What the hell?*

I stood there in the shadows, I didn't want to be seen, and watched curiously as he turned the pages, as if he was really reading them. And then, out of his pocket, a green highlighter appeared. He slowly highlighted some sentences on the page and then took out a small notebook and scribbled something in it. He slurped his fancy-looking drink while he read.

I followed the straw from the drink up to the lips that were wrapped around it, and then onto the face that the lips were attached to. I scanned the face carefully. This whole thing made no sense. It made no sense that the man with the kindest eyes I'd ever looked into, the most perfect straight, white shiny teeth set into one of the biggest smiles I'd ever seen, was wearing . . . *that!* As morbidly curious as I was about his outfit, I really didn't feel like company tonight so I turned and started walking away, mentally planning how much it would cost if I drank everything in the mini bar. But a voice stopped me.

"Val!" he called, and I was forced to turn.

"Hi." Alex had seen me and was standing up. I gave him a noncommittal wave. I *really* didn't want company. "I was just going back to my roo—"

"So good to see you." He started walking towards me and my eyes immediately drifted down to his pants. Tight, black, ripped jeans. So ripped, in fact, that they looked like they'd lost a fight to a lawnmower. But on his feet, he was wearing a pair of sporty white running shoes. *How could this be?* Was he actually part of a conjoined twin set? His twin was fused to him, the twin who was into rock and roll and gold ear studs. The man I'd met last night was merely the wrists and feet twin. I tried to pry my eyes away from the jeans, but it was hard.

"I'm so glad I've found you. I've been looking for you all day," he said.

"Huh? You have?" I asked.

He smiled at me. *Wow.* There it was again. Quite possibly the friendliest smile I'd ever seen. This was the smile of a man who needed to be in a toothpaste commercial, not a commercial for Harley Davidsons.

"I figured out how to pay you back for helping me last night."

"That's really not necessary," I said quickly.

He walked all the way up to me and stopped. "But I insist."

"What is it?" I asked.

"Come to the bar and I'll show you." He turned and started walking away. I wasn't really sure about this at all, but I followed him anyway. Alex pulled one of the barstools out for me. I couldn't remember the last time a guy had pulled a chair out for me and for a second I didn't know what to do. I finally lowered myself into it.

"Would you like a drink?" he asked, waving the bartender down.

"I don't know," I said.

"Oh come on," he urged. "Just one."

I sighed. "Sure." I couldn't believe I was agreeing to this. "What's that?" I gestured to his pink beverage.

"It's called a rosy sunrise, I believe."

"You're kidding, right?" I asked, letting my eyes sweep over him once more. This was getting more bizarre by the second. Dressed like that he should be drinking sacrificial blood from a pewter chalice, or whiskey and petrol out of a human skull.

"I'll have one too, I suppose," I said to the barman, who quickly hurried off. I suddenly got a small stab of panic in my stomach. I hadn't intended on having drinks with Alex. But somehow I now was. I needed to change that.

"You said something about paying me back for last night?" I asked in a businesslike tone.

"Yes." He picked up a small packet from the bar counter and handed it to me. "I've been carrying it around all day in case I bumped into you.".

I opened the packet tentatively. "What the . . . ?"

Alex pulled the packet away from me and tipped its contents onto the bar counter. A latex glove tumbled out, a tube of cream and some plasters.

I stared at the things as strange images rushed through my mind.

"Antibiotic cream and plasters for your knees," he said, opening the cream.

It took me a few moments to figure out what he was saying, but I finally clicked. And when I did, the implications were astounding. "Hang on, you went out and bought that especially for me?" I wasn't sure whether I should feel grateful to him, or whether this was just weird.

He nodded and looked down at my knees. "May I?" he asked, pointing at them.

I pulled them away quickly. "Uh . . . no . . . uh . . . what?" *That would just be weird!* was what I meant to say.

He looked up at me and smiled. "Don't worry, I'm a doctor."

"Reaaallyy," I said slowly and tentatively, not believing him for a second. Doctors didn't dress like that, did they?

"Ideally you shouldn't have let the laceration scab, as it impedes the growth of new skin cells." He said it casually, the medical terms falling off his tongue like everyday words.

"You really are a doctor?" I said.

He smiled at me again and nodded. "So? Can I?"

"Uh . . . sure. I guess." I sounded very unsure still. I was.

He patted his knees. "Put your legs up."

"On you?" I asked. "No. I can't, that's just . . ."

"Oh, come on." He patted them again.

"This is so strange," I mumbled.

"Not as strange as you pulling my facemask off last night."

"True," I nodded, "but still."

"It's already getting infected." He pointed to my knees and I looked down. Large red swollen patches had formed around the scabs and I didn't need my MD to see that he was right.

"Okay, fine." I lifted my legs carefully and guided them up onto him. He draped them across his knees and looked down at them. This was bizarre. More than bizarre. I couldn't quite believe I had my legs up on a stranger at a bar. I looked around to see if anyone was looking at us, but no one seemed to have noticed.

"Okay." He snapped on the latex glove in a way that looked like he'd done this a million times before. And then slowly, gently, he started applying the cream. I watched this semi-stranger in fascination. He seemed to be concentrating so hard, as if my knees were the most important things in the world to him right now. Then he unwrapped the plasters and started placing them onto the wounds with total precision. I flinched when his fingers grazed the back of my knee and sent a shiver through me, despite the hot balmy weather. I couldn't quite work out if this was the weirdest thing that had ever happened to me, or whether this might actually be the one of the nicest things that anyone had done for me in a while. When it was all over I pulled my knees away just as my drink had arrived.

"Thanks," I whispered quietly, half under my breath. There'd been something very intimate about that moment and it was leaving me feeling a little lost for words.

"Pleasure," he whispered back. "It's the least I can do. Take the cream and apply it three times a day," he said in a very doctor-y voice. I nodded and pulled the packet towards me. We sat in silence for a while, until the magazines on the counter pulled my focus. Just as I'd suspected, they were a variety of women's mags in various stages of well-readness; *Elle, Cosmo, Woman's Weekly, Woman's Own, Marie Claire* and *OK!*.

"I hope you're not looking for more samples." I gestured at the magazines and he laughed.

"No. God, no. I think I learned my lesson about that," he said with a smile. He reached up and ran his hand over his cheek. "I must say, it really is very soft today."

"That's because you ripped off the top three layers of skin," I said, taking the first sip of my drink.

"True. And I screamed and cried like a baby."

"Yup. You did." I sipped again and it was rather tasty, *and strong*.

"I suppose I should be embarrassed about all that, but truthfully I've had so much embarrassment lately that that hardly registered."

"I can relate!" I took another sip. God, it really was strong.

"Oh?" He eyed me curiously. "It can't be as embarrassing as mine."

"Trust me. Mine's worse," I said quite confidently, as I bit into the floating piece of pineapple which tasted more like a delivery method for rum than an actual piece of fruit.

"Never. It cannot, *cannot*, be worse than what just happened to me."

I shook my head at him. "No, I win. I'm telling you. You've got nothing on me."

We fell into a silence and eyeballed each other. "Okay," he started slowly, "so picture this." He threw his entire drink back, as if he needed the liquid courage just to tell the story. I understood. I would probably need to be borderline paralytic before I ever repeated my story to anyone. I certainly wasn't going to tell him. "Right," he continued, "she's my perfect girlfriend of seven years. We've lived together for five of them. I bought that apartment just for her, because she liked the view, even though it added an extra half an hour to my morning commute. She's the woman that I spoke about having kids with." He paused for a moment and looked at me as if he wanted me to acknowledge that I was following the story so far.

"Okay. Got it," I said.

"Now picture this; me on a rooftop garden in the middle of London, at sunset, looking out over the city, on one knee, surrounded by the rose petals of a thousand pink roses and over two hundred candles and then holding this in my hands . . ." He stopped talking, reached into his jacket pocket and pulled it out. I gasped.

18 Feb.

Okay. Good news. Researched what the likelihood of couples who meet online staying together is. It is very low! Crossing my fingers and waiting. I'll be here for Matt when things fall apart. Maybe it will even bring us closer? (Am I a bad person for hoping that his relationship falls apart? Of course I am!)

On a different note, I watched a video of a woman sleeping with a male sex doll yesterday. No, I will not be getting one anytime soon. But it was good research for the article. Also, want to write an article about the perils of online dating and how to know whether you're being "Catfished." (Maybe I'll even show it to Matt—out of "concern." Shit, I really am a terrible friend.)

18 Feb. (later that day)

Oh no! Been researching new article and found contradictory messaging.

"Why online love is more likely to last." Internet couples tend to be a better fit than those who meet by traditional means, according to new research

An actual psychologist wrote this. Not me doing research and making things up!

Shit. What to believe? More later . . . (Hopefully research to contradict that last part.)

CHAPTER FIFTEEN

"*W*ow," I said breathily, looking down at the ring in the box he'd just opened.

"I mean . . . Wow." That was really all I could say, because it glinted up at me like the northern lights. A gorgeous round lavender-colored stone, surrounded by pink stones set in a rose-gold band.

"Wow. Yes, that's what she said too." He put the box down on the bar counter. "Only, as you can see, she's not wearing it."

"What happened?" I asked, tempted to reach out and touch the thing of beauty. My fingertips felt drawn to it, like a magpie to pretty pennies.

"Well," he let out a loud, long sigh, "she said no, obviously."

"I'm so sorry," I said.

"Oh, no worries really. It's okay. I mean, she only ripped my still-beating heart out, violently shredded it and then tossed it off the side of the building. No big deal."

"Shit. That's hectic," I said, not really knowing what to say to him.

"But that's not the worst part, though. She then went on to explain that actually she was in love with someone else. And actually, she'd been seeing him for the past six months, and actually she was about to tell me that she was leaving me for him and moving in with him and actually—*God, that's a lot of actuallys*—apparently she's never felt this way about anyone before. And get this, they met in our apartment block, the one we live in, because the guy lives there too."

"Ouch." I physically cringed for him. The image was just so awful. He seemed like a nice guy, somewhat misguided in his fashion sense and beauty regime, but I hadn't had a man pull out a chair for me in ages, let alone attend to my injuries.

"Tell me about it," he said, waving the bartender over and calling for another round of pink drinks. "I bet you can't beat that story." He looked at me challengingly.

"Um . . . *actually*," I emphasized the word and he smiled immediately, "I think I can."

"Really?" He raised his eyebrow in query. "I doubt that."

"No, I'm pretty sure my story is on a par with yours, potentially worse because of one very unfortunate factor."

Now he looked intrigued. "Right, it's a bet then. Whose story is the worst?"

"Okay," I said. "What are we betting?"

"That ring." He pointed.

"No. Never." I shook my head.

"I'm serious. Because if your story is worse than mine, then you genuinely deserve that ring."

"Okay," I muttered, trying to work out if he was for real. "And if yours is worse?" I asked, wondering what I would need to give him.

"Just stay here and have some drinks with me," he suddenly said in a much smaller voice.

"I already am."

"Have a few more. I've been sitting at this bar by myself for five nights and, truthfully, I'm lonely as hell."

"That doesn't seem like a fair exchange, though," I said.

"A new study shows that loneliness is a bigger killer than smoking and obesity. So you'd be saving my life."

"Well, when you put it that way." I smiled at him.

"Okay, great. But we need an impartial judge to decide which story is worse," he suggested.

"Who?"

"What about him?" He pointed over at the bartender, who was already looking in our direction, as if he'd been listening this entire time. The bartender looked like one of those perpetually laid-back kind of guys. Blond surfer hair, golden tan and an unhurried quality to him. He smiled at me and I quickly looked away.

"Noooo," I whispered under my breath. "I can't tell my story to a stranger."

The bartender piped up. Clearly, he had no shame in now admitting that he *had* been eavesdropping. "You won't believe the kinds of things that people tell me. I've heard it all, trust me."

"Like what?" I asked, as the bartender moved closer to us and casually leaned over the bar.

"This one time, a guy told me he'd cheated on his wife the day before their wedding, with her maid of honor who was also her sister."

"What?" Alex and I gasped at the same time.

"You think that's strange, this other time an old woman in her eighties confessed to me that she'd killed her husband sixty years ago and buried him in the rose garden. She wanted to clear her conscience before she died."

"You're kidding?" I said in horror.

The bartender shook his head. "People confess all kinds of crazy things once they've had a drink or two."

"Mmmm, tell me about it," I said knowingly.

"So, what do you say?" Alex asked. "We both tell him our stories and he chooses which one is worse."

I shrugged. "Sure, why not? You go first though." I pointed at him.

The bartender cleared his throat. "Yeah, I already heard that one." He smiled sheepishly at us. "And you're not alone, let me tell you. It's happened to a lot of men who've sat at this very bar."

Alex looked over at me. "Your turn then."

"Okay." I took another sip from my drink and then launched into my story. Leaving out none of the gory, embarrassing details. By the end of it I had two pairs of eyes staring at me in horror.

"Wow," Alex said, shaking his head, "and how many people were there?"

"At least eighty."

I watched them both as they took it all in. "And if you want, you can watch the video online too, since someone filmed and posted it."

"God! I'm so sorry," Alex said, looking at me with genuine concern.

"Yeah, honestly, that's one of the most embarrassing stories I've ever heard," the bartender confirmed.

"So, which one is worse?" Alex asked.

"Mmmm?" The bartender put his elbows on the bar and held his head in his hands, looking from me to Alex and back again. He was taking this very seriously. "So . . . you both had your hearts broken. That's a tie. And one found out his girlfriend was cheating, but the other did spill her guts to the entire world."

"Thanks," I said sarcastically.

"I'd say it's a tie then," he finally said. "Cheating on a par with public embarrassment."

"Wait!" I jumped up, the alcohol swishing through me. "I forgot to tell you that someone live-tweeted the event too, and it got hundreds of likes and retweets."

"Really? Well, that changes everything," the bartender said.

"Wait," Alex jumped in now. "She changed her social media relationship status the very next day to dating him instead of me."

"Also bad." The bartender looked from Alex to me and back again. "I know, you two should just hook up. It would be one of those funny wedding stories you could tell," he said, and then was called away by someone else.

"Hey, who won?' we both yelled after him, ignoring what he'd just said.

"It's a tie," he shouted over his shoulder.

Alex and I sat back in our seats and looked at each other for a while. "I guess you can put that away," I finally said, pointing at the box.

"Yes. I guess I can." He grabbed the ring box and slipped it into his pocket.

"Just out of curiosity, why are you carrying that around with you?"

He looked genuinely confused at the question. As if he'd never considered it before. Then he looked me straight in the eye.

"Honestly," he started nodding his head as if an epiphany was dawning on him, "I think I'm just trying to hold onto something of her."

I nodded. I could relate. Suddenly I could feel the weight of the diary in my bag.

11 April
Dear Diary,

Worst news.

Devastating.

Not sure how to contain myself. Have managed to wipe tears away sufficiently in order to write this but am teetering on the edge of a total all-fall-down.

Sam is moving to Johannesburg. She is moving here and she is moving in with Matt.

Stormy thinks this is a good thing. She thinks this is the final "straw in the coffin." She thinks this will be a great catalyst for moving on from him. Only problem, I have no idea how to move on. How do I move on from someone I've now been in love with for 2 years? Who also happens to be my best friend? Do I even want to move on . . . of course I don't! I'm still holding onto the hope that one day he opens his eyes and realizes how perfect we are for each other!!

IDK. More later. Or not. I'm not sure. Maybe I need a break from writing about this too? In a way, it seems to make the whole thing worse. Who said writing was therapeutic? In this case, it feels like torture. It makes it more real to have it written down like this.

CHAPTER SIXTEEN

"So, a doctor?" I finally asked. The bartender had very kindly put a bottle of tequila down for us "compliments of shitty life." We were probably on our fourth revolting shot, each time we had one vowing. It would be our last as we grimaced and almost choked on the vile liquid.

"Yes," he said in a bit of a slurry manner.

"And she left you? Who leaves a doctor?"

"Exactly." He banged his hand on the counter.

"What kind of doctor?" I asked.

But Alex didn't answer immediately. He poured himself another shot of tequila and downed it. He slapped the shot glass down onto the table and then looked me straight in the eye.

"Colorectal surgeon."

"What's that?"

"I'll give you a moment to figure it out." He crossed his legs and folded his arms casually.

"Ooooh, this all sounds so mysterious," I whispered.

"Not at all," he said. "In fact, there is nothing mysterious about what I do." He fixed his eyes on me expectantly.

"Okay . . . Colorectal surgeon, colorectal surgeon," I repeated the words to myself a few times until a familiar word jumped out at me. "Colo . . . *wait*, rectal?" I asked, putting my hand over my mouth in shock as I said it out loud. It wasn't the kind of word you found yourself saying that much in public. Or ever.

He nodded.

"As in, um . . . rectum?" I muttered under my breath.

"Rectum," he repeated, and my face flushed. *Why is it that when you hear certain words they make you feel instantly queasy? Like vulva or anus, for instance.*

"A proctologist?" I asked slowly. I could now feel the amusement bubbling up inside me. It was small at first, but then it grew until I couldn't quite hold it down anymore. He smiled at me and I burst out laughing.

"Oh my God, that's a good one." The words shot out in between the loud guffaws. I held my hand up for a high-five. This guy was funny . . . *or was he? Shit!* His smile faltered and suddenly he looked serious.

"You weren't joking?" I pulled my high-five hand out of the air.

"No." He shook his head and started pouring more shots of tequila.

"Oh, sorry." I swallowed hard, feeling terribly ashamed that I'd just laughed at this actual surgeon who'd probably studied for a hundred years to become one—regardless of which body part his specialty was based around.

"Yeah, that's kind of the reaction I get from most people," he said. "Feel free to take a few moments to make some jokes about it."

"Uh, like what?" I asked innocently, knowing full well that I could probably really run with this one. I could run far!

"Oh, don't act innocent." He handed me a drink. "Go for it. I don't mind, I've heard it all before anyway."

"Okay," I said slowly and tentatively, sipping my drink. "I'm sure you've been the butt of many jokes."

"No! That's a lame one. You can do better than that, Val." He was smiling at me, egging me on.

"Okay." I thought about it for a while, but nothing came to me.

"I'll give you one for free," he said. "So at the annual medical conference, someone in general surgery thought it would be funny to make a sign that said 'Proctologists do it from behind.' He hung it on the wall outside of our conference room."

I tried to keep my laughter in but couldn't. When it finally tapered off I reached over and touched his hand. "I'm so sorry people make jokes like that. That must suck," I said. "And I really didn't mean to jump on the bandwagon either, it's just, you don't meet proctologists often, *or ever*. Personally, I've never had anyone up there, not that I wouldn't go to one if I needed that looked at, *up there*, and I'm sure you're really good at what you do, *up there,* not that I would ever, *ever*, come to you if I needed that um . . . my rectum . . . *shit!* Can I stop talking now?"

"Please!" He shook his head. "And please stop saying 'up there.'"

I put my finger over my mouth and made a shushing sound. This made him smile.

"Connie, that's her name, by the way . . ." He held his drink up and I clanked mine against it. We tossed the shots back. "Connie thought it was funny too. She once asked me why I couldn't be a cool doctor. She said she was embarrassed telling her friends what kind of doctor I was."

"What's a cool doctor?" I asked.

Alex shrugged. "I don't know. Plastic surgeon, maybe? A neurosurgeon possibly?"

"So basically she wanted McDreamy or McSteamy from *Grey's Anatomy*?" I pointed out.

He laughed loudly. "Colorectal surgeons can be sexy too, right?"

"Yeaaaahh." I stretched that word out and scrunched my nose up a little. "I mean, suuuure. Maybe it could be, sort of, maybe, possibly." I was trying to sound reassuring, but was failing miserably.

"It's not all prostate exams, you know. I do complicated surgery with these special robotic arm things. It's very sci-fi, actually."

"Now that's cool," I said. "You should lead with that. 'I do surgery with cool robot arms.'"

"Okay." He nodded and smiled at me again. "Good suggestion. Maybe I should put that on my business card."

"It's Matt, by the way. His name is Matt."

"Matt," he repeated thoughtfully. "Matt and Connie. Monnie. We should call them that while talking about them." He laughed again; clearly he was as drunk as I was by now. "Or Connt," he suddenly added.

I burst out laughing again at the sound of it. "Let's stick to Monnie." I paused and looked at him. His cheeks were flushed a pretty pink color, and his gray eyes were slightly hooded which made him look rather sexy. This was not how I ever imagined a doctor would be. The back of my knee suddenly itched and I scratched it. "Soooo," I slurred, "how on earth did you become a proctologist?"

"Colorectal surgeon," he corrected me. "We prefer that, makes us sound far more fancy and less proctologist-y."

"Colorectal surgeon," I repeated.

"Truthfully?"

"Total truth." I poured us both another shot of tequila and passed him one. I'd lost count as to how many we'd had. Probably a bad sign. A very bad sign.

"It was to rebel against my parents," he said, between grimaces from the burn of the tequila.

"Isn't rebelling becoming a serial killer, or a member of the Hell's Angels?"

"Not in my family. Both my parents are really well-known surgeons. My mother is London's top cardiologist and my father is this hotshot vascular surgeon that leads teams around the world specializing in separating conjoined twins."

"Whoa! That's intense."

"Exactly!"

"So where is the rebellion in this story?" I asked, my face tingling from the alcohol now.

"Well, I was forced to go to med school. I wasn't allowed to become anything other than a doctor, you see. But I'd once heard my parents make a joke about proctologists at a dinner party with all their other fancy surgeon friends, so I decided to become one just to piss them off and embarrass them!"

I looked at him for a moment and then burst out laughing. I was laughing so much that I clung onto the bar counter and almost toppled over. "Wait," I said, in between snorts of laughter, "you became a . . ." I was screeching now, "a . . . a . . . proc . . .

rectal . . . surgeon . . ." tears were streaming down my face now, "of bums, basically . . . to, to . . . embarrass your parents?!"

Alex started laughing too and out of the corner of my eye, I could see the happy honeymoon couples looking at us.

"Basically," he said, his laughter finally tapering off. "But . . ." He looked thoughtful for a moment. "But it's so much more than that now. When people come to me, they're usually at their most vulnerable. You learn how to put them at ease and make them feel better." He shrugged, more to himself. "It's very rewarding. And it's a less hectic life, I'm not constantly on call like other doctors. You don't have many rectal emergencies coming into the ER . . . *well*, only every now and again." He smiled softly.

I shook my head at him, his story was even more funny because I could actually relate to it. I'd done the exact same thing. "I also became what I am to embarrass my family," I finally said.

"Oh? Do tell me." He leaned closer to me. His eyes were even more heavy-lidded from the alcohol, and he had this kind of sleepy, sexy quality to him. Suddenly, he wasn't so nice and warm and friendly anymore. A guy you could just hang with. Suddenly, he became one of the sexiest men I'd seen in a while. I was completely caught off guard by this realization. Before Matt I used to look at men all the time, but I hadn't looked at one like this in ages. I felt my cheeks go a little hotter. I was glad he'd called me over, despite my initial nonsocial feelings.

"So," I started my story, "my grandparents are these famous Russian poets, very well known. Poetry so depressing you want to crawl into a fetal position and hold yourself after reading them. My dad is a professor of literature at university and my mother is also a poet. They're all very cultured. They all had very high expectations of me."

He was listening to me intently, and it dawned on me that I'd never told anyone this story before.

"So instead of becoming a professor or the next Donna Tartt, like they all wanted, I became a magazine features writer. I remember the moment that I showed them my first published article, it was on . . ." I started laughing at the memory. "On . . ." I tried again but the laughter was still going. "On how to find the G-spot." I finally managed to get it out, way too loudly, and a couple of people turned and looked at me in horror. "You should have seen their faces."

Alex burst out laughing again. "It was probably the same look on my parents' faces when I told them what my specialty was going to be."

We continued to laugh together. "God, we're both so childish!" I hooted.

"We're such rebels," he said, picking up the bottle again, but it was quickly pulled from his hand and whisked away.

"I think I'd better take this away." Our bartender appeared out of nowhere and whisked the bottle of tequila from us. We both protested, almost falling off our barstools while trying to grab it back from him.

"Give it back!" I wailed, but he turned around and shook his head at me. "You're a mean, mean man," I said to him, a distinct slur to my speech. "We're quite drunk, aren't we?" I looked over at Alex, who was slightly fuzzy around the edges now.

"That would be my medical opinion," he said, trying not to slur his words as much as I was. His cheeks were a rich, ruddy color now, his hair was messy and he looked how I felt.

"Soooo," I said, pointing at the magazines, "why are you reading women's magazines?"

"These . . . well, when Connie moved out, these were the only things she left behind."

"So you've been carrying them around because they remind you of her?"

"No, I've been using them to figure out what happened between us. Where the hell I went wrong, and also, to try and get over her."

I looked at him blankly. "You're turning to women's magazines for that?"

"Look." He flipped one open. "Ten Ways To Get Over Your Ex." He pointed at the article and I dissolved into laughter again. I couldn't help it. Because I knew that behind that article was probably a totally dysfunctional woman in love with her neighbor, and desperately making up the last four steps, because she'd run out of ideas at six.

"What?" he asked.

"I write articles just like that," I said. "And look at me, I'm a total mess. You wouldn't take relationship advice from me if I was the last person on Earth, would you? And, news flash, those things are all totally made up too. It's not like we're experts. Take my many literary works of genius on the G-spot, for instance. I mean, just how many ways can you set about finding the thing? It's not like you need GPS coordinates. It's not like you're going to get lost on your way down there . . ." I cleared my throat and put on an official-sounding voice with an American accent, like the lady from Google Maps. "*At the belly button, go south. If you reach the knees, you've gone too far!*"

Alex's eyes widened in recognition, he clicked his fingers together and then flipped one of the other magazines open and held the page up for me. I tried to focus my boozy eyes on the words.

"The Good Girls' Guide To The G-Spot," I read out loud. "Exactly! I mean, how many articles can there be on it? Does anyone have anything new to say about it? The only thing that could ever be potentially newsworthy about the G-spot is if it moved out of its current location and settled inside the belly button. Now that would be an article!"

I waved my arms in the air passionately. "None of those things work. You should not believe everything you read in magazines, trust me."

"Well, I'm here because of what I read." He pointed at step two of the Ten Ways To Get Over Your Ex article and started reading. " 'Jump On A Jet Plane. Stop wallowing in pity on your couch. You need a change of scenery. Why don't you book a ticket for an exotic trip abroad? Treat yourself to sun, sand and cocktails, and maybe even a cute Swedish masseuse.' " He stopped reading and looked up at me. "Hence I'm here. Although, I'm not totally sold on the Swedish masseuse."

I laughed and shook my head at this poor misguided man. "These things don't work," I said again, tapping my hand on the magazine. "Okay, what does the next one say?" I pulled the magazine away and started reading. " 'Number Three. Burn, Baby, Burn.' " I rolled my eyes. It was the kind of title I would have come up with. I continued. " 'It's time to light that match and get rid of everything that reminds you of him. That photo you've been keeping in the back of your wallet or that item of his clothing that you've been secretly hanging onto. And if you don't have anything, write his name down on a piece of paper and toss it into the flames! As you watch the smoke rise up, imagine him disappearing into the sky and never coming back again.' "

I looked at Alex blankly. "Are you kidding me? That would never work." I slapped the magazine closed and dropped it onto the bar counter with a thud.

"How do you know if you haven't tried it?" Alex asked.

"That is a terrible argument," I quickly jumped in. "I don't need to try something to know it's not going to work, just like I don't need to buy that belt that you wear that promises to freeze your fat off from the shopping network to know it's a waste of money and will not freeze my fat."

"I dare you." His eyes twinkled. "Write his name on that serviette over there and let's take it onto the beach and burn it."

"Right now?"

"Yes."

"You can't be serious?"

"Serious as piles." He grinned. "Colorectal humor there," he said with a silly, adorable smile. He passed me his green highlighter and pushed a serviette into my hands.

"Okay, you do it too though," I said.

"Deal." He extended his hands and we clumsily shook them. *Such smooth hands . . .*

We both wrote their names on the serviettes and then walked towards the sea, away from the lights of the bar, until we were in relative darkness.

"You go first," I said, starting to laugh at the ridiculousness of what we were about to do.

"Okay." Alex held the serviette out and flicked the lighter that he'd borrowed from the barman. He raised the flame to the serviette and it caught fire and started to burn.

"My turn," I said. I took the lighter from him and lit mine as well. I suspect mine might have gotten soaked in alcohol, because it burst into dramatic flames.

I squealed in fright and then dropped it. It blazed angrily on the sand. "Oh my God." I picked up my shoe and smashed it into the flaming serviette. It exploded and little bits of red glowing material burst into the air. "Wow, that feels quite . . ." I did it again. Harder.

Alex joined in, swatting at the paper and banging his shoe in the sand, trying to put out the still-burning embers.

"This feels quite—" he started, but I cut him off.

"I know." *This felt fucking good!*

Finally, when all the flames were out and all the flying bits of red paper had settled, we both stood there looking at each other, out of breath.

"Let's do it again," I suddenly said, diving into my handbag and pulling out the secret photo I kept of Matt in my wallet. For a moment I thought about burning the diary, but couldn't. I wasn't there yet.

"Okay." Alex riffled through his wallet and also produced a photo. He lit the photo and held it in his hand as the flames grew bigger. It was dark, and the light from the flames lit up a portion of his face. This man was really good-looking, and nice and fun. It was hard to imagine anyone not wanting to marry him; okay, well, there was that problem with the clothes.

It was my turn now. I took the lighter and looked down at the photo of Matt. God, I loved this photo of him and I'd spent a long time staring at it. He'd gone to get passport photos done and I'd seen them lying on his desk and had pocketed one. I flicked the lighter and held the flame a little way away from it, reluctant to set it on fire.

"Do it," Alex urged.

I nodded, and slowly, slowly brought the flame up. The second the flame came into contact with the photo, it immediately engulfed it. And soon, it looked like Matt's face was peeling off. I stared at it as the flames obliterated it in front of my eyes and a strange feeling whacked me in the gut. I inhaled sharply and then dropped the photo to the floor, where I watched it curl, burn and finally disappear into the sand.

"That felt . . ." I paused, almost frightened to say it out loud. "Good."

"I know," Alex said with a kind of reverence in his voice. And then, with great excitement, he said, "Let's burn it all!"

Suddenly, he ripped the black leather jacket off and threw it to the ground. "I hate this thing," he said, looking at me. "She bought it for me. She said I dressed boringly. She wanted me to be more 'edgy,' whatever that means." He threw some sloppy air commas around and I laughed. Partly in relief, as finally this odd outfit was making sense. *She'd dressed him!*

"Wait, get some sticks!" He ran off excitedly towards a pile of driftwood and grabbed some pieces. I did the same and soon we were piling the sticks together to create our very own bonfire.

"Here." I ripped a few pages out of one of the magazines and scrunched them up, putting them under the sticks.

"This is fucking fantastic!" Alex said excitedly as the paper, and soon the sticks, started burning. And then, he took his shirt off too.

"I can't tell you how much I hate this thing!" He held the shirt over the flames and all I could now look at was his body. It was very obvious that this man had seen the inside of a gym recently, that's for sure. "For the last six months she's been trying to dress me like a Kiss band member," he said, "and I did. I did it because she wanted me to, I even pierced my ear, and then she went and left me for a rock star."

I tore my eyes away from his body and looked into his eyes. "A rock star?"

He nodded, taking the earring out. "Yes. An actual man who sings in a rock band. Apparently, I'm not fun enough. Apparently, I'm too much of a nice guy. Apparently, I'm not cool enough."

"Drop them." I pointed at the offensive shirt and earring. "Set them on fire. Burn, baby, burn!" I almost yelled this last part, getting swept away in the moment. He dropped it, and the shirt burst into flames.

I watched as the smoke billowed up into the dark night sky. There was something so cathartic about it all. Watching it rise up into the air, twisting and flapping in the breeze and then finally disappearing out of sight completely as it melted into the darkness. "Give me that highlighter again." I held my hand out for it.

I tore out more of the magazine paper and proceeded to write Matt's name over and over and over again. I threw the pieces of paper into the fire and delighted in the sight of the flames immediately incinerating them. The flames leapt onto the paper like a pack of hungry animals, devouring it in seconds with a hiss and a crackle and pop. The sounds and smells of the burning paper were strangely intoxicating.

"Fuck it," Alex said. "Let's burn everything." And then suddenly, without warning, he unzipped his jeans, pulled them off—taking the ring box out of his pocket—and tossed them onto the pile.

I looked up from the fire and my jaw swung open as he stood there in his underwear. My sight was a little blurry right now. And granted I was finding it somewhat hard to focus on objects for too long, but I squinted my eyes together to try and get a better look at his body. And it was worth the effort. The warm color of the flames illuminated his torso, casting shadows and highlights on him in all the right places. He had the kind of abs I write magazine articles about, the kind of chest men probably spend their lives bench pressing for, the perfect amount of manly chest hair in just the right spot and . . . I blinked a few times, as my eyes strained and finally I could no longer focus.

"God that feels good," he said. He looked over at me and put his hands on his hips. I nodded at him stupidly. He was almost naked now, apart from those tight boxer brief things he was wearing, that didn't leave much to the imagination, I might add. And then suddenly, a loud whistle pierced the air. We both turned at the same time to find a policeman staring at us.

"No fires on the beach!" the policeman yelled and moved towards us.

"Shit!" I looked at Alex and then, as if we were both thinking the exact same thing, we ran!

12 April
Dear Diary,

I have thought about it overnight. And this will be my last entry. I want to assure you that this has nothing to do with you, it is all me. Well, it's all Matt to be honest. I can no longer write about him like this. This book is a record of our relationship—or lack thereof—and I have to stop it. I have to move on. I have to do something to get over Matt, and soon, because I do not know how much more my heart can take.

No more later. Goodbye. Forever.

CHAPTER SEVENTEEN

⌒

*W*e ran as fast as we could down the beach, laughing hysterically as we went. Alex was in his underwear, which only made the whole thing funnier. This was not how I imagined a doctor behaving. Somehow you always thought of doctors as superhuman, people that were separate to us mere mortals. Not half-naked, drunk arsonists that ran away from the police.

"Stop!" the policeman shouted at us, and we picked up speed. The sand was soft and uneven, and this, coupled with my stiff knees and not-so-sober mood, meant that instead of running, I was swaying clumsily from side to side as I went. Alex grabbed me by the arm and increased his running speed. I could barely keep up.

"Where should we go?" I asked in between massive breaths.

"Hotel!" Alex made a sharp turn and left the beach, and then, without warning, he pulled me to the ground and crouched behind a bush.

"Shhh," he said, trying not to laugh.

I nodded. We both covered our smiles and tried to push the laughter down as the confused-looking policeman ran past us. We watched him go and as soon as he was out of sight, we looked back at each other and burst out laughing again. Even in my current state I knew this was going to be one of those moments that only appears funny when under the influence of serious amounts of alcohol. This was the kind of moment that, when I woke up sober in the morning, I would seriously facepalm at.

Once our maniacal laughter had tapered off and our breathing returned to normal, we started walking back to our hotel together.

"Where's your room?" he asked when we finally got there.

"Number five."

We walked into the fancy reception area and Alex gave me a little shoulder nudge. "Act normal," he whispered.

"You're in your underwear," I pointed out.

"I know." We both smiled and waved as we walked past the receptionists. One looked up and gave us a strange look, but then looked back down quickly. As soon as we were clear of them, we glanced at each other again and laughed. We ran down the corridor together towards my room. I couldn't remember the last time I'd had this much fun, *without Matt*.

"This is me," I said as we arrived at my room. I leaned against my door. My legs were a bit shaky, my kneecaps felt like they were sloshing around in their sockets and my feet felt like they were floating just above the floor. I was *that* drunk! And I was sure it wasn't pretty.

"Number five, hey," he said slowly. He was swaying slightly and his cheeks were so flushed that it looked like he was sunburnt. He leaned forward, supporting himself with an elbow against the wall.

"That was fun." His eyes drifted over me, as if he was unable to focus properly. I felt the same way.

"It was fun!" I repeated. "And I'm so hungry," I suddenly said without thinking. "I wanna get into my room and raid the minibar and lie in a sea of chocolates and eat them all and not care that each one costs the same as a month's salary. That's what I want."

Alex laughed again. "Such a rebel. You know what I want?" He leaned even further against the wall.

"What?"

"You know, when you go down on one knee you really expect the person to say yes, right?" He swung his arm about. "But no! My only memory of the whole event is this horrible NO!" He shook his head. "When a guy is down on one knee, can't you at least say yes? I wish I could erase that part and have a different memory of the whole proposal." He looked sad for a moment, but then looked up at me and forced a brave smile.

"I know," I said, as something that seemed so brilliant and logical dawned on me. "Propose to me, and then I'll say yes and then that will be the last memory of proposing that you have."

"YES!" he half shouted. "That's brilliant." *(We were that drunk!)* And then, before I knew it, he was down on one knee. He opened the ring box and held it out in front of me. The massive rock glistened in the overhead lights and almost blinded me.

"Will you, Val . . . uh, what's your full name?"

"Valeria Svetlana Iv—"

"Sorry, what?" He cut me off. "Svetlana?" he asked, a smile washing over his face.

"Shall I give you a few moments to make a joke, a lot of people do when they find out my middle name. And I've heard it all before . . . sounds like a porn star's name, et cetera!"

He shook his head. "I can see it, though. You have that whole hot Russian thing going for you."

"Hot Russian thing?"

"Icy blonde hair. High cheekbones. Piercing blue eyes. Also looks like you could wrestle a bear in the snow if need be." He momentarily looked like he was about to fall off his knee and onto the floor.

"Okay, okay. Just get on with my proposal," I said, straightening myself up, trying to look pretty for my fake engagement.

"Will you, *I'll just go with Val*, make me the happiest man alive and marry me?" He smiled up at me in a very goofy manner.

"Yes! Yes!" I brought my hands up to my face like those women who win Miss Universe do. "Yes, I will," I replied excitedly. "Oh my God!" I fanned myself dramatically, still thinking of Miss Universe. "I can't believe this is happening. Oh my God, it's a dream come true and it's so much better than world peace."

And then, he took my hand and slipped the ring onto my finger. It fit perfectly and I stared at it. It was strange to have something on that finger, after all these years of nakedness. Alex stood back up.

"How was that?" I asked, quite proud of my dramatic acceptance performance.

"Great," he gushed like he really meant it. "I know it sounds weird, but that felt really good! Thanks!" He laid a big hand on my shoulder. "Anything you want to make you feel better?"

"Yes," I said without even thinking. "You know what I would

like?" The world was spinning more than ever now and the walls were tilting.

"What?" Alex moved closer to me and smiled. "What would you like? Tell me."

"I'd love someone to kiss me, and then remember it in the goddamn morning. Is that too much to ask? Is it too much for a girl to kiss a guy and want him to remember it in the morning?"

And then, without warning, his lips were on mine. They were hard and demanding. I opened my mouth, wrapped my arms around him and pulled him closer. He fell over me, his body pressing into mine, pushing my back into the door. The kiss became frenzied and uncontrollable. His hand came up to the nape of my neck and he grabbed it possessively, holding me in place as he explored every corner of my mouth. In the back of my mind, *far, far back*, a little sober voice whispered at me . . . *"Val, what the fuck are you doing?"* But I was far too turned on to listen to it. So instead, I lifted my leg and wrapped it around him, letting him fall further into me. He grabbed my leg as his lips left mine and explored my neck. I threw my head back, almost giddy with lust as he ran his tongue up my neck, sucked it and bit my earlobe. I ran my hands over his naked back. I dug my nails into it when his lips came back up to mine and devoured me.

"What the?" A voice suddenly stopped us and we bolted apart.

"Shit!" I said, as I looked into the faces of an older couple who were now staring at us. "Sorry, I . . ." I looked at Alex and we laughed again. I flung my door open, while Alex raced down the corridor and disappeared around the corner, still in his underwear. I threw myself onto my bed, the room spun rather fast and then, suddenly, everything went black.

Dear Diary,

Okay, not forever. I'm back with news. It's positive, I think. A step in the right direction, sort of.

I went out tonight without Matt. This is a first for me, I think my entire social life for the last couple of years has centered around Matt. Anyway, I met this guy called John. I could see he was good-looking. He had all the right ingredients for it; sexy smile, brooding dark eyes and carefully tousled hair. The only problem was that I wasn't attracted to him. I know that sounds like an oxymoron. But since meeting Matt, I haven't felt attracted to anyone else. I can still appreciate an attractive man but upon meeting one, but there is never any loin-stirring or heart-fluttering or things like that. John is also a writer, but a sports writer, so we chatted and ranted and raged about editors for a while and the strange world of publishing. Then, we had some drinks, climbed onto the dance floor and before I knew it, we'd pinned each other to the wall of the nightclub.

The kiss was good, technically speaking. Everything moved as it should, no excessive tongue and teeth and spit that covers your chin. His kissing technique was solid, a definite 8 out of 10. But I felt nothing while kissing him and all I could think about was kissing Matt. I even closed my eyes at one stage and imagined it was Matt—I'm somewhat embarrassed to admit this, even to myself. How could Matt not remember that kiss? I know I'm harping and have been for years, but seriously?

I won't go into too much of the sex details with John. It

happened once. I wouldn't write home about it. And yes, I did close my eyes and imagine Matt a few times . . . and yes, I know how pathetic that makes me sound.

Anyway, I'm thinking of asking Matt and Sam out on a double date with John and me. Maybe seeing me with someone else might make something inside Matt's head click.

And who knows, maybe John will become the man of my dreams and I will love him and marry him and one day laugh about this, about how ridiculously in love I thought I once was with Matt.

Okay, I am not putting you away just yet. I want to record how this plan of mine pans out.

So definitely more later . . .

CHAPTER EIGHTEEN

*M*y head was thumping when I finally managed to pry my eyes open. My mouth was drier than the Sahara Desert, and my eyes were stinging as if someone had come in the middle of the night and stabbed them with little pins and then filed them with sandpaper too. I rolled over, and my stomach lurched. *Oh, God!*

I swung my legs off the bed and tried to stand, but I could barely feel my feet. *In fact, did I even have feet?* It felt more like I had large cement blocks strapped to my legs than actual things that could be walked on. Finally, I was up and standing, swaying from side to side as if being pulled in different directions by a million invisible hands. I took a step, and my head thumped even more.

Another step. Another thump. I looked around the room. Everything looked strange, and for the briefest moment, I didn't know where I was. And then it all came back to me and with it all, a wave of nausea crashed through me like an unstoppable tsunami. I tried to stop it. I tried to cover my mouth and make it go away but . . .

I was so classy right now! Hunched over the toilet bowl, gripping the sides of it with my hands and wishing I had a third hand to hold my hair back. When it was all over, I flushed the toilet and collapsed onto the cold bathroom floor.

How much had I drunk last night? I lay there looking up at the ceiling as little pieces from the night before came back to me in bursts. Facemask man had been there. Wait . . . his name was Alex. Hadn't there been a fire too? I raised my hand to my face and something caught my eye.

"What the hell!" I sat up straight and stared at my hand. There was a ring on it, on the ring finger. *Had I gotten married last night?* I crawled out of the bathroom in a state of panic. How? When? Who? Was it facemask man? Oh God, please tell me Réunion island wasn't like Vegas and you could drive through and buy McDonald's while an Elvis impersonator married you? That had *not* been in the inflight brochure!

I scrambled to my feet, walked over to the mirror and looked at myself. As if looking at myself like this might bring back memories of the night before. I could remember the bartender. I could remember us telling him our stories of woe, the fire, burning things, police and then . . . everything went blank. I stepped closer and scrutinized myself. *What was that thing on my neck?* I moved my hair away and looked at what seemed to be a giant mosquito bite. Had I gone bashing through the swamps last night?

My stomach suddenly growled at me. It screamed at me, begging me to put something in it other than tequila. So I had a shower, brushed my teeth—twice—grabbed some clothes that didn't smell like smoke and tequila and headed for the breakfast area.

The food was spread out in front of me in colorful rows, and I went straight for the carbs. Croissants, bread and pastries and all the things I knew would absorb the remaining alcohol that I could feel lurking in the pit of my stomach. I was desperate for them! So desperate that I would have inhaled their sugary, floury goodness right in if I could have. I grabbed a table in the far corner away from everyone else, no need to inflict myself upon people and scare them, and sat down.

"Coffee?" A woman came up to me and asked as I'd just finished shoving the first of the custardy Danishes into my dry mouth.

"YES! Please." I almost screamed this through a full mouth of crumbs. She looked at me like I was a little mad for a second and then rushed off to get the coffee. I hoped it would be strong. Very strong. The kind of strong where the spoon stands straight up. I went back to my carb fest and was just about to shove an entire croissant into my mouth when *he* stepped into the room. I watched him. He looked fresh and clean and perfect. Like a newly cut bouquet of dewy spring flowers. A ray of warm bright sunshine, an effing rainbow arched across a once-stormy sky! *Why did he look like that?*

He glided effortlessly into the room with a smile on his face, nodding politely at people as he went. *Was this my new husband?* Just as I thought that, he caught my eye, smiled at me and waved.

Shit! What the hell had I done last night? I closed my eyes quickly, reaching deep into the dark recesses of my still-groggy mind, trying desperately to draw an image out, especially the one that would explain the rock on my finger, but couldn't find a single one. When I opened my eyes again, Alex was sitting across from me. Still smiling.

"Hi," he said, as if he was totally fine this morning. As if I had been the only one drinking.

"Hey," I managed wearily.

"You don't look great." He looked at me and then reached up and put his hand across my forehead in a very medical fashion . . . *oh wait*, something was coming back to me . . . he was a doctor! A proctologist. He'd fixed my knees last night! *God, that was sweet.* Is that why I'd married him?

"Mmmm, I think I had way too much to drink," I said.

"Me too."

"You look fine, though." I eyed him. He did look fine. In fact, he looked more than fine. Had he been this good-looking last night? Possibly another reason I'd married him? Had I fallen for the hot doctor bit and, *oh shit*, did we have sex? The thoughts whirled through my mind crazily.

"Here." He pulled a handful of pills out of his pocket. "I brought them for you in case you needed them." He dropped them onto the table. Pink, red, blue and a yellow and white one.

"What are they?" I eyed the colorful things suspiciously.

"Just a mix of vitamins and minerals. They kill a hangover, fast. You can trust me, I'm a doctor, remember?" He smiled at me. Killer smile.

"Okay." I took the pills. Normally one shouldn't take pills from a virtual stranger, but there was something about him that just set you at ease.

"So, great news," he said, putting his elbows on the table and leaning in.

"What?" I asked, as I swallowed the last of the pills.

"I remember the kiss!" He held his hand up for a high-five and I stared at it blankly.

"Uh . . . what kiss?"

"You're joking, right?" he said.

"No." I shook my head. "To be honest, it's all sort of fuzzy after the bonfire, uh, and why were we burning things on the beach, by the way?"

"Burn, baby, burn," he said, and I shook my head. "The article in the magazine? How to get over your ex!"

"Aaaaah! Yes," I said as I remembered writing Matt's name on a serviette and burning it.

"It felt amazing," he said.

I nodded as the memory of the feeling came back to me. It had felt rather good, actually. Despite my non-belief in such things like that.

"You really don't remember the kiss?" He sounded disappointed. "The one you asked me to do."

"I asked you to kiss me?"

"Well, you wanted someone to kiss you and remember it in the morning. Which I do, by the way."

"Shit, I'm so sorry, I don't really know what I was thinking. I can't remember that at all."

"Well," suddenly the color in Alex's cheeks warmed a bit, "the kiss definitely remembers you." He pointed at me.

"Huh?" I looked down to where his finger was pointing.

"Sorry . . . I didn't mean to . . ." His voice tapered off and he was definitely blushing now.

"What?" I touched my cheeks and my neck and shoulders, looking for the thing he was pointing to, and then I clicked.

"Nooo," I gasped and placed my hand over the red mark on my neck. "You gave me a hickey?!" I hissed at him.

"Hey, it takes two to tango," he said defensively.

I rolled my eyes. "I can't suck my own neck," I said sarcastically.

"Sure, and I can't do this to myself either." He turned and lifted the back of his shirt up to reveal an unmistakable trail of fingernail marks.

"Oh my God! Did I do that?"

He nodded and dropped his shirt.

I leaned in even more and lowered my voice to a quiet whisper. "Did we . . . ? I mean, we did *just* kiss, didn't we?" Could all of those marks really have come from kissing alone? That seemed unlikely.

Alex smiled at me. "As far as I can remember," he joked.

"This is no time for jokes: did we or didn't we?" I asked.

"We didn't," he said.

"Are you sure?"

"Yes."

"How can you be sure?" I asked, feeling a little panicked now.

Alex's smile faded suddenly. "Val." He leaned across the table too and we were almost touching now. "I would never go to bed with someone when we were that inebriated. Ever."

"Oh." He suddenly looked very serious and I totally believed him. "Well, good," I quickly added. "But why do I have a ring on my finger then?"

The seriousness on Alex face melted away and he smiled again. "You suggested I propose to you."

"I what!" I half shouted this.

He laughed. "Don't worry, it was a fake proposal. You really don't remember any of that, do you?"

"Sorry. I don't."

Alex shrugged his shoulders and then sighed. "Well, that's a pity," he said. "But if you don't mind, can I have the ring back?" He held his hand out.

"Oh God, of course. Yes!" I was suddenly overcome with embarrassment and pulled the ring off as hard and fast as I could. I passed it over to him and he looked at it momentarily before slipping it back into his pocket. We sat in silence for a while and then Alex finally broke it.

"So, you really, really, *really* don't remember that kiss?" He sounded coy.

"No. I really wish I did though." Judging by all the marks we'd left all over each other's bodies, it must have been one passionate kiss!

"You're the first person I've kissed since my breakup," he said almost under his breath as if I wasn't meant to hear it.

I picked up another pastry and popped it into my mouth. "Thanks for those pills, I already feel better."

"Sure. What are doctor friends for, if not free pills?" He reached over and gestured to one of my pastries. "Do you mind?" he asked politely before taking it.

I shook my head silently as he took the food and popped it into his mouth.

"So about last night," he said, some powdered sugar sticking to the side of his face. "I've been thinking."

"Yes?" I asked tentatively.

"Well, we both felt better for the burn, baby, burn thing." He paused and raised a brow at me, as if waiting for me to agree with him.

"True. And?" I said, urging him to continue.

"I was thinking, why don't we go through the list together? Why don't we do all the things on that list and get over our exes?"

"You're serious?"

He looked at me blankly, matter-of-factly. "Very."

"Nope." I shook my head right back. "That's just, just . . ." I searched for the right word, "silly!" Was that really the *only* word my writer brain could think of?

"But doing one made us both feel better, what about the others? Maybe if we go through them all, we'll be over them by the end of it." He folded his arms and sat back in his seat.

"I'm leaving tomorrow for South Africa, though."

"Postpone the flight."

"I have work," I moaned.

"The G-spot is not going anywhere soon, as you pointed out last night. And if you stay, I'll tell you about a whole other spot that you can write about if you like."

"I'd rather not learn about any more spots, thanks. We women have enough already."

"Oh, this isn't a women spot!" He grinned at me. "I'll even let you quote me in your groundbreaking article that shall revolutionize the sex lives of all couples in the world."

"I don't want to know about that," I said, trying not to imagine where this spot was, although I had a pretty good idea already.

"Come on," he urged, reaching over and grabbing both of my hands. "Say yes like you did last night."

"I don't know." I shook my head.

"You've got nothing to lose," he said with a huge smile. *Wow.* He really did have the kind of smile that could knock a woman off her seat. He let go of my hands and then got up. "Think about it, Val," he said and started walking away. "And if you change your mind, I'm in room ten."

"Where are you going now?" I called after him.

"Shopping for new clothes." He gestured to the Metallica shirt he was wearing and I gave a visible cringe. And then he exited the dining room with one last wave at me. I stared after him in thought.

*　*　*

I couldn't, could I?

I sat at the edge of the beach where the grass met the sand, looking out over the sea. The sand was fine and powdery white. The beach was dotted with palm trees, as one would expect for such tropical surroundings.

Could I really stay and work my way through a "getting over your ex" list with a man I didn't even know? I grabbed some sand and opened my hand, letting it run through my fingers and fall back down to the ground. I didn't really have anything to rush home to, and I was definitely going to have to move when I got back, what with Matt and Sam living next door. The idea of going back didn't exactly appeal to me, but the idea of going through a breakup list with someone just seemed so bizarre.

My phone buzzed in my bag and I pulled it out. And when I was done reading the message with tears streaming down my face, I knew what I needed to do.

Sam: *I hope you're happy! You totally ruined my, MY, engagement party. I trusted you. When Matt first introduced me to you, I didn't like you. But I tried. I tried to be nice to you and this is how you repay me. By completely embarrassing me in front of all my friends and family. I should have seen you for who and what you are—you've been trying to steal my fiancé this whole time from right under my nose. I warn you, DO NOT EVER come near Matt again. Your friendship with Matt is officially over, and he agrees with me. Don't ever think you will see him again.*

Dear Diary,

Matt thinks it's great that I'm dating someone. So does Sam, for that matter. She seemed more than thrilled that I'd introduced John to them. I wonder if she suspects how I feel about Matt? She must, mustn't she?

Everyone else thought the date was amazing, including John who has—get this—actually made plans to hang out with Matt some time. The two really hit it off; it was rather revolting to watch the start of the bromance blossoming, to be honest.

Anyway, I will not be going out with John again. It did not have the desired effect and I think Matt wouldn't care if I was staying in and having hot gangbangs all day with male porn stars with eleven-inch dicks. (Note to self; possible article about porn star penis—God I hate that word. Who has the biggest, whose is the most famous, etc? could be fun.) Anyway, I digress . . .

John and I will definitely not be going out again, and I am still pining for Matt like an idiot. And basically, I hate myself for it.

Later . . .

CHAPTER NINETEEN

"*L*et's do it!" I barged in the second he opened his door without even asking. "Let's go through the list and get over them together. I mean, why not?" I started pacing his room, wound up with energy like a spinning top.

"Like you said, we have nothing to lose. Besides, Sam just sent me a message and I can't face going back to Jo'burg. What would I say to people? Or worse, what would people say to me? Let's just do thi—is—" I stopped pacing and talking when I saw him.

"Uh . . ." I mumbled. I'd forgotten for a moment what I was meant to be saying. I was looking at an extreme makeover. Gone were the punk rock clothes, replacing them were smart casual shorts, a simple white T-shirt, a pair of nice-looking sandals. There was no trace of eighties rocker in sight and I stared. Good-looking was an understatement. He looked at me curiously, as if waiting for me to speak again, which I guess he was, considering I'd so abruptly lost my train of thought.

"Yes! Let's do it." I snapped out of it.

"Seriously?" He walked up to me and placed his hands on my shoulders . . . *such big hands*.

"Yes." I nodded. "I mean, *I think so*." My confidence waned for a second and then I remembered that text from Sam. "Yes!" I was emphatic this time. "Absolutely."

"Great! This is great." He ran to the dressing-room table and grabbed the magazine. "Let me see what's next."

"Wait." My stomach plummeted. I knew there was something I needed to do first before I could move onto the next step. Something I should have done last night, but hadn't had the courage to.

"There's still something I need to burn." I slowly pulled the diary out of my handbag and held it up. "It's full of Matt."

"Well," he said, looking at it thoughtfully. "We can't burn it, or we might get arrested. I have another idea though." He shot me a smile and then looked down at my feet. "How are your knees feeling?"

"Fine actually, thanks." The cream had worked wonders on them overnight.

"Perfect," he said and walked over to a small backpack on the floor and started putting things into it.

"Wait, where are we going?" I asked. But he didn't respond. He gave me a mysterious smile and then headed for the door.

* * *

An hour later we were surrounded on all sides by thick, lush, tropical jungle. Vines twisted with fern leaves the size of my head, and every now and then bright pops of color pierced the sea of green. I felt like Alice down the rabbit hole; arriving in a world so foreign and magical.

And the bamboo! I'd never seen bamboo so thick and tall in my life. Standing to attention like soldiers and towering above us like skyscrapers. But what was most interesting about it was that almost every single one was covered in graffiti. You would've thought this would have detracted from their natural beauty, but it didn't. For some reason, each branch became a kind of fascination, with its own unique story to tell, and I couldn't help stopping and reading them as I walked.

"Did you know," I called out to Alex, "that Jim loves Steph 4 eva?" I ran my fingertips over the fresh etching.

"Well, did you know, that a man from Japan was here." Alex pointed to the bamboo next to him.

"Did you know," I continued, "that Jenny is lit as fuck!"

"Good for Jenny." Alex smiled at me. "Hey, we should write something too."

"Like what?"

"We should sign a contract together."

"Contract?"

"Yes, a promise to get through the whole list and get over our exes. We need something to commemorate this moment and make it unforgettable." Alex started scratching in his bag and pulled out a pen. "I don't have a knife, but this should do." He walked up to what appeared to be the only free bit of bamboo space.

"Hey, wait!" I suddenly remembered something. "What's number one?"

Alex looked confused.

"Last night you read me number two and we did number three. What was number one on the list?"

Alex pulled the magazine out of the bag, cleared his throat and started reading again. "'Number One. Don't Jump Into Another Relationship. Your feelings are all over the place right now and it's easy to think you've developed feelings for someone else all of a sudden. This is probably just transference and they are not real. You need to take a break from all relationships and focus on yourself for a while.'"

"That one sounds really important," I said, because it did. It wasn't flippant like burning paper or jetting off to tropical islands, and it really resonated with me. *Focus on myself.* God, I wouldn't even know where to start. Myself had been so wrapped up in Matt for so damn long.

"It is," Alex echoed, "very important." He folded his arms and grew silent and thoughtful-looking. I noticed that while he thought, he brought the pen up to his lips and bit the tip between his teeth. He finally spoke after a few moments of silence. "So that's it then, we make a promise to each other, right here and now, that we'll swear off relationships for a while and go through this entire list together?" He looked at me and raised the pen in the air.

"Well, the first part will be easy for me," I chuckled. "It's not like I'll be meeting anyone anytime soon."

"Me neither," Alex agreed and brought the pen down to the bamboo and started scratching. But it soon became clear that no amount of scratching with a complimentary hotel pen was going to work on the bamboo. This became very evident when the pen snapped.

"Crap," Alex said and then looked up at me. "What now? We need to do something to remember this moment."

"My grandmother used to tie string around her finger when she wanted to remember something," I suddenly said without thinking.

"That's brilliant!" Alex said. He reached into his bag again and pulled out the small promotional notepad that the hotel had given us. Around the notepad was a small green ribbon, that matched the ribbon on the pen. Alex pulled the ribbons off and walked up to me. "Give me your left hand," he said, holding his out.

I lifted my hand slowly and placed it in his. Alex began wrapping the ribbon around my ring finger and started tying it.

"Repeat after me," he said.

"Okay." I watched, transfixed by his hands, transfixed by the fact he was—*for the second time in two days*—putting something onto my ring finger.

"I, Val, do solemnly promise to swear off relationships and work my way through the entire list." He looked up at me and our eyes locked. I swallowed, it felt like something had lodged itself into the back of my throat. Everything around me felt a little more silent all of a sudden.

"I, Val," I repeated softly, "do solemnly promise to swear off relationships and work my way through the entire list." I looked back down at my finger as he tied the final knot. It was just a little piece of green ribbon, but it held so much meaning right now that I felt somewhat overwhelmed.

Then Alex passed me his hand and I began doing the same. I almost forgot to make him repeat the words as I studied his hand carefully. It was big, his fingers were long and his fingernails were perfect. Prominent veins crisscrossed the back of his hand, making it look strong and powerful. When I was done, I pulled away and we stood looking at each other in complete silence. There was this sense in the air that the two of us had just done something significant together. Something important that needed to be respected and could never be undone. His gray eyes seemed to have darkened a little in the shade.

"Come, we better keep moving," Alex suddenly said and started walking again.

I followed him.

I still had no idea where we were going, and no matter how many times I asked, it was still "*a secret.*" It was hot and humid, and got worse the further we walked. The path quickly got steeper, and soon my legs didn't feel like they could go on much further.

"Alex," I moaned, "are we almost there?" My left calf muscle felt like it was about to explode out of the back of my leg.

"I think so." He turned around and smiled at me as he continued his fast stride. I'd been watching him walk for quite some time now, and I was certainly able to deduce one thing from the experience: this man went to the gym! With each step his calf muscles, unlike mine, tensed and relaxed—God, he had better legs than I did!

I confess to allowing my eyes to drift north, to where the legs met the body, aka his arse. And although it was hard to tell through those shorts, he did seem to have the kind of arse that a girl—if she were so inclined—might want to dig her nails into. Not that I was inclined to do such things.

And then, without warning, the incline got even steeper. So steep that it felt like climbing a ladder. The burn moved from my calves to my thigh muscles, which never got a workout, except when hovering over public toilets. The burn moved up further and into muscles I didn't even know I had.

"A . . . le . . . x," I puffed as I tried to keep up.

"Yes?" he replied casually over his shoulder as if he wasn't even moving.

"When are we there?"

"Soon!" he shouted.

I still had no idea what was at the top. And just when I felt I couldn't go on any longer, I could hear something. The distinctive sound of falling water.

"A waterfall?" I asked. "I thought we were here to burn my diary."

"I have a better idea," he said, ducking under a thick, green overhang. We were in the midst of a rain forest now, complete with a green canopy above our heads. Shafts of sunlight penetrated the green roof, sending beams of light down onto the leaf-covered path. And when the warm breeze blew, these patches of light moved around like lights on a dance floor.

With each step the sound of rushing water grew louder until finally the path ended and we stepped out of the canopy and back into the sunlight.

I exhaled loudly when it all came into view. It was spectacular, not to mention so high up that I felt I could reach out and touch the clouds. I was nervous to approach the edge, but I felt compelled to look over it. I moved slowly to where the green grass ended and the rocks began. I could feel the cool spray of water on my face. I finally reached the edge and peered over. A massive cascade of water crashed down over the rocks and into the bluest pond I'd ever seen.

"Now what?" I asked Alex, who was standing a little too close to the edge for my liking.

He turned and looked at me slowly, and pointedly. "I think you know."

I nodded and slowly put my bag down on the ground. And with a very tentative and trembling hand, I took my diary out. This was more than just a diary to me, this was a record of Matt and mine's relationship. I opened it and ran my fingertips over the words on the crinkled pages, as if reading them like Braille. But then panic gripped me.

"I don't know if I can do this." Doing this would be letting him go. All my memories of him, all the records I'd kept for the last three years of my life were contained between these pages. If I didn't have this, what did I have of these last three years?

"You have to do it." Alex walked up to me and placed a re-assuring hand on my shoulder. I clutched the diary to my chest, *my heart*, and walked over to a rock and sat down. I opened the diary onto the last page I'd ever written. Alex also sat. I took a deep breath and for some reason, started reading it out loud.

" '14 Feb. (Six months ago)

" 'I had to drag you out from the bottom of my cupboard for this. You were covered in dust and when I opened you, fish moths ran at me (note to self: maybe need fumigator—or maybe need to clean and dust better). Anyway . . .

" 'Matt is engaged.

" 'To Sam.

" 'He even got down on one knee, he told me. Then to make matters worse, he posted one of those cheesy engagement shoots on Facebook. All 100 of the fucking photos. Matt never struck me as an "engagement shoot kind of guy." That is the kind of thing we would have laughed about together. But he did one. And they were on a white horse in one of the pictures. A WHITE HORSE!

"'Matt is so different now, though. Since meeting her he's started acting and talking differently. He even dresses differently too.'"

At that I heard a mumble from Alex. I continued to read.

"'I think it's because she's super-fancy and from some fancy, rich, posh family. (I wonder if he farts in front of her?)

"'It was so hard to act happy for him. It was so hard not to burst into tears. I don't think anything has ever hurt me this much before.

"'I can't do this anymore. This needs to end. I am torturing myself.

"'No more . . .'"

I turned the page. My mouth was getting dry and a lump was forming in the back of my throat. I briefly looked up at Alex and he gave me a small smile and reassuring nod, the kind that showed solidarity and urged me to continue.

"'Dear Diary,

"'I said no more, and I meant it at the time, but somehow Matt exerts some kind of power over me that makes me forget all the promises that I make to myself. He asked me to be his best man at his wedding and to speak at his engagement party—and guess what I did? I said yes. YES! Of course, I said yes. I always say yes. I haven't been able to say NO to Matt in three years and all I want to do is say it. No, no, no, no, NO!

"'How is this such a hard word to say? But every time he asks something of me, I feel this feeling building up inside and it

becomes impossible to stand my ground and remember everything I'd promised myself the day before.

" 'The sad truth is this . . . I fucking love him and I don't know
how to turn it off and make it stop. And I'm so tired of loving him.' "

I looked up from reading the diary. My eyes were filled with
tears. Alex looked at me as if he knew exactly what I was feeling.

"So, make it stop," he said to me. "We both have to make it stop."

I nodded feebly. I stood up slowly, walked towards the edge
and looked down into the crystal blue pool below. The water was
a bright sapphire blue, except where the waterfall crashed into it.
There it was a frothy, turbulent white, like a cappuccino.

Alex walked up to me and stood by my side. I held the diary
between my hands and looked down at it one last time and then,
with all the might and all the strength I could muster, I threw it
into the air as high as it could go.

The diary soared into the sky at first. It was beautiful to watch,
like a bird flapping its wings and climbing, and then it seemed to
slow down, it paused, looked like it was hovering for a moment or
two without moving, and then its trajectory changed.

It started to fall. Faster and faster and faster towards the bottom. It tumbled and somersaulted in the air. It looked like it was
flapping its wings frantically, trying to stay up, but it was impossible. The inevitability of gravity pulled at it. And then it crashed
into the water.

I stood there and watched as the book floated around for a
while, the current from the raging waterfall pulling it closer and
closer and then, all of a sudden, it disappeared into the foaming
waters. I gasped as the turbulence ate it up violently. It re-emerged
again, only to be dragged back under by thousands of pairs of

frothy fingers. And then, finally, I couldn't see it anymore. It made no more reappearances and it was . . . *gone.*

I imagined it at the bottom of the pool now. Drenched and soaked. I imagined the ink streaming off the pages and bleeding into the water until finally disappearing. Forever. All the words I'd ever written, melting and disappearing off the page, as if turning back time, as if they had never been there in the first place. Erasing three years of memories and stories. I felt a tear slip down my cheek. It was sadness, but there was something else in the sadness too. *Hope? Relief?*

Another tear trickled down my face as I stared at the waters below. It was still hot and humid, but suddenly, a cold shiver ran through me, as if a ghost had just crawled over my skin. Maybe it was the ghost of Matt finally leaving me. I felt the solid weight of an arm around my shoulders and looked to my left. I'd almost forgotten about Alex.

"How do you feel?" he asked in a soft voice.

"Good, I think." I smiled at him. "Something feels different I guess." I said it and meant it this time. Not like all the other times I'd said it over the years. Something did feel different this time. Maybe this list would really work? *I hoped it would work.*

Because trying to get over Matt for these last few years had been like that diet you were always going to start on Monday. Sunday night you would binge on your favorite foods and then swear blind that on Monday morning you would wake up and only drink green kale smoothies for the next month until you lost all the weight.

But around lunchtime on Monday I always slipped and fell off the wagon . . .

And that was Matt.

CHAPTER TWENTY

⟨ornament⟩

"So, what's next?" I said, sitting opposite Alex at the table by the swimming pool. We were back at our hotel, it was evening, and we'd spent most of the day hiking and exploring the forest.

"Well," Alex said, opening the magazine once more. He read. "'Number Four. Commit Murder, On Social Media. His status updates. His thoughts in 280 characters or less. His face in dreamy Valencia filter that really brings out his eyes . . . or worse, him and his new bae in sexy black and white #powercouple #blessed #loveofmylife

"'The last thing you need right now is to have your ex in your social media space which means that's it's time to commit murder. Unfriend, unfollow, unlike and un-everything him from your life.

"'You'll never get over him if you spend your days looking at the time he ate a protein smoothie bowl and posted it on Insta #Chiaseedsarethenewblack

"'And he's going to notice that you unfollowed and unfriended him. But keep your profile open for a while, just long enough for him to go and look there and see those gorgeous pictures of you having so much fun without him. If you can, grab some arm candy and pose with them, and be sure to put it on Insta for him to see that your life continues without him. In fact, whenever you do something fun, post it.'"

"Aaahh, I see," I said, sipping on the pink cocktail—which, in the short time we'd known each other, had kind of become our thing.

"So, let's do it," Alex said. "Let's take ludicrously sexy photos of ourselves and post and hashtag the hell out of them and then order another drink and defriend them?"

I laughed. "I don't think you'll be getting a ludicrously sexy picture out of me anytime soon."

"What?" He almost shouted this part. "Are you kidding? You don't even have to try, you're just naturally smoldering."

"Smoldering?" Now I was really laughing.

"Totally."

I eyed Alex suspiciously. "You don't have to say that to make me feel better, you know that, right?"

"I'm not. I assure you." He sipped his pink drink slowly and looked at me. Scrutinizing me. I suddenly felt a rush of warmth through my body and the back of my knees tingled again.

"You know what your problem is? You lack confidence. This Matt arsehole didn't notice you for three years, which, by the way, I find extremely hard to fathom, and now you think you're not noticeable."

A tightness formed in my chest and all I managed was a slight nod. *Nail on head.* Talk about hitting it. That was exactly how I'd felt for a while now. Somewhat invisible and not worth noticing. Suddenly, Alex looked around and then stood up.

"Come, the lighting is perfect, let's go be smoking and sexy and overly happy." He extended his hand for me to take, the green ribbon looked so prominent on his finger. "Bring that cocktail too. Nothing screams 'over you' like a cocktail in hand."

"Okay. Fine." I picked the cocktail up and slipped my hand gently into his. He pulled me out the chair with a gentle tug. God, his hand was really very smooth, and so soft. Wasn't there a saying about surgeon's hands? "Where are we going?"

"Well, nothing screams 'over you' like a beach either." He led me by the hand to the beach and when we got there, he looked around thoughtfully.

"The sea in background, or the beach in background, or, shall we frolic in the waves?" he asked seriously.

I burst out laughing again. "We might as well go full cheese and frolic in the waves."

"With our cocktails in hand," he added quickly, striding towards the sea. It was that beautiful time just before evening, when the light was at its most vivid. This evening it was a bright, warm orange. We walked into the sea, which was warm and still. Calm. I was wearing a simple, knee-length beachy dress and Alex was wearing shorts, so we couldn't wade in too far. Once we were knee-deep he turned to me and pulled his phone out.

"Okay, frolic." He waved his hand around like he was directing me.

"Frolic?" I laughed. "How the hell do you do that?"

"Splash some water around and throw your head back while you laugh uncontrollably because you're having the best day of your life!"

"This is ridiculous, you know that, right?" I shook my head and rolled my eyes. "This isn't going to work."

"You're right. Wait there!" Suddenly, Alex was running off towards the beach and waving down a passing couple. I watched as he talked to them for a while and then gave them his phone. He ran back and motioned for me to turn around and face the photographers.

"What did you say to them?" I asked.

"That we're on our honeymoon and very in love and need some photos."

"Oh, God. This is so embarrassing." I held my head in my hands.

"I know!" he acknowledged with a grin that looked caught somewhere between embarrassment and excitement. "We'll both frolic together now."

"Fine," I said, feeling sheepish and embarrassed as hell, but hey, if this was going to help me get over Matt, then so be it.

"Smile and hold your drink up," he ordered, as he wrapped an arm around my waist and pulled me closer. My body flinched in response. The other thing I'd noticed about Alex in the short time I'd known him was that he was very comfortable with touching, which he always initiated. Not in a creepy way, but he wasn't afraid to put his arm around my shoulders or my waist. It was nice. I'd put so much thought and effort into trying to touch Matt over the years; accidental leg brushes, arm bumps, deliberate leans and hugs that lingered. And each time I did it, I'd hold my breath with anticipation hoping and wishing that this would be the time that the lean turned into more. But it never did. So there was something nice about this easy, relaxed, no-strings touching.

The couple on the beach indicated to us that they were ready to take the shot. I struck a totally lame pose, one that was meant to give off the vibe that I was *sooo* over it and having the best time of my life. But as I did, without any warning and with seriously surprising strength, Alex scooped me up into his arms. I nearly lost grip of my drink and burst out laughing. Alex did too and suddenly we didn't have to pretend we were having fun. He dipped me and I spilt my cocktail all over myself. I squealed in shock as the cold liquid and ice cubes hit me. Alex lost grip of me and I plummeted into the water below.

"Oh God," I said, looking up at him, laughing from the shallow warm waters. "I can't believe you did that."

Alex was also laughing. He extended his hand for me and pulled me up with such force that I slammed into his chest. I was about to pull away when he wrapped his arms around me, I did the same and then *whoosh*, almost with that actual sound, we both fell into a strange, quiet moment. We looked at each other, arms wrapped around each other tightly, and no one moved. A kind of bubble descended on us that seemed to make all the sights and sounds around more muted and subdued. This only seemed to highlight Alex even more, bringing him into clear focus until it felt like he was all I could see. And then, we both started smiling at each other. I didn't really know why I was smiling, but it felt good. This bubble was only burst by the sounds of clapping coming from the shore.

I pulled away from Alex and looked towards the sound. I'd totally forgotten that we were being photographed.

"Brava!" one of the people shouted. I found myself blushing stupidly at this. We made our way back towards the beach and walked up to the couple.

"Thanks so much." Alex took the camera back and immediately went to photos.

"It's a pleasure," the man said. They were an older couple, if I had to guess, I would have placed them in their mid-sixties.

"Enjoy it while it lasts," the woman said with a smile.

"Enjoy what?" I asked.

"When it's just the two of you and you're very much in love. Soon the kids will come and then everything changes." She gave us a nod.

"Kids?" I felt my eyes widen in shock.

"The honeymoon phase is a special one. Cherish it." She put her hand on my shoulder and gave it a squeeze. "And you two look very in love." And with that shocking statement, they turned and walked away.

Alex didn't seem to have noticed the rather awkward conversation that had transpired, he was too busy flicking through the photos of us. Then suddenly, he stopped and gasped.

"What?" I asked, moving towards him.

"This has got to be the most romantic photo ever taken." He held it up for me to look at and I had to agree with him.

The sun was setting behind us, the water was shimmering with an orange glow, and the two of us were silhouetted against it. It was like one of those photos you might find in an advert for a honeymoon destination, or on a postcard. It was one of the most romantic images I'd ever seen, and if I didn't know the story behind it, I would have guessed that the couple in this photo were head-over-heels in love with each other.

CHAPTER TWENTY-ONE

"*W*e have to post this one," Alex said with a smile. "Hashtag *definitely* no filter."

"Wait!" I stopped him. "No one will believe it's real if we do. I mean . . ." I swallowed. "It kind of looks like we're . . . *in love*, or something like that. It's too much too soon."

Alex looked back at the picture again. His demeanor changed somewhat as he inspected it quietly and thoughtfully. In the short time I'd known him, I'd gathered that he was a great thinker. I could see that he thought everything through. He obviously had a brilliant mind, I mean, he was a doctor after all. And then he started nodding, slowly.

"You're right, we'll save it for later." His finger swished over the screen again, until he came to the shot of me free-falling into the water. "This one." He held the phone up to me.

I laughed. It was a great action shot. I was falling, still clutching onto my cocktail, legs flapping, skirt billowing, genuinely laughing. Alex was also laughing while he reached a hand out to grab me.

"That's a good one," I said. We both began walking back to our table on the beach. I was wet, and before I could do anything about it, Alex ran off towards the pool area and grabbed a big towel. He sprinted back and wrapped it around my shoulders. The kind gesture caught me off guard. He barely knew me and yet he was rushing around getting me towels and fixing my knees. He was a genuinely nice guy. If you had to describe Alex to anyone, the first thing you'd say was, "He's such a nice guy." God, his girlfriend must have been mad to let him slip through her fingers. But what's that saying about nice guys always finishing last? Maybe he was *too* nice.

We sat back down, ordered another two pink cocktails, and Alex sent the photo to me.

"Where should we post this?" I asked.

"Mmmmm . . ." He lifted a finger to his lips. I smiled. He always seemed to put something to his lips when thinking. "Definitely Instagram, maybe Facebook too, or is that overkill?"

"It would be overkill if we changed it to our profile picture on Facebook," I offered after some careful consideration. We were really taking this very seriously. Social media was no laughing matter, and defriending someone these days was as brutal as getting a divorce.

"Good point. But we agree to both Instagram and Facebook?" He looked up at me and raised a questioning eyebrow.

I nodded. "We agree."

I went to my Instagram account and opened it, going straight to my profile in case my news feed had pictures I didn't want to see. I pulled the picture up and looked at it.

"What filter are you using?" Alex looked up from his phone.

"Hashtag no filter," I said with a smile as I typed that.

"Hashtag happiness?" he asked.

I nodded. "Hashtag beach vibes."

"Hashtag happy hour," Alex offered; we were both nodding and typing.

"Hashtag blessed!" I proclaimed, typing away with a smile, even though hashtag blessed was one of the most nauseating hashtags that had ever been invented. In fact, hashtags in general gave me a sense of uneasy cringe. But fuck it, I was going to hashtag the hell out of this.

"Hashtag happy life?" He stopped typing and looked at me.

We both burst out laughing at the same time. To be honest, as much as this was all truly ridiculous, because it was, I was having more fun than I'd had in a while. Maybe this break was exactly what I needed?

"And post it on five, four, three, two . . ." Alex started counting down and when he reached one, I pressed the post button and then started giggling uncontrollably. There was something so deliciously silly about this whole thing, and even if it didn't have the desired effect—throwing the middle finger to our exes (not that Matt was technically my ex; well, I'd been in a relationship with him, even though he hadn't with me)—I didn't quite care at this stage. Three cocktails in, some sand and sun and someone to laugh with, I was starting to feel remarkably okay! I don't think I had felt this okay in a very long time.

But my merriment stopped when Alex suggested we unfollow and unfriend them now. It felt like someone suddenly punched me in the gut. If I unfriended him and unfollowed him, I could no longer look through his photos. Something I did late at night when I felt like torturing myself. In those moments, I always knew I shouldn't be looking, because the results were always the same—it inevitably made me feel like crap. Like a loser stalker. But as much as I told myself not to look, I always landed up doing it, like slowing down at the scene of an accident.

"Can I look through his pictures, one last time?" I asked, feeling the immense gravity of the situation.

"We'll do it together." Alex pulled his chair over to my side of the table. We sat next to each other in total silence, shoulders touching, each one flipping through our Instagram accounts. Matt's Instagram was peppered with pictures of him and Sam, there was the odd one of me and him, but mostly there were images of him and Sam that made them look like the power couple of the year. Once Instagram was complete, we went to Facebook and did the same thing. When we'd both finished we looked up at each other and sighed at the same time. The mood had changed, it wasn't so happy anymore.

"Here." Alex handed me his phone. "You do it for me."

I nodded and did the same, handing Alex my phone. We sat and looked at each other for a while, as if communicating silently. We didn't need words in this moment. We were both on the exact same page and it felt great to finally have someone to talk to, or simply sit in silence with, that understood. Then we both nodded and did it. Cutting them out of our social media lives, which in this day and age is like severing a limb. I just hoped I wouldn't now have a phantom limb that would constantly itch, but that I would never be able to scratch.

CHAPTER TWENTY-TWO

~

$\mathcal{W}$e must have sat in silence for ten minutes after our mass social media murder. I knew it would be hard, but I hadn't anticipated it being this hard. The sun had set, and the colorful twinkling lights of the beach bar came on. Couples started making their way there and taking seats. I looked over, and our friendly bartender from the other night waved at us. I waved back at him. He smiled at me and held up a basket of what looked like bar snacks and put them down. My stomach rumbled at the sight of the snacks. God, I was hungry.

I looked back at Alex, who'd obviously seen the whole thing play out too. "I'm starving too," he said and walked over to the bar. I followed him and we reassumed our usual spot.

"*Bonsoir*," the barman said. My French wasn't that bad that I didn't know what that meant.

"Good evening to you too," I said back politely, while peering into the basket.

"You know you are wanted by the police?" he said, polishing two glasses for us. "Fugitives from the law."

"Really?" I asked.

He placed the glasses down in front of us and instead of producing a tequila bottle, produced a large jug of water. "But don't worry, I covered for you. I said I had no idea who you were. I told him you were probably just crazy Americans!"

"And did they believe you?" Alex asked, pouring me a glass of water.

"Of course! Everyone knows Americans are crazy." He smiled at us and leaned in across the table. "So, what's next?" he asked, looking down at the magazine that Alex had put on the bar counter once again.

"Hey, how do you know what we're doing?" I asked, sipping the cool lemon-flavored water and grabbing for a piece of bread.

"Oh, I told him," Alex said. "Hope you don't mind?"

I shrugged. "You know my most embarrassing moment on Earth and I don't even know your name?"

"Julian." He extended his hand and I shook it.

"Val," I said to him and he nodded.

"So what do you think of this picture?" Alex asked, holding his phone up for Julian to see. "Does it scream 'over you'?"

Julian pulled his own phone out. "What are your social media names?"

"On Facebook I'm Alex Fletcher and on Instagram DrFletcher," he said.

"And you?" Julian asked me.

I gave Julian all my relevant details and within seconds we were all friends. Julian looked at our pictures thoughtfully and started nodding. "So over them!" he declared. "So, what's next?" he asked again, gesturing at the magazine.

Alex cleared his throat, flipped the magazine open and started reading.

"'Number Five. Bitch About Bae. That irritating thing he did in bed which he thought you liked, but you didn't! The way he always insisted that corduroy was having a comeback and his pants were fine to wear out, the way he sat on the sofa in his boxers with his leg up, so his one ball dangled out and rubbed against the communal seating area. The way he got toothpaste on the sink and you had to scrub it off when it dried and went hard. The way he left used floss out, farted in his sleep, snored, said 'Dear Lordy-Lord' when he came . . . take your pick. The point is, rip him off that pedestal with your girlfriends. Remember all the bad, irritating and hurtful things he did (don't leave anything out).'"

There was a collective pause after Alex had finished reading. We all looked at each other for a few moments, and then Alex and I began shaking our heads and laughing.

"Okay, well that one is just ridiculous!" I said, stuffing some nuts into my mouth. "And I can't even pass comments on things like what he did in bed . . . Well," I pondered, "actually, sometimes I could hear them through the walls of my apartment, and he did make a rather strange sound when he came, at least, I think he was coming."

"Wait!" Alex held his hand up. "You did not tell me he was your actual next-door neighbor."

Julian shook his head. "Had you told me that the other night, I might have made you the winner."

"Wait! Let's not jump the gun here," Alex piped up. "My ex lives in the same building as me, with another guy! That counts too."

"But I can hear them having sex through the walls," I quickly added. "And let me just say, she likes him to ride her like a thoroughbred Arabian horse."

Both Alex and Julian recoiled at the image I'd just painted.

"I'm not joking, the other night she said, and I quote, 'Yes! Oooh, yes, baby, yes, ride me like an Arabian horse, baby. Giddy-up! Yes, like a thoroughbred.'"

"You guys' lives are seriously messed up." Julian turned and produced another bottle of tequila. "I was going to suggest you stay off the hard stuff tonight, but it looks like you might need it again."

"Thanks," we said in unison, taking the bottle from him.

"It's all part of the healing process," I exclaimed quickly, just in case he thought we were alcoholics. "The post-breakup drunken bender. Everyone does it. At least it's not crack." I laughed at my own joke.

"You know . . ." Julian leaned in, "if you wanted something a little harder, I could get you—"

"No. No! It's okay thanks." I quickly cut him off and Alex started nodding in agreement.

"Tequila will do." Alex opened the bottle and started pouring us a shot each.

"Just joking!" Julian laughed and then leaned over the bar again. "So, start bitching," he said expectantly.

"Bitching! Yes, I can do that!" I felt confident. "I can bitch!"

"Me too," Alex said.

"Okay, so . . ." I tried to start slagging Matt off, but nothing was coming to me. "Um, yeah, Matt! He was such a, such a . . . um . . ." I tried to think of something negative, but nothing came. *Was I that far gone that I couldn't find one bad thing to say about him?*

"He was so, so, so . . ." I tried to forge ahead. But finally gave up and shrugged.

"Come on, you can do better than that," Julian urged. "Was he selfish, maybe?"

I thought about it for a second and then nodded. "Well, I guess he did slip his laundry into mine sometimes and expect me to do it, and he hardly ever said thank you."

"Selfish and ungrateful!" Julian clicked his tongue and shook his head.

I started thinking again. Really thinking. "You know what, he actually was ungrateful. I did so much for him. Stuff that girlfriends are meant to do. I even went out and bought him a new toothbrush when he dropped his in the toilet. And, oh God, he actually talked me into buying Sam tampons once because she'd run out and he didn't know what to buy."

"Damn! And what the heck did he do back for you, gurrlfriend?" Alex said with a strange accent. He clicked his fingers and snapped his head back and forth.

"What are you doing?" I asked.

He shrugged. "I don't know. Isn't this how women talk to each other when they're trashing their exes?"

"Like Aretha Franklin?" I smiled at him and he smiled back.

"I've never done this before," he confessed.

"Me neither."

"But you're doing so well. Continue," Julian added.

I nodded, feeling a little more confident in my trash-talking abilities. "Okay, I mean, if I think about it, he usually only talked about the things he was interested in. I was always asking him how his day went and I would listen for ages, but he never really asked me back."

"Selfish prick," Alex said, dropping the accent and the dramatic clicking.

"I know, right?" In fact, now that I reflected on it, I could see he was selfish. The relationship had often felt like a one-way street, but I'd ignored those feelings so often.

Julian and Alex looked at me and shook their heads. This was starting to feel really good.

"And, while I'm at it, he didn't sound like he was that great in bed either."

"Do tell." Julian leaned in even more; it looked like he was having more fun than we were.

"Well, I could hear them. And it's not like she was screaming his name every five minutes and banging the wall with her sweaty fists." I threw back a shot of tequila and looked at Alex and Julian. They were both staring at me now.

"What?" I asked.

Alex and Julian looked at each other, as if they were communicating silently.

"What?" I asked again.

"So . . ." Julian started, "your definition of good sex is screaming his name every five minutes?"

"And beating the walls?" Alex added.

I burst out laughing. "What's wrong with that?"

Alex and Julian both shook their heads.

"Um . . . To be honest," Alex started, "I'm not sure I've ever made a woman bang her sweaty fists against a wall."

"Well, then you're probably not doing it right," I said.

"How should we be doing it then?" Julian asked.

"Yes." Alex also leaned in—I had their attention now.

"Helllloooo! Drink, please," a voice suddenly called out and we all turned to see an angry-looking couple waving in our direction.

"I'm busy. Pour your own!" Julian shouted at the startled people and turned back to us. "Carry on," he said to me.

My tongue was a little loose from all the alcohol so I was only too happy to oblige. "Well, all I'm going to say is that sometimes less is definitely more, and slow and steady *does* win the race." I gave them both a wink and a knowing nod.

They looked at me blankly and then shook their heads.

"What does that even mean?" Alex asked.

"Please. Tell us," Julian urged.

"The thing is, sometimes you guys just go for it like you're trying to score a football goal in the first minute of the bloody game!"

"So we shouldn't be trying to score so soon?" Julian asked.

"No. And definitely not with so much enthusiasm! It's a delicate area, it needs some warming up. A bit of prep work before the main event."

"So, lots of foreplay?" Julian asked.

"Not necessarily. But you can't just go for it like a jackhammer. Start slowly . . ." My thoughts trailed off. "Very, very slowly. Like, so slow she almost doesn't even feel you at first. Teasing. And then, only when you've teased her so much that she is about to scream and beg, do you pick up the pace . . . Mmmmmm." I think I needed to fan myself. My body temperature went up a degree or two as I started to imagine all sorts of things.

"*Not like jackhammer . . . slowly . . . teasing,*" Alex said as if he was reading. I looked over at him and he was scribbling my words in his little notepad and I burst out laughing.

"Yes, and here's another tip, when we start looking like we're going to . . . *you know*, you don't have to always increase the speed like a bat out of hell. Sometimes it's all about that slow and steady pace."

"*Slow and steady . . .*" Alex continued to scribble.

"I mean, don't get me wrong, there's a place for jackhammers and bats out of hell, but sometimes I think you guys think sex should look like it does in pornos. Most women don't want to be bent over and twisted into a million positions at one time . . . just saying." I had such a captive audience now. "Also, it's not always about the size of the tool, it's how you use it!"

"So size *doesn't* matter?" Alex asked.

"Not as much as you guys seem to think it does!" I nodded at them both.

"Good to know," Julian almost mumbled under his breath, but then quickly corrected when he realized we'd both heard, "not that I am . . . you know. Deficient in any way down there. At all!"

"No. Me neither," Alex quickly added.

I laughed. "Guys! You're like children when it comes to penis size. Remember, there's only so much space in there anyway . . . and there is definitely a limit to how much luggage one can fit into a suitcase, if you get what I'm saying."

They both looked at me and nodded slowly and thoughtfully in unison.

"Yup." I threw back another shot. My tongue was getting very loose now. "Big, medium, slightly smaller than medium. I'm cool with them all, as long as you know how to use them."

"Thanks," Alex said, "that was very informative. Good to know for step ten."

"Huh? Step ten?" I asked.

"Getting under someone else," he said casually.

"Wait! What?" I said, shocked.

"Didn't you read that far? That's our step ten in getting over our exes." He looked so cool about that.

"Well, I'm not doing that!" I said quickly.

"But we have green ribbons." Alex held his finger up.

"Exactly. What was rule one? No relationships." I held my finger up too.

"There's a big difference between sex and relationships," Alex said.

"Said no woman ever!" I quickly added, because, let's face it, women who can truly separate love and sex are few and far between.

"We made a promise, though. We have to get through the list," Alex insisted.

"I made a promise before I knew I was meant to be having sex with some random person." I wagged my finger at him.

"But don't you want to get over that . . . BLOODY BAS-TARD!!" Alex suddenly broke eye contact with me and screamed. People in the bar looked in our direction and I jumped in my seat, suddenly caught off guard by how emphatic he was being.

"I mean, sure Matt was a bastard . . . But—"

Alex cut me off quickly. "No, not Matt. Look!" He pointed at the TV screen behind the bar and Julian and I swiveled our heads. It was the show I'd seen at the airport, *Big Band Battle*, and the same band was playing from last time. The same cheesy singer was gyrating across the stage to an adoring female crowd, sweat beads glistening on his forehead.

"That's Six Feet Over It," I said, pointing up at the screen. I immediately heard a massive groan emanating from next to me, and when I turned, Alex had lowered his head and was now resting it on the bar counter.

"Not you too . . . please. Not you too," he moaned into the bar, almost inaudibly.

I looked up at the TV screen again and felt my brain doing some kind of mental aerobics until I finally got it. "NO!" I gasped loudly. "That's not . . . ? It can't be . . . ? She left you for *him* ?"

Alex's head was still down, nose and forehead to the bar, but he managed to nod it.

"WHAT!?" I shouted and then coughed a little as I choked on a peanut. "But he's so, so, so . . . lame," I offered. It was the first and only word I could think of in that moment. I was also reeling from the shock from this revelation.

"And their music is terrible," Julian added quickly.

"And his hair! No one highlights their tips anymore, unless your last name is Jovi. Or is it *Bon* Jovi? I don't know."

"And look at what he's wearing." Julian pointed. "No self-respecting man wears pants that tight."

"Or leathery," I added. I shot Julian a concerned look and he nodded at me. No words were spoken, but we both understood what we needed to do!

"It's like if Meatloaf and Billy Idol had a baby." Julian was on a roll now.

"And it was raised by Kiss," I exclaimed.

"Besides, there's no way they're going to win this competition," Julian said.

"Exactly. They've probably bribed the judges to even get this far." I banged my hand down on the bar counter for added effect. "Seriously, you are way, way hotter than him, and more talented—you're a surgeon, for God's sake, and what does he do? Gyrate his pelvis on stage!"

"It's obscene!" Julian started pouring shots and lining them up on the counter with slices of lemons. This was an alcohol emergency.

"But he's cool. He's a rock star," Alex moaned again.

"He's a bad one." I put my hand on Alex's back and started rubbing it in circles. I had to admit that having the man that seduced your fiancée on TV wasn't exactly helpful when trying to get over her.

Alex lifted his head slightly and looked up at us both. "You really think so?" he asked.

Julian and I both began a mutual nod.

"He's terrible," Julian qualified firmly.

"Pure eighties power-ballad cheese." I nodded.

We all looked up at the TV and watched together in silence as the song finally came to an end and he fell to his knees on the floor, again.

"And way too dramatic," I added, pointing at the TV.

"I forgot to tell you, he goes by the name Enigma," Alex said.

"Oh God, what an idiot." I shook my head at the fool who was lying dramatically on the stage in the pool of melancholy blue light.

And then suddenly, it happened. *It!* And it was the worst, worst thing that could ever have happened under the circumstances . . .

CHAPTER TWENTY-THREE

❧

$\mathcal{I}$t felt like we were all watching it in horrific, extra-slow motion.

Enigma pulled himself up onto his knees. And then, he reached into his pocket slowly, so, so slowly. He raised the mic to his mouth again and started speaking, his words deep and blurry, like in a dream. Then his hand reappeared from his pocket clutching a ring box. Julian and I both gasped and then looked over at Alex, whose jaw fell open.

The camera swung wildly into the crowd and found her. Connie. Alex's Connie. She raised her hands to her face, just like I had done during my fake proposal. The camera panned closer to her and Alex gripped onto the bar as if he was going to fall over.

"Connie, you are the love of my life. You are my reason for being. The reason I do what I do every single day. The reason the sun rises and sets in the sky . . ." He paused and looked directly into the camera with his smoldering eyes for what I can only assume was added dramatic tension.

I cringed. God, he really was cheesy.

"You are my Yoko. My muse. My everything. And I really want you to be my wife too."

"Yes! Yes!" she gushed, tears streaming down her face now as she rushed onto the stage and threw her arms around him and they—

Julian turned the TV off quickly and we all just sat there in total silence for what felt like forever. No one dared to speak, I guess we were all waiting for Alex to initiate conversation again, but he seemed glued to the bar. Holding on so tightly that his knuckles had now turned white.

"I . . . I don't think I feel that well," Alex finally spoke. His voice was so soft and reserved, nothing like I'd heard before. "I think I'm going back to my room," he said in a slow staccato rhythm. He stood up, looking a little like a zombie, eyes not fully focusing on things, and began to walk away, dragging his feet in the sand.

"I'll come with." I jumped up and ran to him. I wasn't sure what to do, drape an arm across his shoulders in a comforting way? But how the hell was an arm going to comfort *that*?

I couldn't imagine what he was feeling, at least I hadn't seen Sam and Matt's actual proposal. And on live television, no less. I decided to drape my arm across his shoulders anyway and felt a little bad when I realized just how deliciously broad and muscular they were. I quickly put that thought out of my mind, not appropriate under the circumstances.

We walked in total silence until we reached his room. He stopped, still looking slightly zombie-ish, and turned to face me.

"Thanks," he monotoned.

"Do you want me to come in for a while?" I asked.

It seemed like he thought about this for a while and then slowly started nodding. "Sure. That would be nice. I don't really feel like being alone right now."

"Of course not." He opened the door and I followed him into the room where he immediately went to sit on the edge of the bed.

I sat next to him, shoulders touching once more. Silence.

He finally spoke. "I mean, I knew it was over, but I never thought she would get engaged to someone else. Not so soon anyway."

"There should be a mandatory waiting period between proposals," I said.

"There really should be, right?" He turned and looked at me. "A decent amount of time between heart-breakings."

"Agreed!" I nodded and looked at him. "It's not fair," I said softly.

He shook his head. "No."

"Love hurts."

"It does," he agreed.

"Then why the hell do we do it?" I asked.

"Because when it works, it's the best feeling in the world." He tried to force a small, brave smile and I smiled back at him. My heart felt like it was breaking. It was breaking for him, breaking for me and the general situation we both found ourselves in.

"I can tell you though, I'll be much more careful going into a relationship again," he said softly, staring forward.

"Me too," I agreed and looked down at the green ribbon on my hand.

"I'm certainly not going to be telling anyone I love them again anytime soon." Alex flopped down onto his back on the bed.

"God, I feel like such an idiot. Everyone we know probably saw that." At that, as if on cue, his phone started beeping and buzzing in his pocket.

"Turn the thing off," I said. Sympathetic messages just made you feel worse. I flopped down onto my back too, and we lay next to each other looking up at the ceiling. The ceiling was high and a fan was going round and round in hypnotic circles and as I watched it, I felt my eyes getting heavier and heavier. It was making me feel somewhat sleepy. But I willed them open.

"You know, you haven't bitched about bae yet, and this would be the perfect moment to do it."

"That's true." Alex turned his head and looked at me. "What should I say?"

"I don't know. What did she do that pissed you off?"

"Other than saying 'No' to my proposal, cheating on me and then getting engaged only two months later?"

"Yes. Other than that," I replied. "What else?"

He sighed. It was long and loud and had an edge of defeat to it. "I'm not sure I can do this."

"Sure you can. Where's Aretha Franklin now?" I propped myself up on my elbow and looked down at him. His eyes came up to meet mine and I marveled at how the color of them seemed to change with the light or his mood. Now they were a sad, blue-gray color.

He shook his head. "I'm not that kind of guy. I can't bitch about people, no matter what they've done to me."

I studied him for a while before speaking. "You really are a nice guy, Alex. You don't meet too many these days."

"Apparently, that was part of the problem," he said, turning and looking back up at the ceiling.

"What was?"

"I'm too nice. What did she say . . .? 'Not passionate enough. Not enough fight in me. Too passive.' And I thought the key to a successful relationship was not being a bastard." He sighed again.

There was a small amount of truth to his statement, of course. But I wasn't about to point that out now. A man that was too nice is often seen as boring. But so far, I certainly hadn't experienced him like that. This Connie woman was clearly a mad cow. I almost turned and said that to him, but then stopped myself. He didn't want to bitch about her, even after everything she'd done to him.

We both stared in silence at the ceiling; the soothing circles that the fan was cutting through the air were seriously making my eyes heavier and heavier and heavier . . .

CHAPTER TWENTY-FOUR

The he sound of children laughing and running woke me up. I opened my eyes, the sun was streaming through the gap in the curtains. It seemed late in the morning. I moved my body, but felt trapped under something heavy. I looked down to see what it was, and to my surprise, it was a big, solid hand.

I followed the hand to the muscular arm and turned my head to see whose body this appendage was attached to. I couldn't see all the way behind me, but the head of salt and pepper hair made me realize that I'd fallen asleep on Alex's bed, and now we were spooning!

I became aware of my legs suddenly, and then became aware that they were tangled up in his. God, this was rather awkward . . . but, *mmmm*, well, I must say, it did feel rather nice. I hadn't felt the weight of a man's body wrapped around mine in bed in a very, very, very long time. But although it felt nice now, I knew that the second Alex woke up the nice would become awkward.

So I tried to wiggle my way out of it. But he was too heavy. Still, I persisted. I continued my wiggle, trying to make my body as flat as possible so I could slither out. I made some progress and soon I was slipping lower and lower through his grip. If I carried on like this, I would make it to the bottom of the bed and I'd be able to crawl off. But as I'd managed to get halfway down, Alex moved. He readjusted himself and tightened his grip around me.

Great! My head was halfway down his chest now, and in this position, I had one of his knees poking into my shoulder blade. It was uncomfortable. I stuck my hand around the back of me and tried to push the knee away. But it was hard, and firmly stuck in place. I tried to swat it away a few times, but it just kept coming back.

"Crap," I whispered. I tried to lift my head to figure out how I could untangle myself from this mess, and when I finally did, two knees came into view. They were pressed together, jutting out over my hips. Hang on, if that wasn't a knee then . . .

I reached around again and grabbed it once more. Only this time, when I grabbed it I knew exactly what it was. *Not a knee.* So *not* a knee.

"Val!" I heard a very surprised voice behind me and felt the bed move as Alex threw himself off it. I pushed myself off the bed too and scrambled to my feet. I looked over at Alex. He was standing on the other side of the bed. His eyes were wide with shock, jaw hanging open, almost to the floor. My eyes drifted down, down, down . . .

Dear Lord! There was some serious morning glory happening over there. He was pitching a full-blown tent in his boxer shorts. My cheeks immediately blazed with a mixture of embarrassment and . . . *shit.* My palm started to tingle at the memory of being wrapped around all that. And there was just *soooo* much of it.

Alex grabbed a pillow off the bed and covered himself. He cleared his throat and then turned a strange and disturbing shade of red.

There was no misinterpreting this situation. No spinning this a different way to distract from what had really just happened . . . *I'd touched his penis!* Grabbed it, to be more specific. Held it in the palm of my hand. And what's more, it had been big and hard and thick and had poked into my shoulder with such force that I swear, it could have almost pushed me off the bed. My eyes drifted down to where the pillow was—would I be a total and utter pervert if I told you that I wanted to see what lay below it? Alex turned sideways, as if he knew what I was thinking.

Oh my God! The reality of the situation suddenly came crashing in and I didn't know whether to laugh nervously, or run from the room and hide for the rest of the holiday so I didn't see him again. I could see he was thinking the exact same thing too, as he stood there, cushion covering him, walking sideways now like a crab.

"It's a very natural reaction for a man in the morning . . ." he stuttered suddenly.

Oh God, I didn't want to have this conversation. It was just too damn awkward. "So . . . breakfast?" I suddenly declared loudly. Totally changing the subject. Trying to steer the conversation as far away from his big, hard . . . *Mmmmm.*

"YES!" He almost shouted that. "Yes. That would be a good idea!"

* * *

We sat at a table by the beach looking out over the sea. It had been rather awkward between us since the whole "waking up in each other's arms with a hard-on" thing. We were eating our late breakfast outside today. We'd initially gone to the dining room for the usual buffet, but when we'd walked in and seen what was playing on the TV, we'd both turned and walked straight out.

It would seem that Enigma's live TV engagement was all the news stations were talking about. The video had gone viral overnight, viewed over ten million times. Now I was just suspicious that the whole thing had actually been a giant publicity stunt. But stunt or not, I could see the effect it was having on Alex. And the effect only got worse when on the way out of the dining room we'd passed a group of girls talking about it . . .

"*Oh my God, she's so lucky.*"

"*I hope my boyfriend proposes on live TV like that.*"

"*He's such a rock god. OMG, you guys, he's sooooo haawt . . .*"

At that, Alex and I took our plates of carbs and strong cups of coffee and headed outside.

Despite the fact that the Danish pastries were surprisingly good that morning, the temperature perfect, the air not too humid and the setting spectacular, we sat and ate in total silence. I sipped my coffee, which was exactly what I needed. The caffeine entered my bloodstream and woke me up instantly. I'd been feeling a little groggy from oversleeping and was grateful for every mouthful of the black elixir. I wanted to say something to Alex, but wasn't sure what. *Should I address the borderline hand-job thing, or address the whole public proposal thing?* Both were not easy topics to broach. But before I could decide what to say, and how best to break this silence, something broke it for me.

A loud, piercing scream. I jumped in my seat and my heart thumped, the scream had been so terrifyingly bloodcurdling. I glanced over at Alex, who was sitting up straight. We both looked out to sea, to where the scream had come from, just in time to see an unusually large wave crash against the shore. It was strange to see, because I'd only ever seen a totally flat, calm sea—*until now*. Another scream. More frantic and desperate this time. I held my hand to shield my eyes from the sun's rays and scanned the water. Looking for the source of the scream.

The scream was now a shriek. Primal and guttural and one of the most frightening noises I'd ever heard. Alex and I were both on our feet, as was everyone else around us. The screaming voice started saying words, which at first were distorted, but as soon as they became audible, the entire atmosphere on the beach changed.

"My baby!" the frantic voice screeched. "My baby. I can't find her!" At that, as if an invisible director had just called "*Action*," people on the beach started running towards the sea.

"The wave . . . I was holding her . . . but . . . I can't see her!" the frantic mother wept. "HELP! HELP! MY BABY!!"

Alex and I were swept up in the stampede of men and women rushing towards the water. Everywhere, people were wading in, looking and scanning for the missing child. The sense of panic on the beach and in the air was so palpable that it made me feel sick.

The hysterical mother was now hyperventilating, and looked as if she was about to fall over. A few women had rushed to her side, and were physically holding her up as her cheeks drained of color. Soon, the shallow waters were filled with at least thirty people all rushing around in panic. My heart raced and I felt myself grinding my teeth and wringing my now very sweaty hands together. I had no idea what to do in this situation. I wasn't like all the others who had immediately jumped into action, instead, all I could do was freeze and stare out over the water hoping to see a child's head bob up.

But Alex was in the water. He seemed so calm and in charge, and suddenly he seemed to have assumed the role of leader, telling people where to go and look. He was bringing a calm order to the chaos, shouting things like, "Work from left to right. In a grid."

The fact that Alex seemed so cool and in charge settled my nerves somewhat. But as the time ticked on and the baby still hadn't been found, I began to think the worst. I could see that everyone else was thinking the same thing too, including the mother. She had fallen to her hands and knees and was praying loudly, clawing at the sand and screaming out things like, "Take me instead, God." Other women had also gotten down onto their knees and looked like they were praying.

Then suddenly, another voice could be heard. "I've found her. I've got her." Heads turned and everyone looked. A man began running towards the shore carrying what looked like the lifeless body of a toddler. As he ran, her arms and legs flapped as if no muscles controlled them anymore. I'd never seen a dead person before, and I gasped.

"She's not breathing. She's not breathing!" the man screamed as he picked up his pace. Another gasp. This time a collective one that came from everyone on the beach. Something caught my attention and I turned to see Alex sprinting over.

"Put her down!" he instructed the man. "I'm a doctor."

The man placed the little girl's body down on the sand and then without a second's hesitation, Alex was on her. He grabbed her wrist and looked at his watch, calculating her pulse. Nothing about him seemed even vaguely panicked, instead it was thoughtful. He put his head to her chest and then suddenly, as if this was one of those reality TV shows, started doing CPR. I'd never seen it done to anyone before in real life, and never to someone so small. It looked so violent, as he compressed her tiny chest and blew into her mouth.

In the distance I could hear the screech of sirens getting closer and closer—someone had obviously had the sense to call an ambulance; the thought hadn't even crossed my panic-stricken mind.

I moved closer to watch Alex work, a circle of people had gathered round the little girl now, the mother was clutching her hand and her prayers were getting louder and longer. Alex worked with such intense focus, yet total calm. It was as if he'd zoned the entire world out and all that existed was him, and that little girl. He was literally holding her life in his hands and I had never been so swept up in awe with someone before.

And then suddenly, the little girl stirred. Alex immediately sat her up and endless streams of water began spewing out of her mouth. A massive cheer rose from the crowd and the mother pulled her gasping daughter in to her arms. Alex reached for her wrist again and took her pulse once more, nodding as if he was satisfied.

"I need to examine her." He placed a reassuring hand on the mother's shoulder and then gently pulled the little girl from her arms. I watched in fascination as he began inspecting the girl's body, running his hands up her legs, running his fingers over her ribs, checking and inspecting her head. He was so meticulous and I could almost see the cogs in his brain ticking. Finally, the little girl cried out in pain when he reached her left arm.

"Ssshhh, it's okay," he said to her gently. "I think you bumped your arm a little, let's lie you down again." He gently lowered the girl to the sand and then turned to her mother.

"I think she's fractured her arm, she'll need an X-ray, but she's out of danger now."

As he'd finished the inspection, the paramedics pushed through the crowd.

Alex immediately started talking. "Her pulse is strong and regular. Possible fracture in the left ulna, would order an X-ray and also get a chest X-ray too to rule out any residual water in the chest." The paramedics nodded at him. They didn't need to question who this man was, they could tell he was a doctor. And so could everyone else, that authoritative tone in his voice put him in charge and made you feel safe, as though everything was being handled by him.

And then as quickly as the whole thing began, it was over. The mother and paramedics disappeared with the girl, who was loaded into an ambulance. Everyone on the beach stared after them and watched as the ambulance disappeared around the corner—lights and sirens blazing.

I let out a long sigh, and it was only then that I realized I'd been holding my breath. I turned back and looked at Alex as people descended on him, clapping. Women hugged him, men smacked him on the back and shook his hand and for a moment, he was swallowed up in the crowd.

I stood there, waiting and watching for him to emerge again, and when he finally did, and started walking up towards me, some strange combination of overwhelming emotions rocked me to my core. I was crying. Uncontrollably. I couldn't quite explain why I was crying; coming down from the shocking rush of adrenalin that had gripped me, the relief of seeing the little girl breathe again, the sheer pride and admiration I had for Alex. It was all just so overwhelming and intense.

"Hey, hey," he said, approaching me, "she's going to be okay."

I threw my arms around him, pulling him into the hugest hug. I buried my face in his neck and continued to cry. I felt his hands come up to my back and stroke it in big, long, soothing circles.

"It's okay," he whispered into my ear.

"I've never seen anything like that before." I finally pulled away from him and began wiping my tears. "Now that, *that* was rock-star," I said, grabbing his face and without thinking, planting a firm kiss on his lips. "That was literally the most badass, rock-star thing I've ever seen in my entire life. You just saved a child's life, it doesn't get more fucking rock-star than that." I smiled at him, tears still streaming down my cheeks.

"Really?" His gray eyes lit up. "You think?"

"I fucking know," I said, maybe a little too loudly.

Alex gave me another smile and then pulled me into a hug.

CHAPTER TWENTY-FIVE

I don't know how long we hugged for. It was getting to the point where one of us needed to let go. But for some reason, I just couldn't let go of him. Everything about this hug felt good and I didn't want it to end. Finally, after wrestling with myself, I loosened my grip. I pulled away slowly, but instead of moving off, I looked up at Alex. He looked right back down at me, our eyes locking.

"Sorry. I didn't mean to hug you for so long," I said awkwardly and self-consciously, averting my gaze.

Alex shrugged his shoulders and a tiny smile pulled at the corner of his lips. "It felt good."

"It did," I agreed, a small smile tickled the corners of my mouth.

"Besides, hugging lowers your blood pressure, lowers your stress hormones and increases your sense of wellbeing," he said.

"They should be prescribed by doctors," I said, looking back up at him. His gray eyes looked paler in the bright light of the sun. A dark outline around the iris blended into something that was almost silver in color around the pupil. Apart from being obviously gorgeous eyes, they had such kindness in them too and I felt myself being drawn to look at them. So I did. I only stopped when two men dressed in suits appeared by our sides.

They introduced themselves as the hotel managers and were soon shaking Alex's hand, grateful that he'd saved the girl's life. Alex kept humbly saying things like "it's just my job" but he did accept the complimentary dinner cruise on the yacht that they offered as a thank-you. After they left Alex turned to me.

"Well, at least we know what we will be doing tonight," he said with a smile.

"You want me to come with?" I asked, surprised by the invitation.

"Of course," he said sincerely. "But the question is, what should we do with the rest of the day?"

I looked around. "Well, to be honest, I'm not really feeling very beachy anymore."

"Me neither," Alex admitted. He picked up our empty plates, as well as my bag, and started walking back to the hotel. "Tell me," he said over his shoulder, "would I drop in your estimation from rock star to total nerd if I said there was a museum that I wanted to see?"

"A museum?" I smiled to myself. "I'd love to."

* * *

Musée de Villèle was a short taxi drive away from our hotel. I'd read a little about it on the way. It was a former colonial mansion once owned by a prominent and wealthy family in the eighteenth century, set on the remains of what was once one of the biggest sugar plantations on the island, run by hundreds of slaves. That part left me feeling somewhat cold and queasy, but I was still curious to see it.

We finally arrived and I couldn't remember the last time I'd been to a museum. But I was looking forward to a change of scenery.

The old plantation house was exactly as I imagined it might be, right down to the colors. Cream walls, yellow trims around the windows and doors and pale blue shutters. And it was huge, standing amidst an old overgrown garden that in its day must have been spectacular. With each step closer, I felt like I was stepping further and further back in time.

"It's beautiful," I said to Alex as we reached the entrance.

"I like museums," Alex said. The tone of his voice had changed somewhat, a kind of reverence hanging in his intonation.

"Really?" I asked. "Sounds like there's a story in that somewhere."

He turned and smiled at me as if I was right, there *was* a story behind his love of museums. "I have a bit of a museum crush."

"Tell me." I smiled back at him.

"I find them very calming. Not those big, busy, tourist museums, but the smaller more obscure ones."

"What do you like about them?" I was curious.

"The silence. Have you ever noticed how people always seem to whisper in them?"

I thought about this for a while and it was true. For some strange reason you did feel compelled to whisper in a museum.

"It's the one place where time seems to stand still. It's not about moving forward, it's about looking back." He strode ahead of me, entering the front of the museum.

"Why do you like silence?" I asked as we bought our tickets and began our walk around.

Alex stopped and stood next to me. "Would you think I was boring if I told you my ideal evening would be chilling at home quietly? No TV. No phones and computers. Some wine, food, reading a book, going to sleep?"

"Yeah, that's totally boring," I said with a playful smile. But truthfully, it sounded really, *really* nice. My life for the last three years had felt like a chaotic, wild ride of highs and lows and, quite frankly, I wanted off the ride now. I desperately needed a change of pace, and suddenly I quite liked museums.

"Connie always wanted to go out to dinner with friends to these fancy, busy restaurant or trendy bars."

"Sounds hectic," I added quickly.

"Very." We walked into the first room. "I prefer a dusty, old, quiet museum any day of the week. I've found one or two in London that aren't overrun with tourists, and sometimes after a long day of surgery, I like to go there to unwind."

"Have you ever lost a patient?" I suddenly found myself asking.

Alex paused. He looked straight ahead, not focusing on anything in particular. "A few times," he said slowly. "It's usually cancer, and by the time they get to me, it's too late anyway. It's very hard when that . . ." His voice was soft. It tailed off and he didn't finish the sentence.

"God, I don't know how you do it," I said. A thick lump crawled into the back of my throat. "You're remarkable." Alex turned and smiled at me.

"Thank you for saying that," he said. There was genuine appreciation in his voice, as if he didn't hear that very often. "And what about you? Revolutionizing the sex lives of couples the world over. Helping millions lose centimeters around their waists . . . Did you know that fat around the stomach is particularly damaging to organs and is the most dangerous kind?"

"Oh, please. I haven't written anything truly worthwhile, anything that could make a genuine difference to people's lives, in . . ." I paused and thought about it. "Ever. Maybe I just don't have anything important to say."

Alex looked at me curiously for a moment or two and then a slow smile spread across his face. "I think you have very important things to say and I have a feeling you'll be writing something like that very soon." He walked down the hall and into the first room.

The room looked like the kind you retired to after dinner to drink cognac and smoke cigars. The décor was very French; gold trimmings, low-hanging elaborate chandeliers, old patterned chaise longues and wooden floors that creaked when you walked on them.

There was no one else here and the only sounds I could hear were those of our feet as we walked from room to room.

I looked out the window at the sprawling gardens outside. A massive tree that had almost been taken over by bright orange bougainvillea stood in the center of the garden. I'd never seen orange bougainvillea before. It was so striking, especially against the cool of the green.

"Shall we go outside?" Alex asked, leaning over my shoulder. He was so close that I could feel his breath on the back of my neck and the warmth radiating from his body. There was something so comforting about his presence. He was always calm, his voice soft and soothing and his demeanor always set me at ease. I felt like I could breathe around him. He was like a human tranquilizer, only non-addictive and probably better for your liver and kidneys.

"Yes." I nodded and smiled at him, imagining him as a giant white walking pill.

"What?" he asked curiously.

"Has anyone ever told you how calming you are?" We began making our way outside.

"Maybe." His smile was gone now and he sounded sad even.

"Sorry, did I say something—"

"No," he cut me off. "Connie used to say that too, but not in the most positive way. She called me boring when we broke up."

"Bitch!" I exclaimed loudly.

Alex looked at me and shrugged. "Maybe she was right. Maybe I've got a bit old and boring over the years?" We were outside now and found ourselves standing at the top of an old concrete staircase that crept down to the lawn below.

"Oh, please. You set fires on beaches and run away from the police." I nudged him with my elbow. "Connie doesn't know what she's talking about."

"Honestly, I've never done anything like that before until I met you," he said.

"I must be a bad influence," I chuckled.

"Or a good one." He was smiling again, and then gave me a tiny, playful wink with those big gray eyes. "I think you might be the exact prescription that I need in my life right now, Val."

I laughed. "Are you comparing me to drugs?"

"I suppose I am." We walked down the staircase like the lord and lady of the manor.

"I'm not sure whether that's a compliment," I said.

Alex stopped walking and turned to face me. "It was meant as one," he said seriously.

"Well, thanks," I replied. "I think you might be exactly what I need right now too."

He smiled. "Then it's a good thing we found each other, isn't it?"

"My friend Stormy would call it fate," I commented as we started walking again.

"I don't believe in fate," he said.

"What do you believe in then?" I asked as we meandered through the thick, overgrown garden.

"Science," he said picking a leaf from a tree.

"How boring of you," I teased as we found ourselves walking on a long, wide path. The top of a church steeple was just visible from behind a large tree and we headed in the direction of what soon turned out to be a stone chapel. It looked so unassuming from the outside. So small. Nothing over the top or fancy. But the inside told a totally different story.

It was huge. The outside was deceptive, completely concealing its grand interior. The floor was covered in shiny black and white tiles and a huge vaulted ceiling rose up above us. It was spectacular.

"I don't know when last I went to church," I whispered after our moment of silent awe.

"Me neither," Alex said. He sat down on one of the many pews and I sat next to him.

"What kind of wedding did you want to have?" I suddenly asked.

"Not a church wedding. I've always liked the idea of a very small wedding. Close friends and family, maybe in a forest, or a beach somewhere. Nothing fancy. Simple. Maybe even in an old museum."

"Sounds nice," I said.

"But I guess that won't be happening anytime soon for me." He sounded deflated.

"Me neither," I admitted. "Every single one of my friends is either married, or about to get married. I'm the last single one and I'm no spring chicken anymore either."

Alex turned to me and raised a quizzical brow. "How old are you?"

"I'm almost twenty-nine and I've wasted three years of my life pining for a man who didn't even notice me."

"I'm thirty-seven and I've spent seven years in a relationship that went nowhere. And I'd still like to have kids before I'm too old to walk my daughter down the aisle or play football with my son."

I sighed. "Me too. But I'm beginning to think the right man might not be out there. I might have to take matters into my own hands, fertility-wise."

"I've got an idea." Alex smiled at me. It was a big, playful smile that lit his eyes up.

"What?" I sat up.

"This is the deal: if you and I are still not married in three years' time we'll marry each other and have kids!" he said triumphantly.

I burst out laughing and it echoed through the church.

"Don't laugh, it makes perfect sense. We get on well, we seem to have a lot in common. You clearly have favorable genes and I'm sure the green ribbon thing will have run its course by then." He held his hand up.

"Interesting idea," I said, feeling a little sense of girlish amusement. "But you do know that in order to have babies you need to have sex first." As I said it, I felt a tiny butterfly rear its head and flap about in the pit of my stomach.

"Sex?" Alex sounded thoughtful. "Yeah, we could do that. I mean . . . sure, why not?" I turned my whole body to face him. Now two butterflies were flapping.

"At least I know how to do it correctly, thanks to you," he said, a naughty twinkle in his eye. "Slow and steady."

A warm feeling flitted through me. "But not all the time," I added, going with the sudden flirty nature of the conversation. I must admit, it was rather thrilling to be having a flirty conversation with someone that was actually reciprocating. I was always trying to flirt with Matt, clearly unsuccessfully. Not that Alex and I were being serious, of course. But it was still fun.

We locked eyes and looked at each other for a while. "When we do have sex I'll make sure I'll pull out my notes."

"Don't you get sent straight to hell for talking about sex in church?" I suddenly asked.

At that, we both turned slowly, as if we could sense someone watching us.

"I think you do!" Alex said. We both burst out laughing and ran from the church.

CHAPTER TWENTY-SIX

*T*he afternoon passed quickly. After coming back from the museum, we went our separate ways. I had a long, relaxing bath that took up most of the afternoon. I hadn't felt this calm and relaxed in a long time, dusty museums were clearly the answer. After the bath I got dressed and ready for our dinner cruise. The yacht was leaving at six that evening and by the time I was dressed and ready to go, I was feeling very excited.

I couldn't figure out if I was more excited to see Alex, or more excited for the cruise. We'd had a good time together that day, and I felt like I'd really gotten to know him. I dragged my make-up bag out from the bottom of my suitcase and splashed a few things on my face. I hadn't worn make-up since arriving in Réunion, but I figured some red lips seemed appropriate for a yacht. Not to mention trying to cover up that huge hickey I had on my neck. I grabbed some concealer and dabbed it onto the big purple patch and smiled to myself. I don't think I'd had a hickey since high school. I closed my eyes and tried desperately to remember the kiss, but it was still all fuzzy. I wished it wasn't.

We met in the reception area of the hotel at five thirty, where a car was coming to pick us up. When I got there Alex was already waiting for me. He was sitting comfortably in a chair, legs crossed and reading not a magazine this time, but rather a newspaper. He looked very smart casual in a pair of knee-length shorts, comfortable-looking shoes and a golf shirt. He was clean-shaven, his hair neat and styled impeccably. He looked good. Polished, but not too much. Casual, but not sloppy. Smart, but not overly so.

He was the kind of guy that didn't stick out of a crowd immediately. At first glance he might even blend in, but on closer inspection one realized there was nothing about him that blended. I liked that. There was something subtly disarming about him. Like something that was initially hidden from sight, but once you saw it, you couldn't ever unsee it.

"Hey." As if sensing my presence he suddenly looked up at me.

"Hey! Hi!" I jumped as if I'd been caught doing something naughty and then tried to smile innocently at him.

"You look good." He stood up and pulled a chair out for me. He really was very gentlemanly.

"You too." I gestured at his outfit. "Much better than before."

"Didn't you like my stone-washed jeans and leather jacket?" he asked with a playful smile.

"Um . . . do I have to answer that honestly?"

"That bad, hey?"

I shook my head. "The worst!"

We laughed at the same time. "I was very relieved when it went up in smoke," I said.

"Me too," he said. We both sat down just as the driver appeared. "Time to go."

We walked out the door, passing a couple on their way out. We all waved politely at each other.

* * *

"Wow," I said, looking at the yachts on the pier in front of us once we arrived. They were those grand ones, not the kind for mere mortals. It was the kind you might see in the pages of the *People* magazine. The kind of thing celebs cruise Turks and Caicos in.

"The perks of being a doctor," I whispered over at Alex.

"I don't save people's lives every day, though."

The pier jutted out into the calm, gold-tinged waters. The sun was kissing the horizon now and making it look like orange liquid was bleeding into the surrounding waters. We walked onto the pier and made our way towards the boats. The one at the very end was the largest, it also looked like it was expecting us. A red carpet rolled down the steps and onto the pier, its lights were on and a big "Welcome" sign was posted out front.

"I'm assuming it's that one?" I looked at Alex and asked.

"I would think so," he said as a man holding a tray of champagne glasses suddenly appeared out of nowhere and offered them to us.

"I wasn't expecting this," I whispered to Alex, taking two glasses and handing him one.

"Me neither," he said.

"This way, please," the man then said, waving an arm in the direction of a staircase that I'd only just noticed now.

"Oooooh, exciting," I said, playful. We followed the man upstairs, but I wasn't prepared for what we saw.

CHAPTER TWENTY-SEVEN

*T*he upper deck was full of well-dressed people sipping champagne and cocktails. There was a big blue pool in the middle of it, dotted with floating candles. Rows of fairy lights stretched out over our heads and large colored paper lanterns hung from them. People stood around small tables draped in shiny tablecloths, or lounged on chairs by the pool.

"I didn't know there were going to be so many people," I said to Alex, suddenly feeling a little overwhelmed.

"Me neither," he replied, sipping his champagne.

We both turned as the movement of waving hands caught our eye. The hands belonged to the couple we'd seen at the hotel earlier. He and his wife looked slightly older, in their fifties maybe. Alex and I waved back at them and then the man was on his feet walking over to us.

"Hi, I'm Paul." The man extended his hand and we both shook it. "And that's my wife, Bethany." He gestured behind him and we all looked. Bethany waved. She was pretty. She looked very well turned out and polished, like she was in one of those *Housewives Of* shows.

"Would you like to come and join us?" he asked. It was one of those awkward moments where you can't say no, even if you want to. So Alex and I agreed and soon we found ourselves sitting with Paul and Bethany, two total strangers, having drinks.

But it wasn't that bad. Turned out we had some things in common. Paul was a doctor, the "cool" kind, a neurosurgeon. And his wife, Bethan, had been an accountant before becoming a stay-at-home mom of two. They were British ex-pats living in Dubai and had come here on their annual holiday without the kids, *good to keep the romance alive*, they said. They seemed nice enough, and we all fell into a comfortable, interesting chat. Alex and Paul started talking about something medical-related and Bethany told me all about her glamorous-sounding life in Dubai and how the other day, when she was on her way to fetch the kids from school, she saw a man walking his pet tiger. Apparently, you see those kinds of things rather often in Dubai. After about ten minutes of conversation someone familiar caught eye.

"Look, it's Julian." I nudged Alex and pointed in the direction of the bar. Julian looked up as I pointed. For a moment he looked confused, as if he didn't recognize us, but then smiled and waved.

"Sorry," I said to Paul and Bethany, "I want to say 'hi' to a friend. See you now." I got up politely and made my way to the bar, Alex close behind me.

"Julian," I said as we reached the bar and sat down. "You're everywhere, aren't you?"

"I could say the same for you," he said with a playful smile. "So . . . what will it be?" he asked.

I shrugged and looked over at Alex. I wasn't too fussed at this stage.

"We leave it in your capable hands," Alex said.

"I heard what happened at the beach earlier," Julian said, mixing the drinks together.

"God, you should have seen it. Alex was amazing," I jumped in.

"I was just doing my job," Alex said dismissively.

"Julian, you should have been there. It was the coolest thing I've ever seen in my entire life," I gushed. "He was so calm and in control and methodical. It was insane!"

Julian looked over at Alex. "When I do my job, I just mix drinks."

"And I just write meaningless articles," I added.

Suddenly Alex looked coy. His cheeks seemed to flush a little. "Thanks, guys." He held his drink up and I clanked his glass in toast.

"So . . ." Julian did his bar lean again. The one he was becoming quite famous for. "I didn't know you guys were into this."

"Into what?" I asked.

"Swinging," he stated.

"Swinging from what?" Alex took a sip of his drink and looked confused. So was I.

"Uh . . ." Julian looked from Alex to me and back again. "From each other."

Alex tsked. "What does that mean? How do you swing from each other? Is this a new workout? I can never keep up with them. It's yogalates one day and stretchaerobics the next."

Julian's eyes widened and then he shook his head. "You guys have no idea where you are, do you?"

"We're on a yacht," I said flatly. "We're here for dinner, compliments of the hotel."

Julian smiled at us conspiratorially. "Guys, this is the annual swingers' convention. They come here once a year and book out a yacht. I work the bar, really great tips I might add."

Alex shook his head. He still wasn't computing. My brain, however, was starting to get it.

"NO!" I gasped under my breath. "It can't be. We were just talking to such a nice couple over there."

Julian raised his eyebrows and shook his head, as if in disbelief.

"They were nice," I continued. "And they can't be swingers. He's a surgeon and she's a stay-at-home mom. Stay-at-home moms don't swing!"

"You think?" Julian looked very amused now. "Why don't you ask them?" He looked past me and I turned. I looked over at the couple again, and suddenly, it all became very, very crystal clear. Paul and Bethany were smiling at us. But this time the smile didn't look so friendly.

"Shit!" I turned back to the bar as quickly as I possibly could. "This is a swingers' convention. We are on the wrong yacht!" I whispered over at Alex, who still seemed to be totally oblivious to what I was saying.

"Let me paint a very clear picture for you then, Alex," I said, leaning over to him and gently placing my hand over his for added emphasis. "The people who have come on this cruise are swingers. Not from trees, or ropes or even on swings—*unless they're sex swings*—they have sex with each other. Partner-swap. Drop their keys in a bowl at the door."

Alex's face still looked blank, still processing and absorbing this information. I tapped his hand, hoping the movement would help him along. And then he laughed. Shook his head and smiled at me.

"Nonsense," he said, "that couple over there is too old fo—" He turned and looked at them, and then as fast as I've ever seen anyone move their head, his eyes were back on me. Wide as saucers. "She has her breast out." He reached for his drink and sipped it.

"She's not the only one," Julian chuckled. "Look around."

I closed my eyes tightly and shook my head. "I don't know if I want to look around."

"Well, you're going to see it at some point," Julian said with a laugh in his voice.

Alex and I stared at each other and then both slowly turned our heads around. *Yup, things were really starting to become quite crystal clear now.* The woman wearing nothing but her lingerie at the edge of the pool seemed to help clarify things for me. The naked couple in the pool that she and some others were now watching seemed like a dead giveaway too.

"Alex, we have to get out of here," I said.

Alex didn't speak, he just nodded.

"Bye, Julian," I said, as the two of us quickly made a dash for the other side of the deck where the exit was. But just as we were almost there, we felt the yacht move.

"Oh no." I started to run down the stairs and arrived at the bottom just in time to see the yacht pulling away from the pier.

I turned and looked at Alex in panic. "We're stuck here."

CHAPTER TWENTY-EIGHT

～

*W*e couldn't go back up to the top bar deck, things were really starting to get out of control up there, so we headed inside to look for a place to hide. A corridor stretched out in front of us. Lined with doors, most of them closed, most of them with "Occupied" labels hanging outside. I didn't dare to venture into one, I could only imagine what exactly was occupied.

Finally, we came to an open door right at the end of the corridor. The lights were off and Alex fumbled in the dark for a few moments before finding the switch. He flicked it on and the images and shapes in the room started coming into focus. Alex closed the door behind us.

"Is this a gym?" Alex looked around. *Oh God, this man really needed to watch more films with the word "Grey" in the title.*

"Alex, do you really not know what this is?" I asked.

"No."

"It's a sex room."

"What?" He seemed genuinely shocked. As if it was such a

leap to imagine a kinky sex room at a swingers' party. I looked around at all the things. There were a few of those big round balls that you find at the gym, the ones that work your core, but these were no doubt being used for an entirely different core workout. Straps hanging from the wall that also looked like those things you find in the gym. A few cupboards against the walls, I dreaded to know what was in them.

"Maybe we should leave," I said. But just as the words were out of my mouth three people burst through the door, all of them semi-nude and really just a tangle of arms and legs. A man, that much I could see. Two women, one redhead, one brunette.

"Oh God!" I jumped.

"Well, hello there." The man disengaged himself from the women and looked over at us. *Dear lord, what was he wearing?* I tried to avert my gaze, but couldn't. It was just so, so, so . . . *in your face*. He was wearing a tight shirt and nothing else but a pair of red budgie-smuggler underpants.

"Uh . . . Hi!" Alex stuttered, I could see he was also trying to pry his eyes away from what actually looked a little like a red fire hydrant. "We were just leaving." The two of us started inching our way towards the door.

"You don't have to go. The action hasn't even started yet." The man took a step closer to us and the red front pouch swung from side to side. What was he keeping in there. *An elephant trunk?*

"That's okay," I said as Alex and I continued to shuffle our way towards the door. "We've already had so much action tonight, haven't we?" I glared at Alex and he nodded.

"So much! WOW!" Alex wiped his brow as if he were sweaty. There wasn't a bead of sweat in sight.

Mr Red Bulge raised a brow as if he didn't quite believe Alex.

"Really?" the man asked.

"Yup! She's like a wild animal, this one. Let me tell you." He looked over at me pointedly. I could see he was urging me to say something.

So I did. And it was so almightily embarrassing, but it was such a bizarre, awkward situation, it just kind of came to me. "Meow," I hissed at the three of them and then immediately cringed.

"No worries," the guy said with a smooth smile. "You can always just watch if you want," he then offered.

"No, thanks," I quickly said. We were almost at the door now, just a few more steps to go and then we would be free.

"Suit yourself," the guy said.

"Thanks for the offer though," Alex said politely. "It's very thoughtful of you three."

"Yeah, have a super fun evening," I said. And with that, I felt a tug on my leg and felt myself fall forward.

"Shit!" I went crashing to the floor. I had no idea what had tripped me up until I looked down at my ankle. Twisted around it was one of those straps that was hanging from the ceiling. Alex reached out to pull me up.

"I'm okay," I said, totally embarrassed by my tumble. "I'm totally fine." I quickly untangled my foot and then grabbed onto one of the cupboards to hoist myself up. But then disaster struck. I grabbed the handle by accident and the cupboard door went flying open.

"Crap, crap, crap!" Things felt like they were going in slow motion now; a strange, shiny, black plastic shape seemed to come falling out the cupboard like a sack of potatoes. *What the hell was it?* It pushed me over and then fell on top of me, pinning me to the floor.

"What the—?" I desperately tried to push it off me. But every time my hands came into contact with the thing, it let out a long, high-pitched squeaking sound, like shoes on a squash court. And it was slippery. *Why was it slippery?*

"Val, are you okay?" I felt Alex grab me by the arm and pull. But the strange, big black creature was still on me. It wasn't coming off and, damn, it was heavy.

"What is it? What is it? What is it?" I flapped about in panic now. *Was it a dead body in a bag?* That's what it felt like! I finally managed to wiggle free and climbed to my feet. I looked down.

It was definitely human. That much I could see. The two blue eyes looking up at me through the little holes in the full face mask told me so. The eyes blinked a few times and so did I. I was trying to take it all in. The person on the floor was covered head-to-toe in a black latex skintight suit. The other three in the room had walked over and we all stood staring as it flapped around.

"It's trying to say something," Alex pointed.

"Is it?" I asked. *From what mouth exactly?* It didn't have a mouth. Its whole face was completely covered.

"I can hear it too," one of the girls said. She crouched down and we all followed her lead.

"What are you trying to say?" she asked, leaning in.

We all kept silent as the murmur came out from under the mask.

"I can't hear you, sweetie." She leaned in even more. We all did.

"Mmmm, uhmmm, ffffhjhhaaa . . . yttttthhhhhmmmmmmmgggrrrhhhh," it said. *(Or something like that.)*

"Are you in some kind of trouble?" I asked, speaking slowly and loudly. "Do you need us to get you some kind of help?"

It shook its head at me.

"Look, there's a zip." Alex pointed at the face part and I saw it. A little zip across the mouth area. Alex looked at me and I shuddered. Then he slowly, tentatively, reached out and unzipped him.

"Thanks," the voice from behind the mask said. He had such an ordinary voice. Like he could be the guy on the other end of a call center line, or the man at the bank, or even a school teacher.

He continued talking. "Master won't be happy if I'm out of my cupboard. Can you guys put me back, please?"

I looked up at the other three in the room. They seemed totally chilled and relaxed by all this. The redhead was even chewing on a piece of gum casually and twirling her hair around her finger.

"Sure, mate," the man with the red budgie smugglers said.

"Sure," Alex agreed awkwardly. The sooner we did this, the better. Then we could be out of this strange room.

So we all picked him up. God, he was slippery! We finally managed to get him back into the cupboard where he retreated into the corner, disappearing into the shadows once more.

"Thanks," he said.

"No worries," Alex replied, trying to sound upbeat and nonchalant. We immediately resumed our escape. But he stopped us . . .

"Would one of you mind zipping my mouth shut again and closing the cupboard door?" I looked over at Alex and shook my head. I wasn't going to do that, and the other three were already starting something on one of those swings.

"Of course." Alex moved back to the cupboard, zipped his mouth shut and closed the door on him. Alex looked up at me and he didn't have to say a thing, I could see exactly what he was thinking. We both nodded at each other and then ran straight out of the room.

CHAPTER TWENTY-NINE

*A*lex and I threw ourselves out the door and slammed it behind us. We turned and looked at each other and shook our heads. As if we couldn't believe that had just happened.

"We should probably get out of here," Alex said.

"Probably," I replied. It's not that I was against this kind of thing, in fact, I'd written many an article about swingers and fetishes, but being here with the strange smell of latex and leather in the air was another thing entirely.

We walked back down the long corridor and pushed our way outside and onto the deck. Everything seemed to have dialed up a notch since we were last there. Clothes lay strewn across the floor, so many that it looked like it was made of a patchwork quilt. We moved through everyone and were almost at the bar when we were stopped.

"Hi." It was Bethany in almost all her glory.

"Hey, guys." Paul joined her. "So, what are you into?" he asked, moving closer. "Full swap, soft swap, same room, water sports, MFM, FMF or GG?"

"We're into making an E.X.I.T," Alex spelled and then started pulling me again.

"Yup. We should *definitely* leave," I whispered as we dodged all sorts of strange and sticky things, pushing our way through the crowd.

Alex and I arrived at the bar where Julian was. "How do we get out of here?" Alex immediately asked.

Julian burst out laughing. "You could swim." We both turned and looked at the sea. The shore was in sight, and not a far swim at all, by anyone's standards.

"The water is actually very shallow past that buoy." Julian pointed out. "You could probably walk the rest of the way from there. And the coral reef is out there, so you won't step on anything sharp."

Alex and I walked over to the edge and looked out. The buoy was only about fifty meters away, and maybe another fifty to shore.

"What do you think?" Alex asked.

"I . . . I . . . I don't know." I looked down into the clear blue sea wondering if I should, when something bumped into me. I turned to see what it was. "Oh God!" I jumped in fright.

I was now face to face with a big, blow-up sex doll. It had come crashing into me. Its garish, blue-painted eyes stared at me. They almost had a look of desperation in them. Her big, wide, gaping mouth seemed to be saying something to me . . .

Get me out of here! Get me out of here!

"Let's do it!" I turned to Alex, clutching the doll under my arm. Alex's eyes widened as he looked at it in shock. "Floatation device," I said. I kicked my shoes off and indicated for Alex to do the same. Then I rushed them over to Julian and put them on the bar. "We'll get them from you at the hotel," I said with utter determination, and a blow-up sex doll under my arm.

Julian laughed. "You guys are mental!"

I rushed back to the side of the boat.

"There's a place for you to jump off into the sea over there." Alex had discovered a small platform that jutted off the edge of the boat. We rushed towards the platform and both jumped off it without giving it any extra thought.

I felt my body fly through the air for a few moments, and then I landed in the warm water with a splash. The blow-up doll I was clutching quickly brought me to the surface. I held onto her and started kicking my legs, using it as a board. Alex joined me and soon we were both clutching onto her, kicking. I tried to ignore the fact that one of Alex's hands was now firmly gripping her big balloon breast. We kicked like this for quite some time until our feet finally came into contact with the soft sand and we were both able to stand up. The water was chest-deep for me and I stood still, trying to catch my breath.

"We made it," Alex said. I could hear he was also out of breath.

We both turned and looked at the big yacht behind us. Julian was standing at the railing. He gave us a massive thumbs-up and a wave. I turned to Alex and we both stared at each other for a while. No one said a word.

"Did that just happen?" I asked Alex, breaking the silence.

He started nodding his head. Slowly at first, until it got bigger and bigger.

"That wasn't a dream? That really happened to us?" I asked again.

Alex stopped nodding and then a tiny smile spread his lips. I felt my mouth twitch too. Our smiles began slowly, gaining momentum until they were spread wide across our faces. And then we started laughing. Our laughter was loud, uninhibited and raucous.

"Oh my God," I wailed. "That was insane!"

Alex clutched his sides as he laughed. I couldn't help notice how his wet shirt was now clinging to all the defined lines on his chest and stomach. And when he laughed, they all seemed to ripple and writhe and wriggle around. Suddenly I wasn't laughing anymore. I was gawking at his body through the tight wet shirt. For some reason I reached up and touched my neck. The back of my knees tingled again, almost as if I could feel his fingers on them. He threw his head back and laughed even more and I tried NOT to stare, but his wet pants were clinging tightly to him, you see. I bit my lip and I swear I heard the sex doll next to me let out a little breathy moan, *or was that me?*

"Come, let's get out of here." Alex stopped laughing suddenly and I quickly looked away from his crotch area (God, I was a perv) and started nodding my head vigorously. We walked the rest of the way and when we arrived on the beach, that's when we realized we weren't alone.

"Hi." Alex waved at the couple on the beach, the ones who were sharing what looked like a once very romantic dinner.

"Hi," I mumbled at them and gave a little wave. They looked at us in utter shock and then, simultaneously, their eyes drifted down to my hand. I was still clutching the sex doll.

I looked up at them coyly and gave a small shrug. Alex burst out laughing again and the two of us ran across the beach, sex doll in tow.

CHAPTER THIRTY

~

$\mathcal{I}$ woke up to the sound of my patio door being opened and heard Alex's voice. At first I couldn't make out the words Alex was saying through my sleepy haze, but as I began to regain consciousness words started coming into focus.

"Breakfast . . . Bethany . . . enormous sausage . . . thank me for the cupboard . . . romantic dinner on beach . . . glaring at me . . . and that's why we need to get out of here."

"Huh?" I started to sit.

"Did you just hear a word I said?" Alex asked.

"Not really," I confessed, rubbing my eyes.

"I went to breakfast without you, didn't want to wake you, and let's just say that we don't want to stay here in this hotel any longer. Unless you want to run into Bethany and Paul again. Oh, and by the way, the man we stuffed into the cupboard last night, his name is Dave. He says 'hi'."

"What?" I opened my eyes. "Are they all staying here?"

Alex nodded. "Yup. And they were all very hungry this

morning at breakfast. And speaking of which, here." Alex sat down on my bed and put a plate of pastries in front of me. "And I also got our shoes back from Julian," he said, dropping mine onto the floor.

"Thanks." I immediately reached for one of the Danishes and started eating. I was starving.

"Oh, and the hotel manager wanted to know why we didn't come to the yacht on pier *threeeeee*. Three. Not four."

"What did you tell him?" I asked.

"I told him that you had suddenly come down with an acute case of pneumonoultramicroscopicsilicovolcanoconiosis."

"What's that?" I asked.

"A cough," he said casually as he sat on my bed eating. "Was she a good cuddler?" Alex pointed to the other side of the bed. I blushed when I saw what was there.

"I wasn't . . . I didn't . . ." I stumbled. "It was just . . . I . . ." I stopped talking and looked at him blankly, not sure what to say in my defense. There was a blow-up sex doll lying next to me on the bed, after all. "She was great," I finally said, playing along.

Alex laughed. "Well, in that case she can come with us."

"Where are we going?" I asked, my mouth full of pastry.

"We're leaving the hotel and getting back onto the list." He waved the magazine at me. I'd almost forgotten about the list. We'd had such an action-packed day that I hadn't even thought about it. "But first we are going to hike up a volcano," he said.

"A what?" I climbed off the bed and stood up this time. "You've lost your mind."

"It's not erupting. Besides," he reached into my bedside drawer and pulled out a travel brochure. He flipped it open and held it up to my face. "Hiking the Piton de la Fournaise is one of the *must do* things here in Réunion. I found this in my room too."

"Just because everyone else is climbing volcanoes doesn't mean we should too. It's the same principle that applies to things like jumping off cliffs."

"Well, it's too late to pull out, I've hired us a car, booked us into some other hotels and planned our road trip." Alex laid a hand-written note down on the bed.

"Road trip? Since when was this decided?"

"Since Bethany looked at me seductively while peeling the skin back on a big banana at breakfast."

"Eeeww," I cringed. I looked down at his piece of paper and picked it up. I scanned the words on the page and stopped when I saw it.

"SKYDIVING!" I shouted. "You've written skydiving here, which must be a mistake, right?"

"But look." He grabbed another brochure from the drawer.

"God, I'm kind of wishing that you didn't have access to brochures, or magazines for that matter," I said, sitting back down on the bed.

"Extreme Réunion; paragliding, skydiving, microlight. Everyone is doing it."

"Again," I pointed out, "just because everyone is doing it, doesn't mean we should."

Alex cleared his throat and started reading, "'Number Six. Get The Adrenalin Pumping. Do something that you are completely scared of. Whatever that is; there's nothing like feeling the rush of adrenalin in your veins to make you forget your ex. Be

brave and take that leap, whether it be off the top of a cliff or out
of a plane—' "

"Now you're just making that up," I cut him off.

Alex looked up at me, unimpressed. He then passed the magazine over and folded his arms, waiting. I looked down at the
magazine and continued to read.

" 'Be brave and take that leap, whether it be off the top of a cliff
or out of a plane—' " I paused. "I see, well, I'm not doing any such
thing. I've had enough adrenalin to last me a lifetime, what with
narrowly escaping latex-covered gimps and wild threesomes." I
walked over to the mirror and grabbed a hair band, twisting my
hair into a bun and tying it up.

Alex walked up behind me and placed his hands on my shoulders. He looked at me in the mirror seriously. "It's already booked
for later this afternoon, after we hike up the volcano."

"Mmmmm . . ." I mumbled, "we'll see about that." I put my
most serious, stern face on and Alex just laughed. And then his
hand slid around the front of my neck and my breath got caught
in the back of my throat. He traced his finger over the bruise on
my neck which was a bright violet color today.

"Does it hurt?" he asked softly.

I shook my head, locking eyes with him.

"Sorry about that," he said, looking somewhat concerned.

"It's okay," I said softly, as if something had stolen my voice. We
held each other's gaze for a while and then my eyes drifted down
to the green ribbon on his finger. I'd almost forgotten about them.
Alex moved his hand away and then suddenly walked over to my
cupboard. He pulled my suitcase out and placed it on the bed.

"You should pack, the rental car is already here."

"I see." I turned and faced him.

"Are we taking her?" He pointed at the blow-up doll in my bed.

I smiled. "Well, we can't leave her here, can we?"

"I'll deflate her then?" Alex said, picking her up. Suddenly this was all so funny again.

I nodded and laughed as I watched him trying to squeeze the air out of her by any means necessary. Once she was completely flat, Alex looked up from her and asked, "By the way, you can drive, can't you?"

"Why?"

"Well, I'm from London. Don't think I've driven in years, thought it would be safer if you drove."

"Sure." I gave him a very noncommittal nod, which soon turned into a very committed shake when I saw what it was that I was meant to be driving.

"You want me to drive that?" I asked, looking at the car in horror. "It's huge."

"It was either that or a tiny Renault," he said.

"I don't think I can." I walked around the thing—truly, it was massive.

"Sure you can. I believe in you, Val."

"You know how cheesy that sounded?" I shot him a doubtful look.

Alex smiled at me and put our bags in the car, a huge grin plastered across his face.

"Hey!" I scolded him. "You are way, *way* too excited about this." I walked around to the driver's side and climbed in. Alex climbed in too.

"I am," he said, happily. "I really am."

"Why?" I slipped the keys into the ignition and turned it on.

He shrugged and looked over at me. "I'm having so much fun with you," he said seriously.

I looked at him and started to smile. "Me too," I said and that's when I realized I hadn't thought about Matt once in the last twenty-four hours.

CHAPTER THIRTY-ONE

"Steer it!" Alex shouted.

"I am, I am!" I shouted back.

"Watch the sides!"

"I am. I am!" I shrieked. "Oh my God!"

I could see out of the corner of my eye that Alex had put his face in his hands and was covering his eyes.

"HEY! I wasn't the one who told you to hire the biggest vehicle that has ever been built!" I gripped the steering wheel with both hands and tried to navigate my way down the long driveway. We weren't even out on the open road yet and I was having this much trouble. "You should have got the small one!"

"I thought you said size didn't matter as much as we thought?" Alex looked up at me and smiled now.

"Ha, ha funny," I said sarcastically, trying desperately to maneuver the thing onto the road without causing a major international incident.

"But you did, didn't you?" Alex's tone changed. "In fact, didn't you say you could handle them all? Big, medium or small?"

At this, I burst out laughing.

"What are you doing?" Alex suddenly shouted and I jumped in fright.

"What?" I asked frantically.

"You're driving on the wrong side of the road."

"Really?" I looked around at all the signs and the lights and the markings on the road. He was right! "Shit." I put the massive thing into reverse and readjusted.

Alex started laughing again as I managed to get the car facing in the right direction once more.

"It probably would have been safer if I drove," he said.

"Are you trying to insinuate I'm a bad driver?" I didn't tell him that a few days ago I'd smashed into two parked cars.

"No. Of course not," Alex said, keying the destination into his phone. A friendly British voice filled the car and started telling me where to drive.

After about ten minutes of driving, I finally got the hang of it all. It helped that we were on a very wide road. The road was high, running along a hill. On our right, the sea was far below us and from this vantage point you could see all its different colors swirling together beautifully.

And then the direction of our drive changed. We moved inland, away from the sea. The landscape changed dramatically and quickly. Suddenly, I felt like I was driving in a totally different country. The tropical vegetation was gone and it felt like we were in the English countryside. Rolling hills, cows grazing on the side of the road, haystacks lying in open fields. But as soon as I'd gotten used to these new surroundings, it changed again.

We were no longer driving through open fields, rather a dense wooded area closed in on us. Massive pine trees, so thick and high that they blocked out the sun. The trees surrounded us on all sides, and seemed to go on forever. The road also started getting steeper and narrower.

"Route du Volcan," I read the sign out loud when I saw it on the road.

"I don't need to translate that, do I?" Alex asked facetiously.

"Nope. I've got it." I smiled at him and continued to drive. And then the landscape changed once more. We popped out of the forest and back into the sun. There were no longer any trees, instead, the ground was covered with low, thin shrubs. The road got steeper, and the more we drove the rockier and less shrubbier it became until, *nothing*.

No trees. No grass. Just red sand and black rock as far as the eye could see. This landscape was like nothing I'd ever seen before, it was almost Martian. The road beneath us was no longer tarred either, instead, it was red and sandy. Up ahead of us was a car park. We pulled in and climbed out.

"I guess this is where the walk starts," I said, looking around.

We strolled through the car park and followed a group of people who were already walking. The ground beneath our feet was strange so I bent down to look at it. It was obvious that the lava flow had created rocks that looked rippled, almost as though piles of black satin ribbons had fallen to the floor. I ran my hand over them—they were smooth and strange to the touch.

We continued to walk along the path until we heard someone shouting.

"It's erupting!"

"What?" I looked at Alex.

"It's started erupting," someone else said.

I turned around and was just about to start running in the opposite direction, when out of nowhere, people began running up the path. *Where had they all come from?*

"Shouldn't we be running away from an erupting volcano?" I said to Alex. "Not towards it."

The man next to me obviously overheard and pointed out that this was a very common occurrence and that we would be perfectly safe to watch the eruption from the designated lookout spot.

"A common occurrence?" I hissed at Alex. "I thought you said the thing didn't erupt."

"Whoops," Alex said, his eyes lighting up like a child at Christmas. "Come on." He started moving towards it.

"Not a chance." I stood still as more and more people started coming down the path. People with cameras, what looked like a news crew, old people, people with children . . . *Maybe it was safe?*

"Come on." Alex took me by the hand and soon we were swept up in the crowd of people all racing towards the volcano. We picked up pace, jogging now, down the path, along the dusty road, climbing down the steps, up another set of steps until finally we arrived at the vantage point.

It wasn't what I was expecting. I was expecting Krakatoa, tons of red liquid exploding into the sky, rocks and dust in the air like mushroom clouds. But this was nothing like that. It was the PG version. But still, spectacular. I was in absolute awe as I watched the glowing red lava shooting up a few meters like a fountain might. It looked even redder and more brilliant against the black background. In fact, I'd never seen such a bright red color before, a color that was just so alive.

I was awestruck by the magnificence of it all, this theatre of nature playing out an age-old dramatic scene for us. I gazed over at Alex, who looked equally swept up in this moment. Small trickles of molten rock began to form, sliding down the side the hill. The trickles grew, until they were small red streams. The lava didn't move like a liquid though. It moved like a slow, strange alien creature. It crawled its way across the land instead of flowing. It seemed to take its time too, it was in no rush. *And why would it be?* It was ancient. It had been here for millions of years and had done this thousands of times before, creating, shaping and sculpting the landscape each time. I felt humbled by this great thing. There was something so special about seeing it and, suddenly, I felt strangely emotional. I was watching something so incredibly beautiful, yet destructive. Something that both created, and destroyed.

"I know," Alex said softly to me.

It was only then that I realized I was biting down on my lip to stop the tears that I could feel in my eyes. I looked up at him and he draped an arm around my shoulder and pulled me close.

"I know," he said again, as if he knew exactly what I was thinking. *How did that always seem to happen?*

I put my arm around him and we stood there, side by side, arm in arm, watching in total silence as it continued. No one around us spoke either, and there was something so magical about this moment, a moment that we were all sharing in together. I'm not sure how long we stood and watched, but finally Alex whispered in my ear.

"We need to go, we have a helicopter to catch."

"A wh—" and then I remembered. "You still think it's a good idea to go skydiving?" I asked. "Can't we just tick adrenalin off the list thanks to erupting volcano?"

Alex turned and smiled at me. "Oh, Valeria."

"Valeria? God, only my mother calls me that. And only when I'm in trouble. Am I in trouble?" I asked, turning to look at Alex now. The sun was behind him and I shielded my eyes to see his face.

The bright daylight sun was doing something incredible to his eyes now and I found myself quite transfixed by them again. By the way they seemed to change in such a mercurial manner. He blinked and when he opened them again, I swear they looked a little different once more.

"The helicopter is waiting for us," Alex said, and started walking away.

I snapped myself out of the gray daze I'd suddenly found myself in. "You know there's no way I'm doing this, right?"

"We'll see," he said smugly.

CHAPTER THIRTY-TWO

⌒

"*I* hate you right now, I hate you right now, did I mention that I HATE YOU. Right. NOW!" I screamed over the roar of the blades and the raging winds flying past the open door. I'd never heard such loud, violent gusts of wind before, and I was sure I wasn't meant to either, not unless I was taking a stroll through a hurricane—*and who the hell does that?* No one!

Everything about this moment was completely unnatural. One never expects to be in a helicopter with the door open. Let alone sitting at said open door with legs hanging out! Nothing about this moment was even vaguely acceptable, normal or natural.

Alex looked at me with wide eyes now, all his previous smug smiles gone. "I think I hate myself too, now." He grimaced at me, and the terror that washed over his face did little to soothe me; if anything it totally set me off. How dare he feel terrified! This had been his bright idea!

"I told you this was a bad idea!" I shouted over at him. "I knew it. This is officially the worst idea ever and it's all your fault, Alex. Your fault!" I continued my panicked rant.

"Are you ready?" The instructor who was tightly strapped to my back asked me.

"NO! No, no, no, no, nooooooo." I shook my head violently from side to side and shut my eyes tightly. "I don't want to die, " I wailed frantically.

I heard a chuckle behind me from the instructor and I wanted to turn around and slap him. *How dare he laugh in the face of danger like this?* "You won't die. It's perfectly safe."

"SAFE!" I scoffed loudly. "Safe is not throwing yourselves out of a helicooooo—"

He jumped. I screamed. I clenched my jaw and my fingers tightened into balls of anxiety. The cold wind assaulted my face, like thousands of tiny cold needles poking into my skin all at once. The winds howled against my ears, roaring into them so loudly that it was all I could hear. My cheeks burned, my mouth felt like it was being forcibly pulled open and my nose was about to be ripped from my face. For a second I couldn't catch my breath, as if I'd had the wind knocked out of me. I was totally disorientated as we flipped over and over. Once, twice, three times . . . I looked up at the helicopter, it seemed so far away now and like Dorothy I wished I could click my heels together and magic myself back into it.

I quickly closed my eyes again and let out a long, loud scream. As loud as I could as we continued to fall further and faster. My brain was having such trouble trying to figure out what was going on right now. It was as if it couldn't process all the information I was getting, and why should it? I'd never done anything even vaguely like this before. All my senses were overloaded all at once. From every conceivable angle, all screaming different things. I heard the instructor scream something in my ear, it sounded like *not fighting it, just going with it and accepting it!*

Accept it? Accept that I was falling from a helicopter? Plummeting towards the Earth with nothing but some flimsy piece of fabric to stop me from smashing into the ground at a million miles an hour. My heart was beating against my chest and I could feel the thump of my frightened pulse in my neck and face and ears.

But then suddenly . . . *something happened*. I'm not sure why, or what it was exactly, but everything seemed to slow down. My heart got into a slower, steady rhythm, the winds didn't feel as violent and downright abusive, my ability to breathe deeply returned. I opened my eyes again and looked around.

And I had to admit that it was beautiful up here. I felt like I was in some kind of strange no-man's land. A secret place that existed somewhere between the sky and the Earth. Where I was free-falling completely out of my own control. I surrendered myself to it all.

I untightened my fingers, opened my hands and slowly held my arms out, giving myself over completely to the feeling of falling. The feeling of absolute freedom. All of a sudden I felt like some kind of powerful, kickass superhero, soaring through the skies. I smiled, and out of the corner of my eye saw Alex approaching. We looked at each other and our eyes locked. He was also smiling and I could see he was experiencing the same thing I was. The empowering feeling of total freedom.

All my problems seemed so far away from me now. All those pesky earthly problems like deadlines and meetings and rent and

Matt. The things that kept you locked down and trapped, disappeared. Up here, they just didn't exist. There was nothing here except me, Alex and the big wide-open skies. I reached my hands out towards him and he did the same. We grabbed onto each other so tightly and held on as if our lives depended on it.

We smiled at each other. Stupid, silly smiles. Smiles of complete joyous abandon. To leap through the sky like this was the most liberating, exciting thing I'd ever done. The adrenalin whooshed through my veins like an intoxicating drug and I'd never felt this good before.

We began to laugh as we held onto each other's fingers and twirled through the air. I'd forgotten there were even instructors strapped to our backs. Right now, it was just the two of us. Nothing else in the world existed. *This was what living in the moment felt like!* I was one hundred percent in the here and now. No looking back and wishing things could have been different. No looking forward and wanting to control and manipulate the outcomes of things. I was here. Now. That was all.

And then suddenly, I felt a huge jerk, we were forced to let go of each other's hands and were physically pulled apart. Thrown backwards as the parachutes opened and slowed everything down.

And now I was floating, not falling. It was a totally different feeling. It was soft and slow and gentle as we wound our way back down to the Earth. Trees, houses, hills and roads soon came into view. And the more of them I could see, the more I didn't want to, because I didn't want this to ever end. I didn't want to put my feet on the ground again.

I wanted to stay up here forever. Free from everything. But I knew that what went up had to eventually come back down.

Everything got closer and closer, objects rushed towards me until, finally, my feet touched the ground.

At first I was disorientated as my knees and then hands collided with a sudden bump. It wasn't painful, but it was hard enough to snap me out of where I'd been and bring me back to reality. I scrambled to my feet and immediately looked around for Alex. And there he was. Without communicating our intentions, we both ran and threw ourselves into each other's arms. I held onto him as tightly as I could, I didn't want to let go.

"Oh my God!" I screamed into his ear as I clutched onto him for dear life. I could feel his heart pounding against my chest. It was beating so hard and fast, just like mine. We tightened our grip and suddenly it felt like our hearts were beating as one. I could no longer feel where his heart began and mine ended. I put my face against his. His cheek was cold, and yet, I felt hot. I wasn't going to let go of him, and it felt like he wasn't either, that is until we heard someone clear their throat. We pulled away from each other and that's when we both realized there were still humans attached to our backs. We laughed as our instructors unclipped us.

"Thank you," I said softly, looking into his cool, gray eyes.

"No . . . thank you," Alex replied. And then he did something. A small gesture that for some reason felt so significant in that moment. He kissed his hand, and then blew it across to me.

I smiled, and like a child might do, I reached out and grabbed the invisible kiss. I closed my hand around it, and I swear, I could almost feel something there sitting in the palm of my hand. I didn't want to let this kiss go. Even though I knew it wasn't real, I wanted to hang onto it. So I tucked the imaginary kiss into the pocket of my pants.

CHAPTER THIRTY-THREE

*W*e were back on the road driving and laughing. The excitement in the car was palpable. I tapped the steering wheel as I drove, as if I needed some physical outlet for the energy that was surging through my body right now. The magazine had been right! Adrenalin was the answer. Adrenalin was the answer to everything.

Alex held the magazine up triumphantly and then took his pen and frantically began ticking the step on the page. "Done! Ticked!" He tossed the magazine into the back of the car looking so pleased with himself. He reached out and turned the radio on. An instant eighties hit blasted into the car in all its colorful, permed glory. We both looked at each other and started scream singing. When the song ended, I turned to Alex.

"So where to next?" I asked. "What else do you have planned?"

"We're off to a place called Cilaos, it's up in the mountains and it's meant to be beautiful."

"That's not what I meant. I meant, what does the magazine

have us doing next?" I couldn't believe I'd actually started enjoying this, and dare I say, believing in it. Something inside me did feel like it was shifting. I couldn't quite place it, but I'd barely thought about Matt lately, which was a total miracle in itself.

"Let's see." Alex pulled the magazine out of the back. It was well worn already, the corners were dog-eared and tattered. He was just about to start reading when—

"You missed the turn," he suddenly said, looking behind us. "Quick. Reverse."

I put the giant vehicle in reverse and quickly backed up. The sign came into view. "The RN5?" I asked.

Alex turned his head and smiled at me. This time his smile was mischievous.

"What, Alex?" I asked.

"I forgot to tell you, this road looks quite . . . *interesting*."

"Interesting?" I asked.

He nodded. "And steep."

"Steep? I can see that," I said, looking around. We were really beginning to climb now. Huge imposing mountains surrounded us on all sides, rising up as far as the eye could see. In the distance, carved high into the side of the mountains, a gray line coiled and snaked around them. *Was that the road?* Surely not?

"And the road winds too," Alex said.

"Winds?" I started getting slightly nervous as I looked up at the mountains. "How steep and windy does it get?"

"Let's just say, there are over two hundred reviews on TripTaker about this drive, many of them referring to the fact you need nerves of steel to drive it."

"What?" As he said that, a sudden and dramatic turn made it

look like the road straight ahead of me simply disappeared. To my left, a sheer cliff face dropped down, to my right, a huge rocky cliff rose straight up.

"Oh my Goooooooooddd," I said, inching my way around the thing and feeling like if I made the slightest wrong move, I could lose control of this car and we would simply fall over the side.

"Just keep calm," Alex said in a hushed voice.

"You're not the one driving," I said through my tightly clenched jaw. My eyes were wide. I was too afraid to blink. I was afraid that if I closed them for a second, we might go plummeting off the edge of the cliff.

The road was so narrow that in places it was only big enough for one car at a time. We continued to wind our way up the steep mountain range, curving and coiling with the most intense hair-pin bends I'd ever seen.

The road twisted endlessly up and down the sides of the cliff faces. But when I took a deep breath, and my nerves weren't on a razor's edge, I had to admit that it was beautiful up here. The views were breathtaking; jagged rocky pinnacles rose high into the air. Dramatic, electric-green mountains jutted up in uneven peaks with diving valleys, cutting through the mountainous panorama.

Alex suddenly started reading. "'Number Seven. Reality Check. There's a reason your relationship didn't work. Take a moment to think about the relationship and why it didn't work. Take those rose-tinted glasses off and take stock of what went wrong, as well as what you might have done wrong too. And once you know what those thing are, admit them out loud, own the reality of what happened and then vow to never make that same mistake again.'"

"Wow, that one's quite deep," I said looking over at Alex thoughtfully.

"Pull over here," Alex suddenly said as a lookout point arrived. I pulled over and we both climbed out. It felt good to stretch my legs and arms, and it was only when I was out of the car that I realized how tense all my muscles were from the scary driving. We walked over to the edge and looked down into the green valley below. Everything looked so crisp and clean from up here and the air felt fresh. The sky was overcast and the sun was hiding behind the fluffy clouds. But every now and then, through a crack in the façade, a shaft of bright sunlight shot out and illuminated a part of the world below.

"This is just so beautiful," I said quietly.

"So what's the reality of your relationship?" Alex suddenly asked me.

"I don't know," I admitted.

"What mistake did you make?" he pressed.

"Well that's easy. I loved a man who didn't love me back. I poured everything I had into him, every single last drop and I got nothing back for it, but I just kept going."

"Like pouring water into a bucket with a hole," Alex added.

"Yes, exactly like that." I looked at him. I liked that analogy, because that was how it had felt. "And the more I poured, the emptier I became. The more I loved him, the more it hurt." I sighed. I actually felt empty and drained. Like a part of me had disappeared somewhere along the way. A part I didn't even know was missing . . . *until right this very second.*

This realization hit me all at once. Suddenly, I ached to be whole again. I ached to find that piece of myself that was missing and plug it back in. I needed to fix the leak. I wanted to feel like I'd felt when I'd been free-falling through the sky; peaceful. Whole. Complete. My vision blurred as I felt the sting of tears creep into my eyes. My heart lodged itself in my throat and a tightness squeezed my chest.

"Shit." My voice quivered now. "I didn't realize, until right now, how truly destructive loving Matt has been for me. And how much energy it's stolen from me." I grabbed my chest as a sharp pain pressed into me.

Alex stepped closer to me and grabbed my shoulders tightly with his big hands. The gesture was both reassuring but forceful. He then lowered his head so that he was looking directly into my eyes.

"Val," he said slowly and deliberately, "you deserve someone who will love you back, with as much fire and passion as you love." He gave me a little shake, as if he was trying to snap me out of something. "Promise me you won't spend another wasted day pining for someone who is too stupid to see your worth."

His words hit me like a punch in the gut. "Yes. I promise," I said softly, the words struggling to climb out of my constricted throat. At that, Alex smiled at me. The smile swept across his face, transforming him and all his features. The genuine warmth contained within it spilt out into the world and inhabited the space between us like a bright rainbow after a storm might do.

"And what about you?" I said, lifting my hand up to move a piece of silver hair out of his face. "You deserve that too. Someone who will love you back like that." I didn't stop at moving that one piece of hair though. After putting it back, I ran my fingers through his hair, watching as the separate gray and black pieces mixed together to form a new gorgeous color.

"You know," he said quietly, "the worst part is not the actual cheating. It's feeling that you just weren't good enough for them."

"You are good enough, Alex!"

"Not to her," he said.

"Then she's not the one," I quickly added.

"And Matt's not the one either," he said back to me.

We looked at each other for a while and then Alex walked past me and right to the very edge of the cliff face. And then, before I knew what was happening, I heard the scream . . .

"I proposed to a women who didn't love me and cheated on me and I'll never let that happen again!"

Alex's words suddenly bounced back at us. They hit the sides of the mountains and came straight back.

"Oh my God. What are you doing?" I walked up to him and stood there as the two of us listened to his words echoing over and over and over again, until finally it was silent.

"Okay, your turn," Alex said.

I shook my head. "No! That's ridiculous."

"But we're meant to say it out loud and own it," he said.

"I don't think the magazine meant we should scream it off a mountaintop."

"Do it," Alex urged.

I looked at him for a while, weighing it up. It did seem totally ridiculous, not to mention embarrassing. But Alex was looking at me in a way that for some reason made me feel it was okay to do it. "Fine." I sighed. I readied myself and then screamed . . .

"I've loved a man for three years who didn't love me back and I will never do that again because I deserve MORE!"

My words hummed and buzzed around me in the air, filling

it with energy. There was something so cathartic about this, so I did it again. This time I screamed as loudly as I could, until my throat hurt.

The words flew back at me. "*More, more, more,*" they echoed. *I deserved more.* Those three words ran through my mind and for a moment, I actually believed it. I did deserve more, didn't I? I deserved someone who would love me back. Someone who would see me, really see me. Someone who would remember kissing me and would want to kiss me again.

Alex joined me and screamed again too.

We stood there and listened as our invisible words knocked into each other, reverberating through the valleys below and back up the mountains.

Hearing our words repeated in that way, a strange feeling began coming over me.

Alex yelled again. And then so did I. And soon, we were both yelling our realities to the mountains in front of us over and over again. And then I found myself inexplicably crying.

Alex took a step closer to me and suddenly his hands were on my face, wiping my tears away. It was the nicest, most unexpected gesture. And it felt good. I closed my eyes for a moment and savored the feeling of his soft hands on my face.

Something was happening. Alex. This view. The echoes of our words. This journey. Us. Something inside me was stirring and moving and shifting. I could physically feel it. A weight was slowly being pulled off me and I seemed to be feeling lighter and lighter with each passing moment. *Was I finally getting over Matt? Could this really be working?*

I opened my eyes slowly and looked up at Alex again; he was

looking down at me with such care and concern etched across his face.

"I think we can do this together." He said it with such conviction.

I nodded. "I think we can." And I really meant it this time, because for the first time in years, I felt Matt slipping further and further away from me. And it felt good.

CHAPTER THIRTY-FOUR

The mood when we got back in the car was different. More reflective, as we sat in silence and continued the rest of the journey. The winding road soon came to an end as we finally arrived in the small mountain village.

The quaint town looked like it should be on the side of a chocolate box, or one of those old vintage biscuit tins. The first thing you noticed was all the color. There is one thing I can say about Réunion island, it pops and explodes and bursts with color. I'd done some more reading on it and its fascinating history might have had something to do with its colorful present. The island was a mix of different cultures, a melting pot of French, Creole, Tamil, African and Chinese influences, all coming together to form something so unique, I wasn't sure it existed anywhere else in the world.

I looked out at the town. It was surrounded on all sides by mountains. Dotted at the foot of these mountains were small wooden houses painted in a bright array of colors. Yellow houses with bright green shutters. Pink houses with bright red roofs, colors you would never think of mixing together, but they worked. Some of the houses were almost totally swallowed by overgrown gardens; huge ferns and palms and bougainvillea that only added to the rainbow that this little village town in the mountains was.

"Where are we going?" I asked Alex, who was also staring out the window at the sights.

"We're checking into our hotel and then I have something else planned."

"Does it involve volcanos, helicopters and dangerous roads?" I asked. "Because I think I've had enough excitement for one day."

"No, on the contrary." Alex keyed the hotel address into his phone and soon we were listening to the polite British lady again. I followed her instructions. We wound our way through the somewhat sleepy town. It had a charming, slow atmosphere about it. People here seemed to walk a little slower even. Finally, we arrived at our hotel.

"Wow." I looked up at the building. It was beautiful. A triple-storey painted in bright yellow. An intricately carved bright teal balustrade ran the length of its upstairs balconies. Flower pots filled with flowers clung to the balustrade, creating a carpet of bright pink that swept across it. The hotel was right on the street and small tables and chairs had been placed on the pavement like a street café in Paris.

We parked the car and walked inside. Alex immediately strode up to the reception and started speaking in French to the lady behind the counter. She seemed all smiles and only too happy to help. Alex started digging in his back pocket and soon pulled out a wallet. This was my cue to rush up to him.

"Wait," I said, pulling out my wallet, "how much is it?"

"Don't worry." He shrugged, pulling out a shiny card. It was way shinier than mine, but just because it was shiny and mine was more matt, didn't mean I wasn't paying my way.

"I'll pay for my room," I said, sliding my card across the table towards the receptionist, even though I knew my emergency fund would be very depleted by now.

Alex looked over at me and gave a small smile. "Of course," he said. Once we were booked in, the receptionist showed us to our rooms. But instead of being inside the hotel, we were led through the back and outside.

Stretching out in front of us was the most beautiful garden. It was the smell I noticed first. There was a soft breeze, and riding on it, the sweet, sticky smell of frangipani and fresh-cut grass. The garden sloped up steeply and was filled with so many different shades of green. And in between all that green, explosions of flowers in various shapes and sizes and colors; bright purples, cotton-candy pinks, oranges and big white trumpet-shaped flowers.

We walked further into the garden and the chalets came into view. Scattered in the garden, small free-standing cottages all in bright Creole colors. The sound of trickling water made me look down—a stream cut through the garden and we walked over a wooden bridge.

"This is so beautiful," I said, as we followed the woman up the path. We passed the first few cottages and then she finally stopped outside one and passed me the key.

"Thanks," I said, looking over at Alex. Suddenly the idea that we were being separated felt wrong. We'd spent so much time together.

"Where's yours?" I asked, because for some reason I needed to know.

The woman pointed and spoke in French. I looked over at Alex for a translation.

"Number eight," he said, "up the path and to the left."

"Okay." I nodded at him. "Well, goodbye then." I started turning the key in my lock.

"Not goodbye," he said.

I raised a brow at him.

"I have something else planned for us, remember?" He gave a tiny smile. "Meet in the reception in ten minutes?"

"Why?" I asked.

"Because we are about to cross another thing off our list."

"Haven't we crossed enough off the list today already?"

"Trust me. You'll want to do this one." He winked and continued to walk up the path and finally disappeared.

* * *

Ten minutes later, after off-loading my bags and changing into a comfortable skirt and T-shirt, I walked back down to the reception and found Alex waiting for me. It was late afternoon and the air was thick and hazy.

"So where are we going?" I asked when I saw him and we started walking out of the hotel and onto the street.

"'Number Eight. Have A Spa Day With The Girls,'" Alex said, handing me a brochure. "I know I'm not one of the girls, but I should do, right?"

I smiled across at him. "You'll do," I said, looking down at the brochure in my hands. I started reading out loud. "This town is known as a spa town. Water from thermal springs is heated by volcanic chambers far below the surface. The water is packed with minerals and is said to hold great healing powers for many ailments, from arthritis to relieving stress, and is a natural pain-killer." I looked back up at him. "Did you book?"

He nodded.

"You are a busy bee, when did you get all of this done?"

"This morning, when you were sleeping in."

"Are you always this prepared for everything?" I asked, opening the brochure.

"Unfortunately," he said.

"Unfortunately?"

He shrugged and we started walking out the hotel together. "Don't you know by now, Val? I'm Mr. Stable and Reliable."

I laughed. "You make it sound like a bad thing."

"Isn't it?" he asked. He sounded serious.

"Mmmm," I muttered, "not all woman are looking for tattooed, rock-star rebels. In fact, I must say, predictable sounds really good at this stage of my life."

He smiled playfully. "Well that's good to know. Since we'll probably be getting married and having kids in three years' time."

I laughed. "And who said you're predictable and boring?" I looped my arm through his before I realized I'd actually done it. I almost pulled away but Alex moved closer and tightened the loop.

"You're probably the only person I've ever met that thinks that about me," he said.

"Oh, please. I doubt that. We went skydiving today. You made us throw ourselves out of an aircraft!"

"I've never done anything like that before, not until I met you anyway. These last few days something has changed for me. I feel . . . *different*," he said, his voice soft and slow. Out of the corner of my eye I could see him looking at me as if he was thinking something important. "I think this list is really working."

"You know what I feel?" I suddenly said without thinking. I stopped walking and turned to look at him.

"What?" he asked.

"Over the last three years, I spent so much time and energy pouring water into that leaky bloody bucket, that I've done nothing for myself. These last few days have been the first time in years I've actually done anything just for myself. The magazine was right, I need to focus on myself."

"Me too," Alex admitted. "Stay away from relationships and focus on ourselves." He said that last part with a strange tone in his voice and I looked over at him. Suddenly, he looked very thoughtful.

We walked quietly through the quaint streets together until we arrived at our destination. A spa on the edge of the town. We walked inside and then I saw the sign. My French wasn't so bad that I didn't understand that it was saying something to the effect of *No clothes beyond this point.* I could see Alex was also looking up at the sign too.

"Did you bring us to a spa, or a nudist colony?" I whispered.

"Shit," he whispered back, "I totally forgot we would need bathing suits."

"You think?" I looked around at all the people walking past us in their big white fluffy gowns.

Alex turned to me and shrugged again. *"C'est la vie,"* he said with a smile. "When in Rome." He let go of my arm and walked right in.

CHAPTER THIRTY-FIVE

⌒

$\mathcal{W}$e received our spa menu and I read through it. We were set to soak in a mineral bath, then have an aqua massage—I didn't really know what that was, but it sounded good. After that we were scheduled for a manicure. I looked down at my nails, which were in desperate need of help. All this stress lately had been making me pick.

I was in the ladies' changing room and opened the locker that had been assigned to me. In it hung a big white gown and a pair of slippers. I slipped my clothes off, wishing that one of us had thought to bring a bathing suit, and put the gown over myself. My bra and panties would have to suffice for now.

I followed the signs out of the bathroom and found Alex waiting for me once more. He too was dressed in his gown. I looked down at his feet, which were too large for the standard slippers provided and so his heels hung off the back of them. He wiggled his feet at me and smiled. The phrase about men with big feet suddenly ran through my mind, not that I didn't already know he was rather well endowed in that area. My cheeks tingled and flushed. *Why was I thinking about Alex's* . . . Shit! I stopped myself.

"After you." Alex gestured for me to walk in front of him. We followed the therapist in her white coat. She led us into a room where a natural Jacuzzi made of rock sat. Huge windows on the other side of it ensured we had a view over the mountains and valleys below. It was simply breathtaking.

The therapist smiled at us. "I'll fetch you in thirty minutes for your treatments." She exited, closing the door behind us. Alex wasted no time getting in. Why wouldn't he, he was wearing big boxer shorts that could have easily been mistaken for swimming trunks. Mine weren't so simple though . . .

"The water is amazing, and this view," Alex said as he slid into the Jacuzzi. "Join me."

"Seriously?" I clutched my white gown tightly to my body.

"Just get in. I won't look, if that's what you're worried about."

"I'm not worried." I shrugged, not wanting to come across as shy or self-conscious. "I'm fine. I mean . . . I don't care if you see me in my . . ." I opened my gown and dropped it to the floor as quickly as possible, lest I lose my nerve.

"Wow. Nice underwear," Alex suddenly said.

"What?" For a second I was taken aback, and instinctively covered myself, but then something dawned on me.

"Oh my God, thank you!" I exclaimed throwing my hands in the air. "Finally! I cannot tell you how much sexy lingerie I've bought over the last three years, in case Matt and I ever had impromptu sex somewhere. And no one, and I mean *NO one*, has ever seen it, let alone complimented it!"

"It's a pleasure." Alex smiled and his eyes swept over my body.

I was wearing particularly sexy undies that day. A black lace push-up bra that did some rather special things to the ladies in a "lift and separate" sense. The bra had a deep purple ribbon that was tied in a cute bow that sat between the cups. The panties were black lace too, tanga style, and tied on the sides with the same matching purple ribbon. I looked down at my exposed body and then back up at Alex as something dawned on me. It had been so long since anyone of the opposite sex had seen me like this and I wondered if I shouldn't take advantage of the situation.

"So, you're a guy," I suddenly said to Alex, keeping my arms tightly at my sides, covering at least something of myself. I was feeling rather awkward, naked and exposed.

He looked at me curiously. "Last time I checked."

"What I mean is," I continued, "you're a male and I'm a female."

"Mmmm?" Alex muttered with an amused smile on his face.

"So imagine that you and I *weren't* friends, and you saw me like this, as a guy, if I was a girl." The idea was so crystal clear in my head, I was just having trouble articulating it; I tapped my fingers anxiously against the sides of my thighs.

"Okay?" He leaned back and folded his arms across his chest, watching me with what I could see was amusement.

"What I'm trying to say is that imagine we were *not* road trip buddies right now. Imagine that you were just a guy and I was just a girl and we'd just met and you were looking at me in a purely sexual manner. I know it's hard to imagine but—"

"It's not hard to imagine, Val," he cut me off and I swear my heart skipped a beat.

"Oh?" The word slipped out of my mouth.

"It's not hard to imagine. Trust me." He uncrossed his arms and moved closer to me. Be still my fast-beating heart! *No seriously, be still.*

"Uh . . ." I stuttered stupidly as I looked down at him.

"You look good, Val." He looked up at me and smiled. "Really good."

I nodded slowly. "So if you were a guy and I was just a girl that looked like this and—"

"Yes." He cut me off again.

"Yes?" My heart pounded as his eyes swept over my body again, slowly.

"If you were a girl that looked like that and I was just a guy I would definitely walk across the room and talk to you."

"You would?" I slowly pulled my hands away from my sides, exposing all of myself. Alex seemed to notice this gesture and his eyes moved down to where my hands had been. I was suddenly filled with a giddy sense of happiness at the thought that someone actually found me attractive. Not just someone though, *him.*

"Th-thanks," I stuttered. "So I've still got it?" I asked again, just to be sure.

He chuckled. "You got it."

I nodded my head at him and smiled. "I've got it." I clicked my fingers and wiggled from side to side happily. "I've *soooo* still got it!"

Alex laughed. "I can't believe you ever thought you didn't."

"Well, it's been so damn long since someone actually looked at me like that, a girl needs some reassurance sometime."

"Are you reassured?" he asked, his voice was low and slightly husky-sounding.

I nodded. "Well, when someone that looks like you tells me I've got it . . ." My voice tapered off and I looked at him.

"Mmmm, so you think I'm good-looking, do you?" Alex asked playfully.

"Oh, please, you know you're good-looking."

He smiled at me as if he did know it, but was shy to admit it. "I try and stay as healthy as possible." He ran his hand through his hair and a flash of green ribbon caught my attention.

"Healthy?" I tutted. "I'd say having an eight pack makes you a little more than just 'healthy.'" I grinned at him and started playing with my own green ribbon that I'd suddenly become very aware of.

"Have you been counting?" he asked.

I shrugged. "Maybe," I admitted, and took a step closer to the Jacuzzi.

"The water's really good," he said, moving over to let me in.

I stepped in. And he was right. The water was warm and felt amazing. It also felt different, thick, and softer; I guess it must have been the high concentration of the vitamins and minerals. "Can I tell you something? I've never told anything this before. It's really, *really* embarrassing."

"Yes," he said. "I won't judge you. I promise."

I shook my head. "No. I think you might if you knew what I was going to say."

"Val," he moved closer and looked me straight in the eyes. "I would never judge you."

"Okay." I nodded and took a deep breath. "So . . ." I hesitated, "I once took a sexy photo of myself in my underwear and . . . I sent it to Matt by 'accident.'" I gestured air commas. "Obviously it had been on purpose, but I pretended I'd meant to send it to someone else."

Alex nodded. Showing no visible signs of judgement on his face at all. So I continued.

"I thought that maybe if he saw me differently, if he saw me as a woman looking sexy or, whatever . . . it was stupid. I feel like such an idiot when I think about that."

"Don't feel stupid," he said.

"I do, though. I can't tell you how many times I'd wished so hard that Matt would finally see what was in front of him. That he would realize that he loved me and confess it and leave Sam and chase after me, or something. It's been my dream for so many years."

"Matt's just mad and blind," Alex said.

"Is that your professional doctor opinion?" I asked.

"No. It's just common sense." He said this part with such sincerity in his voice, and with such a smile in his eyes, that I couldn't help but feel a lot better.

"Thank you." I looked at him, his gray eyes were a different color once more. They were pale and pearly, with a dark black ring around them.

"Your eyes change color, a lot," I said.

"Funny. I was just thinking the same thing about you."

"Really?" I felt a little warm rush in my cheeks.

He nodded. "They're startling."

"Startling?" I repeated the word. I couldn't remember the last time someone told me I had startling eyes.

I smiled over at Alex. "Yours too. Startling."

He smiled at me coyly this time, it showed off the dimple in his cheek. "You are aware that this is the perfect selfie moment, right?" he said.

"You're right," I agreed.

"Luckily I come prepared." Alex reached out the Jacuzzi and grabbed his phone from inside his gown. He held it up and I moved closer to him. He started a countdown and for some reason, as the countdown reached one, I tilted my head to the side so that my cheek pressed up against his . . . *smooth*. So smooth.

He took a picture and held it up for us to inspect. "I'm going to send it to you and we can post it. Hashtag rock-star life," he said with delight in his voice.

"Sounds cool," I said, looking at the photo as he chose the different filters. "That one." I reached down and stopped his hand.

"I was just thinking the same thing. Makes us look gorgeous as hell," he chuckled and posted it. We both looked at the picture for a while before he put his phone down.

I knew we were just posting to make our exes jealous, and because the magazine had told us to. But this time, it didn't really matter as much to me as it had before.

It was more important that Alex and I capture this moment we were having together and post it so *we* could keep it permanently.

CHAPTER THIRTY-SIX

$\mathcal{W}$e took a taxi back to the hotel when all our treatments were over. It was dark and cold and the fact I had wet underwear on didn't much help. But I was feeling relaxed. More relaxed than I'd felt in forever. So relaxed that as we drove in the taxi, I was melting and sliding off the seat.

The aqua massage had been heavenly. Lying on my stomach, jets of warm spring water being sprayed over my body. My skin felt creamy and soft, as if the spring water really did have an effect on it. The manicure had done me the world of good too, not to mention also being a source of great entertainment, as I watched Alex getting his first one. He'd hated the way the nail file had felt and had cringed the whole way through it.

By the time we got back to the hotel we were both starving. So after a quick change, we met at the restaurant inside the main hotel. But before our menus came, the waitress asked if we wanted to choose our own wine.

I gazed over at Alex. "Fancy, but I know nothing about wine," I said.

"Lucky for you then that I do," he replied, standing and following the waitress. The fact that Alex knew about wine added to that air of sophistication that he had, I think without even knowing he had it. People with those kinds of airs are usually only too aware of them, changing that sophistication into something resembling snobbishness. But Alex didn't have that. Instead, his was subtle and very attractive. We followed the waitress into the old cellar, which looked more like a creepy, underground crypt, the kind you might find skeletons lurking in.

"We make and bottle our own wine here," the waitress said, pulling out several different bottles of red wine. "This area is renowned for its vineyards and wineries."

A big, old wooden table stood in the center of the room, Alex and I pulled up two stools and sat down. The waitress took out some glasses and laid them in front of us. The air in this room was old, dusty and woody, much like the museum had been.

She uncorked one of the wines and poured us two small glasses. "I've never really liked red wine," I whispered over to Alex, hoping the waitress wouldn't hear me.

"Then you've never drunk the right kind in the right way," he whispered back to me.

"And how is it meant to be drunk?" I asked.

Alex turned. His eyes sought out mine, and once he'd found them, he locked onto them. "Just like this. In a dusty cellar, surrounded by old bottles and barrels and, the most important part, it needs to be drunk with good company." He smiled at me.

"So, I'm good company then?" I asked playfully. His next

response stopped my playfulness immediately, as well as my heart.

"The best." He said it with such authority. As if this was an irrefutable fact, like who the current president was or that the sky was blue.

"Oh," I managed feebly. My voice had a slight coy edge to it. "You're good company too. The best," I said.

Alex looked over at me. The warm orange light in the cellar was making his gray eyes a shade of brown. Not a muddy, dull brown, but something rich and vibrant and chestnut. We smiled at each other. His smile was different somehow. Broad. Unrestrained. Open. As if he was trying to show me something. Out of the corner of my eye I could see the waitress smiling at us.

"So I've poured you our famous Pinot Noir," she said. Then she took another bottle out and placed it on the table. "This is our Malbec, and this . . ." she placed another bottle on the table, "is our blend." She started moving away from us and I wondered where she was going. "I'll leave you to it." She smiled again. "You can come back up when you've tasted them and when you're ready . . ." She said that last part with a smile in her voice and then closed the door behind her. She was gone.

The atmosphere immediately changed. And as if they too were responding to the change, the lights flickered on and off quickly. A little shiver passed through me, but I didn't feel cold. Suddenly the room felt so much smaller than I knew it really was, as if the walls were closing in and moving us closer towards each other. I became acutely aware of Alex next to me. The back of my knees itched and I scratched them quickly.

"I would find this place totally creepy right now if you weren't here," I said, reaching for the glass of wine and raising it to my mouth.

"Whoa!" Alex reached out and stopped me with his hand dramatically. "What are you doing? There is a way of doing this," he said, forcing me to lower my glass back down to the table.

"First we look at it." Alex swirled his glass around and held it up, looking deeply into it. I copied him, not sure what the hell I was looking for.

"We're looking at the color of it." Alex held a white napkin up behind the glass and scrutinized it further. I did the same while trying to bite back a smile. I felt so silly and out of my depth doing this.

"Now swirl," he said, swirling the wine around in the glass elegantly. I tried to copy him and splashed it all over my hand.

"Ooops," I said, and licked the wine off my finger.

Alex shot me a playful, disapproving look. "Definitely, *not* how you do it." He shook his head at me. "Now we smell." He raised the glass to his nose and took a deep breath in. I watched in fascination for a moment. He looked so committed to this moment, as if he was concentrating one hundred percent on it. I lowered my nose to the glass, taking a whiff. Again, I had no idea what I was smelling for.

"And now, we sip. Put it in your mouth for a while. Swirl it around slowly, and then only do you swallow."

I lifted it to my lips and finally took a small sip. I swirled it around my mouth, as I'd been instructed to do. And then swallowed.

"Do you taste it?" Alex asked.

"What?"

"Currants and plums," he said seriously.

I burst out laughing. "No! I don't taste that at all. I taste red wine."

Alex shook his head at me and tutted. "Oh, Val, you're not trying hard enough. Take another sip."

"Fine." I sipped and suddenly Alex was up and standing behind me. He placed his hands over my eyes and whispered in my ear.

"Think about eating a sweet, juicy plum," he said, his breath caressing the side of my ear.

I giggled at this and he shushed me. "You have to take this seriously," he urged in a stern, yet teasing voice.

"Next you'll be telling me to imagine myself running through a field of lavender in Tuscany and dancing in the sun."

"No, that's only with the Merlot," he said. I laughed again. This whole thing was cheesy, and funny and there was also something so damn cute about him getting so into his wine.

"Fine. Fine. I'll be serious," I said. His hands were still over my eyes and this seemed to make all my other senses sharper, especially my sense of smell. I could smell Alex's cologne now. It was slightly woody. It had an earthy quality to it, fruity, mossy, maybe even a little citrusy. It wafted into my nose and as I sipped, the smell somehow heightened the flavor of the wine. I concentrated hard, the warmth from his hands on my face made me more relaxed. Relaxed and in tune.

"Plums?" he asked again, softly, right into my ear. I could feel his breath on the side of my face like thousands of tiny ant footsteps rushing over my skin. His smooth face slowly grazed my neck and a warm sensation set my skin ablaze. And then suddenly, I could taste it. *Plums!* It was so subtle you could almost miss it, but it was there.

I turned around and looked at him. "Plums!" I nodded, excitedly. "I taste them. It's amazing. Delicious."

Alex smiled at me and went back to his seat. He looked so pleased with himself right now.

"I told you. You've just being doing it all wrong. You just needed to be in a dusty cellar, surrounded by old bottled and barrels—"

"And in the right company." I cut him off.

"Yes." He nodded.

I felt a tingle rush through me as the wine warmed me from the inside. *Or was it something else warming me?* "Clearly, I've just never been with the right person before . . . *until now*," I said softly.

His smile faded a little and he looked at me seriously. "Until now," he echoed, and then he broke eye contact with me and fiddled with the green ribbon around his finger.

I looked down at mine too, and suddenly it felt tight and so did my throat.

CHAPTER THIRTY-SEVEN

∽

"*T*his place doesn't seem real," I said. We were standing on the hotel balcony upstairs sipping our wine together after our meal. The view was incredible from up here in this little mountain town. The island of Réunion was full of surprises, that's for sure. A couple of hours away were the warm, tropical beaches, and a little way inland was this. Suddenly, a white trickle of cloud started rolling down the side of the mountain, bringing with it a cold mist.

"Look at that." I walked over to the railing to get a better look. Alex joined me.

"That mist," I said as a massive wall of ghostly whiteness started creeping noiselessly over the top of the mountains and came towards us. Where had it all come from so quickly?

"It's kind of creepy," Alex said. He was standing next to me now.

"Don't say that." I nudged his shoulder playfully with mine.

"But it is." He turned and leaned against the balcony railing, turning his back on the mountains and looking straight at me. He was holding a glass of red wine in his hand. "It's like the start of a horror movie," he whispered. "Two lonely travelers get trapped in a small, mysterious mountain town when a strange, thick mist rolls in, blocking all the exits in and out."

"Stop it." I smacked him on the shoulder this time. "Don't say stuff like thaaa—" My eyes widened as I looked at the mountain. The thick fog was moving even faster now. Flowing smoothly and quietly, a faceless creature eating up the mountain as it went. I swallowed hard. He was right. This was creepy as hell.

"Do you think it will come all the way up here?" I asked, crossing my arms around myself. The temperature had definitely plummeted.

I fixed my gaze on the foot of the mountain, where the row of brightly colored houses sat. In my mind, they became a kind of boundary, as long as the mist didn't make it that far, we would be fine. Only, within minutes, the thick white veil began to flow over the roofs of the houses, almost as if it were a liquid, dribbling over them. Coating them, until finally, even the almost luminous lime-colored house had disappeared completely. I shivered.

"I guess we know the answer to the question then: it *is* coming for us," he said in a creepy horror voice.

"Stop it," I said to him again.

Alex smiled at me. "Wait, you really are scared, aren't you?"

"Well, look at it. It's a big, mysterious mist and it's coming right for us."

Alex took a step closer to me. "Why are you so scared of a little bit of mist?"

"My grandmother," I said. "She used to tell me these terrible, terrible, awful Russian folktales when I was younger. And they scared me for life. So yes, I am terrified of mist."

"Oh?" He raised a curious brow. "Like what?"

"The bloody Baba Yaga for one. This evil ogress who comes and takes disobedient children to her little wooden house in the misty woods where she cooks them and eats them," I said.

"Sounds terrible."

"It is. And don't get me started on Koschei the Deathless. She's not great either."

"Awful," Alex said.

"They are!" I said, keeping my eye on the creeping mist that was now rolling down the street towards us. In a few moments, it was sure to climb up onto our balcony and then plunge us into its whiteness. "She used to tell me them in Russian, which made them even more creepier."

"Do you speak Russian?" Alex asked, looking at me strangely now.

"A little. Why?"

"This might sound strange, but I've never thought French was the sexiest-sounding language." He paused and stared at me.

"And you think Russian is?" I was amused by this. "Russian sounds like Klingon."

"Not when spoken by a beautiful woman." Alex took another step towards me. "Say something," he said slowly and softly, gazing at me intently. His gray eyes seemed darker in this light. They were mesmerizing and I felt myself being pulled into them.

"*Chto ya dolzhen skazat?*" I said softly. It meant, *What do you want me to say?*

Alex's eyes widened and a small smile crept over his lips. "Okay, I have no idea what you said, but it was . . . wow . . ." He looked at me seriously. "You're a really interesting woman, Valeria." It was said slowly and purposefully.

"I am?" I asked. My stomach tightened.

Alex nodded and raised the glass of wine up to his lips again. I watched him closely as he sipped. The blood-red liquid ran down the side of the glass and then flowed into his open lips. He swallowed, and then the very tip of his tongue came out to lick the tiny red drop that was clinging to the side of his mouth. Suddenly, I forgot about the mist and all I could see was Alex and his lips and the wine. I let my eyes drift up from his lips, drift up his face until I reached his eyes. He was already looking at me. His eyes were an even darker gray now, it never ceased to amaze me how the colors changed so much. Like a chameleon, changing color with each and every emotion.

I suddenly shivered. Something cold nipped at my ankles. I looked down. "It's here," I said. The first white finger of mist crept up onto our balcony. I took a step back as more seemed to move in, like the smoke of dry ice moving across the floor, it soon pooled and danced around my feet, as if it were ready to swallow me.

I looked back up at Alex. Right behind him, almost like a solid wall moving towards us, the mist came. It moved over his shoulders and around his torso, as if it had hands that were reaching out. We both looked down at the space between us, as the mist pushed its way in and began to smother us. Alex put his hands into it and swatted, the mist reacted immediately, swirling and coiling as if it were angry. And then, it was everywhere.

I shivered again as the moist cold droplets completely surrounded us. I looked over at Alex, he was soft around the edges as the mist blurred him.

"God, it's freezing," I said. A moment later, I felt something warm and firm on the side of my face. It took a second to realize what it was. Alex had reached out and put his hand on my cheek. Without so much as a second thought, I reached up and placed my hand over his. I slipped a finger between his and he tightened his grip on it.

"You have nothing to be afraid of," he said with such care and sincerity that I think I wanted to cry, but I pushed that feeling away.

"What, will you fight off all the evil creatures when they descend from the mist?" I said teasingly instead.

"For you . . ." His voice was even slower and softer now. The warmth from his hand radiated out across my cheeks and into my lips. "I'll fight them to the death."

My first thought was to burst out laughing at this, but something stopped me. Even though Alex had said this with the slightest smile in his voice, there was something so sincere about his comment too that I felt truly touched by it.

"Thank you," I said, meaning it entirely. The mist suddenly got even thicker, swirling around us now and causing his face to blur even more. "We should probably try and get back to our rooms before we can't find them," I said, feeling a genuine sense of worry that we might never be able to make it out of this mist.

"Good point," Alex said.

CHAPTER THIRTY-EIGHT

 ᶜ

*W*e stepped outside into the garden where our rooms were situated. By this time, visibility was almost zero. I felt disorientated, until I felt the big hand on my lower back.

"This way," the calm, authoritative voice said. It was Alex's voice, of course, not some voice from above or anything. But it was a voice I would listen to. There was something about it. It was the tone. The words he chose, the way he said them. If Alex had to tell you something truly awful, like there was a giant spider clinging to you, it would probably still sound like music to your ears.

We stumbled forwards together, but couldn't see a thing. The mist was so thick now that you could feel it with your hand. As if it had a weight to it. It was also wet, it clung to my skin and coated me in a thin layer of icy, cold moisture.

"Shit!" I tripped over something and landed on the floor.

"Val?" Alex asked. I could hear his arms flapping and see the trails they were making through the mist, even if I couldn't see him properly. I reached up for one of the hands but couldn't find it. I climbed onto my hands and knees and then tried to stand, only my head hit something on the way up.

"Val!" Alex shouted and I felt him jump back.

But as he did, a razor-sharp pain radiated through my scalp like fire.

"OH MY GOD!" I screeched. "Don't move. Don't move. Don't move." I was frantic and crawled forward on my knees. I found Alex's legs and quickly wrapped my arms around them tightly, pulling him as close as I could, not caring that my head was now fully in his crotch. Face first.

"Val!" Alex tried to push me away but I clung on even tighter. "What the hell are you doing?" he asked.

"What do you think I'm doing?" I wailed.

"Uh . . . I don't know," Alex said.

"Well, I'm not suddenly trying to go down on you if that's what you think!" I said, in between winces of pain. "Stop moving, please," I begged and grabbed onto his legs even harder. "My hair is stuck on something. And it's fucking sore!"

"Your . . ." I felt his hands come down. On the top of my head at first, then they slid over my cheeks, over my face, into my hair. "Where?" he asked.

"Here." I pulled my head away slightly, pulling back my free hair and exposing the strand that was stuck. It stretched from my head right to his crotch area, there was just no making this up. I was attached to Alex's crotch! I felt his hands fumble some more, his thumb clipped my lip, his palm squished my nose, he poked a finger in my eye. Finally, he had the strand between his finger and located the problem.

"My belt buckle," he said. "It's stuck in my belt buckle."

"Great!" I threw my arms in the air and almost lost my balance. I grabbed onto Alex once more.

"Uh . . . those aren't my thighs," Alex said awkwardly.

I squeezed. The things beneath my hands felt hard and firm and . . . "Oooohhh," I said, suddenly realizing that I was gripping his backside. I released my hands, not before giving it the tiniest little squeeze again.

"God, I hope no one sees us like this." I sighed and then shook my head a little.

"Whoa!" Alex grabbed the top of my head with his hand and held it firmly in place. "Please don't do that."

"Don't do what?" I asked.

"Don't move like that."

"Like what?"

"You know," he said with a strange tone in his voice. "*You know*." Great vocal emphasis was placed on this last "you know."

"No, I don't know," I replied. "I don't know, *know*, you know."

"Just stop moving your head like that," he said, sounding exasperated, or was that desperation in his voice?

"What, like this?" I moved my head again and this time his hand came down a lot harder on the top my head.

"VAL!" he said loudly. "Every time you move your head like that it's causing some friction . . ."

"Oh." I thought about it for a second and then got it. "OH!" I said, biting my lip. "Sorry, I don't mean to be . . ." My voice tapered off as I looked straight ahead of me, *and yup*, it had grown somewhat. I tried to bite back an awkward smile, but couldn't. This was the second time in a few days that I'd had an encounter with his surprisingly large package—was the universe trying to tell me something? Well, if it was, it wasn't being very subtle about it, that's for sure. In fact, it was being very in your face about the whole thing. Literally.

"Let's just get you loose, shall we?" He sounded determined, and fiddled with my hair until he finally managed to free me.

"Thank God," I exclaimed loudly as I felt the tension on my head relax. Alex then pulled me up so forcefully and quickly that I smooshed into his chest. I lost my breath for a moment as the wind was knocked out of me by his solid frame. Instinctively, I placed my hands on his shoulders and held myself in place. I pressed myself into him a little, even though I knew I shouldn't. But his body was hard and firm and he smelt good and was so nice and kind and fun and I was a little warm and fuzzy around the edges because of all the wine. My inhibitions were down, my morals slightly looser and there was something so romantic about this mist all of a sudden. Alex slipped his hand around my back and held me in place. It didn't feel like a very friendly hand, though, not the kind of hand that helps friends to their feet and stops them from falling backwards. It felt like a totally different kind of hand. The kind that cups a woman's back possessively as if she were theirs. The kind of hand that was both firm and reassuring and frightening in the way it made my knees weak and mind swirl with thoughts that I was sure I wasn't meant to be having. His hand slipped down a little lower and gripped me tighter.

"Mmmm." I let out the tiniest breathy moan, which I actually hadn't meant to make. *What the hell was I doing?* I didn't know. We were meant to be getting over our exes together, not getting into each other. This was crossing a line. A big green, ribbon line.

A line that was firmly placed around our fingers. I could almost feel the ribbon tightening on my finger like an anaconda, as if it knew that this moment was happening and it was telling me to stop. I pulled away from him quickly.

"Sorry," I suddenly said. "We should find our rooms." I started making my way through the mist once more. It was a little thinner now and we found my room first.

I turned to look at Alex before opening the door. A part of me didn't want this evening to end, or the moment to be over. "Goodnight, I guess?" It was definitely a question and I paused and waited for the answer.

"Good night," he said back to me. There was an awkward lull in the conversation. I reached for the door handle pointedly, hoping it would make him say something to stop me from opening it. Only he didn't.

"Okay. Good night," he said.

"Good night." I said it again, giving him one last chance to tell me not to open the door. The ribbon on my finger tightened and I shook my head to myself, trying to dislodge all that was running through my mind right now. I finally opened the door and without looking back at him, slipped inside and pulled it closed. I waited, my back to the door, and listened intently at the sounds of his footsteps getting further and further away from me.

I sighed, and a feeling of emptiness rushed in as I stood there all alone in my room looking around. I started taking my clothes off and was just about to climb into bed when my phone beeped. I reached for it. I was sure it was one of my friends, I'd been sending them the odd message here just so they didn't worry. But it wasn't. My heart started beating faster.

Alex: I forgot to say thank you

I typed back.

Val: For what?

Alex: This has been one of the best days of my life.

I smiled to myself, almost giddy.

Val: Me too.

Alex: Sleep tight.

Val: You too.

Alex: Looking forward to tomorrow.

Val: Me too.

Alex: Sweet dreams.

Val: Thanks.

Alex: If you get scared, you know where I am . . .

I sat up a little straighter. Wait. *Was this an invitation to join him?* I lowered my fingers to the screen and was just about to start typing something flirty back when the green ribbon caught my attention. Rule number one went running through my mind: *don't jump into another relationship . . . feelings are all over the place . . . easy to think you've developed feelings for someone else . . . just transference . . . not real . . . take a break from relationships . . . focus on yourself for a while.* Clearly, I was letting myself run away a bit here and needed to reel myself in. I wasn't sure what I was feeling right now was even real. *Wait, what was I feeling?* I brought my fingers back down and typed something else entirely, something that every part of my body was telling me not to . . .

Val: I'll be fine. I'm a big girl.

Alex: I know.

Val: See you in the morning.

Alex: Can't wait.

Alex: Good night, Val.

Val: Good night, Alex.

CHAPTER THIRTY-NINE

"So . . ." Alex laid the magazine out on the table in front of us and took out his trusty pen and green highlighter.

I ate my breakfast and looked down at the magazine. I'd had a great sleep the night before, despite the mist, and had woken up feeling refreshed and starving.

"We only have two more to go." Alex circled them and I stared at the magazine.

"Really?" I pulled it away from him and looked. "Oh God, I can't believe we're almost through the list already." And then a thought hit me uncomfortably in the ribs: what would happen when we finished the list? This adventure with Alex would be over and that would be it. I looked up at him. He was looking at me too.

"There's no rush to get through them, though," Alex suddenly said, pulling the magazine away as if he was thinking the same thing.

I smiled happily. "No need to rush," I repeated.

"So shall we go exploring the town after breakfast?" Alex asked, fighting me for the last croissant on the plate. I managed to grab onto the end of it before he pulled it away and it tore in two. We both laughed at this and stuffed the food into our mouths.

Alex sat back on his seat and rolled his shirt up, looking down at his stomach. "I'm really going to need to get back to the gym when I get home."

"Oh, please!" I tutted. "Says the man with an eight pack and a rock-hard chest of steel."

Alex suddenly stood up and held his hand out for me. "This place is meant to have really nice walks."

"A walk?" I shook my head. "I've already walked once this holiday."

"Once is not enough." He grabbed my hand and started pulling me out of the chair.

But—" I started objecting but was quickly interrupted.

"But nothing, Val. But nothing."

I giggled as Alex wrapped his arms around me and pulled me forcefully. We bumped into someone else's breakfast table on the way.

"Sorry." Alex held his hand out. The couple eating gave us a slightly disapproving look which made me laugh.

We stumbled outside the hotel and found ourselves back on the street once more. There was no sign of the mist from the night before. It was as if it had never been there at all. The day was warm, not too hot though. A perfect temperature that made it pleasant to walk.

"Look," Alex suddenly said, pointing at a sign that indicated a walking trail off the road and into a wooded area.

"Uh . . . But it's just pointing into a forest," I said, looking into the tall thick trees.

"Don't worry, we won't get lost." Alex took my hand and pulled me up the path and into the woods.

"Famous last words," I said, as I glanced around. Just like the mist the previous night, this was, once again, the perfect start to some kind of horror movie. Two hikers going into the woods for an innocent walk. All goes well until a madman with an axe jumps out from behind a tree and decides to turn their skulls into little ashtrays.

We walked through the forest, the tall trees dwarfing us on all sides, rising up so high that when you looked up, you couldn't see their tops. It was silent here, except for the sounds of our feet crunching down on the carpet of pine needles. The sweet scent of pine permeated the air and a slight breeze made the leaves rustle.

We continued to walk on in silence for a few more minutes before something made us both stop. Soon, the fresh smell of pine needles was no longer what filled the air.

I inhaled deeply and looked over at Alex, trying to ascertain if he was smelling the same thing, or was I just imagining it?

"Is it?" I asked, taking in another whiff.

"It can't be, can it?" He looked at me, also sniffing.

"I think it is," I said. I looked around to find the source of the smell. I didn't have to look for too long because, suddenly, raucous laughter broke through the air.

Soon, two distinct voices could be heard. The voices sounded young. They were laughing and talking in French. We smiled at each other and followed the sounds until we found what we were looking for. Two teenagers slumped against one of the trees, smoking something that was definitely *not* a cigarette.

Alex and I shared another smile and continued to watch the two teenagers.

I tutted softly. "Naughty-naughty," I whispered quietly to Alex. It was obvious what they were up to. The distinct smell, the hysterical laughter, the angry-looking teenage clothing coupled with the fact that they were loitering in the woods, dead giveaway. Alex took a step and something loud crunched underfoot. Suddenly, two pairs of startled teenage eyes were on us. The looks on their faces changed immediately; surprise, shock and then panic. Then one of them said something in French and, at the speed of light, they were off, running through the forest. Clearly these weren't career criminals.

I looked over at Alex and laughed but he wasn't looking in my direction and suddenly he ran forward.

"What?" I asked. And then I saw it too. The thin column of smoke curling up from the ground. The joint was sitting on a big bed of dry pine needles, and it was only minutes away from going up in flames.

Alex picked the joint up and then began smashing his foot down on the pine needles.

"They could have caused a fire," he hissed as his foot extinguished the last of the smoke. "So irresponsible." He shook his head angrily.

"Totally!" I agreed, walking over to him. And then, we both suddenly became very aware of what Alex was holding between his fingers. We looked down at it. Thick, white, rather crudely rolled and burning. We both looked up from it and made eye contact.

"When last did you . . .?" I asked, not finishing the sentence, rather letting the question hang in the air, much like the pungent smoke wafting around us.

Alex looked serious. "I never have." It wasn't a question, it was a statement, and yet, the inflection at the end of his sentence made it feel like one. *What was he asking me exactly?*

We both looked down at it again. A breeze blew through the

forest and dragged some of the smoke with it. It twirled and twisted in the air, like smoke coming from a genie's lamp.

Our eyes lifted once more and we looked at each other again. "Do you think we . . .?" I asked.

"We could . . ." Alex replied, looking back down at the thing between his fingers.

"It's just a plant," I quickly said, in an attempt to justify this.

"And it's used a lot in medicine these days too," Alex added.

"Canada just legalized it," I offered up.

"It's legal in the Netherlands," Alex added.

"Totally," I confirmed.

"And medical marijuana is legal in most of America, you can basically get it for strep throat. I've had a few cancer patients on it during chemo."

"See!" I said. "It would almost be criminal *not* to."

"Exactly," Alex said.

"So we agree then?" I asked.

"Why not?" Alex replied and then slowly started raising it to his lips. Then he paused. "I've never smoked weed before. Ever." He looked to me, questioningly.

"Just put it between your lips, inhale, and then you have to inhale again otherwise it doesn't go down into your lungs."

Alex nodded and tried, but all that happened was a massive fit of coughing and chest banging.

"That's awful!" He continued to cough. "How do people do it?"

"I don't think you got any," I said, taking the joint from Alex and raising it to my lips. "Like this . . ." I inhaled the distinctive-tasting smoke, held it in my lungs for a while, and then blew it out. "Easy," I said, and passed it back to him.

Alex tried again, but the same coughing fit occurred. He shook his head and passed it back to me. "I can't do this," he said.

"Wait!" I held my hand up dramatically. "You can't back out now. I've already done it."

"But I can't physically do it."

"I know." I took the joint from him, remembering something from my college days. Not that I was a big smoker, but I'd partaken here and there—*who hadn't?* Clearly the serious med students hadn't, that's who.

"I'm going to blow it into your mouth," I said. "All you have to do is inhale as I blow in. Okay?"

Alex nodded and I indicated for him to come closer. I inhaled, careful not to keep it in for a second longer than it needed to be, and then brought my mouth down over his. I blew into his mouth and heard the sound as he inhaled in. But even once I knew Alex had inhaled, I didn't move my lips. Instead, I kept them there. Letting them linger. Alex moved closer to me, the movement caused our lips to rub together. A static-like tingling sensation prickled on my lips. The sensation grew, until my whole face tingled. It crept into the back of my neck and raced down my spine. I pulled away, almost surprised by how intense the sensation had been. I looked at Alex. He had a slightly surprised look in his eyes too.

I cleared my throat. "Did you get it?"

He nodded as a thin puff of smoke curled out of his mouth and rose up into the air.

I looked back down at the joint, it was nearly finished. I brought it up to my mouth again and took a slightly bigger breath this time. I held it in until it felt like my lungs were going to explode, and then quickly brought my mouth back down to Alex's.

This time Alex's hand came up to my cheek as our lips met. He opened his mouth slightly and I placed mine over his, breathing the smoke into it, as he inhaled. Again, I didn't move my lips off right away. Instead, we both seemed to close our mouths slowly at the same time, causing our lips to rub together gently. The tingling feeling was back and it felt so good that I didn't want it to end and then suddenly, it felt like we were kissing.

Were we? No one was moving their tongues or lips though. Alex lifted his other hand to my cheek and held my face in place. I moved closer to him, until our chests touched. I was so aware of our lips. His against mine. Mine against his. It was all I could feel. We kept them so still, that when they both finally started moving, it was very obvious. My lips curled into a smile, and I felt Alex's doing the same. We smiled against each other's lips.

"Whoa!" I said softly and slowly against his mouth. My words sounded dreamy and slow and heavy.

"Whoa," Alex imitated me as we slowly pulled away. We looked at each other, stupid smiles plastered across our faces.

"Whoa," we both said at the same time and then started looking around. The forest appeared more beautiful than it had a few moments ago. The greens were greener and almost shimmery now. I watched Alex, he seemed to be gazing straight ahead of him with a faraway, distinct look on his face.

"Alex, are you okay?" The words came out of my mouth, but it didn't sound like me. My voice wasn't mine, it was as if someone had hijacked my vocal chords and was speaking through me. Someone with a strange, slow, mechanical, voice. "Oh my God! I'm channeling Siri!" I suddenly said, putting my hand to my lips to see if they'd changed shape. "Helloooo." I was surprised by the sound of my voice again. "I'm Siri!" I looked up at Alex. He looked at me and smiled.

"Hello, Siri," he said. *And that was it.* The world's funniest moment. The joke to end all other jokes. A punchline like no other punchline that had ever come before it, well, that's how it felt anyway as an explosion of laughter filled the space between us. It was so loud and frightening that I'm sure we terrified all the forest animals.

Alex moved towards me, he was laughing so much that his shoulders were rising and falling and he looked unsteady on his feet. We reached out and grabbed each other by the shoulders, clinging on tightly.

"It hurts!" I cried, as tears started pouring from my eyes.

"Me too!" Alex said, as his laughter became hysterical.

I pulled Alex into a hug and we held onto each other, screaming with laughter until we were both crying tears.

"Let's walk," I suddenly said, pulling away from Alex.

"Which way did we come from?" he asked.

"I don't know." I shrugged and then an idea hit me. "I know!" I closed my eyes and stuck my arm out, pointing one of my fingers, and then spun around and stopped.

I opened my eyes and looked at my finger. "Siri wants us to go that way." I turned and looked at Alex. He started nodding in agreement.

"I trust Siri," he said and then we both stumbled off in that direction together.

CHAPTER FORTY

*W*e were surrounded by forest and the world was moving in slow motion. Somehow everything looked crisper and clearer, yet muted at the same time. The colors all seemed to hum at me, as if each one had a different sound and I swear, I could feel some kind of vibration moving through the air. *Maybe this was mother nature whispering to me?*

"Wow!" I said breathily.

"I know. It's so like, like . . ." Alex held his arms out and wiggled his fingers around. "It's like I can feel the air."

I burst out laughing again, and soon Alex joined in. We stumbled and cackled through the undergrowth like two people who'd escaped from a mental asylum, almost insane from all the laughter. We walked a little more and luckily "Siri" had chosen the right way, because suddenly we found ourselves standing at the edge of the forest, the town stretched out in front of us just behind the row of trees.

"Where does Siri want us to go next?" Alex asked.

I closed my eyes again and spun around, this time completely losing balance and falling to the ground. As I hit the floor I began screeching with laughter again. I could hear Alex laughing too, then I felt two arms under mine and a firm tug. I stumbled back up to my feet and then crashed into Alex. He wrapped his arms around me and then we both fell backwards onto the floor again.

We both cried with laughter. The kind of laughter that renders your body useless. We were gasping for air now and I'd never known laughter like this. It was so intense I thought I might actually die from it.

"Are you okay?" Alex asked, still holding onto me. I was lying on top of him now. I lifted my head up and looked him in the eye. This time his gray eyes looked slightly purple, not a garish bright purple, but as if they had a touch of lavender field in them. His lids were heavy, giving him a cute sleepy look. I propped myself up on his chest and looked down at him. I could feel myself smiling, as if it were out of my control.

"You have purple eyes," I said, lowering my face all the way up to his, touching my nose with his.

Alex widened them so I could look even more. "Your eyes are blue," he stated. And for some reason, this was again the funniest thing I'd heard all year. I burst out laughing so hard that I could barely hold my head up. It crashed down onto Alex's shoulder and he began to laugh again too.

"You're so hot," I suddenly heard myself say into his neck. His laughter stopped and he moved his head to the side to look at me. Suddenly, I wondered if I should have said that at all.

"Val . . ." he whispered breathily.

"Yes?" my equally breathy voice whispered back.

"You're so beautiful." He smiled at me, not the silly goofy smile of before. A warm, genuine, and dare I say, sexy smile.

"Really?" I lifted my head so that I could look at him better.

"So insanely beautiful." He looked at me and my heart stopped. Wait! This was *the look*, wasn't it? The look that I had always wanted to see on Matt's face, but never had. I blushed. I couldn't help it. Little prickly flames licked my cheeks and I was sure I'd gone a bright shade of crimson. This was the drugs talking. It must be. Alex and I were travel buddies, *weren't we*? And the green ribbon! The fucking ribbon. Rule number one! *What was happening?*

"*VAL!*" a voice screamed at me from my subconscious and at first I looked around to see if someone was talking to me.

"Yes?" I replied into the air.

"*You know the answer*," the voice said.

"What?" I asked, looking up into the sky this time, as if this was where the voice had come from. Was it a divine voice? Not that I believed in the divine, but bloody hell someone was talking to me, *weren't they?*

"Did I say something?" Alex asked, looking confused

"Did you?" I asked, equally confused now.

"I don't know." Alex looked around too.

"I think someone is speaking to us," I whispered in his ear, leaning forward so the voice couldn't hear me.

"Is it Siri?" Alex whispered and I started laughing again. Alex joined in and once again we were gasping for air. We finally stumbled back up to our feet and smiled at each other goofily.

"Do you really not remember that kiss?" Alex suddenly asked, totally changing the direction of the conversation.

"You sound like me now," I said with a smile. "Wondering if Matt remembered the kiss."

Alex stuck a finger out at me and waggled it. "If Matt forgot that kiss, then he has a serious problem. No one can ever forget kissing you. You are, like, the best kisser ever."

"The best kisser?" I burst out laughing again. No one had ever called me that.

"I'm being serious." Alex took a step towards me. "That was literally the best kiss of my entire life."

"No!" I gasped. "You're kidding. Was it?"

"Yup." He nodded and his eyes drifted down to the hickey on my neck. My hand automatically came up and touched it as it burned.

"I wish I remembered it now," I said.

Alex stepped backwards and leaned against one of the trees, his arms were folded, his eyes locked on me. They were almost the color of liquid mercury now. Swirling and glistening and dancing in the ever-changing light. So beautiful to watch. So hypnotizing, so, so . . .

"We could do it again." I suddenly heard some version of myself say.

He smiled. "We could," he stated matter-of-factly. "But what if you forget it again?"

I pulled my phone out of my pocket and waved it at him. "We'll record it," I said, walking over to him.

His eyes widened in surprise. "Interesting idea."

I stepped closer to him. Then he stepped. I stepped. He stepped again and soon we were face to face. Only a few centimeters of nothingness separated us. We looked at each other and smiled. I looked down at my phone and flicked my finger across the screen until I arrived at the video. I turned the phone around, as if taking a selfie, and held my arm out to the side. We were still smiling at each other. I could feel the effects of the weed really kicking up a notch now. It pulsed through me, making my body warm and relaxed. I felt like I was standing on a sunny beach somewhere, soaking up the sun. I pressed record and leaned in until our lips touched. His lips brushed mine. Not innocently or softly, but in a hard and demanding way. And then he pulled me closer and before I knew what was happening, his lips slammed into mine, covering my mouth with a hot, hungry kiss.

I opened my mouth and soon he was kissing me harder and deeper, with an urgency that spurned me on. I wrapped my free arm around the back of his head and slid my fingers through his hair, tugging on it tightly as I changed the pace up and took control. Slower this time. I ran my tongue over his lips, tracing them, caressing them. His breathing quickened and he let out a moan. I could feel his sharp breaths against my mouth as I teased him relentlessly with the tip of my tongue, darting it across his lips.

My arm-holding phone was getting tired and I was struggling to keep it up as the kiss intensified again. Our tongues met in one magical moment and suddenly, as they massaged each other, glided over each other, I felt like I was floating on air. My feet were no longer in contact with the ground. His arms were on my hips now, pulling at them. Pulling them closer until they slammed into him. I opened my hand and my phone tumbled to the ground, I didn't care. I brought my hand down to the side of his face, running my thumb over his lips, pulling at them as our tongues explored the depths of each other's mouths.

"Oh fuck," I whimpered in total mind-numbing ecstasy as his tongue left my mouth and his teeth came down on my lip and tugged. I pulled away teasingly, and he grabbed my lip between his teeth again. I giggled this time, as I bit him back. Hard. *Oh. My. God.* I felt like my I was losing myself in this kiss. I'd never kissed anyone like this before, ever. Not even Matt in the lift. The kiss overwhelmed and overpowered all my senses and I wanted more, more, more of it . . . *him.*

But nothing seemed like it was enough. No matter how much I sucked, and licked and nibbled and how deeply I explored his mouth, I was still totally unsatisfied. I wanted so much more, *of him.* I was drowning and he was the oxygen I needed. I was burning and he was the water. I was lost and he was the way. I felt some strange bubble come over us. A hazy, thick, dreamy space that surrounded us and wrapped us up in it. I melted into the space, into him, and I never wanted to leave—

The sound of a car horn suddenly cut through all that and made us both jump backwards from each other in shock. Our eyes met and we stared at each other. I was out of breath, my heart was thumping in my chest and it felt like I had lava pulsing through my veins. Alex looked out of breath and dazed too. His cheeks were flushed and his hair was messy from where my hands had been. We simply stood there and stared at each other for the longest time. Finally, I spoke.

"Wow. Okay," I said, swaying from side to side. The intoxicating kiss had only made me feel even more stoned now.

"Wow," Alex repeated, a slow, giddy smile sweeping over his face.

"Wow," I said again, smiling back at him.

"You already said that," he chuckled. A deep, low chuckle.

"I know," I said. I looked down and noticed my phone was on the ground. I picked it up, dusted it off and put it in my pocket.

"Soooo . . ." Alex asked, stretching the word out slowly, languidly, fluidly. So it sounded like liquid letters spilling from his mouth. For some reason this made me giggle.

"Where to now?" he asked.

"We just kissed each other," I said with a giggle in my voice.

"I know." Alex smiled at me. "We did. And it was hot." He looked me up and down and I felt a little giddy. I stumbled on my feet and then spun around again, sticking my finger out once more. I came to a stop, my finger pointing upwards. "That way!" I declared.

Alex nodded at me, slipped his arm through mine and the two of us started walking across the road to the quaint shopping street in front of us. The streets and the shops and buildings looked even brighter and more colorful now.

We walked in total silence for a while, and I felt so in tune and in touch with Alex that I was sure I could read his thoughts. This was confirmed when we both suddenly stopped walking and stared straight ahead . . .

A revelation revealed itself unto us. Like the magical hand of fate swooping down. I'm sure the heavens were busy opening, angels were polishing their trumpets ready to sing and blow and dance and any moment now, a grand ethereal light would no doubt break through the clouds and bathe this place in its glistening glow of glowiness.

We both turned and looked at each other slowly. And then, we started nodding at the same time. Slowly up, slowly down. There was no need for words. No! We didn't need such pedestrian things as words, this transcended words. This transcended sentences and paragraphs and entire encyclopedias. No words needed. We both knew what the other one was thinking.

"Yes," I whispered over to Alex. This hallowed moment felt like it needed whispers.

"I agree," Alex whispered back.

"Then it's decided?" I asked dreamily.

"Wait," Alex said. "We need to read it first." He looked at me with a serious deadpan look plastered across his face. "Reading it makes it real."

I nodded at him. Of course this made total sense at the time. I dug in my handbag and pulled the magazine out. It was so well read that the pages automatically opened at the right spot. I scanned the page, trying to bring my heavy eyes into focus, and started reading.

"'Number Nine. Get Lit, AF! Get a makeover. Get a cut; there's nothing better than stepping out with a brand-new hairdo when feeling down in the dumps. But make sure you take your BFF, in case you go full breakup mode and decide to shave your head or dye it mermaid. Splash out on new make-up, experiment with colors you've never used before. Nothing makes you feel better than sexy red lips.'"

I rolled the magazine up and slipped it into my bag again. We gave each other one more nod and started walking to the shop in front of us.

Salon Très Chic.

We'd almost reached the door when I heard that voice again. I stopped. I looked around once more to see if I could find the source of it. But there was no one near us.

"*VAL!*" it screamed at me. "*Step away from the salon. Do not, I repeat, do not go inside. You are high as a kite. Do not get a makeover when high! Do not do this.*"

But as soon as she'd finished, another voice joined in.

"*VAL!*" it screamed. "*Don't worry! Do it! It will be fun. Besides, you are at your most creative right now. Do it.*"

The other voice answered back. It was almost pleading with me now not to do it. But I wasn't having any of it—

I grabbed Alex by the arm and we marched inside the salon.

Of course, little did Alex and I know at that stage how much we would regret this terrible decision in the morning.

CHAPTER FORTY-ONE

~

The next morning

*T*he strange knock woke me. *Where the hell was I?* Everything was so unfamiliar, and hard! What the hell was I lying on? Where was I lying and why was there a policeman staring at me through a window . . . wait, *what window was this?*

It was small. Not like a hotel window. It was dirty, also not like the hotel window. I rubbed my eyes, trying to remove the sleep from them, trying to make sense of what the hell was going on. I sat up and banged my head against something hard. I grabbed it and rubbed it. I looked up. A roof. A material-covered roof. I looked around. I was in the car. The seats had all been pushed down and I was in the back of the car.

Another loud knock on the window. "All right! All right!" I waved my hand at them, indicating I was coming. I tried to move, but something heavy was draped over my leg. I looked down. Another leg. A big, muscular, hairy man's leg . . . this was *not* my leg! I followed the leg from the calf, to the thigh and higher still. Up and up and, *mmmm*, it was attached to a really nice-looking lower back, *and wow*, great, big broad shoulders. Alex had such a nice back, I'd never really noticed it until now. The back went up to a head . . . *a blond head!*

Oh my God!? Whose head was this! I threw the big leg off and crawled to the door. I opened the window and stuck my head out. The two police officers were looking at me now, as if I was in trouble. *Was I in trouble?* My nose itched and I scratched it, a familiar smell filled my nostrils and I quickly put my hand behind my back. My fingers smelt like marijuana, as if I had been . . . !!!! A moment of clarity! Multiple exclamation marks flying into my mind. Flashing lights. An alarm. *I'd been smoking pot!*

"Hello, officers," I said as sweetly as I could. I was trying to radiate innocence.

"You cannot sleep here," one officer said, looking over my shoulder into the car.

"We can't?" I asked, unsure of where the hell we were. I stuck my head out of the window even further, and that's when I became aware of the fact that we were parked on the side of the road.

"Shit!" I hissed under my breath.

"Can you step out the car, please," the policeman said, opening the door for me.

"Sure thing, sir." I smiled up at him, forcing myself to exude all the sugarcoated goodness of the word. I was dew on a spring morning, freshly picked blossoms and your grandmother's home-made cinnamon biscuits! But when I climbed out, a loud din rang out around me. I jumped as I saw things falling, *nay*, cascading out of the car and onto the ground. The stuff pooled around my feet.

I looked down. A junk food graveyard lay scattered at my feet. Empty cans of fizzy drinks, polystyrene hamburger boxes, chocolate wrappers, a half-eaten rather tasty-looking pastry, more wrappers, a bottle, crisp packets.

"Sorry," I said, completely embarrassed, and bent down to grab the stuff, shoving it straight back into the car.

"Can you move the car, please, you cannot park here." The policeman sounded a little firmer this time and my heart began to pound in my chest.

"Yes! Yes, of course!" I said quickly.

"Can I ask what you're doing here?" the other one asked me. He was looking into the window suspiciously, possibly at the strange blond-haired man who was stretched out in it.

And then it came to me in a whoosh. "We were looking for the campsite, we couldn't find it," I said with confidence, because that memory had suddenly come back to me. Alex and I had been looking for a campsite last night, *why* . . . I do not know though.

Both the policeman stared at each other and then turned and pointed. I followed their arms and looked at where their fingers were pointed.

"Aaaah." I nodded solemnly when I saw the sign only twenty meters away. A large, *you cannot bloody miss it* sign with a big tent on it and an arrow pointing down a road. "Must have missed it," I said sheepishly this time.

"Have you been drinking?" the other policeman asked.

"No!" *Had we been drinking?* I wasn't so sure.

"And what about your friend there?" he asked, pointing at the man behind me.

"Oh no!" I gushed. "He hasn't drunk. No!" *Who was that man?*

I had a cold, sinking feeling this wasn't going well and suddenly I had images of being hauled into a police station and thrown into jail.

"Look," I said really calmly. "I'm here on holiday from South Africa, my friend and I *(no name yet)* were looking for the campground and we couldn't find it. It was getting late and we didn't know what to do, so we parked the car here and slept. That's all. I'm really, really sorry, sir. I mean, sirs."

The policeman glanced at each other once more and another look passed between them. Shit! This was not going well.

"It was really dark," I suddenly said. "No street lights here, we must have stopped just before seeing the sign, but we'd driven so long and far and we were really tired and it wasn't safe to keep driving like that. I'm really sorry." I was trying to reason with them. I didn't want to go to jail.

They looked at me and then their faces seemed to soften somewhat.

"Okay," one said. "As long as you drive off, no harm done."

"Yes! Yes of course." I was so happy to hear this that I had to fight the urge not to run up to them and hug them both. "We'll move now. Thank you. We won't do it again."

The policeman began to move off. They climbed into their car and pulled away. I smiled and nodded at them and then, when they were out of sight, I turned my attention back to the blond man who was asleep in the car.

Who the hell was he?

CHAPTER FORTY-TWO

I slowly, tentatively walked up to the car and looked in again. He was the same size as Alex. Same muscular physique, but his hair was a bright, brilliant bleached white. I stuck my head into the car again . . . *What the hell was that sound?* A faint, clinking. Like a wind chime.

I cleared my throat, hoping to make the person stir. They did not. I leaned in a little more . . . *What the hell was that sound?* I cleared my throat again, much louder this time. Still nothing.

I picked up an empty can and very softly tossed it at the sleeping back. The can hit and bounced off. The back flinched and stirred. The man moaned sleepily. He wiggled. He moved his legs and then he slowly turned.

I gasped. The sight was so awfully horrifying. It was a nightmare. The worst thing I'd ever seen in all my living years. It was shocking and terrifying and truly utterly undoubtedly horrendous. It was Alex. But not like I knew him.

It was Alex with a full head of bleached white hair. He looked like a nineties raver en route to Ibiza. I started shaking my head

from side to side; the shock of it was so overwhelming that I—
what the fuck was that sound?

I looked around. I could distinctly hear the loud clinking of a
wind chime, but coming from where? I turned my head again,
and that's when I caught sight of myself in the mirror.

"NOOOOOOOO!" I screamed. "Nooooooo!" I put my
hands on my head and felt them instantly. "What have I done?" I
wailed, running my fingers over the tight cornrows in my hair.
My hands trailed down, down, down and I felt something
attached to the hanging ends. I lifted the ends and was utterly
nauseated with what I saw . . .

I wanted to cry. Hanging from the bottom of each braid was a
luminous collection of plastic beads. Pink, yellow and green, just
dangling there.

"Whyyyyyy?" I wailed, looking at Alex, who was staring at me
in total horror. "What have we done?" I asked, pointing at his hair.

Alex scrambled to his knees and moved to the front of the car.
He looked into the rear-view mirror and gasped. And then he
turned to me.

"What have we done?" he asked, looking pale. More pale than
I'd ever seen him. Pale as a corpse without a drop of blood in it.

I shook my head, tears welling in my eyes. "And why didn't
anyone stop us?"

The previous night . . .

"Oh my God, this place is *soooooo* beautiful," I said walking into
the salon. It was not beautiful, though. Let's be clear about this. I

was obviously seeing things through rosy-rainbow, weed-tinted glasses and had I been even vaguely in my right mind, I would have seen the signs immediately. The signs that I should have run and left. There were several signs . . .

1. The interior of Salon Très Chic was painted pink. Not a trendy dusty-rose color with cute gold accents or anything like that. It was bright, hot pink! Candy, Barbie, bubble-gum pink.

2. The heart-shaped mirrors were wrapped in bright purple LED lights, making it look more like a cheap disco than a place to get your hair done.

3. At the hair stations, they had those old-school hair-dryer things. Those bulbous big ones. The ones that came out on arms and were placed over your whole head. They looked more like UFOs from a bad sci-fi film. And they were also a bright turquoise.

4. The floors also were covered in fluffy zebra-skin-patterned carpets.

* * *

I should have immediately looked at those four simple signs and run straight out the door. But we did not. We didn't run, instead we told "Salome," the owner of Salon Très Chic, *also the only woman I've seen still rocking a perm*, that we were there for makeovers. And what is worse than all that, was how we chose our makeovers.

"What should we do?" Alex looked as excited as I felt. "I've never had a makeover before." He was almost squealing now.

And then I said it. The stupidest thing I've ever said before, but at the time, it seemed like the most brilliant idea on the planet. My mind was just swirling with "brilliant" ideas, and I felt like the love child of Elon Musk and Steve Jobs and was seriously wondering why no one had picked me out as the next creative genius who would revolutionize the world.

"We should ask the magazine," I said in a strange, deep and poignant voice. One that had a sense of gravitas to it. A smack of the mysterious.

Alex gasped. "Yes! Let the magazine guide us." *(Who says that? No one who isn't stoned, that's for sure!)*

But we continued and what happened next would be the ill-fated thing that would land us in this braided, bleached mess.

"Let's open it randomly and whatever pictures we see, we get," I said. *Oh God, it had seemed like such a good idea at the time.*

At this stage, you would have thought Salome would have had the sense to stop us. You would have thought that even she could see that we were in no way sane enough to be making any kind of aesthetic choices. But she didn't. In fact, she seemed only too excited to be a part of this insanity.

We flipped the magazine open and . . .

Bands We Loved In The Nineties.

I wish the voice had screamed at me again. *I might have listened.* I wish it had told me that Beyoncé's Destiny's Child braids would not be a good look on me, no matter how much I liked Beyoncé and had belted out "Say My Name," in my bedroom with a hairbrush with the door closed. And I really wish the voice had spoken up when Alex and I had pointed at Justin Timberlake's over-bleached mop of NSYNC hair and I wish I hadn't egged him on when I shouted, *"Oh my God, I had such a crush on Justin when I was younger."*

Why had no one stopped us . . . *why?* I ask with tears in my bloodshot eyes.

CHAPTER FORTY-THREE

Present day . . .

$\mathcal{W}$e both sat in the front seats holding our heads in our hands. We'd driven up the road and found a legitimate parking spot for the car. Neither one of us could remember why we'd been looking for a campsite the night before.

"It's not *that* bad," Alex said, breaking the long silence that we'd been sitting in.

"Are you kidding?" I wailed. "It is *that* bad. In fact, it's worse than *that bad*! *That bad* would be if I'd cut bangs which everyone knows would not look good with my face shape, that would have been bad. This, however, is so much worse than bad."

Alex turned and looked at me. I stared at his head. It was hard not to stare. It was almost all you could see. It was so bright and reflective that it almost changed the lighting inside the car. The bleach job was a very bad one to begin with. It was white in some parts, fading into a yellowish color, radiating outwards to bright orange. All these colors, coupled with his gorgeous gray eyes, slightly olive complexion and chiseled face that was now sporting some very sexy stubble just looked so damn . . . *wrong*. He looked like a rubbery Malibu Ken doll!

"Oh my God, I can't take you seriously with that hair!" I slapped my hands over my eyes, which caused my braids to clank together and the car was filled with the sounds of wind chimes once more. I cringed and then wanted to cry.

"My hair makes a noise," I whimpered weakly.

"My hair blinds people," Alex offered with a resigned sigh.

I kicked something with my foot and looked down at the floor, and there it lay. The thing that had caused all the trouble. I picked it up and it fell open on the page. There were fresh scribbles and notes all over the page.

"Uh . . . Alex?" I asked nervously. "Why have we got lots of multiple ticks next to number two again? Commit murder on social media as if we did something else last night? Oh God, did we post pictures of ourselves?"

Alex and I stared at each other and then both jumped at the same time.

"Oh my God!" I scrambled into the back of the car looking for my phone. Alex did the same, finding his phone under a seat.

"We didn't, we didn't, we didn't . . ." I pleaded with myself out loud as I opened Instagram. But I had a bad feeling about this. *Very bad.*

"We did!" Alex held the phone up for me to see.

"Oh God," I gasped as I looked at the picture of the two of us and started shaking my head. "How bad does it get?" I was terrified to know the answer. Alex looked back down at his phone and started flipping through the pictures.

"A lot worse," he admitted, holding the phone up for me to see.

This time I didn't gasp. A gasp was not adequate for this moment. A gasp would not have sufficed, even though I was fully aghast and it was a very gaspy moment.

"How many did you post?" I asked, my voice quivering.

Alex started counting and he only stopped when he got to six.

I looked down at my own Instagram and simply shook my head in utter disbelief. I'd posted about ten selfies of the three of us in various places around town. And when I say *three*, I mean Alex, myself and "Sally," which is clearly what we'd decided to name the sex doll who was in every picture with us. It wasn't bad enough that we had actually documented our very ill-conceived makeovers and posted them on social media, but to have done it with a sex doll . . .

"We changed our Facebook profile pictures too," Alex said.

I bit my lip and opened my Facebook App, terrified of what I was about to see. And when I saw it an awkward silence filled the car.

I finally spoke once I'd taken it in. "Well, it can't get much worse than that." I pointed at the picture of me kissing Sally on the cheek, her big, gaping mouth staring into camera.

"Hey, you sent me a video on WhatsApp," Alex suddenly said. "Let's see what it is." He moved to sit next to me and then pressed play.

"Okay!" I said, slapping my hands over my mouth as I looked at it.

"Wow!" Alex said.

"We are really going for it, aren't we?" I stared at the video in shock. Alex and I were kissing. But not just kissing, I mean, really,

really kissing. Tongues, open mouths, hands . . . We both watched in total silence and jaw-dropping shock, until the video cut out.

There was silence in the car after that.

"Well, that was—" I started but didn't know what else to say.

"Interesting," Alex offered up.

"That's definitely one way of looking at it," I said.

We sat in silence again. And then both of our phones beeped with a message at the exact same time.

CHAPTER FORTY-FOUR

⟋⟍

$\mathscr{F}$ive words.

That was all. That was all we needed to be back on the road once more and heading straight back to where we had come from.

Julian: My wife is a hairdresser.

We drove in total silence back to the tropical beaches of Saint-Gilles where this whole adventure had started. The mood in the car was strange. We cast awkward smiles at each other and tried to make small talk the entire time, but nothing was really clicking.

Two words.

The video.

Images from that video were running through my mind over and over again, and whenever I looked at Alex, all I could see was his mouth. Lips. Tongue. Soft hands. Face. And I wanted them. I wanted them all, and not necessarily in that order and that thought made me feel very unsettled and somewhat confused.

We finally arrived at the address that Julian had sent us.

Immediately, I could see that this was a much more civilized place. A row of pretty shops were set along a strip by the marina and hers was the third one. Its front was painted in a bright turquoise with gold lettering written above the door . . .

Halo.

Now that, that was a much better name for a hair salon. We walked inside and were greeted immediately by a bubbly redhead. She introduced herself as Emma, Julian's wife. She had even cleared her schedule to help us, since this was such an " 'emergency," and we were Julian's friends.

My hair was not that hard to undo. The plaits that Salome had put in weren't very good and some had already started coming loose. But once all the plaits were out, I had something that resembled a poodle. Emma gave me a quick wash and blow and soon my hair was back to normal. No one would ever know that I had once rocked braids and beads . . . except all those people who'd seen my social media over the last twenty-four hours, which was a lot. I'd also received some fairly interesting messages from my friends, mainly wondering if I was okay, had I lost my mind, why was I playing with a sex doll and why did I look like Destiny's Child? The usual thing you would expect from caring friends. Except for that one message where Stormy-Rain actually thought I looked amazing.

Emma started on Alex. She said it would take a little longer, so I excused myself and went for a walk along the marina. It really was quite beautiful here. A row of palm trees ran the length of the water's edge. Small boats bobbed up and down in the crystal-clear waters, swaying to the invisible current. The air was warm and smelt fresh and salty.

I continued my walk; all the way up, and then back all the way down. A pharmacy caught my eye, and I quickly went inside. I can't resist a pharmacy, they always have interesting things, besides, I needed some more deodorant. I walked the aisles and found the deodorant, then something caught my eye and I moved over to them. Various boxes and packets of wax.

"Mmmm." I bent down and took a closer look. I might need one of those. So I grabbed one. With all my stuff safely in a bag, I headed back out, just in time to see a dark-haired Alex walk out of the salon and into the sun.

I stopped and watched him. His hair wasn't the same as before. That gorgeous salt and pepper hair was gone, now it was a dark, rich, warm, brown. But he looked amazing. *God, he was really hot, wasn't he?* I mean, I knew he was hot, but all of a sudden, he looked even hotter. Hotness level . . . killing it. Hot AF. So damn . . . and he was nice. More than nice. Kind, funny, interesting and he'd kissed me like *that* and told me I was beautiful. Now why couldn't I have met a man like him instead of one like Matt? My finger itched and I scratched it, something caught on my nail and I looked down. The ribbon was starting to fray around the edges and a long green thread had come loose. I tried to snap it but it didn't work and now I had a long thread dangling from my hand. I sighed and looked back up just in time to see Alex run his hands through his hair. The muscles in his arm and shoulder rippled through his clothing. Then he pulled his phone out of his pocket, almost in slow motion. He flipped his hair again and then raised his phone to his face. His big, strong, smooth hands holding the phone tightly. His fingers moved deftly over the phone screen. Nimble perfect fingers, surgeon's fingers. I watched him, totally intoxicated by everything he was doing right now. And then suddenly . . .

"AAAHH!" I screamed, jumped and dropped my packet on the floor when my cell phone rang in my bag. It was so loud and had caught me so off guard that I'd almost fallen over in fright. The shout had caused Alex to look in my direction. He smiled over at me and waved his phone in the air, indicating that he'd been the one calling me.

I scrambled to pick my shopping up off the floor as Alex came running over.

"Let me." He bent down and grabbed my things, slipping them back into the bag.

"Thanks." *So nice.* "Your hair looks good." I indicated.

He smiled. "Much better."

"Much." I smiled back at him.

"I managed to get us back into the same hotel we were staying at, by the way. I hope you don't mind?" he asked politely.

"Oh. Thanks," I said.

"So we should go and book back in."

"So much for our big road trip," I said, shrugging and starting to walk back towards the car.

"What do you mean?" he asked.

"Well, it's not exactly like we adventured very far and long. And we don't really even remember a whole chunk of it either. Other than some very embarrassing bits."

"At least we have all the photos and the videos to fill in the blanks," he said. His voice had an edge to it. Teasing, yet . . . something else.

His voice made me stop walking. "At least," I whispered back to him, feeling my blood heat.

"So let's go home." Alex draped his arm around my shoulders then stopped.

"What happened?" He raised my hand to his face and looked at it.

"The ribbon seems to be unraveling," I said.

He looked at the ribbon intently and then raised it to his mouth. "You mind?" he asked.

I shook my head. Alex gripped my hand tightly, raised his teeth to the string and tried to bite it off. It didn't work, though and only made it unravel more. Alex started pulling the loose thread, and with every pull, the ring became thinner and thinner and thinner, until the thread finally snapped. We both looked down at the ribbon on my finger.

"Mmmmm," Alex mumbled.

"What?" I looked up at him, he was still staring down at my hand.

He shrugged. "It's almost gone," he said quietly, thoughtfully.

"It is," I echoed.

He raised his other hand and put it next to mine. His ribbon was still very much intact.

"Yours is fine," I said. It was almost a question, although I wasn't sure what the answer to that would be, or what I was really asking with my question.

"Good," he said, pulling his hand away from mine.

Something stabbed me in the stomach. A painful, uncomfortable feeling. "Good," I echoed. "Maybe I should tie a new one around me?" I asked.

He looked up at me momentarily, our eyes locked for a second and then he looked away. "I'm sure we can find another one in the hotel," he offered.

"Sure," I said, feeling somewhat sad, I didn't quite know why.

We started walking back to the car in total silence and then headed for our hotel.

CHAPTER FORTY-FIVE

After checking in, we headed back to the bar. Julian was there to greet us with two pink cocktails. We slid into our usual seats and sat down.

"You guys look much better," Julian said, sliding the drinks over to us.

"Your wife is amazing," I said, taking a much needed sip.

"She is. But you don't have to tell me that," he said sweetly. "You know, I met her right here. She sat exactly where you guys are sitting now." He then looked at us strangely. "Who knows, maybe this is a lucky spot to fall in love." He met my eyes and seemed to be trying to convey something to me. Then he looked at Alex, giving him the same kind of look.

"Are you okay?" I asked him.

"Are you guys okay?" he asked back.

"We're good," I said. I tried to sound casual and chilled but somehow it hadn't come out exactly in the way I planned for it to.

It sounded more panicky and on edge, which was how I felt. I just wasn't too sure why, though.

"Really? Anything happen that I should know about?" He looked from Alex to me and then back again.

Alex seemed to stiffen up in his seat a little, then shuffled from side to side a few times. "No. All good," he said, sipping his drink.

"If you guys say so," Julian teased.

I scrunched my face up at him. *What was he getting at here?*

"So what's next on your list?" Julian asked.

What was next actually? That was a good question. I took the magazine out of my bag and laid it on the bar. I ran my finger down the page. Everything was ticked. Except for the last one.

"Shit!" I said.

"What?" Julian asked.

"We've done them all, except for the last one." How the hell had I forgotten about this last one?

"What's the last one?" Julian asked.

I started reading. " 'Number Ten. Get Over Him By Getting Under Someone Else. Well, you have come to the end of the list, and are now probably ready to take the biggest and most important step of all! This is the final step, the one that will launch you over the threshold and into your new life without him. It will turn you from pining ex to whining ex (whining someone else's name in bed, that is). Because it's true, the best way to get over someone, once and for all, is by getting under someone else. So book a sesh with the waxologist—and we don't mean for your brows. Pull out the lingerie and find someone else. He doesn't have to be a keeper—in fact, it's better if he's not. This isn't about getting into another relationship (remember number one). He just needs to be there to help you ride over that last hump—pun intended. And don't worry, it really is like riding a bicycle, once you're in the saddle, it should all come back to you.'"

There was a general pause after I'd finished reading as I think we all let it sink in. And then, suddenly, Julian burst out laughing.

"What?" I looked over at him.

He continued to laugh and shake his head at us. "Of all the people I've met here at the bar over the years, you two have to be the weirdest!"

"That's not true. You met a woman that killed her husband," I whispered over at him.

Julian continued to laugh. "You're so gullible. I only told you those stories so you would tell me yours."

"Bastard!" I exclaimed playfully.

Julian shrugged. "What can I say, I love a good story. So . . . where are you going to go to get laid?"

"Laid?" I suddenly flung my hands over my mouth and giggled uncontrollably. "That's such a trashy word."

"Well, it is what you're doing," he said to us.

Alex and I looked at each other and then Alex turned to Julian. "Any suggestions?"

"Well, it depends what you're into." He leaned over the bar, looking very comfortable. "The metal heads and the ones that dress in black hang out in Club X, the hipsters are all twirling their moustaches and sipping their artisan teas at This Is Not A Club, then there's Club Dungeon, but I wouldn't go there, unless you're into that kind of thing." He paused. "I mean, you could be?" He looked at us and raised his brows in question.

"What kind of thing?" Alex asked.

"You know . . . whips, chains, leather, latex, the occasional bloodletting and sex dolls?" Julian burst out laughing again.

Alex shook his head. "No, thanks. I think I've had enough of all that to last me a lifetime."

"I know." Julian snapped his fingers. "Go to Liquid. It's quite fancy, so you'll need to dress up, but the people there seem normal."

"Okay, thanks," I said.

Julian pulled out the famous bottle of tequila and three shot glasses.

"What's this for?"

"We'll have a drink together, to toast this moment." He poured us each a drink and we all held it. Then we threw the drinks back and brought the glasses back down to the bar with a loud thud.

"You guys won't go through with it, though," Julian said, sliding away from us.

"What?! Of course we will," I called after him.

"Sure you will." He sounded very sarcastic now.

"We will," Alex called after him. "We will both get laid tonight!"

"Whatever you say, but I bet it won't happen," he continued to tease.

"Watch us! Watch this space, Julian, you naysayer!" I shouted after him.

Julian threw his head back and let out a loud belly laugh.

"Val and I are so getting laid tonight," Alex said. Maybe a bit too loudly, though. Because suddenly people were looking at us. I tried to hold down a giggle. Alex turned slowly and through his clenched teeth said, "I think I said that too loudly."

"You think?" I quipped sarcastically. "I think that's our cue to leave," I whispered back to him.

"I think you're right." We got up and made our way back to the hotel. We checked in again—this time we were in different rooms. Alex walked me to my door.

"Meet in the reception in two hours?" he asked.

"Sure."

"All dressed up and looking beautiful," he said.

"I'll try my hardest." I opened the door and as I closed it I heard . . .

"You won't have to try very hard then."

CHAPTER FORTY-SIX

⌒

I walked into my room, and then collapsed onto the bed. Some of my hair fell into my face and I inhaled its scent. It smelt good, like jasmine. At least I would have good hair tonight, the rest I wasn't so sure about. I walked over to my suitcase and pulled out the dress that I'd worn to the ill-fated engagement party. It was the smartest thing I had. I pulled my engagement shoes out too, one still had dry mud clinging to the heel so I walked outside to clean it on the grass. I rubbed it several times before the thick mud started coming off. And then a familiar rustle in the bushes again . . .

I didn't even need to look up to know who was there.

"What?" I asked, tilting my head up and coming face to face with him. "Mmm?" I implored. He tilted his head down, as if he was looking at my shoe. Again, he looked like he was mocking me. Judging me.

"What? You also think I won't get laid tonight?" I asked him.

He raised his wrinkly little head and looked me straight in the eye as if he didn't believe me.

I scoffed. "Wait and see, my wrinkly friend. Just wait and see." I turned and walked back into my room, determined now. It was time to start getting ready. And if I was going to be scoring tonight, a little bit of pruning might be in order. I took the wax strips to the bathroom with me and closed the door.

I looked down at the box. It was a happy, pink-looking box. In retrospect, the box should have been red, with bright letters on it: "WARNING: this product has been forged in the flames of hell and will scald your vagina," or something dramatic like that. It promised *No mess, no fuss, no hot wax and clumps*. But it lied.

Still, I was getting laid tonight! That's right, people. L. A. I. D. Capitals. Laid. So there was no way I was going to let anyone navigate down there with it looking like the Amazon rain for- est. Besides, if I was hoping the guy was going to at least find the C-spot, there was no need to distract and confuse him with all the other things that were standing in the way of an actual orgasm. I'd almost forgotten how those felt, what with the lack of action I'd seen.

I pulled the strips out. I'd used these cold wax strips a few times before, they were usually pretty easy. I rubbed the strips between my hands and pulled a few apart, laying them carefully on the counter.

I was already in my underwear and pulled my panties down. Then I got myself into the right position, i.e., one leg up on the toilet seat. I tried not to look at myself in the mirror, this was by anyone's standards an incredibly undignified pose.

"Right. Okay." I looked down at it thoughtfully. *Which part to tackle first?* I wasn't going for a full bald eagle here, just a neat short back and sides. "Right," I said again, bending my head as far forward as I possibly could in order to get a full picture of the situation.

Once I'd decided to start from the outside and work my way inside, I grabbed a strip and placed it on. I patted and smoothed it down and then took a deep breath. This was going to hurt. I pulled the skin taut, as taut as I could. I could do this! I was a woman of the world, a brave traveler. I was *She-who-jumps-out-of-helicopters* and *She-who-runs-from-police*. I could do this. And then I ripped . . .

OMG! "Fuck, fuck, fuck it!" The pain. The agony! It exploded through my body and into my brain. I saw stars! I saw fuzzy white spots behind my eyelids, it was so intense I swear I lost conscious momentarily. The pain was blinding. It was disorientating, it was utterly destabilizing and suddenly I found myself falling backwards. I grabbed hold of the counter to stop myself, only to slide off it when one of my hands came down on a strip and slipped across the marble countertop. The other strips all fell to the floor and so did I.

"Ouch!" I winced. There was pain everywhere. My vagina felt like it was on fire, that was a given. My back and head had come into contact with the hard bathroom floor, and on my tumble down, my elbow had collided with the edge of the bath.

I lay there, flat on my back, looking up at the ceiling, catching my breath and coming to terms with what I'd just done to myself. Finally, once I was more *compos mentis*, I lifted my hands up and looked at them. In one hand was the wax strip that had caused all the pain. I was at least pleased to see it covered with a layer of hair—at least the pain hadn't been for nothing. On my other hand, a strip was stuck to my palm. I pulled it off and finally stood up.

I looked at myself in the mirror. "Bloody hell!" I had a neat, clean landing strip running down the left side that didn't match anything on the right! I couldn't leave it half undone now, *could I?* But I certainly didn't want to wax anymore since the landing strip was a rather alarming shade of red that I was hoping would simmer down before tonight. I turned and was about to reach for the soothing aloe vera cream that had come with the wax kit when I saw my back.

"Nooooo!" I tried to reach behind me, but my arms were not long enough. There, dotted across my back, right in the middle, were three wax strips. I'd seen them fall off the counter and I'd obviously landed on them.

"Shit!" I hissed, trying to bend my arms backwards in yoga-like positions that I had no business even attempting, since I'd never been to yoga in my life. But they remained *just* out of my reach. I took my bra off, hoping that would help. It didn't.

I looked around the bathroom and saw the detachable shower head. "Yes!" That would do. I climbed into the bath and detached the shower head. And looking over my one shoulder into the mirror, I tried to push the strips off with it, but they were stuck.

"Crapping hell!" They were going nowhere. And now I was left with only one other choice . . .

CHAPTER FORTY-SEVEN

"Hey, Alex," I said sweetly into the phone.

"Hey, Val," he imitated right back.

"So . . . you know how on the first night we met I sort of helped you out with an issue?"

"How can I forget?"

"Well, you know how you said if I ever needed help . . .?"

"Yes?" He sounded tentative. "Are your knees sore again?"

"No, it's not that body part, per se."

"What body part do you need help with this time?" His voice had a little lilt to it and for a second I wanted to say something else entirely, but didn't. "My back," I said. "I kind of have a waxing emergency."

"A what?"

"It's hard to explain, but I need your help," I said, turning my back to the mirror and looking at the strips again. They had been on there so long, they were making the skin pucker in horrible ripples. "I think you need to hurry. And please bring a razor too, if you have a spare one." I would need to take a different approach when it came to removing the rest of the hair.

Moments later Alex was knocking on my door. I wrapped a towel around me and waddled to the door. My vajayjay was still stinging and the friction from walking wasn't helping either. I hoped it would cool down soon, because no one in the club would want me if it looked like I was walking with a bird cage dangling between my legs.

"Hey." I opened the door and peered at him sheepishly.

"What happened?" he asked, coming in.

"Uh . . ." I turned around and then lowered the towel, exposing my back. "

"Ouch." I heard him wince and then felt a warm hand come up and touch my back. "Lie down on the bed," he said.

"Okay," I said feebly. I walked towards it and climbed on, careful not to let the towel slip too far. I tensed my body and waited.

"Try to relax," Alex said, sitting down next to me.

"That's all well and good for you to say," I mumbled into the bed. "You don't have strips of sticky devil paper stuck to your body."

I heard a small chuckle from Alex.

"Hey," I turned my head, "was I laughing when your face was suffocating under a layer of black muck? No! I don't think so."

"Sorry," he said. "But in my medical experience, I find things really do tend to hurt less if you're relaxed, if you know what I mean."

"Eeew!" I shook my head and buried it in the duvet. "Fine. I'm relaxing," I said, trying to convince myself of this, even though every single nerve and fiber and cell in my body was screaming something else entirely. "I am so relaxed right now," I whispered in a Zen voice. "I am soooo relaxed . . . like a leaf in a breeze, so, so relaxed soOOOO—"

I screamed as the first strip was ripped off. "WhYYY?" I wailed. "Warn me next time you do that!"

"Sorry, I thought it would be less painful if you didn't know it was coming."

"OWW!" I arched my back in pain once more as he ripped the next one off—again, no warning.

"Jesus, Alex!" I screamed. "I asked you to warnnnOOO—"

I screamed again as he did it a third time. This time I felt tears come to my eyes. I blinked a few times in absolute agony.

"All done!" Alex said quickly.

"Oh. My. God," I whimpered. This waxing had been the worst idea, ever. Well, that wasn't really true, now was it? The braids had been the worst idea. But this was a close second. I swear, if I didn't get laid after all this effort, pain and humiliation, then damn! I would be furious.

"It's okay, it's all over." And then, I felt his hand on my back once more. But this time it felt different. *Very.* It was warm and soft. He placed it on my shoulder at first, and then slowly, gently it trailed down my back, all the way along my spine, coming to a stop on my lower back. Suddenly, all the pain was gone, especially when his fingertips retraced the length of my back again. Up, up, up, down . . . down . . . down . . .

His fingers weren't stopping where they'd stopped before. This time they travelled further south. I felt the towel slide back a bit and his fingertips move even lower. I shivered. My skin pebbled and the hairs on my arms and back of my neck stood straight up.

His fingers finally came to rest right at the very bottom of my back, right where my back curved into my bottom.

"It's still sticky," he finally whispered after what had been a long silence. His voice sounded small and far away now.

"Yes," I replied, with an equally small, whispery voice. Truthfully, I was feeling somewhat entranced right now. The feeling of his warm hands grazing my back had left me spinning. And then, I felt him stand up. I heard him walk away. I looked over my shoulder, careful not to lift myself too far up that the towel exposed my naked front. *Or wait, did I care?* Did I want him to look at me there?

I raised myself up on my elbow, slightly exposing the side of my breast. *What was I doing?* I wasn't quite sure, but for some reason, I wanted Alex to look at me in that way. I didn't want him to see the fun girl that he'd been hanging out with, I wanted him to see me as more than that . . .

Alex walked out of the bathroom and stopped when he saw me. His eyes moved down to the spot I wanted him to look at. They seemed to linger there for a while, going from a light silvery gray to a darker stormy color that sent an excited shiver through me. And then, his eyes drifted up to mine and he held my gaze with such intensity and purpose that I felt myself melting into the mattress below him.

He broke eye contact and cleared his throat awkwardly. He moved towards me and I put my head back down. Soon, I felt a warm, wet soothing cloth being dragged over my skin. His movements were slow, gentle and the warm water felt good against my skin. He didn't say a word, and neither did I. Instead, he silently wiped the sticky patches off my back. I lay there, breathless and wordless. Something about this, no, *everything* about this felt less like wiping sticky patches and more like . . . like . . . *what?*

I felt his fingertips brush my lower back once more. A ball of hot energy exploded inside my stomach and radiated outwards from there, sort of making me . . . *oh God*, wait, what was going on . . . *was I* . . . ? Yes! Oh, yes. I was.

Turned on.

Big time.

I closed my eyes and let the feeling wash over me. It seemed to build with every slow stroke of the cloth on my back. And before I could stop myself, a breathy whisper escaped my lips. *Shit!* I hadn't meant for that to happen, and it had sounded so sexy and moany, the kind of noise you make during sex. Suddenly, with some panic, I wondered if Alex knew what I was feeling. And then I wondered if Alex was feeling the same thing too? *Was he doing this on purpose?* It felt like it.

The pressure on my back got firmer suddenly. Alex seemed to have moved from a gentle wipe to a somewhat firmer massage. And all of a sudden, nothing about this felt like Alex and me. This felt like two totally different people doing something else entirely.

His hands continued to work the length of my back, his fingers glided over my shoulders and he ran them up into the nape of my neck and up into my hair. I tilted my head forward to give him even more access. His fingers tangled in my hair and then his fingertips traced the side of my ears.

My body physically reacted to his touch. He'd never touched me like this before, and once again, I was overcome with a desire to roll over and look at him, and let him touch me somewhere else. His hands left my neck again and moved over my shoulders once more and then, it really changed, when his hands moved to the sides of my back. I held my breath with anticipation. I didn't have to wait long. His hands worked their way down my sides, and slowly, softly, his fingers grazed the side of my breasts . . .

I inhaled sharply as a wave of pleasure vibrated through me from head to toe. So intense and heady that I felt drunk on the pleasure.

What was happening? I wanted to turn around so badly. I wanted his hands on the front of me, my breasts, my face, my . . .

And as quickly as it started, it stopped. I felt him get up. I heard his footsteps on the floor and then heard the door. I looked up just as he closed the door and walked out of the room.

I sat up in bed and stared after him. *What the hell had just happened?*

CHAPTER FORTY-EIGHT

⌒

I was ready. I looked at myself in the mirror. The pretty pink dress that I'd worn to the engagement party and the high heels looked different with my hair and make-up like this. I'd found some red lipstick in my bag and put it on. I'd also given myself a very dark smoky eye. My hair was down, tumbling over my shoulders, and I looked good. I *did* still have it. I just hadn't realized that in a while. Alex had brought a razor and I'd managed to even myself out. I took a deep breath and walked out my room, heading down the long corridor towards the reception where, yes, as always, he was waiting for me.

"Wow." He stood up and stared at me as I walked in, my heels clicking loudly on the marble floor.

I spun around for him slowly, careful not to fall off my heels. "I clean up well," I joked.

"Yeah. You do." He was staring at me. Eyes sweeping up and down, looking at me as if he'd never seen me before. As if this was the first time he was looking at me. I froze and I let him look. I liked the way it felt. My body responded, the places where his hands had been earlier seemed to wake up and twitch and tingle. I exhaled slowly and then started walking up to him.

"Shall we?" I stopped in front of him and looked straight in his eyes. I could almost see myself reflected in them they were so silvery. He didn't say a word. He just nodded and we walked out together.

Half an hour later we were seated at a bar at the nightclub. The club was an assault on all my senses. Strobing lights, the loud repetitive sounds of bassy house music, the throngs of hot, sweating scantily clothed people who all looked at least five to ten years younger than us. And to make matters worse, things between Alex and me felt strange. We hadn't spoken in the taxi here, and we were hardly speaking now. No one had mentioned what had happened in the room and I was starting to wonder if maybe I'd imagined it.

"So . . ." I finally had to break this enduring silence. "Now what?" I asked.

"I don't know. I've been off the market longer than you have, I'm hoping to take your lead on this."

"My lead?" I sipped my drink (more like slurped it). "God, if you're thinking of following me on this one, we'll be here all night," I said after another long slurp.

Alex shrugged. "I've never gone out to a place looking for sex before."

"Me neither," I confessed. "I mean, there have been times where I've gone out hoping that that could potentially be where the evening went, but I've also never done this."

Alex nodded, and I could see him faltering. If he backed out of this, I would too, and I would be relieved.

"NO! No!" he suddenly said. "We made a promise to get

through this whole list." He held his hand up and wiggled his ring finger, green ribbon firmly in place.

I nodded slowly, disappointed that he'd suddenly pulled himself together. "We did," I said softly. We sat in silence for a while longer, and although we sat right next to each other on the barstools, I could sense a massive elephant sitting between us.

I looked at Alex. He was sipping his drink and looking down at his shoes. For someone who'd come looking for sex, I didn't think he would find it down there. He looked up slowly and our eyes met again. I tried to think of something to say, but the elephant seemed to be holding my tongue.

"Okay." Alex sat up a little more confidentially this time. "Okay!" he repeated.

"Okay?" I asked.

"We can do this," he said. "We can do this." He said it again, a little slower this time, as if trying to convince himself.

I nodded. "Okay. Shall we do it then?"

"Yes. Cool." He put his drink down on the counter and turned his attention back to the people in front of us. "What about her?" he asked, pointing at someone across the floor.

"Eeeww, no!" I shook my head. "I don't want you to catch a dreaded disease."

"Not her then." Alex scanned the dance floor some more. I did the same thing. But this was so bizarre. We were sitting here choosing people to potentially sleep with, and honestly, I had no desire whatsoever to sleep with any one of them. *And I didn't want Alex to either* . . . But I played along. I had to.

"What about him, for me?" I asked, pointing at a man at the other end of the bar.

"What?" Alex almost shouted. "For you?" He shook his head. "Not good enough."

"Really? I think he's quite hot, though?"

"No. Definitely not." Alex turned my face away from him and forced me to look somewhere else. "Over my dead body." He sounded rather firm.

"Fine," I conceded and continued to scan the room. "Him?" I pointed at another guy sitting alone at a table.

Alex tilted his head to the side. "He looks like a serial killer."

I threw my hands in the air. "If you're going to disapprove of every one, how am I going to do this?"

Alex looked around the club. "But they're all so . . . so . . ."

"So what?" I asked, tapping my fingers on the bar counter.

"Not good enough for you." Alex's eyes met mine and something shot through me.

"How do you know that?" I asked.

"Because I know you and . . . look at them." Alex waved his hand from left to right.

"We *are* in a nightclub. This is not exactly the kind of place one comes to when looking for a quality Prince Charming. Besides, isn't that kind of the point?"

Alex looked at me again and sighed. The colors from the flashing lights lit up his gray eyes that just seemed to be acting as mirrors now. "Fine. That one in the other corner looks somewhat okay." He gestured and I looked. I took another sip of my drink and stood up. I was going to do this. I was going to walk over to him and say "hi".

I looked at Alex, hoping he might stop me. But he didn't. So I turned and started a very, very slow walk across the club. Down the steps onto the dance floor, across the dance floor, past some tables, past another bar and then . . . I stopped. *What was I thinking?* I couldn't fucking do this. This wasn't me. I turned around and was just about to walk back when I saw Alex . . .

He wasn't alone anymore. My stomach tightened. That hadn't taken long. I hadn't been gone for two minutes and he was already laughing and drinking with a hot brunette. I watched them for a while. She put her hand on his shoulder and then giggled.

"Pppsht!" I tsked loudly. She flicked her hair and then leaned forward; I'm sure aware that her dress gaped in the front. Bitch!

Well, now I had to do it!

I wasn't *not* going to have sex tonight if Alex was! I turned back around and walked to the man in the corner.

CHAPTER FORTY-NINE

One drink. Two drinks. Some laughter. Some hand-touching. Another drink. More laughter—*mostly his*. A hair flip. Another drink. Another drink.

His name was George. He lived here. He was single. Twenty-seven. Good-looking. And I was trying really hard to flirt and like him. But an hour in, I just wasn't feeling it. At some point I happened to look over my shoulder, to see what Alex was doing and . . . *he was kissing her!*

My mouth fell open. This couldn't be happening. I was not going to let this happen. Alex getting lucky, and me not. I turned back to George, looked down at his lips and then just went for it. I smashed my lips into his and kissed him. He tasted like brandy and mint and the combination was making my stomach churn.

I kissed him with one eye open as I watched Alex and the tarty brunette get more acquainted. It was revolting, *she was basically eating his face!*

And then Alex started walking over to us. I stopped kissing George as Alex appeared.

"Hey," I said to him. Tart-a-lot was now draped across him like a cheap feather boa.

"Hey." He sounded somewhat awkward. "I think we're going to head back to the hotel, will you be okay here—"

"I think we'll come too." I jumped up. "Right, George?" I looked over at George who seemed confused for a moment or two and then shrugged.

"Sure, sounds good."

* * *

I arrived at my room with the guy that I was now meant to have sex with. Alex was also there with Alessandreeeeee (eeeee eee e eeee). That was her name, by the way. She was French and oh God, she was awful. And it wasn't just her name that was rubbing me up the wrong way with its too many vowel sounds, it was absolutely everything about her. I don't think I've ever taken such an instant dislike to someone before as I had to this woman. We all stopped at my door and stood there in complete silence, until I broke it.

"Well, this is me," I said awkwardly, opening the door to my hotel room and looking over at Alex. I was waiting for him to say something, I just didn't exactly know what. "This is me," I said again.

Alex nodded. "Indeed it is. Number twelve," he said, looking at me as if he wanted me to say something. This was confirmed when he raised a brow in query.

"Mmmmm?" I asked, rising my brow back at him.

"What?" he asked back.

"Huh?" I replied, looking at him pointedly.

Alex started nodding his head. "Nothing. All good."

"You sure?" I continued to press him.

This time he shook his head. "Yup." But he continued to shake his head. "Everything is dandy."

"Dandy?" Alessandreeeeee suddenly giggled. "You English-men are très cute." She kissed his cheek and Alex widened his eyes at me. I quickly looked away.

"We better be getting inside then," I said.

"Unless . . ." Alex started speaking and then paused.

"Unless, what?" I asked quickly.

"We could all go for another drink first, I mean . . . if you . . . uh—" Alex said.

"I've already had a drink," Alessandreeeeee said coolly. *I hated her.* This trashy French temptress that was hanging all over Alex like a pair of crotchless panties on a washing line.

"I'm okay, thanks," George said.

"Okay, then." Alex looked over at me. "You heard them." He smiled at me. It was a large, broad toothy grin that seemed more like the kind a court jester might give.

"Coooooool." I really extended that word. "I guess we better be going inside then." I stumbled over the words awkwardly, my mouth feeling drier by the second.

"Sure. Us too," Alex said. Alessandreeeeee sighed and tapped her impatient high-heeled foot. I wondered if it would be rude to step on her little pink toes?

"Good!" I said, and then did something fairly cringeworthy and horrific. I shot Alex two thumbs-ups.

"Yes. Great!" Alex shot me a thumbs-up too and I turned and started walking into my room, George hot on my heels.

"So, see you at breakfast," I heard Alex say from behind me and I turned.

"Sure."

"Table for four?" He gave me another corny thumbs-up and I did the same again. "Or as you guys say, *quatre*." And then he burst out laughing. A strange laugh that seemed more like the kind you make under dire circumstance; like you cut your finger off in a woodwork accident and land up laughing nervously when you see it lying at your feet. No wait, no one laughs when they cut off a finger, *what was I thinking?* Shit, I wasn't thinking.

I looked over at George. *Seriously, what the fuck was I thinking?* Could I back out of this now, or had I taken it too far already? Of course I had, curious George was now walking around in my hotel room looking at things.

I shut the door behind me, not before looking down the corridor one more time. When I did, Alessandreeeeee giggled as she smacked Alex on the bum. I think I tasted vomit in my mouth.

"So . . ." I turned to George who was sitting on the bed expectantly and, *Oh dear Lord*, the man had started unbuttoning his shirt.

"A DRINK!?" I screamed and rushed over to the minibar, bending down to get something out of it. "Yes, a drink will definieeeee—"

I jumped when I felt a hand on *my* bum. It felt so foreign and unexpected and *wrong*. Alex hadn't jumped at Alessandreeeeee's hand, though. In fact, I bet he'd liked it. Loved it.

"Oooh, uh . . ." I took a few big steps back. George was peeling his shirt off now and advancing towards me. He had a hairy chest,

I didn't mind that, the thing I did mind was the shiny gold medallion that was nesting in it like a buried treasure. I couldn't take my eyes off it. It glinted and glistened in the overhead lights and now it was absolutely all I could see. George didn't have a face, or arms, or legs anymore. George was just a big gold medallion coming towards me. *I should never have brought him back to my room.*

"You're so sexy," he whispered seductively as he moved towards me like a sleazy Casanova. *Oh God, oh God, oh God. What was I doing?*

"Mmmmm." I nodded and kept walking backwards. He kept advancing, he tried to look me in the eye and send me smoldering, sexy vibes—at least I think that was what he was doing. It was all so confusing and suddenly I didn't quite feel like I was even there. I was with Alex, imagining what he was doing. He was probably knee-deep in Alessandreeeeee already. I wondered what kind of things she would be saying to him.

"*Oui, oui. S'il vous plaît. Je voudrais une grande baguette.*"

Or whatever else she would scream out while banging her sweaty fists on the wall, since I'd let Alex in on the secrets of fist-banging.

"Your lips . . ." Casanova was upon me now, mere inches from my face. All husky voiced and dreamy, sexy-eyed. "So succulent and juicy," he continued.

"Mmmm," I mumbled, trying to hide the sheer cringe that I was experiencing right now.

And then his hands were on my face and his lips were on mine. His lips were so moist and big, and they covered the entire bottom half of my face. His tongue was so large and wet. He was not a good kisser. I bet Alessandreeeeee was a good kisser.

"Shall we get a little more comfortable?" George pulled away and led me to the bed.

The moment had come! This was it. He sat down on the bed and then he pulled me onto his lap. This time I definitely tasted vomit in my mouth. I bet Alessandreeeeee wasn't tasting vomit right now. I bet she was tasting something else entirely—

"I'm sorry!" I launched myself off George like a rocket. "I can't do this. I thought I could, but I can't. I'm sorry."

"What are you talking about?" he asked, looking totally shocked.

"I shouldn't have brought you here. I'm just not ready for . . . uh, this. I think you should go."

George looked at me and soon his shock gave way to profound confusion, which then gave way to something else.

He stood up and put his shirt back on. "It's that other guy, isn't it?"

"What guy?"

"Alex?" He sounded a bit pissed now.

"What?" I spat out. "NO! God, what do you mean? Pppsshhtt." I made a strange sound that I wished I hadn't made because it sounded so ridiculous.

George eyed me suspiciously. "Sure." His voice dripped with sarcasm. "Whatever you say." He started walking for the door and I was totally and utterly relieved. Then he turned and looked at me.

"Good luck with him." He smiled. Cruelly. "I don't think he's put an end to what he's doing." He exited and I was left standing all alone in the room feeling terrible.

CHAPTER FIFTY

⌒

I walked through the garden, an itchy, sick feeling brewing in my stomach. The thought that Alex was having sex with someone else made me feel queasy. And not just anyone else, but heeeeeeer. The girl with way to many "eeeeeee's" in her name. But I bet she was good in bed, one of those uninhibited French types. Up for anything. A real fun-time kind of gal!

Every time I imagined what was happening, my skin crawled and my heart raced. It wasn't pleasant. And not even the tranquil surroundings of the garden that I'd been walking in for ten minutes already were helping. So I headed to the beach hoping that the soft sounds of the lapping waves would help quell the quease. I tried not to look in the direction of Alex's room, but couldn't help it. The door was closed, the blinds had been dropped and the light inside was dim . . . definitely set up for sex.

My mind ran away with me for a second as I wondered what kind of sex they would be having. *Shit!* Stop imagining him having sex, I mentally scolded myself and kept walking towards the beach. But as I got closer a familiar figure came into view. I stopped and looked at it. He looked at me with such cool, calm, flat, dead wasteland eyes that it made me furious. I stormed up to him and crouched down on the floor so that we were eye to eye.

"You were right, okay? Are you happy now? Is that what you want to hear, you beastly, prehistoric devil turtle? Huh?" I glared at him and he didn't blink.

"Val?" I heard a voice and my head snapped up. At first I couldn't see where the familiar voice was coming from.

"Is that you?" the voice asked. I stood up and looked around. And there, in the distance . . . Alex. He was dripping wet and standing in the calm sea.

"Alex?" I called out.

"Who were you talking to?" He started walking towards me and stepped straight into a cool shaft of soft moonlight. *Wow!* Breath stolen. Heartbeat skipped. He was drenched in a silvery light and I had never seen him looking so good before. There was something almost ethereal about him.

He came even closer. "Well, that was quick." He cleared his throat and looked awkward.

"You too," I said, sounding equally awkward.

I walked onto the beach and stopped. Alex was now ankle-deep in the water. He wasn't wearing a shirt and drops of water were sliding down him like warm, gooey chocolate. I stared in awe. *What else was I meant to do?* He was just so magnificent and manly and wet and hard and I wanted to reach out and touch him. In several places.

"I didn't . . ." Alex suddenly said. "We didn't . . . have sex." He closed the gap between us.

"You didn't have sex?" I asked, the inflection of my voice shot up, as if I was excited.

"But well done to you!" He gave me another strange double-thumbs-up; it looked so forced.

I shook my head. "I didn't either," I admitted quickly. "I tried. But I couldn't."

"Me too," he said. "I don't think picking women up in bars and bringing them back to my hotel room is my thing." He smiled.

"Oh, so Alessandreeeeee is not your kind of thing?" I couldn't help the sarcasm in my voice.

"Not really actually."

"I thought Alessandreeeeee would be everyone's kind of thing." Still with that sarcasm.

Alex smiled. "She might be everyone else's, but she's not mine."

I smiled back at him. "George wasn't my kind of thing either."

We both looked at each other and then, perfectly timed, both let out long, loud sighs. I put my hands on my hips and stared at Alex.

"I feel like we've come this far, though . . ." he started. "I mean, we've done everything else on the list, except this." His eyes drifted down to his hand and he started picking at the green ribbon around his finger.

"I know," I said. "And I even waxed and shaved my . . . *you know!*"

He smiled. "And I read all your articles on the G-spot in preparation, just in case I needed some refreshing."

"Really? Where did you read them?" I asked.

"Online. I Googled you and I've subscribed to the magazine online, so whenever you write something, I'll be notified immediately."

"You did?" Something about that made me really happy. "Well,

I'm sure if you'd gone all the way, Alessandreeeeee would have really appreciated that."

"I thought so too. It's a pity I didn't get to try all my newly acquired tips. And I'm sure George would have appreciated all the landscaping you went to such painstaking effort to do." He smiled playfully.

"Thank you, I appreciate you saying that." I smiled back at him. "It's just such a waste that it remains unseen."

"I couldn't agree more." Alex started nodding, and then mid nod, his smile began to falter and he started looking at me in that way that he'd looked at me the other day.

"What?" I asked nervously. My heart starting pounding in the back of my throat.

"When last did you go for a midnight swim in the sea?" he asked.

"Never."

"It's very refreshing. And it clears your head." He started walking backwards into the sea once more.

"Is that why you were swimming? Clearing your head?" I asked.

He held his hands out and beckoned me. "Come."

I looked around to see if anyone was there. The coast was clear. So I pulled my dress off over my head and tossed it in the sand.

"Nice underwear," Alex said.

"Thank you." I stepped into the water. It was so warm and clear.

Alex continued to walk backwards until the water was at his waist. I followed him in and soon I was standing opposite him.

"We did make a deal though," he almost whispered. "To get through the whole list, together."

"We did."

"It would be criminal not to honor it, wouldn't it?" Alex said.

"Definitely." I swallowed hard, the tension that was building in the space between us was electric.

"I mean . . ." He paused for the longest time. Tension building and building until I almost felt sick from it. And then he finally spoke, "*We could?*" His words instantly set me on fire.

"We could," I replied breathily.

"Only if you wanted to," he added quickly.

"Do you want to?" I bit my lip; the excitement was almost too much to contain inside me.

"Only if you do." His eyes drifted down to my mouth and I felt them burn.

"We did make that other promise too," I said, letting my eyes drift down to his lips too.

"Rule number one?" Alex asked, still staring at my mouth.

"Mmmm," I mumbled.

Alex took a small step towards me. "It wouldn't be like that," he pointed out, bringing his eyes up to mine. "It would be two friends, helping each other out." He started leaning towards me. "Just two buddies helping each other out," he said again, softly and slowly. He'd leaned so close that his lips were mere centimeters away from mine, I could feel his breath on my face.

"Two buddies . . ." I echoed.

He nodded. "It's the least we could do for each other. After everything we've been through."

"The very least," I said breathily.

"The absolute least," he echoed.

"It's just sex," I said.

"Just sex," he repeated, and then his lips came down on mine.

CHAPTER FIFTY-ONE

I was expecting fireworks, and explosions, and crazy heat and hunger like that video of us, but it wasn't like that at all, and it threw me.

The world stopped and everything ceased to exist. The only thing that existed were his lips on mine. His lips . . . so slow and searching. As if they were trying to pull something out of me. Fetch something from deep inside. He brushed them against mine softly, like the touch of a butterfly wing. I parted my lips because I wanted, *needed*, more of him.

He paused and exhaled into my mouth. I breathed in deeply, filling my lungs with the sweetest smelling air. And then he slid the tip of his tongue into my mouth. Warm, wet, soft. My tongue met his and as if they had known each other their entire lives, they started engaging in a complicated, intricate, sensual dance. Somehow they knew every step.

His hands were on my back. Squeezing, kneading my flesh

between his fingers. Gripping at me hungrily. I pulled him closer until my breasts were flattened against his hard, strong chest.

The kiss deepened. It didn't speed up, we stayed in that slow, steady rhythm that made my limbs feel like they were floating and melting all at once. The dance in our mouths reached a crescendo; our tongues stroking, massaging, lapping at each other.

But when we realized that there was no way of being buried deeper in each other's mouths than we were right now, the kiss changed.

Fast. Hot. Demanding. Furious and needy. Greedy for more. Any rhythm we had was gone now. It was rough and the movements jagged. His hands travelled lower and he cupped my ass, squeezing hard. And then, in one swift movement, he lifted me. I gasped immediately but wrapped my legs around his waist tightly, clinging on like I never wanted to let go. I wrapped my arms around his neck, laced my fingers in his hair and pulled his head back. I kissed his exposed neck and then he moaned as I ran my tongue up the length of his neck. I tasted cologne. It was bitter on my tongue.

Alex held onto me tighter. He started moving me up and down against him. Against his big hard length. This time I moaned as the pleasure shot through me like lightning. The waves around us lapped violently as he moved me faster and faster. I clung onto him, unable to kiss now I was so overwhelmed by pure pleasure of this moment. And then . . .

"Oh God," I moaned loudly. This hadn't happened in a while! In a long, long, *long* while. But that didn't mean that I'd forgotten how good it felt. It hit me hard and fast and unrelenting. Not stopping. My muscles stiffened and I clung to him. My body shook uncontrollably as the last wave rushed through me; up my stomach, across my breasts, up my neck, into my face, lips, eyes and out the top of my head.

And when it was over, I was rendered limp. Like a marionette puppet with its strings cut. With my head buried in his neck I tried to catch my breath again. My heart pounded against his chest like it was trying to escape. Like it wanted to crawl into him and be a part of him in some way.

After a few moments, Alex let go of me and I slipped slowly down his body and back into the water. Like melting ice-cream down the side of a cone in summer. I was almost in a liquid state now and think I would have puddled into the sea had Alex not wrapped an arm around me and kept me standing.

I slowly raised my head and looked at him.

He was looking down at me now as if I was the only thing that existed to him. No one had ever looked at me like that before. With such singular, intense focus.

He lowered his lips back down to mine, planting a small kiss.

"Come," he said, extending his hand for me to take.

"Where?" I asked dreamily.

"We're only just getting started." He took my hand and we began walking back to the beach together.

CHAPTER FIFTY-TWO

*M*y skin was hot, but his fingertips were cold against my back as he unclasped my bra. He pulled it down slowly, letting the rough lace graze my nipples as he went. A dizzying sensation was building in me, and had been since we'd walked into my room. *But he did nothing.* My hunger was being teased and tormented. My patience was being stretched to breaking point. Anticipation grew until it was a caged animal that begged to be released. I'd told him to tease, but I needed him to release me from this torture as I stood in front of him, breasts bare and exposed, and all he did was look at me.

"Please," I finally whispered when I couldn't take any more of it.

"Please what?" he asked. His voice was sex and desire.

"Touch me." I reached out and took his hands in mine, bringing them down and placing them on my waist.

"But then I would have to stop looking at you," he said. His voice was laced with the kind of awe and admiration that a woman can only ever dream of hearing.

His obvious desire for me filled me with a kind of confidence that I had never known before, so I took a few steps backward, until he could see all of me. Head to toe. I'd never done anything quite like this before. But I was going to do it now. *For him.* Because he was looking at me like *that*, making me feel like the sexiest woman that had ever existed.

I placed my hands on my stomach and then slowly dragged them down until my fingers slipped into the top of my panties. Alex's eyes widened as he stared at my hands with such concentration. Slowly, teasingly, I pulled just the one side down over my hip. Alex let out a long breath, I could see how turned on he was. How he was hanging on my every move. But what I didn't realize was how turned on I would be showing myself to him. Fireworks were going off inside me, shocking back to life parts of me that had been dead for so long.

I started to pull the other side down and I didn't stop this time. I let my panties fall, pool around my feet, and I stood there in front of him totally naked. His eyes moved over me in slow circles. Looking at every single inch of me. My body was now throbbing for him. My chest was rising and falling as my breath came out in short, sharp bursts as if I was panting. He wasn't even touching me yet.

"Please," I begged again.

Alex walked up to me slowly. His shirt was off, but he was still wearing his bathing trunks. I wanted them off. He stood in front again and just as I was about to reach out and pull those pants off him, he dropped to his knees in front of me.

"Oh my God," I gasped, shuddered, and my whole body shook as he placed a kiss on my inner thigh. The kisses moved higher and I reached down and gripped the top of his head as it nuzzled between my legs, pushing them open a little more.

"Since you went to so much effort . . ." he whispered against my inner thigh. I started giggling but stopped the second his mouth came down on me. His lips and tongue came into contact with that place that made me cry out immediately. I looked down at him, worshiping at my altar. I gripped his head tighter, holding it in place as he worked some kind of magic that made me feel like gravity no longer existed. I was floating and then I was clenching every muscle in my body and panting until I finally moaned. Loud, long guttural. Coming from a primitive place inside me that I wasn't able to hold back.

He slid back up me, dragging his fingertips over my body as he went. But as soon as he was there, I dropped down to my knees. Before I'd even touched him, he let out a breathy moan. I tugged at his pants, pulling them off and immediately, without any hesitation, I drew him into my mouth. His entire body shuddered and the more I did it, the more he seemed to shake and tremble, until he stopped me and pushed my head away.

"Stop," he said breathlessly. And I loved it. I loved knowing that I had almost taken him there just with my mouth. He pulled me to my feet and walked me backwards until I reached the bed. Then he pushed me forcefully and I fell back onto it with a bounce. He quickly climbed on top of me, pressing his body into mine. The weight of him crushed me into the bed. I felt so overpowered now, in the best way possible.

He brought his mouth down and kissed me slowly and gently once more. His mouth left mine and he trailed small kisses over my chin and onto my neck. The kisses moved down to my collarbones and then lower, until he reached my breasts. I arched my back, making it quite clear what I wanted. That I wanted his mouth on them, his tongue circling and his teeth nipping. And he gave that to me. And more. It all felt so delicious and I was almost delirious from all the pleasure crashing through me. A ball of frenzied energy was starting to build deep inside me now. It set my insides on fire and made me writhe and thrash and it made me want more . . . I only wanted one thing now, though. I needed him inside me, touching that energy inside.

"Please," I was begging again. I pulled his head back up to my mouth and opened my legs for him to slip between. I reached behind me and grabbed at my bag, it was on the bedside table. I scrabbled frantically for the condom that I'd found in the club bathroom. "Please," I begged again and almost threw it at him.

I closed my eyes. I heard the wrapper being ripped open. I heard the snap of the latex and I braced myself. *Anticipation. Want. Need.* I felt like I was going to explode if I didn't have him. Now.

And then in one movement that caused me to cry out, he drove inside me. I threw my head back as he moved in and out of me with a hard, fast, deliberate rhythm. I heard myself saying his name over and over again in a whimper as he pushed my knees up against my chest as that ball of energy inside me ignited and exploded.

And then he stopped moving. "Look at me. Open your eyes," I heard Alex say when my head stopped spinning and I stopped seeing stars behind my eyelids. I obeyed him. He was so close to me now. His nose touching mine. His eyes boring into me. And then, slowly, so slowly, he started moving inside me again. Oh God, was this really *just* sex?

I grabbed the sides of his face and held him in place, looking into his eyes. His pupils were big and dilated and his eyes dark and stormy. Our hearts started beating together as one, beating against our chests as we rocked back and forth in a motion so slow, small and subtle.

"Val," he whispered, not breaking eye contact.

"Yes?" I whispered back.

He shook his head slightly. "I don't know," he said, a tiny moan escaping his lips.

"What?" I asked, raising my hips up and grinding them against him slowly.

"I don't know if I can put it into words," he said. His voice coming out in jagged little bursts.

"Then don't use words," I said breathily.

At that, everything stopped. He stopped moving and everything went very still. As if the world suddenly froze. The bed melted away, the chairs and the tables, all disappeared. Once more, it was only the two of us. He held my gaze intensely and I wondered what was coming next. The mood between us had suddenly changed. Like a switch that had been flicked on, or off. Alex looked different. He smelt different. His body felt different. I felt different and everything suddenly felt so unfamiliar yet . . . *right*. I felt myself stepping over some kind of boundary and entering uncharted territory where nothing was the same as before.

This was really starting to feel not like *just* sex.

He started moving again and I moaned, caught off guard by the sudden motion. His movements grew faster and faster again and I joined in, lifting my hips up and down to meet his thrusts. We moved as one and it felt like we were seeping into each other's pores, becoming a part of each other as we stared deeply into each other's eyes.

And suddenly we were rising up together. Up, up, up, up like a rollercoaster climbing to the top. We teetered at the top for a while, holding our breaths and waiting for the inevitable fall . . .

And then we fell. Plummeted. Raced down together screaming as our stomachs dropped and we struggled to catch our breath.

That *definitely* wasn't *just* sex. And every single part of me knew it.

CHAPTER FIFTY-THREE

*W*e lay on our backs looking up at the ceiling. We hadn't said a word since falling out of each other's arms after having the best, best, *the best*, sex of my life. Sex where I had actually said his name over and over again, and sex that had there been walls to beat with my sweaty fists, I would have.

We were holding hands, but that was our only physical contact. We were both completely naked, my hot body was covered in a layer of sweat and when the sea breeze blew through the open window, a pleasant cooling sensation made me shiver slightly.

Finally, Alex stirred. He turned to face me. He propped his head up on his elbow and looked down at me and then smiled.

I turned my head to look at him better and found myself smiling back. "Well." It was only when I opened my mouth and spoke that I realized how dry it was. "I guess we can tick that off the list."

His smile grew. "I guess we can." He lowered his head and planted a small, soft kiss between my breasts.

"You taste salty," he said, keeping his mouth there, letting his lips linger on that sensitive part.

"I'm sweaty." I laced my fingers through his hair again. It was damp and sticky.

"Me too," he said, moving his lips over my nipple and blowing on it.

I winced, a mixture of cold pain and hot pleasure stabbed me. He lifted his head back up to me and smiled again. The heady scent of sex lingered in the air. Sex and sea air and cologne and sweat.

"You're so beautiful," he said, pushing a wet strand of hair out of my face. I reached up and grabbed his hand. Brought his fingertips down to my lips and kissed them one by one. Everything about this moment felt so natural and normal and comfortable. It didn't feel awkward in any way at all. My body seemed to instinctively know what to do with Alex in a way that I had never known before.

I pulled his hand away and looked at it, tracing it with my fingers. "You have such beautiful hands," I said, admiring them. I'd always liked them, but it was only now that I was getting to see them up close. "This is loose," I added, looking at the green ribbon on his finger.

"Take it off," he whispered to me.

I turned and looked at him. Our eyes met and he looked at me like he'd never looked at me before. I tugged at the little knot and the ribbon immediately loosened, and fell from his finger onto the bed. Our eyes both drifted down to where the ribbon was now lying; there was something so final about it lying there like that, as if it was dead. Alex picked it up between his fingers, then lowered it to my face. I closed my eyes as the tip of the ribbon came into gentle contact with my skin. It tickled. He ran it down my nose, over my lips, down my neck and I arched my back once more as he trailed it teasingly over my breasts.

I opened my eyes again and looked at Alex. He opened his mouth as if he was about to say something, but then stopped himself.

"What?" I raised my head.

"I just wanted to say that this last week has really, *really* meant a lot to me," he mouthed quietly.

"Me too," I said. "It's meant the world."

This moment. Right here, right now. Suddenly, it felt like everything we'd done over the last week had somehow been building to this exact moment for Alex and me. As if this was meant to happen. As if it had somehow been ordained from the very first moment we met. A realization hit me, well, part of one—I wasn't sure I had the full picture yet, I could only see parts of it. Fragments.

"You mean . . ." I started talking, "you've come to mean so much to me, Alex." I said softly. I knew I wanted to say more, but I wasn't quite sure exactly what I wanted to say, or if I should say it?

"You, Val," Alex brought his lips to my forehead, "have come to mean so much to me too."

I waited for him to maybe say more, but he didn't. Something was lurking on the tip of my tongue. They were words that I suddenly felt rather frightened by. Words that I dared not speak out loud . . . the words seemed so inappropriately big. So unexpected that I wasn't sure I trusted them just yet. My thoughts suddenly drifted back to number one on the list . . . *were these feelings I was feeling even real?*

And then Alex stood up and extended his arm for me to take.

I sat up on the bed and looked at him. Totally naked and so fuck-ing gorgeous it was a sin. A sin to waste that naked body by not doing something with it.

"What say we shower?" Alex asked.

I smiled. That was more like it. I could definitely do something with that body in the shower.

The warm water rushed over us, washing away all the sweat and sex and the beach sand that I'd only realized now was cling-ing to my ankles. Alex picked up the bar of soap and then started washing me. Every inch of me. Running the soap all the way over me from my feet to the tips of my fingers. When he came to my finger, he looked up briefly, and then slipped the ribbon off, drop-ping it onto the floor. The feeling of the hard slippery bar on my breasts was amazing, and it got that ball of energy all coiled up inside me again.

He took his time making sure that every inch of my breasts were clean. I closed my eyes and put my arms up on the wall behind me, giving him full access to every possible part of them. The sides, underneath them . . . everywhere. The warm water trickled down my body, caressing it softly, and at that moment Alex took a nipple between his fingers and squeezed. Hard. I jumped with surprise, the pain was ecstasy. I opened my eyes and looked at him again and he did it again to the other one. Pain and pleasure melted together to create something new and intense that needed exploring.

And then suddenly Alex turned me around and pressed the front of my body against the cold, hard wall of the shower. He suddenly kicked my legs open and a hand dived between my legs. He came up behind me, his lips to my ear and he whispered something that I couldn't hear through the sound of the falling drops and then I felt him inside me again. Alex was definitely *not* too nice, after all. Nice guys didn't do . . . *this*.

He pinned me to the wall even harder, holding my hands in place as he thrust into me. My body smacked into the cold wall with force and then he said something into my ear again. I was just about to ask him to say it again when my body started tensing again and all I could do was keep still and let the feeling crash through me. It was so intense it made my legs shake. I could feel Alex was starting to lose control too, his movements were getting more erratic and frantic. I was just about to remind him that he wasn't wearing a condom when I felt him slip out of me. He moaned into my ear and I don't think I'd ever heard such an amazing sound before. I smiled. It had been quick, and dirty and totally satisfying.

We stayed like that again for a while until Alex turned the water off and then turned me around to face him once more. I couldn't help smiling at him.

"What?" He smiled back.

"Doctor Alex Fletcher, you are a sex god." I let out a girly giggle.

"Only because I've been reading all your articles," he said putting both his hands on the wall behind me and leaning in for another kiss.

I kissed him back and we didn't stop. Even while drying ourselves with the towels, we were kissing. Even while walking back through to the room together, we kissed. Even as we both climbed into bed, we kissed and even as we fell asleep in each other's arms, *we still kissed*.

CHAPTER FIFTY-FOUR

~

I had this crazy dream. I dreamt that Alex and I were getting married. Which was insane of course, but it felt good. I walked down the aisle towards him and he looked at me with *that look*. That look that made the words tingle on the tip of my tongue again. And when that moment came, that moment to say our "I do's," a fog started rolling in. A heavy mist suddenly made visibility hard. Alex's face was blurring, but I could see his lips were moving, he was trying to say something to me. I leaned in to listen, but all I could hear were whispers again. I opened my mouth to speak, words wanted to come out, but they didn't and then . . .

A knock on the door.

I sat up in bed with a fright and looked around. Alex was gone but the little note on the pillow told me that he'd gone to fetch breakfast.

The knock again.

I smiled. Excited to see him I climbed out the bed, grabbed a gown and raced to open the door. I swung it open excitedly, expecting to see Alex standing there. But it wasn't Alex.

"MATT? What the hell are you doing here?" I stumbled backwards from the door in total shock. Matt looked so foreign here. So out of place. And I couldn't quite reconcile him being here.

"Val. Oh my God, I'm so happy to see you." And then suddenly, he was inside. Rushing towards me. Pulling me into a hug.

I pushed him away. "What are you doing here? Where's . . . uh . . ." I looked behind him to see where she was lurking, "Sam?"

"She's not with me," he said, a massive smile sweeping over his face. I stared at him. I had no idea how the hell to interpret that smile.

"Where is she?" I asked,

"She's back in Cape Town," Matt said, moving closer to me again. "Permanently."

I shook my head. Nothing about this was making any sense.

"We're no longer together." Another massive smile swept across his face.

"You . . . WHAT?"

"I know now!" Matt started walking towards me again. I stepped backwards. Backing away from him.

"Know what?" I asked, as the back of my knees bumped into the bed behind me. I was trapped and couldn't walk any further.

But Matt continued to move closer, until he was right in front of me. Close. So close. He reached out and put his hands on my cheeks, cradling my face gently and coming even closer.

"It's you," he said, his eyes sweeping over my face. "It's always been you."

"Me?" My mouth dried as I stared into his eyes. I knew those eyes so well. I'd studied them so many times before. Stared into them and wished that they would look back at me with that look that I'd been longing for for so many years . . . hang on—

That look!

He was looking at me with *that look*.

"Wh . . . what . . ." I stumbled over my words. My stomach was churning, but not in the way that I would have expected it to churn in this moment.

"Val, you were right about us." He stepped closer to me. His face now inches from mine.

"Right? About what?"

"I've been so blind. It was like I couldn't see what was right in front of me this entire time. But now my eyes are open and it's so clear to me. As if I'm wearing a new pair of glasses and everything has come into focus since the engagement party—"

"I don't want to talk about that." I cut him off and tried to move away from him, but he held me in place.

"I do." He tried to make eye contact again, but I couldn't. I looked to the floor. He placed a hand underneath my chin and tilted my head up, forcing me to look at him once more.

"I haven't stopped thinking about what you said. That we're perfect together. We *are* perfect for each other."

"Forget I said that," I quickly added.

"I can't, because you were right. And I can't believe it took me three years to see it. But when Sam gave me that ultimatum, it all became so clear."

"What ultimatum?"

"She said I could never see you again. That it was you or her, and I chose you, Val. I choose you because I can't imagine not having you in my life."

My mind was racing at a million miles an hour. Thoughts and images swirled through it like an uncontrollable whirlwind was raging inside my brain. I didn't know what to think. *Was this really happening?* Was this it, the moment I had dreamed about, prayed for, wished for, obsessed over for so many years? Was it finally, finally happening?

"What are you saying?" I asked.

"That I love you," he said.

And just like that, it rolled off his tongue.

Those three words.

The three words that I'd pined for. The words that I'd said to him silently in my head so many times before. I'd opened my mouth to say them to him so many times before, but never had. They were always on the tip of my tongue. Residing there. Waiting to be freed. But now they weren't there anymore. *Where were they?* I no longer felt the unstoppable urge that was so great that sometimes I had to bite my lip so tightly that it hurt.

"Matt, I . . . I—"

"I know," he said, cutting me off. "You've always loved me and I'm so sorry it took me so long to see it."

"But you're getting married, Matt. To Sam," I said.

"It's over between us."

I was about to open my mouth to say something, anything, I wasn't sure. But suddenly his lips were on me. His lips felt hard and cold and a chill ran through my body and into my feet. I felt sweaty and clammy and confused.

I tried to pull away from the kiss, but Matt obviously took it as something else, and pulled me in even more. *This was what I had wanted. Wasn't it?* But it felt so strange; his lips on mine, his tongue pushing its way into my mouth, his hands running down my back, pulling me closer to him. I felt as if I was out of my body, floating above myself looking down at what was going on.

"I love you," he whispered against my mouth. It sounded so genuine and so sincere and he said it with the exact tone I'd always imagined he'd say it with. Something in me stirred.

"Say that again," I said. "Say that again." I wanted to know if this was real.

He pulled away from the kiss and held my face between his hands. He looked deep into my eyes and were those . . . ? *God, he had tears in his eyes.* This was the exact script I'd written in my head. He would look at me, tears in his eyes, and tell me how much he loved me and what a terrible mistake he'd made all these years and how he needed me.

"Val," he started speaking slowly. 'I love you. I can't believe I didn't see it before, I've made such a mistake. But I need you. Please . . ." A tear left his eye and rolled down his cheek.

"Matt," I whispered back to him. My voice shaking with emotion. So many different emotions I wasn't even sure I knew or understood them yet. I'd wanted this for so long . . .

I leaned in and placed my lips over his. I'd always wanted to know what it would feel like to be able to do that. To be the girl who could just kiss Matt whenever she wanted to. I'd always wanted to know what it would feel like to run my hands through his hair . . . *so I did.* I kissed him and I ran my hands through his hair. I'd always wanted to know what it would feel like to splay my fingers across his chest . . . *so I did that too.* I'd always wanted to know what it would feel like to have him desire and want me and lust for me. So I pushed myself into him just enough. I could feel he was hard, *but was this what I wanted?*

"Val?" A voice from the doorway. I knew exactly who it was the second I heard it.

I pushed Matt away from me and stared at the door. Alex was standing in it holding a plate of breakfast in his hand. "Alex," I said.

Alex looked at me. His face dropped and then he looked over at Matt.

"I should go now," Alex said and turned away.

CHAPTER FIFTY-FIVE

I ran out of the room leaving Matt behind me. "Alex, wait!" I called after him as he walked briskly down the corridor towards the reception area. But he ignored me and kept on walking, leaving the hotel and marching straight for the beach.

"Wait, Alex. I can explain!" My words came out in desperate bursts. *Why was I explaining? And what exactly was I explaining?*

Alex finally stopped when he reached the beach. He swung around and faced me. His face was cool and calm and betrayed nothing of his feelings. What was he feeling?

"It's Matt," I said. "He's left Sam. He's here. He says he's in love with me. He cried." The words cascaded out of my mouth. "I didn't know he was coming here. I didn't know." I sounded frantic and panicked and I didn't quite know why. Nor did I quite know what these feelings rushing through my body were. Hot, cold, anxious, angry . . . Everything buzzed and whirled and my heart pounded.

"I see," he said. And then he got very quiet and thoughtful for a moment. My heart raced, waiting for him to say something back to me. "It's what you've always wanted, isn't it? It's what you dreamed of?"

I hesitated. "Yes." I nodded. "It is what I wanted."

"And now it's happening." Alex smiled. Not a warm, friendly one, but a smile that made my chest feel tight. "He left his fiancée and he's come all the way here to tell you he loves you and sweep you off your feet."

"Yes."

Alex paused. He looked at me for the longest time and then his body language seemed to change somewhat. "I'm happy for you, Val. I really am," he said.

"You are?" I asked, completely taken aback by his answer. Suddenly, something felt like it exploded in my chest. It took my breath away momentarily.

He nodded. "Sure. You've been in love with him for so long. This is your dream come true, right?"

"Um . . . I guess," I acknowledged. This had been my dream for so long, *so why was there a part of me that felt like it was a total nightmare too?*

"I . . . I . . ." I stumbled over my words again, they were barely coming out. They were barely making sense in my head, so how was I even meant to speak them out loud? *Nothing was making sense right now.*

"But the list." I took a step closer to him.

"What about it?" He shrugged.

"We made a promise to get over our exes together. We made a promise not to get into a relationship with anyone with the ribbons . . ." I raised my hand and realized the ribbon wasn't on it anymore.

Alex raised his hand and his finger was empty too. "Like you said at the very beginning, Val, don't believe everything you read in magazines."

"But . . . but . . ." I grasped for words. They were not coming. And then some did. "Last night?"

"What about it?" Alex finally looked up at me. His gray eyes were almost black. A turbulent, stormy black color.

"It was—" I stopped. Not knowing what word to put in that sentence, hoping that maybe he'd put a word into it for me.

"It was two friends helping each other out so that they could move on," he said, looking away again.

"Was it?" I asked. That heavy feeling in my chest again. "Was it just sex for you?"

Alex swung around and looked at me again. This time he looked angry. "What do you want me to say, Val? That I felt something? Because I did. Okay. I felt something. I still feel something. I've felt something for days now."

"So what are you saying, Alex?" I asked, the sound of my heart beating was so loud.

"That the list worked for me. I'm over Connie. I'm totally over her, and this last week with you has made me realize how we were never suited for each other in the first place because I've met you and you and I are so—" He stopped talking abruptly.

"We are so what?" I asked.

"Well, I thought we were anyway," he said sadly. "But it's clear you don't feel the same way, because you're not over Matt. In fact, you're kissing him. You're running your hands through his hair, you're rubbing yourself against him . . ." His voice trailed off.

"I . . . I . . ." I stuttered again. "Alex, please?" I said.

"Please what?" he asked.

Please tell me what I should be feeling. Please tell me exactly how you feel. Please tell me what to do, what to think. I shrugged. "I don't know."

"Val," Alex took a step closer to me, "since meeting you, I feel alive. I've done things that I never ever thought I would do before. I feel like I've woken up. That before meeting you I was sleeping and now . . . I'm awake."

"Awake?" I asked. But I wanted to hear more than "awake." Surely "awake" didn't override years and years of love that I'd felt for someone?

"Well, what do you feel?" he asked.

"I . . . I . . ." I tripped over my tied tongue. "Confused," I admitted.

Alex sighed and then shook his head. "So here I am again . . . I feel like I'm on the rooftop all over again asking the girl to pick me and then she doesn't."

"Is that what you're doing, Alex? Asking me to pick you?" I asked.

"Maybe . . ." he said. He looked at me. I could see he was wrestling with something in his head and then he just blurted it out. "I think I might be feeling a lot for you, Val . . . that I might be . . ." he paused for the longest time, "falling for you." Alex threw his arms in the air. "Is that better? Is that what you want to hear? Even though I said I wasn't going to be saying that anytime soon, I think I might be saying it again."

A warm rush swept through my body and my heart started thumping in my chest. "You are?" I asked.

"Yes . . . Jesus!" He turned away from me and walked in a

small circle. "Talk about falling for the wrong women. I seem to have a habit of that. One cheats on me seven years into the relationship, and the other one is kissing her ex the night after I made love to her." And then Alex paused and looked at me curiously. "And you are confused." It was a statement. Not a question.

I locked eyes with Alex, I could feel a tear dislodging itself from my eye and start rolling down my cheek. *I was confused. So confused.* I couldn't quite sift through what I was feeling right now. It was all just too overwhelming and sudden. Matt arriving and breaking up with Sam. Alex telling me he was falling for me. I needed a moment to process this all. But I didn't get it, because I heard my name being called.

I turned and looked at him. *Matt.* He was smiling at me. Waving. I looked back at Alex, his eyes seemed to be beseeching me.

"Val?" Matt called again and I turned around once more. He was looking at me with *the look*.

Shit! I looked back over at Alex. He looked expectant, waiting for me. Waiting for the answer. I started shaking my head at Alex. "I don't know wh—"

He cut me off by holding his hand up. "Then let me do it for you."

"Do what?" Panic gripped me.

"The last week has been amazing. I will never forget it. And I will never forget you. And I wish you only the best, Val. I wish you all the happiness in the world, wherever and whoever that may be with."

My heart snapped. Broke. It shattered into a million pieces in my chest and I wanted to cry. He turned and started walking away.

"Wait," I called out in panic.

Alex turned again. "You don't know what you want, Val." He said it so firmly and I knew he was right.

"I just need a few moments to think," I said. I needed a second to catch my breath and fucking process this all.

"You shouldn't have to think so hard about this. I know I don't have to." He turned again and continued to walk away.

"Val?" I heard Matt call me again. I turned and looked at him Matt had left Sam. *For me.* He'd come all this way to tell me he loved me. I'd spent more than a thousand days loving that man and surely something that had happened over the course of a week could not erase that?

I turned and looked back at Alex. He was far down the beach now, jogging. I wanted to run after him and stop him and . . . and . . .

"Val, are you okay?" Matt called from behind me again.

"I'm fine," I called back to him. "Give me a minute. I'll meet you inside." I turned and he smiled at me. I smiled back because that's what I always did when he smiled.

"Sure." He nodded and walked back inside. I looked back to where Alex had been. But he was gone now. I scanned the beach and the garden, but couldn't see him anywhere. So I turned and started walking back towards the hotel. Towards Matt. I walked towards Matt, because that's what I'd done for the last three years of my life. Matt was my default.

A rustle in the bushes made me stop. I didn't even turn to look, because I knew exactly what it was.

"WHAT!" I shouted.

I waited for a response, but of course I knew I wouldn't get one. So I turned and looked at him. His head moved from side to side, almost as if it were shaking it at me.

"Fuck!" I hissed quietly to myself and then wanted to turn around and run to Alex again. But Matt was waiting for me. *Matt*.

"I'm doing the right thing," I whispered at him. "I'm doing the right thing," I said again.

Wasn't I?

CHAPTER FIFTY-SIX

*S*everal very confusing hours later I found myself standing at the airport once more. But this time, I wasn't alone. Since leaving the hotel, I'd been in some kind of strange detached space where I felt completely separate from everyone else and everything around me. In a kind of surreal, fuzzy no-man's land. Today was Wednesday, one of the days there were flights back to South Africa, and this time there had been space on the flight, was that a sign?

I looked around the airport. A week ago I hadn't even known that this island existed and now that I was leaving it, I realized how attached I'd grown to it. I looked around at the massive boards and pictures everywhere advertising the many beauties of the country.

A huge underwater scene was splashed across one. A scuba diver swimming around a brightly colored coral reef. *Dive Réunion*, it read. Yellow fish swimming around the diver, bubbles escaping his mouth rushing to the surface and then . . . *What the hell was that?*

The bloody bastard. Lurking in the corner of the billboard, so, so far in the corner that you might miss it, a beady little brown eye attached to a long wrinkly neck. I shook my head, feeling like there was a conspiracy against me. All the shelled creatures of the world were conspiring against me. Stalking me. Staring at me . . . *judging me.*

I huffed and turned my back on the billboard, but there, plastered across the other wall . . .

Welcome to Réunion. Visit the Tortoise Sanctuary. More beady eyes. More wrinkly necks. More judgey, pursed-mouth beaks.

"Bloody hell." I turned my back on this billboard too and folded my arms.

"Are you okay?" Matt asked, putting his hands on my shoulders. I flinched in fright. I'd almost forgotten Matt was even here. *How had I forgotten that?* For the last three years all I had wanted was him here.

I spun around. "Ever get that feeling you're being watched?" I asked.

Matt burst out laughing and pulled me into a hug. "God, Val. You say the funniest things. That's one of the reasons I love you."

I lifted my arms feebly and wrapped them around him. I closed my eyes and buried my head in his shoulder and inhaled his scent. He smelt like he always smelt. Bleu du Chanel. But this time, the scent wasn't doing what it usually did to me. It wasn't giving me that feeling. The feeling that used to make my stomach leap and cartwheel and plummet.

Matt took my face between his hands again and raised my lips to his, kissing them softly.

"God, this feels so good," he whispered softly against my mouth. "So right."

"Mmm," I mumbled, "it does." I said this even though I wasn't entirely sure it did.

"I know what you were doing with that Alex guy, and don't worry, we don't have to speak about it. I get it," he said suddenly.

"What was I doing with Alex?" I asked, surprised by his statement and genuinely interested in what he thought I'd been doing.

"I know you just did it out of anger and pain," he said. "I know it didn't mean anything." Matt looked deeply into my eyes again as if he loved me. As if he *really* loved me. "Shall we go home?"

"Home?" For some reason that word had such gravitas to it and seemed laced with meaning.

"Your place or mine?" He smiled at me. Sexy. Flirty. Dirty. And it suddenly occurred to me what he was getting at. *Sex.* Matt and I were meant to have sex now. But I'd just been with Alex the night before, and I wasn't sure I could be the girl who slept with two different men in twenty-four hours.

Wait. What the hell was going on here? My mind was swirling. So many thoughts, so many feelings, so much confusion clouding everything right now that I wasn't sure what was right or wrong and what I wanted or didn't want.

I pulled away from Matt gently. "Would you mind if we took this slow? It's all a bit overwhelming still," I whispered quietly.

"Sure. Of course. No pressure." Matt quickly corrected defensively. "Sorry."

"It's okay. This is all just so strange and I'm still trying to get my head around it," I said, moving a little further away from him without even knowing.

A boarding call came through the intercom. "That's us," Matt said. "It's time for us to go."

Time for us to go. This was all so strange. But I followed him towards the plane anyway.

CHAPTER FIFTY-SEVEN

ↄ

Dear Diary,

I bought a new one of you because the last one of your kind is lying at the bottom of a pool in Réunion. I've needed to write. To try and get all the thoughts out of my head and onto paper so I can make sense of them.

Matt and I are officially together . . . I think? Well, we are. I just didn't think it would feel like this. We are doing the same things as before, pizza, beer, TV, chilling . . . and kissing. We kiss a lot. Last night he ran his hands over my breast and it felt really weird. Matt has been talking about the future, saying what a waste it is that we have two flats. That we should move in together. I told him I thought that was a bit fast, he laughed and said it's been three years in the making though.

It's been exactly five days since I've come home. Five days since I saw Alex, but I can't stop thinking about him . . .

I got a message from Julian the day after I arrived home. Well, a photo. He'd taken a photo of Alex and sent it to me with the word WTFAYT? written below. In brackets (What the fuck are you thinking?) The photo showed Alex slumped over at the bar. He was drinking his little pink drink again. He looked miserable. He had facial stubble and his hair was a mess and it broke my heart.

I don't know. I don't know what to do! I don't know what to think or how to act or how to feel! I wanted something so badly for so long and now that I finally have it . . . IDK!

More laters . . .

Dear Diary,

It's been two weeks since I got back from Réunion. Matt has been away on business for the last five days and I know I shouldn't say this, but I feel relieved. Guess who I bumped into today at the mall: THE BOSS and DIVORCED! They saw me and wanted to thank me, because now they are in love. They say. (I crashed both their cars at Matt's engagement party, you'll remember.) Matt wanted to have sex with me the night before he went away on business. I told him I wasn't feeling that well . . .

On a totally different note, my editor wants me to start writing a weekly column for the online magazine. Something "personal" she said. (She heard what happened to me at Matt's engagement party, apparently we have some mutual friends. She thought it would make a great story, especially now that Matt and I are together. She says this is a total miracle. She said I must be so happy. She said this must feel like a dream come true. My perfect Hollywood ending . . .)

Guess what . . .? Alex seems to have pulled a number four on me. He's murdered me on social media. I am blocked from all his online profiles. The last picture I saw of him was one he posted the day he arrived back in London. It showed a massive pile of unopened envelopes on his couch saying something to the effect of, "Welcome home!" I saw he'd tagged his location and I went to see it. I think I know where he lives now. I've found myself staring at a picture of his apartment building on Google Earth trying to guess which flat is his and hoping I could see him through the window. I know that's lame. But I just feel like I need to see him. If only for a moment. I hated that the last time I saw him was when he'd looked at me like that, and then run away down the beach. I hate that the last memory we have of each other is that moment.

I haven't seen any of my friends since coming back. I guess I'm a bit worried what they'll say to me about everything that has happened. For some reason, I feel strange trying to explain to them why I am suddenly with Matt now. By the way, have I mentioned that I feel really bad about Sam? I keep thinking about her, and not in the way that I used to think about her, in the whole "I wish she would blow up and disappear" way. I hope she's okay . . . what am I saying, of course she's not okay. Her fiancé left her for his best friend who ruined her engagement party . . . I'd started feeling so good about myself and everything while I was in Réunion, and now I just feel crap about everything. Including myself.

Later . . .

Dear Diary,

So two things happened to me today that have left me feeling—what is the right word—unhinged maybe? One, I bumped my knee on a chair and ripped the old scab off it. There was blood everywhere. Matt tried to help me with it, but he didn't have any plasters and landed up wrapping my knee with toilet paper and for some reason this made me so angry with him that we had a fight about it. I apologized later, I don't know what got into me. I'm just not feeling myself. And then, two, I got a message from Julian today. The message was another photo. It was a photo of the magazine that Alex and I had been using. He said he found it at the bar. He took a photo of one of the other articles in the magazine. The article was called, "How Do You Know If You're In The Wrong Relationship?"

1. You think of someone else when you are with him.

2. You can't wait for him to be gone so you can enjoy your own company.

3. When he phones to chat, you zone out and pretend you're listening, but you aren't.

There were more, but I think you get the picture . . .

So here's the thing, I'm pretty sure I've made a terrible, terrible mistake and I don't know what to do to fix it. I'm not even sure I can fix it. I feel like I'm drowning in my mistake and the more I drown, the more I'm starting to realize some things that I wish I'd realized a while ago. Anyway, I'm going to my friend this afternoon to chat to her. I need her advice and if there's one person who knows how to tell it like it is, it's her. I'm off to see her now.

More later . . .

CHAPTER FIFTY-EIGHT

I pulled up to the house that Stormy shared with her boy-friend Marcus. It was a pretty house, perhaps the prettiest on the block. Large windows, lots of plants in the front garden and a fresh paint job that made it look brand new and immaculate. I walked up to the front door and found a note attached to it. I opened it.

> Key under pot plant with pink flower. Come in. I'm in the back garden.

I shook my head as I read the note which any would-be burglar would have been only too thrilled to have received. I walked inside, looked around and laughed.

The house was a strange mix of Marcus and Stormy. In between big screen TVs, immaculate leather couches and an open-plan modern kitchen, were dots of Stormy. A purple dream-catcher in the corner, a bright pink fluffy pillow on the couch, a painting of

God knows what on the wall and a pair of bright yellow sandals discarded carelessly in the middle of the floor.

"Stormy?" I called out, walking through the house to the large French doors that opened out into the garden. I didn't see her at first, but when I finally did, she seemed to magically emerge from the undergrowth; mud besmeared, branch in hand and leaves in hair and, *Oh My God!*

"What the hell have you done to your hair?" I gasped.

"Do you love it?" she asked, twirling around, the beads all knocking together and making that dreadful clanking noise that I was all too familiar with.

"Mmmmm," I mumbled, "it's great. What's not to love about green braids with beads on the ends?"

"I know, right? I was so inspired by your hair that I decided I had to have it too."

"It looks good on you," I lied. Not even Stormy-Rain could pull this one off.

She skipped over to me, holding a massive pair of garden shears in her hand which made me incredibly nervous, since she was known for her clumsiness.

We made some tea and a few moments later were sitting on the back porch sipping it—*well*, she was sipping, I was pretending to sip. It was the most hideous thing I'd ever tasted in my life, I didn't care that it was organic, magnetically charged, crystal infused and good for your cholesterol, or whatever else it no doubt claimed to be.

I'd been explaining for the last ten minutes, non-stop, the events that had transpired in Réunion and transpired the day I left Réunion. I told her about Alex walking away, about wanting to stop him but not being sure. I told her about Matt and how I was so thrown by the fact that I wasn't feeling for him what I always thought I would feel. She listened intently. I paused for a while to catch my breath.

"I just don't know what to do," I said, shaking my head. "I don't know how I'm supposed to feel and what I am supposed to feel and for who?"

"You don't need to know that now," Stormy replied. "The universe will provide a sign."

I scoffed. "A sign?" I looked over at her and raised an eyebrow. "I came to you because you're the one person that always tells it like it is and speaks the truth and all you have to say is that I will get a sign."

She nodded. "I'm afraid this one is beyond me. You're going to have to keep your ears and eyes open for it."

"God!" I was frustrated and put my tea down. "How will I know it's a sign?" I asked.

"You'll just know," she said almost mysteriously, as if she knew something I didn't. She probably bloody did. She always seemed to know things that others didn't know.

"No." I shook my head. "I'm so confused right now that I'm not sure I would get the sign if it slapped my face."

"I doubt that," Stormy said, crossing her legs and pulling them up onto the chair. I was just about to argue further, when I heard a rustle in the bushes. I almost shot out of my seat when I saw what came next.

A small, beaked mouth. Thick leathery skin, a wrinkled neck, a shell and . . .

"Oh my God!" I pointed at the tortoise that had just emerged from the bushes.

"It's Elvis," Stormy said casually. "Since I had a garden, I brought him back."

"I know!" I gasped. Everyone knew Elvis, he was Stormy's pet tortoise. She used to take him with her everywhere she went.

"But . . . but . . ." I stuttered as I looked down at him. And then, as if he too had gotten the bloody memo that was clearly circulating amongst his kind, he slowly raised his head and looked up at me. Our eyes locked and I swear he said something to me deep in my subconscious mind, but not that deep that I could hear it.

My brain started screaming things at me. It started showing me pictures like I was scrolling through an Instagram feed; Alex and I in the sea together with the sun setting behind us, Alex and I holding hands diving through the air, tasting plums, standing in the mist, shouting at mountains, the way he smiled, the way he laughed, the dimple in his cheek, the way he made me feel, the way we'd made love, and worst of all, the look on his face just before he'd walked away. And it was all so, so, so clear to me and I wasn't sure why it hadn't been clearer to me until that very moment. And then it started showing me something else. A magazine had gotten me into this trouble, and a magazine would get me out of it.

"Oh my God!" I jumped up and down. "It's the sign." I turned to Stormy, and her eyes widened. "I know exactly what to do! I know exactly what I want!" I was so overjoyed in that moment that tears started streaming down my cheeks. Stormy was suddenly on her feet too, jumping up and down as if she was also as excited.

"Then go out and do it." She swooshed her hand around. Her bangles clanked together as she did and I ran up and threw my arms around her.

"Thank you." I hugged her and she hugged me back.

I turned and started running towards the door, but her voice stopped me midway.

"By the way," she yelled after me, "Marcus and I are pregnant!"

I stopped dead in my tracks and turned around. Her statement had caught me so off guard that I wasn't sure what to say to her. Trust Stormy to drop a bombshell like that in the most inappropriate way ever.

"Ah . . . ah . . . uh . . ." I stuttered. My brain was trying to change gear from what I now knew I needed to do, to this major announcement.

"Congratulations!" I said almost awkwardly. And then it hit me. "Shit. Have you told Lilly yet?"

She shook her head and looked at me solemnly. "No. I don't know how to."

"Shit," I whispered. Lilly and Damien had been trying for a baby for years now and nothing they did seemed to be working. They had even gone through months of fertility treatment and still nothing.

Stormy looked suddenly tense. She never looked tense. I walked back towards her.

"Have you spoken to Annie and Jane?" I asked.

"Not yet," she said. "It doesn't help that Annie is popping them out at a rate of one per year though."

A small chuckle escaped my lips. It was true. Annie had just had her third child with her husband after swearing blind she would never do it again. She swore blind after the first one, and then again after the second one.

"And Jane and Dimitri just got engaged, they'll probably start trying soon," she added, shrugging her shoulders.

Lilly had always been the one out of all of us that had wanted to be a mom the most. In fact, it wasn't that long ago that Stormy had also sworn blind she would never have kids.

"But go! Go!" Stormy insisted. "Go do what you need to do, we can talk about this later."

I nodded at her. "Lilly will be happy for you," I said.

"I know," Stormy replied sadly. "But she'll also be sad."

I nodded at Stormy, because I knew she was right. Lilly would put on a brave face, she would host the baby shower and be there at the birth if she could. She would love that baby to bits and be the first to offer her babysitting services, but under all that, there would be a part of her that was devastated.

"We need to talk about this later," I said to Stormy, I didn't want her to think I was rushing out of this big moment.

She nodded at me and gave me a big smile and a thumbs-up.

"You're going to be such a great mom," I said to her.

"I know!" she said with a smile. "My star sign told me so."

I ran out the house and climbed into my car. I knew exactly what needed to be done.

But it wasn't going to be easy . . .

CHAPTER FIFTY-NINE

*"M*att!" I burst into his apartment the second he opened his door and walked all the way to the other end of the room as if it was a stage and I was ready to give a monologue. Which in a way, I was. I'd been practicing it over and over in my head the entire drive.

"What's wrong?" Matt asked, moving towards me.

I held my hand up. "No. Stay there. I need to tell you something."

"What? You're worrying me." He looked genuinely concerned.

"The thing is . . ." I started, ready to spew out all the words that I'd been rehearsing in my head. "The thing is, this isn't what I want."

"What isn't?"

"This. Us. You and I." I started pacing the room now. "Oh God, and I can't believe I'm saying this, because it's all I've wanted for so long, and now that I have it, it couldn't be more wrong for me if I tried."

"Sorry, uh . . . what are you saying?" Matt folded his arms tightly.

"It's not you, Matt. It's me. I've changed. Someone changed me for the better and now I no longer want what I thought I did. I want something else."

"What do you want?"

"Alex," I said. "I want him."

"Uh . . ." Matt unfolded his arms and the look on his face was pure and utter shock. "But I thought . . . I mean, you said at the engagement party and . . . you said it!" His voice had an edge of panic to it.

"And at the time, I thought I meant it."

"You thought?" He sounded angry now.

I nodded. "How did you not notice me for three years, Matt?"

"I made a mistake," he said defensively.

"No. I don't think you did. I think you didn't notice me for three years because you and I are not meant to be together. We're not right for each other, Matt. And it's taken me looking at a tortoise to figure that out."

"What the hell has a tortoise got to do with this?"

"Everything!" I said.

"Uh . . ." Matt took a step closer to me. "You sure you're okay? You don't sound like you're thinking straight."

I shook my head. "On the contrary, Matt. I have never thought so straight in my entire life."

"But I broke up with Sam for you." Now he sounded like he was pleading with me.

"And you shouldn't have," I said.

"But I did!" He said it a little louder this time. As if he was angry with me. "And she will never take me back now!"

"And she shouldn't," I said to him. "And you shouldn't either. Because if you broke up with her because you thought you had feelings for me, then she wasn't right for you in the first place either."

"What?" He unfolded his arms and grabbed his head in his hands. "I called off my wedding for you, Val."

"I know. And I'm sorry." I rushed over to Matt now and tried to lay a hand on his shoulder. He pulled away from me.

"Shit. You are not doing this, Val! You can't be doing this."

"I am doing this, Matt," I said. "I am finally saying *no* to you. I haven't been able to say no to you for years, even when I wanted to. And I'm saying it now. No."

He shook his head and I continued.

"Matt, you and I, we're not right for each other. Don't you see that?" I asked. I walked over to him and this time he let me lay my hands on his shoulders. I looked at him.

"You are going to make someone really, really happy one day. That someone is just not me."

"But I called off my wedding for you," he said again, as if this was the most important part of all this. The crux of the matter.

I sighed. "I put my entire life on hold for you for three years, and I'm sorry, but I am not going to waste another second of it." I turned and walked out of his apartment for the last time.

* * *

I sat back in my chair, my finger hovered over the "Publish" button. For the first time in my life, I'd written something worthwhile—just like Alex said I would. I'd written something that would hopefully change people's lives; mainly mine and Alex's. I knew that he'd subscribed to the mag, so the second I published this, he would get a notification. I closed my eyes, took a deep breath in and then lowered my finger to the button.

DEAR DIARY: A WEEKLY COLUMN BY VAL IVANOV

Dear Diary,

I've made a terrible mistake. Huge mistake. You see, a couple of weeks ago, I made the wrong choice. And no, it wasn't choosing what to watch on Netflix, this was much bigger than that.

Because I chose the wrong man. And not just any man. *The man.* The kindest, funniest, smartest, sexiest man I've ever met in my entire life. And this man stood right in front of me and he told me that he was falling for me and I did the unthinkable, I let him slip through my fingers. I let him walk away.

I should have run after him. I should have chased him down the beach and to the ends of the Earth, if need be, shouting at the top of my lungs that I had fallen too. *That I loved him.* But I didn't. And now I've lost the most magical person that I've ever known.

And what is so magical about this person, I hear you ask? *Everything.*

He came into my life when I needed him most and least expected it. He came into my life when I didn't even know that he was exactly what I wanted and needed. He took me on an adventure like I've never been on before and on it I found myself . . . *and him*. And now that he's gone, I can only look at my life in one way; before him, and after him.

Because he's changed me. Changed every single part of me. And now that I'm changed, I can never go back to the way I was before him. He has awakened a part of me that I never even knew existed. He reached right into my heart and soul and left his mark there and I can never, ever erase it. I thought I loved a man once before him, but I realized that in loving that man, all I was doing was giving parts of myself away. And it was exhausting. But it's not like that with *him*; being with him, and loving him, only adds to my life and I want him back more than anything I've ever wanted in my life before. Because loving him comes so easily.

I'll let you in on a secret, I'm not really writing this for you to read. I'm writing this for him. I'm hoping that he will read this and realize how truly, deeply sorry I am for not choosing him.

Because he is everything.

So please . . . come back to me. Because I feel lost without you.

I love you.

More laters . . . *hopefully*.

CHAPTER SIXTY

~

Dear Diary,

Hi, diary. Real diary. Private diary. It's been a week since I published the column and I haven't heard a thing from Alex. Of course the column seems to have catapulted my career, it became the most read and shared thing last week. Everyone has read it and is talking about it, except for the one person that I need to read it.

I even tried to call Alex, and it looks like he no longer has the same number. Julian said he'd also tried to call but it was the wrong number. Seems that Alex has gone to great lengths to keep me away. So at this stage I have two options:

1. I give up. I forget Alex and move on with my life and try to find someone who will one day live up to him (never going to happen), or

2. I can go and find him.

Can you guess which one I've done . . . ? I'll give you a clue, let's just say that I'm writing this from International Departures. In fact, I have to go. Right now.

Wish me luck. More to come . . .

* * *

I didn't sit still the entire flight to London. *How could I?* An entire ten hours of tapping my foot, pacing the aisle, twirling my hair around my finger and repetitive toilet visits, even though I didn't need them—I'm sure I burnt more calories on that flight than an hour at the gym.

I had a pent-up ball of energy in my stomach that was twisting my insides into knots that felt like they were going to explode. I felt like that terrible Monty Python sketch, where the man in the restaurant eats too much and explodes. Except mine would be an explosion of emotions that would fill the entire plane, coat its walls and windows and cover everyone in its sticky, messy goo.

And by the time I landed, I was an absolute wreck. The airport bustled with a manic energy, which only served to set my nerves on edge even more. But after what felt like another few hours of pure torture, I finally found a taxi. I leapt in and handed the driver the address. *I hoped this was Alex's apartment.*

We finally arrived at the building and I immediately raced up the steps to the front of it. I looked at the wall in panic—there was a massive panel of buzzers for all the various apartments and I had no idea which one was Alex's. I was just about to start pressing them randomly when I saw someone come out the elevator and walk towards the door. I ducked behind a massive pot plant and when they exited, I grabbed the door and slipped in. It was all very cloak and dagger-y of me.

I walked around in the large reception, my feet clicking loudly against the fancy marble floor, wondering how the hell I was going to find him, when a row of postboxes on the wall caught my eye. I walked up to them and started scanning the names, and there he was. *Just like that*. Apartment 66. I raced towards the lift, the anticipation building inside me like a coil. *Tighter, tighter, tighter* . . . I was sure there was a limit to how tightly this thing could be wound, and I was sure I was about to discover where that limit was as the lift seemed to climb the floors like a sloth.

Could it not go faster? Was that too much to ask? I stared, tapping my foot impatiently as the lights for the floors seemed to illuminate in slow motion.

"Oh, come the F on!" I cursed the buttons loudly when the lift seemed to slow down even more. *How was it possible for something in the universe to be so perversely slow?*

Finally, after what felt like an eternity in hell, it arrived on the right floor. I threw myself out the door and started running down the corridor, reading the apartment numbers as I went.

62, getting closer, 63, nearly there, 64, almost there 65 . . .

There! I was here. And I didn't waste a second. I banged on the door like a mad person. I heard a footstep inside, I saw the door handle begin to turn and my heart climbed into my mouth. This was it. This was the moment that I had been waiting for. I was about to see Alex and I couldn't waai—

"You!" My jaw fell open when I saw who was standing on the other side of the door.

"Uh . . . who are you?" she asked. She had that air of snarky superiority, the kind that made you instantly dislike her.

"Connie?" I asked her, even though I knew the answer to that already.

"Yes, that's me," she said sarcastically.

"What are you doing here?" I asked.

"Uh . . . I live here," she said snappily.

My heart climbed out of my mouth and committed suicide by tossing itself on the cold, hard floor. "You . . . you . . . uh . . . you do . . ." I stammered, walking backwards. My feet were just carrying me there on autopilot. As if I had no control over them whatsoever. *No wonder he didn't respond to my article.*

"What do you want?" she asked, raising a perfect brow at me.

"I want . . ." I stopped walking backwards now and paused. *I wanted what I couldn't have. I wanted what I'd lost. And it was all my fault.* That's what I wanted to say to her, but I didn't.

"Never mind." I turned around and started walking towards the lift, feeling like I was dragging my now very broken heart with me. I could almost hear it whimpering as it slid across the cold floor, trailing behind me.

I heard a long, loud sigh from behind me. "Are you looking for Alex?"

I turned back to her and nodded. Tears in my eyes now . . . no, tears streaming down my cheeks. God, I didn't want to cry in front of her, but I was.

She leaned against the doorframe in a defeated kind of manner. "He doesn't live here anymore," she said, almost sadly.

I shook my confused head and then my eyes drifted down to

her finger where the massive celebrity engagement ring had once been. But her finger was bare. "He moved out," she said flatly.

"Where?"

"I don't know."

"So you and him are . . .?" I couldn't bring myself to say it out loud.

"No. I was with someone else who, well, let's just say when his circumstances changed, I was no longer what he wanted." She looked so sad in that moment and suddenly I felt desperately sorry for her. I could kind of guess what had happened; Enigma won, he scored some major record deal and was now banging someone far cooler than her, some up-and-coming rock chick covered in tattoos with labia piercings.

"I'm sorry," I said. I actually meant it.

She shrugged. "What can you do, hey?"

"So why are you here?" I asked.

"It's temporary. I had nowhere to live, Alex had a month on his lease, so he let me stay here while I found a new place."

I smiled. That sounded like Alex. The guy who didn't have a bad bone in his body, even when it came to people who'd hurt him.

Then she looked up at me and met my eyes. "I lied. I know who you are."

"How?"

She rolled her eyes at me. "You were all over his social media pages. How could I miss you? Although your hair is considerably better in real life."

I nodded.

"Don't make the same mistake I did," she said slowly to me.

"What mistake is that?"

"Letting the one good man around go." She gave me a small look and then started closing the door.

"Where can I find him?" I asked frantically as the door started closing.

"St. Mary's hospital is where he works."

Of course! Why hadn't that dawned on me? "Thanks," I said to her and turned and ran out the building.

CHAPTER SIXTY-ONE

"I'm sorry, the doctor can only see ye next weeeeek," the receptionist said in a very thick accent that I was struggling to understand.

"Next week? But I need to see him right now," I said, feeling frantic. I could see that my raised panicked tone had caught the attention of the taxi driver, who was now looking at me in the rear-view mirror.

"I'm sorry, but the doctor is fully booooooooooked." *What accent was that?*

"But it's an emergency!" I wailed down the phone.

"If ye're experiencing an emergency, perhaaaaps ye aught ta go down to the emergency room," she suggested. *Was she even speaking English?*

"It's not that kind of emergency," I said. I could see the taxi driver was really paying attention now.

"What kinda emergency is it, luv?" she asked.

"Um . . . I think I've . . . uh . . ." I looked up at the rear-view mirror and the taxi driver was no longer even trying to be subtle. He was blatantly staring at me. I placed my hand over my mouth and tried to whisper into the phone. "I think I may have something in there," I whispered.

"Sorry, what?" she asked.

"I said," I tried to whisper a little louder this time, still not too loud, "I think I may have something in there."

"Sorry, you need to speak up, dear!"

"Fuck!" I glared at the taxi driver and this time he did look away. "I said, I think I have something stuck in there . . . you know. *Up there!*" I said that last part pointedly.

"You have a rectal foreign body?" the woman replied coolly, as if she said this kind of thing all the time. She probably did.

I cringed at the sound of it and wanted to die, but pulled myself together when I remembered the reason I was doing this.

"Mmm-hmmm," I mumbled. "I think so."

"You think so, or you know so? The doctor can't squeeze you in for 'I think so,'" she said.

"Definitely!" I suddenly shouted. "Absolutely! Totally lodged in there. In there . . . so far in there . . . deep!" I hid my face in my hand as I said it, I could see the taxi driver had perked right up.

"What is it?" the lady asked.

"What is what?" I asked.

"What is it that you have in your rectum?" Again with that cringey word.

"Um . . ." my brain raced but I couldn't think of a single thing. "Who knows!" I finally said, face-palming as I did. "Could be anything, really . . . Could be many, many things. You know how it goes?" I squeezed my forehead between my fingers and wanted to bite down on my tongue to stop myself from talking. But I needed to see Alex, and I'd do and say whatever I needed to do to make that happen.

"Aaaaah, I seeeeeeee," the woman said in a knowing voice, as if this had happened before. *Dear God, did this happen?*

"So, that's why I'd rather come to the doctor than go to the emergency room, if you don't mind," I said. "It's a delicate issue, if you know what I mean."

"I understand." I heard a page flap. "The doctor could see you now if you can be here in fifteen minutes?"

"Perfect!" I almost shouted this last part down the phone and jumped in my seat with excitement.

"What's your name?" she asked.

"Uh . . . my name?" But I didn't want to give it to her. "Uh . . ." I looked around the taxi and outside and said the first thing I thought of. "Sally." The sex doll.

The taxi driver eyed me suspiciously. "Oh, keep your bloody eyes on the road and your ears to yourself!" I shouted at him. He finally had the grace to look away.

After a few more minutes we finally pulled up to the hospital. I paid as fast as I could and threw myself from the taxi.

"Good luck with whatever it is," the driver called after me with a sarcastic smile. I wanted to run back and wipe it off his face, but I had more important things to worry about. I raced into the hospital, scanned all the doctors' names on the board and once I'd located Alex's room number, I rushed to find it. It was easy to find and soon I found myself standing in his waiting room.

The room was full of people sitting around reading the paper. People looked up momentarily and then looked away, as if no one wanted to make eye contact, as if no one wanted to admit why they were here.

I walked up to the counter. "Hi, I'm Sally."

The woman looked up from what she was doing. "The emergency patient?" she asked. Too loudly. I looked around to see if everyone was looking at me again . . . *they were*. You could only have one emergency in this kind of doctors room!

She stood up and walked me towards a door. "Change into the gown and wait for the doctor, he'll be through to see you soon," she said.

I walked into the room and looked around. So this was where Alex worked. Suddenly I was flooded with pride. Alex was a doctor. He worked in the hospital and saved lives and probably did it with a smile. The gown was hanging on the wall and I wasn't about to change into it so I sat on the bed and waited for him. The door opened and the receptionist stuck her head around it.

"Well, what are you waiting for? The gown," she said, pointing at it.

I stood up quickly and grabbed the gown this time, taking my clothes off and changing into it. It was one of those terrible bright green hospital gowns that open in the back. It was cold and I shivered while I waited for him.

It felt like forever, but finally the other door opened. I heard the voice before I saw him. "So, Sally, I believe you have a bit of an emer—"

Alex looked up and stopped talking. Our eyes locked and my God, he looked amazing. Truly. He was wearing a crisp white doctor's coat. His name was smartly embroidered onto the jacket pocket. He had a stethoscope casually hanging around his neck and he was wearing a cute pair of glasses I'd never seen him in before. They drew even more attention to those gunmetal-gray eyes of his. *His eyes* . . . God, you could get so lost in them. Fall into them, swim in them, live in them and never want to leave.

"Alex," I said quietly to him.

"Val," he said back. His voice was cool. "Why are you here?"

"Um . . . I'm here because I have this pain in my chest," I said slowly. "I've had the pain for exactly three weeks now and it won't go away."

Alex looked at me and sighed. "I'm not that kind of doctor. Maybe you would be better suited to a cardiologist," he said.

I shook my head. "No. You are the only person in the world that can fix this pain."

"Why?" he asked, taking a step closer to me.

"Because . . ." I felt the tears welling up in my eyes. "Because I think my heart is broken and only you can put it back together again." A tear rolled down my cheek.

Alex's face softened somewhat and he took a small step towards me. "You came all this way to tell me that?"

"Well, my article didn't work so I had to."

He shook his head. "What article?"

"The one I wrote about you. Didn't you see it? You subscribed to the magazine?" I asked.

"I lost my phone," he said softly. "I didn't see it. What did it say?"

I got up and walked over to him. "It's you, Alex," I said. "It's everything about you. It's your eyes and the way I feel when you look at me. It's the way you smile and the way my heart skips a beat every time you do. It's the way you make me feel about myself when I'm around you . . ." I paused and took a moment to wipe my tears a little, they were blurring my vision and I wanted to see him when I said this next part. "I love you and I made a terrible mistake."

"Really?" He stepped closer to me.

I nodded. "I'm an idiot for choosing Matt and nothing happened with him, *nothing*."

"You mean that?"

"Yes! With every single part of my heart, every single tiny fiber in my body and nerve cell and everything!"

"That's a lot," he said.

"So . . . ?" The moment of truth had arrived. "Will you forgive me for being a total idiot and can you give me another chance?"

Alex looked at me. I could see he was thinking, weighing things up. He didn't say a word.

"Oh God, say something. Please," I begged. My heart felt like it was going to explode out of my chest with anticipation. I took another step closer to him and then reached out and took his stethoscope. I put it in his ears and then pulled the cord towards me, placing it onto my chest. "Listen," I said.

"It's beating fast," he said.

"And it's beating all for you." I placed my hands on his chest and moved closer to him. He took the stethoscope out of his ears and then I felt his hands on the sides of my face.

"You kind of broke my heart a little bit," he said quietly.

"Then let me put it back together," I said. "And I promise I won't do that again."

"Promise?" he asked. He seemed so vulnerable right now and I wanted to hug him and tell him that everything would be fine and hold him and care for him and never let him go again.

"Promise," I whispered. I brought my lips all the way up to his and rested them there. "Besides, Sally misses you too."

I felt his lips smile against mine. "Really?"

"Mmm," I mumbled, dragging my lips over his. God, he smelt good.

"I'm not into threesomes." He took my lip between his and kissed it teasingly. "I'm too selfish. I wouldn't want to share you."

"She could watch," I offered, and then burst out laughing.

"From the cupboard," Alex added and we both laughed. "I lied, by the way. I just wanted to hear you say it out loud, I did see your article. It was beautiful."

"Then why didn't you get hold of me?"

"Because I realized something too when I read it."

"What?" I asked.

"I never actually said the words to you, so I never gave you all the information."

I shook my head.

"I never actually said I love you. And I should have. And then I shouldn't have walked away, I should have stayed and given you a minute because I could see what a strange and confusing moment it was."

"Really?"

"So I bought a ticket to South Africa. I was going to fly there this week and barge into your apartment and fight Matt for you, if I had to."

I laughed and cried at the same time. "You were going to do that?"

"Fight him to death if necessary." Alex smiled at me.

"I love you," I said again and it felt so good to say.

"I love you." He kissed me softly on the lips and I melted. "By the way, I take it you don't have a, um . . .?" He pulled away and looked at me pointedly.

"NO! No," I laughed.

"So no need for me to—"

"No need." I cut him off. "No need at all. And for the record, there'll never, *ever*, be any need to . . ."

Alex laughed. "Noted." He let go of my face and slipped an arm around my back. The gown was open and his hand immediately slid under it.

"I never thought I'd be so happy to be wearing a hospital gown," I said.

"Me neither." He slipped his other hand around me and into the gown. I moaned as his hands travelled down my back.

"God, I missed you so much," I said, finding his lips again and kissing them.

And then he pulled away from me. "I have something for you." He stuck his hand into his pocket and pulled out his wallet. I watched as he opened it and reached into the coin pouch. "I found them in my room, and I couldn't bear to leave them there." He pulled them out and I immediately started crying.

The green ribbons.

I held my hand out for Alex and he reached for it. "Can we try this again," he asked, "with new promises that we make to each other?"

I nodded.

"So repeat after me then: I, Val, do solemnly promise to enter into this relationship and never follow lists in magazines again." I burst out laughing, tears streaming down my face at the same time as he tied the green thread around my finger, there was hardly anything left of the ribbon.

"Yes," I said, looking down at the ribbon on my finger once more. Only this time, it meant something totally different to me and I swear, I was never going to take it off again. *Ever.*

EPILOGUE

WhatsApp Group: Lilly's Birthday

Damien: Hey guys, I've added you to this group, please keep it private. I want to organize something special for Lilly's birthday. And I'm going big.

Annie joined the group.

Val joined the group.

Jane joined the group.

Jane: Hey!

Annie: Hey Dame.

Val: Yay. Howzit?

Stormy joined the group.

Stormy: Hh,jf'pkhf'k q . . . dg . . . Hi

Jane: Oh for God's sake! Someone is going to need to help Stormy with this.

Damien: I'll add Marcus to the group and she can communicate via him.

Annie: HAHAH!

Val: You can't see me, but I am rolling my eyes.

Marcus joined the group.

Marcus: Hellooo. This is me. Stormy. Not Marcus. But Marcus is typing, I'm just telling him what to say and he is typing for me. So it's me. Not him. In case you are wondering. This is Stormy.

Val: Hahah! Hey.

Damien: I don't think anyone will confuse you two.

Annie: I hate to be a party pooper here, but I have one child trying to get at my boob and the other two look like they are about to eat the dog food, it's dinner time here.

Damien: Overshare.

Marcus: Didn't need to know that.

Marcus: That's me. Marcus. Not Stormy.

Annie: Sorry, I forgot there were men on the group.

Jane: As one tends to do . . .

Damien: So, Lilly's birthday . . .

Damien: As you know, it's been a tough few years, what with the baby thing.

Damien: Lilly's been a bit down, so wanted to do something really special for her birthday.

Annie: Great idea!

Val: Love it.

Damien: But it's a surprise and no one can tell her.

Marcus: Oooh. Ooh. What is it? (That's me. Stormy)

Damien: I'll let you know the details closer to the time. But keep the first week of October open.

Marcus: That's like a million months away. You can't keep us in suspense. Give us a clue.

Damien: Okay . . . we're all going back to the beginning. To where it all began . . .

* * *

Want to find out more about Damien's plans for Lilly's birthday? Visit Jo's website to find out how you can read a free bonus novella!

www.jowatsonwrites.co.uk

Author's note

⌒

I've seen a few cool things in my life, but one really sticks out for me and I knew I had to write about it one day. Some years back we went on holiday to Réunion Island, one of the most interesting places in the world. But more than that, we got to see its volcano erupt. It was sheer chance and perfect timing that we arrived just as it started. We then got to take a helicopter ride over it and watch the lava spewing out. It was one of the most amazing and strangest things I've ever seen, an image that I can't ever forget. I hope I've adequately described it in this book and encapsulated the magic of it all. I hope the island sweeps you up and away as much as I was swept by it and if you can, I recommend a visit.

I feel very sad to be finishing this series and saying goodbye to Lilly, Annie, Jane, Stormy and now Val. These friends have been with me for years, and in some strange way I feel like I've gotten to know and love them. I've become friends with them. I'm also sad to leave all the islands and the sea and sun and sand that has been so fun writing about. I'll miss Stormy's mixed idioms and

Lilly's dramatic inner monologues. I'll miss them all and I wish
I could write each and every one of them a sequel. Who knows,
maybe one day they'll all come together for a reunion, but for
now, it's a big goodbye to this group of friends and all their wild
adventures finding love. I hope you've loved them as much as I have
and I hope you'll join me on my next adventure with new characters and new books. If you want to read one last bonus novella
about them though, be sure to go to www.jowatsonwrites.co.uk to
get a free copy sent to you.

Jo x

Love funny, romantic stories?
You don't want to miss

Love
to
Hate
You

Read on for a preview . . .

CHAPTER ONE

BAD TASTE IN WIGS

～

*D*on't ask me how the hell it happened . . .

I could blame it on the vodka.

Maybe I could blame it on JJ and Bruce. Maybe it was the strobing lights of the nightclub and the repetitive *doof doof* of the bass that triggered some kind of chemical reaction in my brain, causing me to go temporarily insane.

Maybe it was my outfit (NOTE: Never let a drag queen dress you for an evening out). I was wearing a sequined blue *thing* that could barely be described as a dress, and the famous "Marilyn wig" which they'd brought out especially for me, *God only knows why?* I looked like a crazed, transvestite prostitute with bad taste in wigs. Maybe that's why it happened?

But what are the chances?

To find a straight guy at a gay nightclub? Possibly the only one. And to find such a ridiculously hot one, who somehow knew my favorite drink and bought it for me all night long. Who kissed me like *that* on the dance floor and now had me pinned underneath him in the back seat of his car.

I *never* did this.

Someone else was half naked and sweating and moaning and grabbing at his tattooed shoulders. Someone else was licking Vodka Cranberry cocktails and sweat off his chest and having the best sex of her life—*deliciously dirty sex*—with possibly the hottest man that had ever walked the planet.

He'd made me feel like the sexiest woman alive, and that, coupled with the fact that I didn't know his name and would never see him again—*all that strong alcohol helped, too*—saw all my inhibitions fly right out the back window of his car. I did and said things I didn't even know I was capable of. With my face pressed into the seat, I told him how I wanted it. And he willingly gave it to me . . .

As well as several variations on the requested activity.

And when it was all over, he lay on top of me gasping for air and sweating beautiful glistening drops (God, even his sweat was sexy). It was easily the hottest experience of my entire life. But then he did something very odd, something that tipped me over the edge. He lifted his head and met my eyes with such intensity that everything around me went silent and blurry. He was look-ing at me like he knew me. Really, *really* knew me.

My mouth opened and an almost inaudible whisper came out, "Do I know you?"

He smiled at me. A naughty, skew, sexy smile. "Not yet." And then he kissed me. No one had kissed me like that before. It was the kind of kiss shared by long-lost lovers.

But when some nosey drag queens knocked on the car window

and made loud *oohing* noises and one of them mimed a comic blowjob gesture, I nearly died. I flung the door open and ran, leaving my Sex God shirtless and with his trousers still around his ankles. While I, the girl that never does stuff like this *(I reiterate)*, had to make an embarrassing run of shame across the now crowded parking lot. I could feel every single dramatically drawn, raised eyebrow watching me as I went.

Before I could get far, I was stopped by a distinctly masculine wolf whistle. Sex God clearly had NO inhibitions.

He was now leaning against his car, zipping up his jeans and doing it completely shirtless—*with a very appreciative audience, I might add*. He lit a cigarette, inhaled slowly and let the smoke curl out of his mouth.

He was like an advert for cool, in that *I-don't-give-a-flying-fuck-who-cares* kind of way. An advert for everything deplorable and lascivious, but downright filthy-sexy in a man. *Who the hell was he?*

I really had to go!

I climbed into my car and pulled out of the lot, allowing myself one last glance in his direction. The cigarette hung out of his mouth seductively; his wet hair clung to his face; he was leaning across the bonnet in such a way that he looked like a model from an X-rated Calvin Klein billboard. As I sped away, he blew me a kiss and shouted after me.

"I'm in love!"

CHAPTER TWO

I Heard He Was Raised By Wolves . . .

⌖

*I*n my head-pounding, hungover daze, I rolled, slipped, and fell out of bed, feeling like someone had poured sand into my eyes and pushed me down a steep cliff. I got up and pulled the now very itchy sequin dress off and got the fright of my life when I realized I wasn't wearing any underwear. I knew I'd left the house with panties on last night. *Hadn't I?*

I was already running late for work—I had accidentally pressed the snooze button on my phone way too many times—but I couldn't rush to work looking like I was.

I grabbed some cotton wool, dunked it in make-up remover and attempted to wipe the thick, chalky layers of black smoky eye make-up off my face. My red lipstick was smudged and one of the false lashes was clinging on like a dry spider. The make-up was coming off, but the glitter was more stubborn. "A highlighter, babe. Fab," JJ had said as he'd emptied the entire jar onto my face. The glitter was sticking to my face like glue and some bits had even lodged themselves into my hairline. The wig was even worse.

The clips holding it in place had twisted so badly that everything was completely stuck—*no doubt from rubbing my head back and forth in the back seat of a total stranger's car.* Instant nausea rose as I started to think about it again. *Crap, what the hell had I been thinking!*

But the wig was my top priority right now, and I was left with no choice but to painfully rip it off. I yelped in pain as tufts of brown hair came out in chunks, then I cursed the wig and tossed it onto the floor. I couldn't believe I'd actually worn the thing—it looked like a dead Maltese puppy.

I dissed my usual middle part, scraping my hair back into a ponytail. Contact lenses out—after inventing some new yoga poses to pry them from my dried-out eyes—and glasses on. Black pantsuit, white-collar shirt and a pair of semi-high heels. Then one last mirror check before running out.

On my way to grab my laptop bag and a handful of headache pills, I passed JJ and Bruce's room, but before I could give them a vengeful wake-up knock, my passive-aggressive attempt at punishing them for their part in my early-morning state, I saw the note.

Sera,
  You naughty, naughty girl! We heard you caused quite the parking lot spectacle. Dinner tonight, we want all the juicy details.
  XX
  J&B

I sighed and, as I went out to my car, my face went red-hot at the thought of telling them what had happened.

My twenty-year-old Toyota had been acting up lately. Another thing to add to the growing to-buy list, along with socks without holes, black pumps with non-peeling soles and now some new undies. But I just couldn't afford a new car right now—*or ever*—not between paying back loans and secretly sending money home to my sister Katie.

"*Please start, please start, please start,*" I pleaded with the hunk of metal junk.

My job was the most important thing in my life. Without it, I wouldn't be able to help Katie and she'd be at our dad's mercy. And there was no way I was going to let that happen. I simply couldn't afford to do anything that would jeopardize it especially since I was one of two interns vying for a permanent position at the company. Being late didn't exactly scream "hire me."

I also knew what being late meant. I would surely walk slap bang into an apocalyptic crisis lifted straight from the Book of Revelation. Working at an ad agency means going from one emergency to another. High stakes, lots of money on the line, demanding clients, demanding creatives and deadlines tighter than the skinny jeans they all wear.

My car finally started after a few smoky chugs and I threw a few thank-yous out into the universe. But as soon as I drove out of my apartment complex and turned onto the highway, I was assaulted by bumper-to-bumper Jo'burg traffic, made even worse by minibus taxis and their "creative" driving techniques. Currently I had one only centimeters from my bumper with a painted sign on his back window that read, "*What goes surround, Comes surround.*" At least something about this morning was vaguely humorous. But the static traffic gave me too much time to think and reflect . . .

What the hell had happened last night? Most of it was a blur, but every now and then an image flashed through my mind.

Vodka. Lots.

"Is this seat taken?" That smooth move and that husky voice . . .

Slowly grinding himself into me on the dance floor of Club Six, running his hands up my thighs, creeping way, way too high for public decency laws, until his hands were . . .

"You're so fucking beautiful," he'd whispered in my ear, his hands coming up and cupping my face.

"I want you so badly, Sera." Hang on, how had he known my name?

"I need you." That was the moment I melted completely and decided to walk outside with him . . .

Fumbling for his car keys . . .

On him . . .

Under him . . .

Windows steaming up . . .

"Fuck, you're amazing." More words that made me lose my mind as I writhed on his lap and totally forgot myself in the moment . . .

His tattoos . . .those dark piercing eyes . . .

"I could do this forever," he'd whispered in my ear seductively.

"Sera." He rasped as he came on top of me, the weight of his body crushing me into the seat.

Oh. My. God.

Had I really fallen for every lame jackass line in the book? He probably said that to all the girls he had anonymous back-seat sex with. Was I really that stupid, or sex starved, or mad, or drunk, or all of those to have actually bought into his smooth-play-boy moves. *Mortified* AF. My only consolation was that I'd never see him again.

After a frustrating hour in traffic, I finally arrived at work, but the only parking space I could find was all the way on the other side of the office park, so I was forced to run with a pounding head and lurching stomach.

But when I finally got inside, I was downright shocked. Something was *very* wrong.

I was expecting to run straight into the usual office chaos: people screaming at each other, screaming into the phone, screaming at the coffee pot or the copy machine. But something bizarre was going on today. People were sitting around lazily . . . *chatting?*

It was as if someone had come in the night and tranquilized all my co-workers. Had someone put Xanor into the air conditioning system? That was surely the only explanation for this eerie calm. I inched my way to my desk feeling very uneasy—*was this the calm before the storm?*

Before I had a chance to pull out my chair, Becks slunk up to me and whispered conspiratorially into my ear.

"Have you heard?" she asked.

I half turned to her but she cut me off quickly before I could manage to respond.

"They hired a new Creative Director. Apparently he's a fucking rock star. Blake something I think—"

At the sound of that name, one of the junior copywriters who happened to be walking past quickly corrected her, "Isn't it Blade? I heard his name was Blade?"

Next thing I knew, an equally excitable art director joined the conversation, "Blaze? Isn't it Blaze? Or Slash?" She was practically squealing.

I looked from one glowing face to the other. Their eyes were lit up like firecrackers and their cheeks were flushed a bright shade of pink.

"I heard they offered him a huge financial package to come here," Becks said with a wild, wide-eye look. Becks, short for Rebecca, always seemed to know exactly what was going on in the office. I think she made it her business to know. She was also my toughest competition for the permanent job here.

The other creatives simultaneously nodded in agreement, declaring that he was probably worth every cent, maybe even more. *Yes*, he was definitely worth more, they concluded. Then they walked off—no doubt to spread more legends of this creative man-God.

In an ad agency, creativity is king. It's the currency and the Holy Grail. So when one of these so-called creative geniuses comes around, it whips everyone into a star-struck frenzy. He might as well have been an actual rock star because everyone here at JTS was whipped. I was too hungover to be vaguely interested, but the rest of the office buzzed like the static on a television.

"I heard he doesn't sleep . . . ever," the strange pale vampire girl from layout said dreamily.

"He's going to bring in a lot of new accounts . . . not to mention awards," two senior managers said as they passed.

"I heard he nailed all the chicks at his last job," two guys from IT said before a macho fist bump.

I sighed and started to roll my eyes, but they hurt too much.

I opened my email and there it was: "Meeting in the Canteen to introduce new CD" *(Creative Director)*. The meeting was in ten minutes. I lay my head on my desk and waited for the headache pills to kick in.

I must have drifted off to sleep though because I thought I heard someone say, "*I heard he was raised by wolves.*" I opened my eyes and looked around, but no one was there. I glanced at my watch—*Crap!*

I jumped up and ran to the canteen as fast as I could without tripping and landing on my face. When I finally got there, everyone was already inside and standing around a black-clad figure. I could only see the back of him from where I was. I glanced around looking for Becks and finally saw her standing in the front row with the other starry-eyed women. I carefully pushed my way forward trying not to be seen, but when I got there, he turned and suddenly I couldn't breathe—

WARNING: Being jilted at the altar in front of 500 wedding guests can lead to irrational behaviour, such as going on your honeymoon to Thailand alone. Recovery will lead to partying the night away at Burning Moon festival – and falling in love with the person you least expect . . .

Don't miss *Burning Moon,* the first book in the Destination Love series.

Available now from

HEADLINE
ETERNAL

Newly single.

Holiday of a lifetime.

Bumping into 'the ex'.

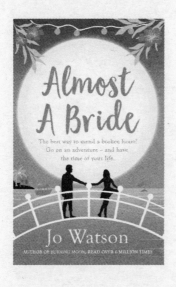

For more laugh-out-loud, swoon-worthy hijinks, check out *Almost A Bride*, the second book in the Destination Love series.

Available now from

When you go to Greece to meet your family but end up snogging your smokin' hot tour guide. #sorrynotsorry

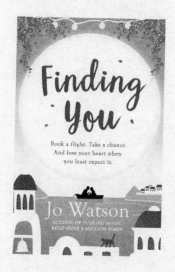

Get ready for a rollercoaster of a rom-com on the beaches of Santorini with the third Destination Love book, *Finding You*.

Available now from

She believes in Fate.
He believes in logic.
But this unexpected journey could change
everything . . .

Take the road trip of a lifetime in this hilarious
opposites-attract rom-com, as the bestselling
Destination Love series continues with
After The Rain!

Available now from

One night can change everything . . .

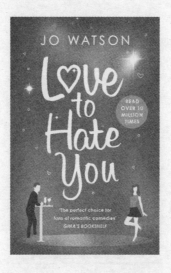

Love funny, romantic stories? You don't want to miss *Love To Hate You*

Available now from